THE SMILE HAS LEFT YOUR EYES

DANIELLE N. DAWSEN

Paperback ISBN: 979-8-9851095-0-4

www.daniellendawsen.com

First Edition

For people like me, who sometimes like feeling sad.

Chapter One

Aspen

I GRIPPED THE RED-AND-WHITE BALL between my fingers, holding it inside of my worn glove as I glanced at second and third base through the thick wires of my mask. It was the bottom of the seventh inning and we were winning six to five.

The sun shone down on all the players, heat radiating off the packed dirt. I would've been blinded by the reflection if it weren't for the thick lines of eye black drawn at the tops of my cheekbones, the ends smeared downward. Sweat dripped from my hair, salty water trickling down the back of my neck and adding to the already-drenched long-sleeve compression shirt under my jersey.

I stepped on the plate, throwing the ball back to Rafe, who caught it swiftly, turning around in the motion and kicking at the dirt surrounding the white rubber rectangle. Taking my place directly behind the batter's box, I squatted, balancing on the balls of my feet. I blew out a slow, deep breath in an attempt to calm my quickening heartbeat. The count was three-two with a runner on second and third; one more ball and the bases would be loaded. If the guy at bat got a hit, the game could be tied, and we'd have to go into extra innings. *As if everyone here wasn't already exhausted.* But if Rafe got a strike, we'd win and become one step closer to going to States and then Nationals.

Based on the batter's past three at-bats, he liked outside pitches, which was exactly why I was calling for a low and inside pitch. If we jammed him and directed his hit toward third, our third baseman, Jason Wright, could get the out there with a tag. If Jason was late, his throw would be fast and accurate enough to get the out at first. He was good like that. There was a reason he was one of our starters.

Rafe and I made eye contact, cueing me to drop my hand between my legs and punch out a short combination of numbers on my fingers. I got a quick nod from Rafe, who adjusted his greyish navy-blue baseball cap.

Rafe dug his toe into the dirt while settling his left foot onto the pitcher's rubber. He twisted the red seams of the baseball in his fingers, quickly finding the perfect position with his pointer and middle finger on the seam and his thumb below it—the standard fastball grip.

His baseball hat cast a shadow on the top of his face, making his dark-brown eyes disappear. He cocked his hands just behind his left ear, his left hand hidden behind his glove. With a fast and fluid motion, Rafe lifted his right leg, planting it firmly into the ground and swinging his left arm down and toward his right hip. It all happened in slow motion. My eyes followed the spinning baseball traveling at a diagonal angle, making the pitch similar to a crossfire. The batter knew the pitch was in the zone; his swing blinded my vision momentarily, but I could see more than enough of what I needed to. The ball slammed into the net of my glove with the most satisfying 'thwack.' The batter's eyes followed suit as he finished his swing.

The silence was deafening as my eyes focused on the flawlessly delivered strike. It was on the very edge of the zone and the speed was close to Rafe's top from the day. I waited for the umpire, even though it was a done deal since the batter had swung and missed.

A loud "Strike!" was bellowed from behind, the ump's hand forming a solid fist.

I jumped up from my spot and threw my mask off. Rafe came running toward me and wrapped a firm arm around my shoulder, causing my head and neck to jerk downward. Jason and Devin met us halfway between home plate and the pitcher's mound, clasping each of our hands in a quick handshake with big smiles.

"Great call, Aspen. And nice fucking pitch, Rafe," Devin, our captain, praised as our players made their way to the dugout.

Devin Meyers was one of the best things that had ever happened to the Cedar Heights baseball team. Besides their lucky draw of pure, raw talent over the past three years, that was. Just an inch taller than both Rafe and me, the six-two dirty-blonde captain made all the gears turn. A skilled first baseman with polished leadership skills, he was the reason we won States last year. But now, with a fresh batch of juniors on varsity, I hoped he'd lead us to Nationals once again.

As the other players packed their stuff into their bags, I sat on the long metal bench. I unhooked my leg guards first, followed by my black-and-grey chest protector. I placed everything inside my catcher's gear bag and relished the new, light feeling of not being weighed down as the cool breeze blew against my damp uniform.

Our coach gave us a quick speech, congratulating us on the win and dismissing us to the locker rooms. I let the rest of the team go ahead first; it was my lame attempt at trying to steer clear of changing at the same time as the others. That was something I avoided like the plague.

Rafe noticed me lingering behind. He said something to a couple of guys who gave him a slight nod before continuing on their path.

Rafe turned around and walked back toward me. "What are you waiting for? Don't you want to get out of this heat? It's so damn hot, and you're even wearing an extra layer," he said as he took off his hat that had a cursive CH etched into the dull blue in white thread. Rafe wiped the sweat off his forehead, his tanned skin glistening from perspiration. He ran a hand over the top of his head, messing his hair around to fix the sharp indent the cap made on his coarse black hair.

"Yeah, I just wanted to reflect on the game a bit before my adrenaline dies down," I lied, giving him a fake smile.

Rafe gave me a weary look, but the downturned corners of his mouth soon vanished. "We just finished a pretty intense game. It's over ninety degrees out here and you're wearing that damn undershirt again. You can change and then rewatch the game. I asked Amelia to record it."

There was a painful tug at the bottom of my heart. I smiled again, slightly squinting my eyes to make it look more genuine. "Tell your girlfriend I said thanks."

"Sure." Rafe patted my shoulder and I winced, but it seemed like he didn't notice.

He placed himself behind me and pushed me forward, guiding me to the locker room, gently shoving me all the way to the entrance, where I stopped resisting—it'd be weird if I refused to go in.

I made my way to my locker, placing my gear under a nearby bench. My changing teammates surrounded me, wearing the bare minimum amount of clothing or nothing but a towel wrapped around their waists as they headed to the showers. Not everyone rinsed off after a game, but the hot weather encouraged more guys than usual. I averted my gaze, keeping my eyes to the ground or on the clean clothes I was fishing out of the locker. I wasn't interested in any of them, anyway. Although Rafe's naked torso was slightly distracting.

"I gotta take a piss," I muttered to Rafe, who gave me a small nod of acknowledgment as he slipped his dirt-stained white baseball pants off, leaving him in his tight black underwear and long socks.

"Is there something wrong with your bladder? Why do you always go to the bathroom when we're changing?" He furrowed his brows, bending down to slip off his right sock. His toned abs flexed with the movement.

I gulped and turned my head away. "Yeah. Something like that." I waved his comment off.

It was nothing new, me going to change in the bathroom. I'd started doing that before high school, although there wasn't a baseball team at our middle school, so Rafe and I played on a competitive team and only changed with each other at long tournaments.

I closed the stall door behind me, sliding the tiny metal bar into the lock. The dark-blue cubicle was somewhat large as I opted to go into the smaller of the two handicap stalls.

I didn't actually have to go to the bathroom, of course. There were several reasons that I hid. No one would know I liked men if I kept my mouth shut, but some secrets were more visible, yet just as dangerous.

I unbuttoned the front of my short-sleeved jersey, shrugging the fabric onto the floor. Undoing my belt and pants, the dirty material fell on top of my jersey, leaving me clad in my underwear and black shirt. I tugged on the wet, sticky material that was practically glued to my skin. It wasn't that I wanted to wear extra layers when I played, especially not at this time of the year, but I didn't really have a choice.

I carefully slid my arms out of the sleeves, gently pulling the shirt over my head. With a heavy sigh, I placed the sweat-drenched shirt on the ground. I held my arms up and stared at the white bandages on my forearms. Because of the sheer heat of the day, the tape keeping the gauze on my skin was peeling up from the ends.

I should've brought some to school so I could redo them. *Stupid.*

I sucked in a breath as I peeled the long bandage off, knowing it wouldn't have stayed even if I left it there. The cuts on my wrist were raw and irritated, but the slight sting didn't bother me. I was more than used to it.

I shouldn't have done that this morning, but sometimes I couldn't help it. It was an abysmal habit I'd picked up when I was fourteen and trying to cope with my shitty life; unfortunately, it'd spiraled into something much more than I could handle, and the insides of my thighs, my abdomen, and my arms from my shoulders to the wrist took the brunt of my unhealthy coping mechanism.

It was bad. I knew it was bad, and even when I recognized things were getting worse, even when I noticed how the small lines on my wrist became more compact, longer, thicker, and started venturing onto other parts of my body, I couldn't stop. Even when I wanted to. Even when I tried.

It was something completely out of my control, yet at the same time, it gave me the control I so desperately needed.

Sometimes it bothered me during games if the marks were fresh, or an old scar was acting up. I dressed in long sleeves whenever I played to hide it. Well, I always wore long sleeves because even if it wasn't just my wrists that were exposed, the undersides of my arms were just as littered with swollen white-and-pink marks. It was fine when it was a cold or rainy season, but with summer approaching, the humid weather made it almost unbearable to play with an undershirt or even just compression sleeves.

Unfortunately, there were other things that got in my way more when I tried to play baseball: My left shoulder sent dull, aching pains throughout my entire body, the bruise the size of a small bowling ball and all sorts of deep purples and blacks. But it would fade with time. They always did.

I hastily put on a loose, black long-sleeved shirt and a pair of black shorts that stopped just above my knees, slipping on a pair of crew socks and a pair of black, battered Vans, the plethora of dark colors setting the mood. Gathering all my dirty clothes into a pile, I slipped my old, bloodied bandages into the middle so no one could see when I walked out.

I passed a trash can on my way back to my locker and discreetly tossed the two long white-and-red pieces into the grey bin.

I shoved my baseball clothes into my bag as Rafe placed his foot on the bench, tying his shoes, asking, "Are you ready to go?"

Rafe was my ride practically everywhere, carting me to and from school every day. There was a car I was supposed to share with my older brother, Alex, but the day I got my license, he made it very clear that it was *his* car and bad things would happen if I were to use it.

"Yeah, just let me wash my hands real quick," he replied, straightening his back and heading toward one of the many sinks that lined the wall. I watched him from behind, his muscles flexing underneath his tight shirt. He threw his used paper towels into the trash can. Eyes narrowing for a split second, his thick brows tightly knit together as he turned his head, glancing at me and then looking back into the trash.

He lightly clenched his jaw and quickly made his way toward me. "Did you throw out those bandages covered in blood?" His voice was stern, looking for a clear answer.

"What?" I laughed nervously. "Of course not."

"I saw you throw something in there earlier and those bandages were the only thing in the trash can."

I dismissed his subtle interrogation. "I had a bloody nose earlier." Dodging questions and making up reasonable lies had become a very handy skill I'd developed over the years.

Rafe stared at me. His whole body tensed and he let out a huff of air. "Fine. Okay. Let's just go."

The walk to his car was silent besides the scuffle of our sneakers against the gravelly concrete. But Rafe was used to it. I wasn't a particularly talkative person. Well, I used to be.

I opened the passenger side door and slid onto the soft, faded fabric covering the seats. Rafe stuck the aged key into the ignition. The engine roared and quieted down, repeating the same thing three times before a beeping noise filled the air and the vehicle finally started. It was his dad's old car and it barely worked, but a car was a car and both Rafe and I were thankful for it.

"Is there anything you want to do?" Rafe asked. It was Friday night and the social butterfly that was my best friend wasn't interested in staying home alone.

"No, just..." I trailed off.

"Just not your house?" He finished my sentence.

"Yeah," I murmured.

I didn't let him come over anymore, especially not if my brother was home. Alex was a sophomore at a local college and always came home at unpredictable times. It wasn't that I wanted to keep Rafe away from my brother, but more so that I needed to keep my brother from seeing me with another guy. *Alone* with another guy, especially Rafe.

Rafe sighed once again. He was probably getting tired of me, and I didn't blame him. You see, depression had this way of sucking the personality right out of you, leaving its victims nothing but a shell of their former selves.

I didn't talk a lot. I had nothing interesting to say, and added essentially nothing to conversations. I was simply *there*. A boring shadow that followed Rafe around like a lost puppy. But what else was I supposed to do? Life had me numb and he was the only person who made me *feel*. I knew he was bored of me, and I knew he was tired of me. But unless I heard those words straight out of his mouth, I'd just keep being that burdensome shadow.

"We could go to Jason's house. A bunch of the guys are going over. Apparently, his mom's making dinner for anyone who shows, and you know that his mom's cooking is better than Gordon Ramsay himself." Rafe licked his lips at the thought.

It was something I couldn't deny. Jason's parents were both professional chefs. Damn good ones at that.

"If you want to," I replied with a low chuckle while giving him my signature smile, making sure to flash my dimples.

Rafe's face fell. "Actually, let's just go to my house. My mom's making pozole tonight." He pronounced the dish with a Spanish accent.

"Sounds good to me."

Rafe only lived about six minutes from our high school, so he pulled up next to his house in no time. He parked his car on the street just in front of his house, his parents' cars occupying the small driveway.

We went in through the front door, taking our shoes off and placing them on a small shoe rack, setting our bags down just past the entryway.

"Mamá, estoy en casa," Rafe shouted to his mom in her mother tongue as we made our way toward the kitchen, announcing that he was home.

The familiar scent of Mexican laundry soap permeated the air of the relatively small, two-bedroom, two-bath house with a decent-sized living room and small kitchen, all visible from the front door. I looked up at the familiar white of the popcorn ceiling, pulling out a chair from the old wooden table and sitting down as Rafe went straight to the white fridge. He scanned the contents, seemingly unsatisfied.

His mom came bounding into the room, her feet making thumping noises on the bare tiles. She rushed over to her son, whacking him on the head and releasing a string of curses that I couldn't understand.

"I'm already cooking dinner! Why are you looking for food? You'll spoil your appetite!" She was about half a foot shorter than Rafe, her body slightly pudgy, with a red apron tied around her waist. Rafe's mom had greying hair that she re-dyed black now and again, and there were small wrinkles forming around the corners of her mouth and eyes. She was from Mexico; her first language wasn't English, but if I ignored her thick Spanish accent, she was completely fluent. Although Rafe's dad was born in the states, all of his grandparents were from Mexico as well.

Rafe raised his hands, trying to protect himself as I laughed at the amusing situation.

The noise garnered his mom's attention and she craned her head to see me, her open palm that was about to hit her son still raised in the air. "Oh! Aspen, I didn't know you were here." She gave me a warm smile, glaring daggers at Rafe before moving away from him. "I'm glad you came. I made an extra portion for you."

"Thanks, Teresa."

"Of course!" she cooed. Besides the fact that we'd known each other since Rafe and I first started playing baseball together when we were four, I think the reason she liked me so much was because I kept Rafe out of trouble. "Dinner's not ready quite yet, so you two should wait in another room so I can have a bit of space."

Rafe and I removed ourselves from the cramped kitchen. He headed straight to his room and plopped himself onto his double twin bed. The dark-blue covers were messy and random papers lay around his room. Next to his closet were numerous shelves full of trophies, medals, and signed baseballs on display. I had a lot of the same awards. On the other side, he had a brown, rectangular desk with a laptop, along with random knickknacks here and there.

He lay on his back with his arms spread like a starfish and his legs bent at the knee, hanging off the end.

I stood just past the doorway. "Do you have some band-aids I can use?" After I threw my bandages out, the burning sensation turned into an intense itch as the newly forming scabs continued to rub against the fabric of my sleeves.

"Hmm?" he mumbled, bending his neck upward and moving into a sitting position. "What do you need a band-aid for?"

"Oh, I have a cut on my ankle from when someone slid into me."

"Yeah, let me grab you one." Rafe picked himself up and sifted through the bottom drawer of his desk, handing me a single, normal-sized plaster.

"Can you just hand me the box?" I asked softly.

"Yeah, I guess..." He paused, looking down at the socks that covered my ankles. "I'll get something to disinfect it. Let me take a look at the cut." He gestured for me to take off the crew sock.

"N-no, that's okay. I can do it myself," I sputtered.

"Is it on the outside or inside?"

"What?"

"If it's on the outside, it'll be kind of awkward for you to reach it," he said.

"No, I'm alright. It's on the inside. I can reach it just fine."

"Okay..." Rafe sounded unconvinced. He handed me a large box that had multiple different sizes.

When I turned to leave the room, Rafe's voice had me glancing over my shoulder. "Is this also something you have to hide in the bathroom to do?"

We made eye contact. His gaze bored into mine, filling me with a sense of discomfort. Eye contact was a dangerous thing to do. When I laughed, I could fake smile lines. But when you truly looked into someone's bare orbs, nothing remained hidden. There's a saying that eyes are the gateway to the soul, and in many ways, that's true: Eyes are the essence of a person. They tell a million stories, and if you know someone well enough, they can reveal *everything*.

I averted my gaze, not replying to him before walking to the bathroom down the hall, clutching the box in my hands.

I shut the bathroom door behind me, sandwiching myself between the towels hanging from the hooks on the door and the sink. I set the band-aids on the counter and rested my hands on the edge of the sink, my shaggy bangs falling over my eyes and obscuring the man I saw in the mirror. I didn't necessarily dislike my appearance... it was just hard to look at myself at times because I never recognized the person staring back.

I knew that some people found me attractive, but I didn't really get it. I'd been told it was because of my dimples. I had one on each cheek, deep and heavily defined, and most prominent when I smiled. They were charming, apparently. Distracting. And that was why my dimples were my favorite feature: They drew attention away from my eyes. They used to be a vibrant green, with specks of gold littered around the pupil, but now they were nothing more than a dull, ugly grey. When you stared at them too long, you could tell something was... *off.*

I wondered how everyone would react if they knew it was all fake. All our friendships, all the shared smiles and laughs. Would they be mad when they realized I didn't care about them—about anything? Would my sexuality completely overshadow the lies? When it all came to light, what would they do to me? Jump straight to blackmail like Alex? Would they beat me, too? Probably.

Would Rafe join in with them?

I glanced down at my arms. *I could always just try to kill myself again. Then I'd never have to know what would happen if more people found out.*

I chewed on the inside of my lip, rolling up my sleeve and grabbing as many large band-aids I could find. Rummaging through the cabinets until I found a spare pair of scissors, I cut the sticky ends off half the band-aids, attaching another one to the top to make them bigger while keeping the part that sticks to the skin off my cuts. I covered large portions on both my forearms and threw all my trash into the tiny bin next to the toilet, filling it to the brim. I grabbed the box and went back to Rafe's room, placing the plasters on his desk.

"Why'd that take you so long?" His eyes didn't leave his phone when the words left his mouth.

"I went to the bathroom, too."

He hummed in response, only paying half-attention to what I was saying.

"Is there anything you want to do?"

"Not particularly," Rafe said absentmindedly, probably annoyed that I was here. He wanted to hang out with the other guys from the team, after all.

I didn't enjoy being around them. Sure, they were great at baseball and we were part of the same friend group at school, but I knew the second they found out I was gay, not a single one of them would still be my friend. If their homophobic slander was anything to go by, then I was truly fucked. Not just by them, but by everyone. I was just so *lucky* to have been born in a town where I hadn't met a single person who didn't talk about gay people like they were scum walking the earth.

I didn't hang out with people unless Rafe was there; there was no point otherwise. They included me in plans, but I tended to flake out when there was no promise of alcohol or weed.

"Do you want me to leave?" I struggled to keep my voice even.

"No. Don't go. We can watch a movie or something."

Come on, Aspen. Stop holding him back. "You should go to Jason's house. I wanted to look over the tapes today, anyway..." I practically whispered.

"Or, you could come with me."

I looked down and fiddled with the hem of my sleeve. A silent answer.

"I don't get why you don't like them." He shook his head, his thumbs moving speedily on his screen, probably letting them know he was coming over.

Of course, he didn't get it. And I hoped he never would.

"I do like them. I'm just a little tired from the game. Uhm, I guess I'll see you later then?" I asked in a hopeful tone.

"Sure." Rafe's voice was monotone, his lack of excitement evident.

"Okay." I chewed on my cheek even harder, penetrating the skin and drawing a small amount of blood. The flavor of iron invaded my taste buds and the walls of my mouth became raw and jagged, joining the other parts of the pink skin I'd accidentally gnawed off.

I slowly made my way out of his room, my steps sluggish as I scolded myself internally. *I shouldn't have suggested leaving. But it isn't like Rafe really wants me around...*

I'd been in love with him for as long as I could remember. Literally. I couldn't remember... Before I knew it, I was already head-deep in an unrequited love that would never be returned.

The thing about having been depressed for so long was that I'd become hyper-observant. I noticed every little thing. Body language or slight changes in tone, and I took those things and analyzed them, especially with Rafe. *What does it mean? Does he hate me? Should I stop talking now? Does he know...*

I slung my bag over my shoulder, momentarily forgetting the giant, tender bruise and swearing as the wiring of my catcher's mask pushed against my back. I choked on a cry and quietly muttered, needing to release the feeling of pain in some way. "Shit!"

"What's wrong?" Rafe came jogging out of the hallway.

"Nothing, I just stubbed my toe." I looked him up and down. "Why'd you come back out?"

"I forgot to ask if you needed a ride home."

"Oh. No, I'm good. I can walk." I gave him a small smile, avoiding his eyes.

"But your house is a thirty-minute walk from here."

"I'll just use it as some time to go over plays," I reassured him with no actual plans of going home—not this early at least. I didn't know if my brother was home or not.

"Okay," Rafe sounded unconvinced.

"Well," I slipped my shoes back on, "bye."

"Yeah. Bye..."

Maybe Rafe was happy to see me go.

Chapter Two

Aspen

I MADE MY WAY OUT the front door with my backpack and baseball bag hanging off my shoulders. I lumbered toward the park a couple of blocks from my house, the sun just beginning to set and the sky full of sun-kissed clouds, creating a nice, warm array of colors. Setting my stuff down next to a pole, I walked across a sandpit and placed myself on the rubber seat of a swingset.

I didn't swing, though. I didn't kick my legs or bask in the feeling of hot wind blowing through my hair. I simply sat there, staring at nothing. It wasn't hard to pass time. My mind had a way of making hours seem like seconds.

The sky had quickly shifted into a dark blue, my surroundings illuminated by streetlights. The post-sunset night sky clued me in that my parents had probably gotten home from work, meaning it was alright for me to head back.

I went through the garage, quickly throwing my dirty uniform into the wash on my way in. It was eerily quiet, making me assume that neither my parents nor brother were here. *Seems like going to the park was a waste.*

The door to the garage connected directly to our kitchen. I wound around the center island that mirrored the marble counter and the brown cabinets stacked beneath it, passing the dining table just feet away. The sound of television filled the empty living room, the only actual sign of human life in the pristine house. Even the long couch placed under the picture window was spotless, minus a single stain covered by the purposefully placed decorative pillows. My dad believed it was a wine stain, and I'd never bothered to correct him. Lightly stomping up the creaky staircase with a tight grip on the railing, I ignored the false images of a happy family of four garnered on the white walls. There was one in particular that always made me shiver: Alex's hand rested on my shoulder, and to any unsuspecting individual, we looked like two close brothers, but when I saw it, all I could see was the way his fingers dug into the thin fabric covering my bicep, leaving bloody nail marks across the bruise in the pressure's wake. It was his way of telling me not to let my smile slip.

Once through the long hallway on our second floor, I entered the last door, throwing all my bags on the floor of my room. I felt like getting straight into bed and passing out; I didn't know how I managed to do the things I did every day. My tank was always running on empty. School, baseball, hiding my true self, being surrounded by people that probably didn't even like me... it was a lot.

I stripped and went straight to my shower, where I spent the next hour reveling in the scalding hot water with throbbing, stinging wrists.

When I got out, I stood in front of the hulking mirror that covered the entire wall. I used my hand to wipe away the condensation, focusing on my blurred body. I hated looking at myself, yet somehow, the scars made me proud—a warped type of pride that brought about a sense of disgust and self-hatred.

I was in good shape. Great shape, even. As a catcher, squatting was practically a part of me, resulting in my thighs being thick and made of nothing but muscle. It didn't matter though. Not really. It wasn't like I could show them off; there was no one I wanted to see my bare skin beside Rafe, but after I'd mutilated myself like this, I didn't want him to see, either. The insides of my thighs were adorned with long, white, jagged marks. Some of my oldest scars. I rarely cut there anymore because it chafed against the rough fabric of my baseball pants too much. My stomach... I regretted doing it there, sometimes. And my arms, they weren't even comparable to barcodes at this point. The lighter undersides looked like they'd been through a shredder. I didn't regret that at all.

Sometimes there was this voice in my head. It wasn't my own, but at the same time, it was. It told me to *do it*.

End it.

There's no point.

You're miserable and could make it all stop, just like that.

Ah. There it was again. That feeling. Like I was going to explode if I didn't somehow release it. I stared absentmindedly at the drawer I kept my razors in, my face blank and void of expression, finally relaxed and matching my eyes for the first time today.

I shouldn't. I knew I shouldn't. I'd already had my share this morning and if I did it again so soon, the cuts would never heal. That would be an issue when playing baseball. A welcome issue...

It was painful and nearly impossible to drag my eyes away from the thing my head was telling me I wanted—*needed*—so badly.

One foot after the other, I pried myself away, grabbing a towel and exiting the bathroom. I threw on another clean long-sleeve and a pair of shorts. My wet hair, now a dark, chocolate-brown, dripped onto my clothes.

The droplets falling from the tips of my messy bangs and onto the floor fascinated me, occupying my attention and allowing me to unfocus in a dangerous way. There wasn't a lot left for me anymore. I may still have had baseball, but I was slowly losing Rafe more and more every day. Soon, I wouldn't have enough excuses to convince my mind to stay alive.

Fourteen years. That was how long we'd been best friends. At eighteen now, we'd spent the majority of our lives next to each other. Over a hundred and sixty-eight months. I knew it was just a matter of time until the long clock stopped ticking... since the boy he became friends with was long-gone. Now, I was playing a waiting game. One day, I'd wake up and find myself alone. This wasn't an *if* type of situation. It was a *when*.

The growling of my stomach disrupted my thoughts, forcing an annoyed grunt out of my mouth. Teresa had even made me food. I could've stuck around after Rafe left—they wouldn't have minded.

I made my way down to the kitchen and silently poured a small bowl of cereal. I scrolled through social media as I shoveled spoonfuls into my mouth. The baseball team looked like they were having fun, if Rafe's story was anything to go by. He had an enormous smile plastered on his face as he recorded himself and the guys playing a prank on Devin in the background.

He didn't smile like that with me anymore. But why would he? I didn't do anything to make him smile. *Jokes?* I scoffed at the thought. My sense of humor disappeared a long time ago.

Not wanting to see any more, I shoved my phone into my shorts' pocket.

The creaking of the front door startled me and in walked Alex.

"Where's mom and dad?" I was hesitant with my words, my heart rate already picking up. It thumped in my chest and pulsed throughout my entire body.

His light-brown hair bounced as he snickered, "They're going on a business trip."

"How long?" I asked in a quiet voice.

"They'll be back Monday." He closed the door behind him.

"Why didn't they tell me?"

"Mom texted me and told me to tell you." The corners of his mouth twisted into a sinister smile.

"Oh," I gulped.

"So..." he drew the word out, slowly making his way toward me while dragging his finger along the table. "Did the fag win his little game today?" He cocked his head to the side with a disturbing glint in his eyes.

"We won," I mumbled.

"You won? Hmm, that doesn't sound like a fair game." Alex clicked his tongue.

I furrowed my brows, my worry spiking.

"To lose to a fag? *They must have really sucked.* I wonder how they would feel if they knew what you were. You're a catcher, right? Doesn't that mean you sit right behind the batters?" His jaw ticked and it was like a switch flipped in his mind. "Don't tell me," he said with a haughty laugh, "do you play catcher just so you can stare at other guys' asses?"

"W-what?" I stuttered. "Of course not!"

I'd been playing the position since I graduated from t-ball, and no one had those sorts of feelings and thoughts at that age. And even if I *was* old enough, it was still absurd.

"Holy shit. You're so fucking *disgusting.* Maybe I should just tell everyone. I wonder what your little friends would do when they find out you're a filthy cocksucker. Oh! And our *parents!* Shit, they'd probably throw you right out!"

I clenched my jaw.

"I have no reason to not expose you. Should I just... *leak it?*" Alex teased.

"Don't," I said in a quiet-yet-firm tone.

"Don't *what?*" he drawled. "Don't tell everyone the *truth?* You want *me* to *lie* for *you?*"

"I'll do anything, so *don't,*" I pleaded. "You *promised.*"

"Hmm, well, I guess our past arrangement wasn't so bad. It's kinda fun, don't you think?" He smiled. *He smiled. That sick fuck.* "Come on, Aspen. *It's fun, don't you think?*" Alex seethed, the words overenunciated as a threat.

Shit.

Shit. Shit. Shit. Shit.

Damn it... *Here we go again.* No matter what I replied, the outcome was always the same.

I kept my mouth shut, the bit of pride I had left keeping me from giving him what he wanted.

"Hey, Aspen. Answer. Me." My brother had a crazed look in his eyes.

I didn't look up to meet them and instead stared at my half-eaten dinner.

"Fucking answer me!" Alex's palm came slamming onto the table, rattling my bowl, and causing the spoon to fall onto the wood. I jumped at his outburst. "Are you scared of me? *I'll give you something to be fucking scared of!*"

His hand flew to my head, clamping onto my hair, and yanking me to my feet. I wanted to scream, to yell, but that would just make it last longer. I could fight back, I really could. I was a couple of inches taller than him and we were about equally muscular. But the price of fighting back was being outed, and that was something Alex had been reminding me of since I was in seventh grade.

My hands tried to grab onto my brother's arms to lessen the hurt of the pull, but it did little to help. Once I was standing, he let go and sent a closed fist into my face. The force sent me to the ground and before I could get back up, his foot dove into my rib cage, kick after kick.

Alex didn't stop until I was coughing and gasping for air.

"Come'ere!" He grunted as he grabbed my hair with one hand and my shoulder with the other, his fingers curling into the large bruise he gave me the other day. "Don't want to get any blood on the floor, now, do we? If mom and dad see anything broken or dirty, I'll have no choice but to tell them the truth," he chirped.

I willed myself not to cry. *I'll just take it like I always do.*

Alex didn't give me a chance to ground myself and instead *dragged* me up the stairs. I felt the burn of my skin scraping and being peeled off by the rough wooden steps. Large, painful bruises were already forming where my body hit the harsh ridges of the step above, primarily the vertebrae at the base of my neck and the small of my back. The bastard didn't even give me the opportunity to get up and walk on my own two feet.

When I got stuck on a step, Alex swore and told me to stop making things difficult before shoving the heel of his foot into the area where my shoulder and neck connected. I clenched my teeth, muffling the pain, trying to find release through my voice. By the time we were finally at the top, my entire body shook.

"What? Done already?" my brother scrutinized. He was *disappointed.* "Don't be such a goddamn baby. You're literally fine. There's no need to overreact."

I kept silent, not wanting to agitate him any more. With one last kick, Alex wandered back down the stairs and out the front door. It was fine. I was *fine.*

I crawled to the wall, struggling to prop myself against the cool surface. I set my legs out straight in front of me and stared at the red marks on my calves and shins. Looked like shorts were out until they faded... *Fucking hell,* that was the only part of my body I *didn't* need to cover.

I stumbled trying to stand, using the side of the wall as a crutch as I slowly hobbled back to my room. I closed the door behind me and collapsed onto my bed, fishing my phone out of my pocket to be met with a thoroughly cracked screen; it was just after ten p.m. I placed the device on the side of my bed next to my pillow and let the darkness consume me.

Whether that resulted from my physical fatigue or the deep, depressing abyss that was my thoughts and mind, they both led me to the same place.

Chapter Three

Aspen

THE LIGHT BUZZING OF MY phone startled me awake yet again. I'd lost count of how many times this had happened, but I hadn't bothered to pick it up or see who it was.

I wasn't really in a position to care at the moment.

I didn't think I'd left my bed in a couple of days. It might have been Sunday, but that could be off. I hadn't showered, eaten, drunk, or simply gotten out of bed. It was warm under my thick, heavy blankets. They felt like a shield, and as long as I was covered, nothing could hurt me.

Except, deep down, I knew that wasn't true. My brother could come in at any moment and decide he wanted to have some more *fun*. With my parents gone, he had free range to do whatever he wanted. When they traveled, I usually stayed out... But this time I didn't feel like getting up. *I couldn't.* My curtains had remained closed and I'd spent my time in the dark, sleeping and trying to forget about everything that hurt.

My weekend was full of nothing but pain. Physical, mental, the whole shebang. My brother didn't come home and I'd never been so thankful in my life.

I'd gotten lucky—there were no bruises on my face from when he punched me, although the same could not be said for the rest of my body. At least those parts could be hidden by clothes.

My boisterous alarm rang out, adding to my already-intense headache and cluing me in that it was, in fact, Monday morning, which meant another day of being around people that would hate me if they knew I was gay, and another baseball practice that would push me to my limits on the pain spectrum. Despite knowing the weather was going to be over eighty degrees today, I wore a navy-blue, nearly-black long-sleeve with a square-graphic image in the center. I paired it with regular denim jeans. My outfit was practical and, above all, comfortable. Minus the fact that it made me ten times more likely to come down with heatstroke.

I grabbed my unbearable amount of gear and headed through the front door to be met with Rafe's car parked outside. I threw my stuff into the backseat and climbed into the passenger seat.

I wanted to avoid the topic of why I'd been MIA all weekend, so I started the conversation first. "Did you have fun with Amelia?" I asked, fully aware that the two had gone on an obnoxiously sweet date whilst I'd hidden from my brother and struggled not to kill myself.

"Holy shit, dude, Saturday was great. We went to the beach, and damn, her body is *gorgeous*. There aren't a lot of girls with asses like hers. And after that, we went to a drive-in movie and cuddled in the backseat wrapped in blankets. I even gave her my sweatshirt. She looked so adorable swimming in it!" Rafe rambled on and on about the pale girl with waist-length brown hair and greenish-hazel eyes, who he'd been dating for about two weeks now.

I couldn't think of an emotion to describe how I was feeling. It was like a painful tingle radiating through my body and settling into the pit of my stomach. Rafe's definition of a perfect date... all the things I'd never be able to do. The beach? I'd rather be caught dead than have to take my shirt off in front of him, so that was a hard no. I could go to a drive-in movie, but we wouldn't be able to cuddle, not in this town. And his sweatshirts were the same size as mine, so there'd be no point.

"I'm taking her out to dinner this weekend and she said her parents are going to be out of town." Although the sly smile on his face stung a bit, I was unfazed. This wasn't the first time he'd had a girlfriend and I could guarantee it wouldn't be the last. Rafe hadn't been through a lot of girls or anything, he just seemed to have some issues with commitment.

"Looks like someone's gonna get lucky!" I tried to offer some form of enthusiasm. My best friend liked to share details I'd have been better off not knowing, but at least he seemed happy.

"So," Rafe started as he pulled into a random spot in the parking lot, "when are you going to get a girlfriend? I could name three people right now that are super into you."

"I'm not really interested in dating right now." *False. I'm not interested in dating girls.* "I'm just kind of focusing on baseball."

He snickered, "I call bull. You already accepted your offer from the University of Rowland. You're going to one of the highest-ranked schools for baseball in the nation with a major scholarship grant. High school baseball doesn't matter for us anymore. In less than four months, we'll both be playing for colleges. It's a done deal."

"No, I know."

Baseball was a great distraction. It gave me something to focus on rather than thinking about how much I loathed myself. Not only was it a game of tactics and strategy, but also strength and physical skill. As a catcher, I got to play my own game by putting chess pieces exactly where I wanted them. I used to find that exhilarating.

"I wish we were going to the same school, though. It sucks that we won't get to play together," Rafe sighed.

Even if he said that, when the time came, I didn't think he'd give me a second thought. Rafe would finally be able to move on with his life without worrying about a background extra.

I hopped out of the car and we went straight to the locker rooms where we stored all of our gear before meeting up with our friend group in front of a specific cluster of lockers. Jason Wright and Isabella Singh were in the middle of an intense argument. I couldn't tell if they hated each other and wanted to commit murder or were secretly in love and the sexual tension was killing them. Next to the pair were Devin and our other friend, Jamey Hinge. We'd all played baseball together at Cedar Heights since we were freshmen, except for Isa, who swam competitively.

"Aye, Alvarez, Ace, what's up?" Jamey removed himself from the wall he'd been leaning against, giving us each a nod of his head.

"Did you guys hear about that freshman that just transferred here?" Isa shoved her hand in Jason's face, pushing him away as she turned to ask us the question.

"Nah. Why?" Rafe asked.

"I heard he's an ice skater!" she laughed.

"Ice skating? That's kind of cool though, isn't it?" I asked.

"Yeah," Isa rolled her eyes. "But he does *figure skating!* You know, the one where people wear those super tight outfits with sparkles and sequins."

"And it's a guy doing that?" Jason scrunched his nose in disgust.

"That's so fucking gay." Devin made a gagging motion, which brought small laughs from the group. I had no choice but to do the same.

What was wrong with a guy doing figure skating? A sport didn't define someone's sexuality. And plenty of other sports had guys wearing tight uniforms; wrestling made guys look like they were dry humping each other.

"Should we go knock some sense into him?" Jason suggested.

The group seemed to be seriously considering it.

"Wait, guys. Hold on a second. You can't just beat someone up, and you don't even know if he's gay, so just chill out a bit." I wasn't sure if Rafe's comment was comforting or scary.

"Aspen!" A high-pitched shriek interrupted their conversation. Amelia jumped on my back, which had my eyes bulging out of my head and my body screaming in pain. I grabbed the five-eight girl's long legs so she wouldn't fall as she took hold of my cheek in her fingers and pinched.

I faked my smile, making sure my dimples showed while crinkling my eyes as I let out small laughs to hide my discomfort.

"How's my twin doing today?" she giggled as I stood up straighter, getting her to slide off gently.

Amelia liked to joke around that we were related because we had some similar features. We both had baby faces, for example, and our eyes were both unusually large and round.

I glanced at Rafe to see how he reacted. Even though I was aware Amelia wasn't into me like that, sometimes the way she acted seemed like flirting, and the last thing I needed was Rafe thinking I was trying to steal his girlfriend. If anything, it'd be the other way around—I'd much rather steal him from Amelia.

Unlike us, Rafe's eyes were somewhat narrow and had a slight almond shape stacked with thick black lashes, making it seem as if he was wearing eyeliner. The brown of his eyes was a distinct color, not light and not dark, but a perfect in-between. His nose was prominent, the bridge inhumanly straight, the tip a soft L shape that made his features more delicate.

"Why don't you two just date already," Isa snickered.

I shot her a glare. "Don't say that. You know Amelia and Rafe are together."

"That's right." Amelia slung a stretched-out arm around my shoulder, doing the same to Rafe and forcing us to bend down so she could reach us. "Don't tease my boys." She let go of me and Rafe wrapped his arm around her waist, pulling her body closer to his.

The first-period bell rang, forcing the couple to separate. We all waved our goodbyes and headed off to our classes. I walked into my physiology class with Isabella in tow, taking our seats at a shared desk.

We made small talk while waiting for our teacher to show up when one of Isa's friends from the swim team joined us. "Isa, either put those heart-eyes away or ask him out already." The blonde shot us a playful smirk.

"Shut up, Megan. Stop trying to project your fantasies onto me." Isabella's voice was high-pitched as she made fun of her friend.

I sat there awkwardly, throwing out small laughs here and there.

"Oh, come on, don't lie! I know you fell for Aspen's smile *ages* ago!" The blonde was loud and drew attention from some others in the class.

"Well," Isa tilted her head to the side, "his dimples are to die for... but my parents would stop feeding me if I brought home a white boy," she clicked her tongue. "They want a nice Indian man that'll blend right in."

"I thought you and Jason were dating," I teased, trying to get under her skin.

"Jason? He's black, not Indian, dumbass."

"I know that. But if your parents do stop feeding you, Jason's parents will take care of that. If anything, that's even better for you."

"Ugh," she moaned. "The thought of Mr. and Mrs. Wright's cooking makes me drool. Unfortunately, Jason's too much of an ass. His ego makes me want to barf."

"I definitely understand that," I said as I watched other students pull out their notebooks. I had no reason to do that, though. As a second-semester senior going to college on a sports scholarship, anything better than failing was an A in my book.

"Where does he even find that confidence?" The sheer thought of Jason irritated her.

I grinned. "All the guys on the baseball team are like that."

"Stop smiling!" Isa's friend whispered. "Unless you want to be hit on by every single girl in this class," she winked at me.

Isabella ignored her. "*You* aren't though."

I plastered a cocky smile on my face, getting ready to retort, when a voice snapped, "Mr. Ace. Ms. Singh," our heads whipped up to the teacher, "If you two don't want detention, I suggest you stop talking while I'm trying to lecture."

Isabella raised her arms in defense as we quieted down, putting an end to our discussion.

The day passed by slowly. The heat had been getting to me since my second class, and I could feel sweat dripping down my back. I walked with Devin and Rafe to the locker rooms to get ready for practice, slipping into the bathroom unnoticed. I tucked my white compression long-sleeve into my grey belt and white baseball pants that completely covered my grey socks. I wore the same black cleats I always did and matched it with a grey cap. Even if I was wearing a lot of layers, I'd do whatever I could to make it easier to deal with the weather.

Gradually, everyone made their way onto the field and started warming up while waiting for the coaches to show. Rafe and I lightly tossed the ball around on the grass in right field. Before I had time to put on my catcher's gear to help Rafe get his shoulder going for pitching, Coach Gale called us over to sit in a circle to the side of our dugout.

I was overly conscious of Rafe's knee resting atop my outstretched leg while he sat with his legs crossed in a pretzel shape. The warm touch made it challenging to focus on Coach's words.

"We have our game against Riverside tomorrow and I'm sure you're all aware, but if we win this last playoff game, we'll be heading to States. I have no doubt you'll pull through, since we did the same last year. Our fielding, our batting, our pitching and catching, and our overall teamwork are better than Riverside's. But that doesn't mean you boys can slack off. A win is never guaranteed, so let's practice hard and earn it!" He knew what we needed to do and there was no room for negotiation.

We worked on refining various plays for the entire practice. It was a harsh workout, but just mellow enough that we wouldn't be exhausted going into the game tomorrow. It was an away game, which meant we'd have to drive to Riverside High School. The school was within our district, but was one of the farthest from us. To make it on time, we'd get to skip our last period.

I wouldn't say that I was excited when I played baseball. I think 'excited' was too strong of a word. Baseball used to be one of the few things that still made me happy, but my emotions weren't exactly what they used to be, and I no longer experienced the same eagerness or enthusiasm when I played. I was fully aware that my interest and love for the sport was slowly fading; baseball had been a part of me for my entire life, and at this point, I only still played because I didn't know what else to do.

It was the last part of my being that had survived life's tribulations, the last semblance of my life before it'd gone to shit, the only string holding me together. I'd watched those strings break, one by one. And this one, too, was thinning. Soon, it'd snap.

Chapter Four

Aspen

"I GOT IT! I GOT it!" our left fielder shouted as the baseball fell perfectly into the net of his glove.

That was the third out.

My team jogged back into the dugout to prepare for our first at-bat. I sat at the end of the bench and leisurely took off my bulky gear while our first batter stepped up to the plate. Jamey dug his foot into the box, hunching over slightly in his stance. His job was to get on base and steal when our second batter gave him an opportunity.

The third person in our lineup was Devin, the most consistent and reliable power hitter on our team. I stood in the on-deck circle behind the third base foul line, taking practice swings and trying to ignore any soreness in my muscles and joints.

Devin connected with the ball, sending it just over the second baseman's head and landing where the dirt met the grass. That hit sent Jamey home and our second batter to third base, while Devin was called safe at first.

Now it was my turn. I placed one foot inside the box, turning my body to look at my coach for a sign. *Swing away.* As always. I'd held the fourth spot as the cleanup hitter in the lineup since I joined the varsity team as a sophomore. My job right now was to get the biggest hit I could to send our runners to home plate.

I let out a slow breath to focus my mind. I raised my bat, placing it above my head as I adjusted my grip on the handle. The pitcher started his windup, probably hoping a faster ball would be more likely to get me out, but the catcher's way of thinking was too simple. When his arm came swinging down and the ball was released from his hand, I took a step with my left foot and cocked my bat.

My eyes followed the ball as it spun toward me. I didn't blink and waited until the ball was in an ideal position. I swung my bat, making sure my form was perfect while the barrel hit the lower center of the baseball. *How stupid.* Calling for a fastball from a pitcher with weak control against a slugger with a high batting average. The catcher must've been green.

I sent the ball flying into the outfield so high it got lost in the sky, dusk encasing the sphere and rendering the baseball invisible in the purples and peaches of the darkening mosaic of clouds. I sprinted toward first, rounding the base and going straight for second. My teammates cheered as the ball landed well behind the center fielder, allowing our two runners to cross home base. It would've been a home run if they'd had a fence. The third-base coach flailed his arm around in large motions, urging me to keep going. I rounded second and darted toward third. The coach yelled at me, telling me to go down. I started my slide off to the side of the base just as the third baseman caught the ball. When he slammed his glove down to tag me, I glided straight past the base; the fielder missed me by a hair as I twisted my body and grabbed the white rubber with my hand.

"Safe!" the field ump shouted from between second and third.

I looked into the dugout at the gleeful guys pressed up against the chain-link fence, slapping the helmets of the runners I sent home. Rafe stood just feet away from me, getting ready for his at-bat. The proud smile on his face was enough to pump me up for the rest of the game.

We crushed them. Riverside was barely even competition for us when we were at our best. I ended the game with two triples and three doubles, Rafe getting on bases with one triple, two singles, and two walks. Our battery only allowed five of their batters to get on base throughout the entire game. It was nearly a complete shut-out, and damn, it felt good. Our season wasn't over yet; we won our league's playoffs, which meant our next game would be at States.

I talked to Rafe on the side of our huddled group after shaking hands with the other team; he was so animated and excited.

"Weren't you the one who said high school baseball didn't matter anymore?" I questioned.

Rafe gave me a coy smile. "Just because it doesn't matter doesn't mean it's any less fun."

"Understandable—" cool water suddenly gushed down my head, drenching my clothes and leaving small, partially melted ice cubes on top of my hair and between my jersey and undershirt. My body went rigid at the icy feeling, my arms and fingers pointed toward the ground as straight as possible, and my jaw hung open. Rafe took a similar position, shaking his hair out like a dog.

Our teammates and coaches surrounded us, screaming and laughing as they celebrated. They'd dumped the water from the orange cooler onto Rafe and me for carrying the game.

"Okay, okay," Coach Gale shouted over the boisterous team, raising his hands in the air to get everyone's attention. "Quiet down. I'm sure you're all tired, so I'll keep this short. I'll be receiving our schedule in a day or two. Our first States game will be this Saturday. I'm not sure who we're playing yet or if we'll have to travel, so keep your agendas open and plan nothing for this weekend."

A thrill shot through me at the prospect of being away for the weekend. It'd be a much-needed break from Alex and having to worry about him.

The coach continued his speech and explained our upcoming practice schedules. While he talked, my gaze wandered downward. My eyes widened and a slow panic began bubbling in my gut. My white sleeves had become see-through, making the unbandaged old and new cuts visible. I shifted my catcher's bag toward the front of my body, awkwardly hugging it with my arms in an attempt to hide the undersides that hosted countless scars.

My expression contorted as the players continued to listen to Coach Gale. "It's single elimination, so we can't afford to lose..."

Rafe tapped the top of my shoulder and I winced; the bruise, while fading, was still tender.

My head whipped to the side to look at him. Rafe surveyed me before asking, "Why are you holding your stuff like that? Did you hurt your shoulder?"

That sentence caused Devin to snap his neck toward us. He brooked his weight right next to Rafe, so it wasn't difficult to overhear.

"Aspen, is your arm hurt?" Devin took injuries blisteringly seriously because if someone played on one and made it worse, there was a chance they could ruin their chances of playing in the future.

"No, of course I didn't. Rafe was just asking why I didn't have my bag on my shoulder," I explained.

Devin took my words with a grain of salt as he crossed his arms over his chest and hesitantly placed his focus back onto our assistant coach who was talking about the highlights of our game.

"So?" Rafe spoke, pushing me to answer his question.

"Am I not allowed to hold my bag in my arms? Why are you being so nosy?" My words came off harsher than intended.

Coach Gale dismissed the team and people either headed to their cars or the guest locker room.

"*Nosy?* I'm worried about you!"

"I'm literally just holding my bag! What's the big deal?" I didn't understand why our conversation was escalating. I could guess that it was because Rafe was tired of my roundabout replies, tired of me.

"All I wanted to know was if you were hurt! Why are you getting all defensive?!"

We were yelling at each other, but after our lengthy celebration, the other team had vacated the area, leaving just me and Rafe in the giant backyard of their school.

"I'm *not!*" I shouted back.

"You *are,* Aspen! You made it *painfully* obvious that you are the second you got defensive over a simple question!" His arms flew around, a more-than-livid look on his face

"It's a fucking bag, Rafe. *Get. Over. It,*" I seethed.

It's not that I didn't understand where he was coming from. I did. It was that I couldn't have him invading my psyche like this. He'd never understand the consequences. I couldn't remember the last time we'd fought or even argued. Rafe was always putting up with me, despite how tough I made everything. I should've been thankful. It was a wonder he'd lasted this long.

"Is it that difficult to tell me what's wrong?" Rafe's voice cracked, as if he was wounded.

I looked at him apprehensively, but stayed silent.

"Fourteen years, Aspen. It's been fourteen years and you're getting mad because I asked you *what's wrong?*" His raspy tone was soft and low-pitched.

"It's because nothing's wrong. You're being annoying. There's no need to overreact."

"*Overreact?* Fucking *overreact?* You're the one who's overreacting! I was worried about you so I asked a question and all I get for that is being called *annoying?*" Rafe said, exasperated. "If you're so fine, then prove it. Just put the bag where you usually do and I'll forget you said that."

"*Holy shit, Rafe.* I called you *annoying.* Stop acting like I actually did something to offend you!" I took an unsteady step backward, my heart pounding in my chest.

"If you don't let go of that fucking bag, then I'm going to assume you're lying and are injured. I won't stand for you ruining your dream because of a damn *high school team.*" He took a threatening step toward me and I took another back, nearly tripping on the grass behind me.

"I told you I'm not injured! Why won't you just believe me?!" A lump formed in my throat, the one that always warned me when I was about to cry.

Rafe was *scaring me.*

"It's a *bag!* Why can't you just do what I'm asking! I *never* ask for anything from you! *Ever!* Just this once, I'm asking for a favor. *Please,*" Rafe begged as he got even closer to me.

I clutched the gear tighter, knowing the dripping fabric encasing my arms revealed everything from my wrists to the base of my jersey sleeve.

Rafe reached an arm out to snatch the bag.

"JUST FUCKING BACK OFF!!" My shout echoed around the empty field, my eyes squeezed shut.

His hand froze, hovering just above my catcher's bag. I slowly peeled open my eyes, Rafe hesitantly retracting his arm. The look of hurt that flashed across his face pained me, but I didn't have a choice. *Rafe didn't give me a choice.*

The corners of his mouth quivered, and the ends of his eyes seemed to droop downward in defeat. "I'm sorry that worrying about you makes me such a shitty friend."

"Come on, Rafe! Don't pull this bullshit! I set my boundaries loud and clear and you chose to ignore them."

"I just don't understand why you need those boundaries in the first place! You don't tell me shit about your life! With how you've been acting, it feels like we aren't even friends anymore."

"... *not friends?*" I muttered, staring daggers into the ground as my vision clouded with salty water. Those words muddled my mind. My thoughts became muggy and all I could hear was Rafe's voice on repeat, as if it was stuck on an endless loop.

He let out a deep, aggressive puff of air, like he was dumbfounded by my presence. "*I can't deal with you right now.*" His words were like a stab to the heart. Rafe threw his frustrated hands into his hair, glancing from me to the distant parking lot. "*Fuck this.*" He turned on his heel and left me behind.

I watched Rafe chuck his gear into the trunk of his car, not looking back once as he got into the vehicle and drove away.

He left me.

He left me in Riverside all alone, with no way to get home. No money and a practically dead phone.

I couldn't remember the last time I'd cried; a numbness had taken over years ago, forcing certain emotions to become foreign. But today, tears pricked my eyes. A single drop slid down my cheek, followed by a plethora of others. I didn't cry out, but I wept in my own, silent way.

It wasn't like I expected him to stay forever. I knew that one day we would separate from each other and go our own ways. I was well-aware that I was nothing more than a troublesome shadow following Rafe everywhere he went. *It's just a matter of time.* That was what I kept telling myself.

I sniffled, pushing my bag back to my shoulder and wiping my runny nose. I pulled my phone out of my backpack and pressed call on Devin's number. He usually drove a bunch of guys to games so they could all save gas, but he didn't pick up. I assumed it was because he was driving, but Jason and Jamey didn't pick up either. I decided it would be best to convince myself they were just blasting music so loud they didn't notice I called them. It'd make me feel better that way.

I pulled up my GPS, punching in my address. I let the device in my hand fall to my side when I started lifting my feet.

A two-hour walk...

My battery wouldn't last that long. I'd probably get lost, too.

I closed all the open apps on my phone except for the navigation, turned the brightness down, and pressed the Low Power Mode button. As I was doing so, my phone began to ring.

It was my mom, who was supposed to get home yesterday. I hurriedly wiped the tears off my face despite knowing she wouldn't be able to see me.

"Hi, mom," I answered the phone, raising the tone of my voice to get just the right amount of happy inflection.

"Hi, Aspen! How was your game?"

"It was great, we won!" A phony smile appeared on my face. It helped to get into character.

"Congratulations, sweetheart! I'm so proud of you!" I heard her whispering something to someone else in the background before asking me another question. "Are you home yet? Did Rafe give you a ride?"

"Yeah, I'm in the car with him right now."

"Okay, okay. Tell him I say hello."

"Will do," I chirped.

"No, Jessica! I told you this has to be done in a larger font, our client is older and will have trouble reading this." She paused for a second. "Sorry, Aspen. I know I said your father and I would be home Monday, but we had an emergency at our office in Turin, so it looks like we won't be able to come back until Thursday or Friday."

"Oh." *Crap.* "That's fine. I can manage on my own, I'm not a little kid."

"Ask your brother to bring home some dinner if you're not going out with friends. Even if you spend all your time with Rafe, don't keep mooching off of Teresa. You can rely on your brother a bit more since we'll be gone for a couple of days this time," my mom rambled on. "If you go into the fridge, you'll find some—" the phone cut off.

I pulled it away from my ear; the screen had gone black. I sighed and put my phone in my back pocket. I ogled the sky; I somehow always found myself walking home and away from Rafe whenever the sun was disappearing.

I knew the general direction to Cedar Heights, but there were so many turns along the way that it'd be impossible for me to remember the specific roads I needed to take.

———

I'd been right. I got lost. Thirty minutes into my walk in the grueling heat and I was already met with a view I'd never seen before. I'd definitely never driven past this block of houses, and the surrounding streets were unfamiliar. Overall, I had no clue where the hell I was. I had no choice but to go back the way I came and try a different route, hoping something might look familiar while I tried to avoid getting mugged.

The sky turned black as nighttime approached. There were no visible stars in the sky due to the heavy pollution in the city. I couldn't tell how much time had passed when I finally got to the major intersection just blocks from my house. My feet ached and I shivered from the chill, bits of dew collecting on my socks as I treaded through grass.

The main issue arose when I saw the sun peek out from behind the clouds to the east. My lack of sense of direction really came to bite me in the ass. I couldn't say I was particularly surprised. It didn't feel like I'd been out all night—my endless thoughts had this strange way of making time pass.

If the sun was up, then it was probably just before five a.m. Even though I was frustrated and upset that Rafe had left me to find my way home, I couldn't find it in me to be mad at him. It was my fault anyway. Every time I went the wrong way, I decided to backtrack, which added several unnecessary hours to the trek.

He probably assumed I'd be able to catch a ride from one of the guys or even my brother. Maybe he thought I could take the bus, and there was also the possibility that he'd forgotten that I had the sense of direction of a newborn baby that hadn't even opened its eyes.

If I was going to lose my best friend, I'd rather it be from something like this than going through the pain of him finding out I was gay, let alone in love with him.

Would he call me a creep? Disgusting? Would Rafe be repulsed and dread the fact that he'd *changed* in front of me?

The natural light made my fatigued eyes burn. Alex's car wasn't in the driveway, so I assumed he'd stayed out again. *No complaints here.*

I made my way up the stairs sluggishly, tossing my bags into the corner of my room and throwing all of my clothes into my laundry basket. I lumbered into my bathroom with a fresh towel wrapped around my waist.

It was like it was calling my name, *that drawer.*

What was the point? I'd pushed away the only person keeping me alive.

He hated me... thought I was annoying, nothing but a nuisance.

Do I really have anything left to live for?

What about baseball? *No...* I played baseball because it was an excuse to stay close to Rafe. I'd lost interest in the sport long ago, around the same time I'd lost interest in everything else that used to make me happy.

Should I just... *do it?*

Chapter Five

Aspen

I DIDN'T KNOW WHAT IT meant at first. I didn't understand it. But the older I got, the more I was able to recognize that feeling.

It wasn't my gaze that shifted. No, I'd always looked at Rafe differently. The second I realized exactly what that meant, I wanted to make it go away.

I didn't like the idea of being gay, of being attracted to guys. I tried everything that came to mind to change it, to reassure myself that it wasn't the case. My family, friends, and the people in this city had drilled this ideology into my skull: Being homosexual was a sin.

Being gay was disgusting.

Unnatural.

Wrong.

I tried to brainwash the haunting revelation out of me. Video after video. I stared and studied the naked women, but there was nothing. No arousal, no attraction, nothing.

That was the last straw that made everything finally click. Of course, I felt nothing. The sexual aspect of women had nothing to do with me... and I wanted nothing to do with them.

I couldn't be gay. I didn't want to be gay...

Yet I was undeniably in love with my male best friend.

"*Aspen!*" The voice startled me and had me slamming my laptop shut. Rafe peeked his head into my room, his body still standing outside the door. "*What are you doing? I called your name like five times. My dad's here to pick me up. I'll see you Monday!*"

"R-right," I stuttered as my best friend turned on his heel. I couldn't help but watch him leave, my eyes raking over him from head to toe. "See you later..."

I couldn't like Rafe like that. I shouldn't.

But I did.

"What was that?" Alex knitted his brows together tightly with a mixed look of confusion and disgust on his face as he leaned against the short stretch of wall between our bedroom doors.

"What?"

"Why were you looking at Rafe like that?" he snarled, stomping into my room.

I turned my desk chair to face Alex. "L-like what?"

"Like you were checking him out."

I held my breath, creating a long pause between us. "Hey, Alex," I started, "can I tell you a secret?"

"What is it?" He placed himself on the edge of my bed.

"Promise you won't tell mom or dad?"

"Just tell me what it is," he huffed, crossing his arms over his chest.

"I—" nerves stunted my voice. I'd never said the words out loud before: "I'm gay."

Alex's head snapped up to mine, his eyes staring daggers into me. "Gay? You can't be gay. You're not gay, Aspen."

"I am, though..."

"Why would you think that?" Aggression slipped into his sharp tone. "You're only in seventh grade. You're too young to know."

"I—like Rafe. Like, I think I have a crush on him..." My words were breathless.

"You're not gay!" Alex's voice rose as he spoke through clenched teeth.

The weird feeling I got when he denied my sexual orientation only made me more certain of it. "I'm gay, Alex."

"My brother is not a fucking faggot!"

Hearing slurs was not uncommon in this household, but it somehow felt different when I realized the hurtful words were directed at me. "Why would you say that?" I yelled back.

Alex stood, his body looming over me, forcing me to tilt my head up to look at the guy a foot taller than me. His expression was something I'd never seen before. His eyes were filled with pure hatred and repulsion, his face contorting like he was about to explode. His disgust drained the color from his face, leaving his skin an uneven, ghostly white.

"If you are gay. Then you. Are. Not. My. Brother." A crazed expression glinted his eyes as he harshly jabbed his finger into my shoulder. "I can't believe you're a filthy cocksucker! What, don't tell me you wish you were a girl. Seriously? You want a pussy? Is that so you can whore yourself out like a little bitch?"

"No! That's not it! I'm a guy, I don't want to be a girl." I tried to reason with him, but Alex was blinded, his mind closed off and no longer caring about the things I said.

"How the fuck did I get stuck with a fag?"

Alex's body hunched over with one of his arms pushing against the armrest, holding him up, and simultaneously trapping me against the back of the chair. His face was inches from mine when he slapped me, my head snapping to the side.

My mouth hung open, the side of my face now pointing toward my brother. I turned my head to look at him and he slapped me again, harder. "Don't look at me, you fucking bitch."

My hand cradled my now-pink jaw. "Why—" I choked on my words. "Why would you hit me?"

He leaned back, removing his weight from the chair. This time, a closed fist came down on the top of my cheekbone, his knuckles making a small cut just under my eye. "Who said you could speak? A homo like you has no right to talk to me."

I clamped my jaw shut, my eyes focusing on the carpet beneath me with furrowed brows.

"Are you about to cry? Seriously?" he laughed. "You really are a fucking pussy." Alex cocked his head to the side, ticking his jaw. "I wonder if I can beat the fag out of you."

A pang of fear struck me at his seriousness, at the sheer level of his hatred.

"Come'ere," he growled, grabbing the collar of my shirt and yanking me off my chair. He dragged me out of my room, and I clawed at his hands, but he was fifteen and I was thirteen. He was taller and stronger than me, and no matter how much I struggled, I couldn't get him to release his grip. Tears streamed down my face and I hiccuped, begging him to let go.

Alex pushed me inside of the spare, square-shaped room we had upstairs. The area was generally untouched, near-empty with nothing in it besides a couch lining the wall, a cheap-looking rug sprawled over the hardwood floor, and a glass coffee table collecting dust in the center. He slammed the door shut behind him and locked it.

He pulled me around, every movement jerking me in different directions. His unbudgeable grip treated me like a weightless rag doll. Fear coursed through my veins as Alex pushed me backward, his back to the door. He snarled and shoved me, sending me flying onto the table, shattering the glass on impact. I gasped, my breath hitching in my throat before oxygen could fill my lungs. My body froze, paralyzed with pain shooting through the nerves in my body.

The glass splintered into countless shards, digging into my skin and simultaneously ripping holes in my shirt.

A momentary flash of bewilderment and regret crossed Alex's face, but those thoughts in his head vanished before the seed could take root. "Fuck! You broke the damn table!"

I shuddered. Why? Why was he doing this to me? What was so bad about being gay? It wasn't wrong, and I didn't deserve this.

But I could blame myself.

I was stupid. I was so stupid. It wasn't like I was unaware of my family's views on homosexuality, yet I went ahead and told Alex, anyway.

I didn't think he'd simply accept me and tell me he loved me no matter who I was attracted to. But this...

Alex wasn't a violent person. He had never been. So why?

My breathing became labored as I stared up at Alex's face peering over mine with a semi-satisfied look. "You think this is bad? Just wait until our parents find out. I'm curious... what exactly do you think they'd do if they knew their son was a faggot?" Alex already knew the answer. He was toying with me.

I wanted to deny it, but deep down, I knew.

If this was Alex's reaction, then my parents' would be ten times worse.

My eyes went wide and I choked on a sob. "Please! Y-you can't tell them! Please," I begged as tears slid from the corners of my eyes and down the sides of my face and into my hair.

"Why the hell not?"

"I'm—I'm your brother!" I wanted him to realize that nothing had changed, I was still the same as before.

"I don't care, Aspen," he deadpanned. "It doesn't matter if we're related by blood. That changes nothing."

My back uncontrollably twitched. A sharp pain shot up through my neck and I closed my eyes as tight as I could.

"Someone like you doesn't deserve to have the same things I do. A fag like you doesn't deserve to live a nice life. Give me one good reason I

shouldn't tell mom and dad right now." There was a slight smirk on his stony face—disappointment mixed with intense amusement.

"Any-anything you want," my voice came out in a raspy whisper. "I'll do anything you want. Just—don't tell anyone else. Please."

"Anything, you say? Are you sure about that?" Alex sneered.

"Yes... Just don't tell anyone." My words were laced with defeat. I shivered from the pricking stings and throbs, my body hovering on the edge of unconsciousness.

Alex stepped over me and walked toward the door. "Make sure to clean this up when you're done. If mom asks me what happened, I won't lie for you."

I gazed at the ceiling, random splotches of black with flashing green and purple littering my vision. My arms were sprawled out at my sides and my legs lay still, lifeless.

My brother placed his hand on the doorknob and turned it. Before he opened the door, he craned his head over his shoulder. "You have a deal."

He upheld his side of the bargain. Alex kept my secret, and in exchange, he'd beat me up whenever he felt like it.

Alex rarely touched me when our parents were home, but they traveled frequently for work. Sometimes it was just a day trip, and occasionally, a full week.

Madelin and Garret Ace. Co-founders of a successful business enterprise focused on consumer travel satisfaction. White and devout in their faith. And unfortunately for me, homophobic. Well, not just homophobic. They hated anything that didn't fit their definition of acceptable.

And I did not fit into that small box.

What I didn't understand the most out of everything was why Alex tortured me. Why—how he could possibly enjoy it.

When I came out to him, his violent tendencies surfaced, like he'd been wrestling with anger, the emotion bubbling under his skin, just waiting to burst out. And it seemed like I was the perfect outlet.

He knew he could do whatever he wanted to me and I would never tell a soul. Hell, I'd do everything I could to hide it. Which also meant I had to do everything I could to cover for that monster.

I sprinted as fast as I could, trying to ignore the intense pain in my leg. Each step intensified the twinge tenfold, and it was getting harder and harder to ignore.

"Aspen, slide!" the third-base coach shouted through cupped hands.

I didn't want to. It would make everything hurt so much more than it already did, but if I was called out here, then we wouldn't score a run and we'd have to go into another extra-inning that I knew I wouldn't be able to handle.

I ground my teeth as I dropped to the ground, sticking my left leg out and tucking my right leg under it. My foot slid across the flat home plate as the opposing team's catcher caught the ball and slammed his glove onto my leg.

A loud shout came from the umpire, "Safe! That's the game!"

I could hear the cheers coming from my teammates, coaches, and parents in the stands. We'd just won our first 15U tournament of the season.

They celebrated, but I couldn't get up. I rolled to the side as the catcher removed the pressure from my leg. Noticing that I was still on the ground, the umpire threw his mask off to the side. He raised his hand in the air and called for my coach. The rowdy team went silent and my coaches rushed toward me. My mother and father trotted down the bleachers as fast as they could, running through the dugout to where I withered, clutching the lower half of my leg.

My breathing shallowed and I squished my body into a fetal position that somehow eased the pain.

"What happened?" my coach asked urgently, crouching down next to the lower half of my body, gently removing my hands.

I didn't answer him.

He placed his hands where mine had been and I yelped in pain. He immediately retracted his arms.

My face pushed into the beige dirt and tears stung my eyes.

"Garret, we need to take him to the emergency room!" My mom touched my dad's shoulder, her words scrambled.

"Okay, go get the car, I'll try to pick him up," came my dad's gruff voice.

He scuffled one hand under my backside, scraping it on the hard rocks in the dirt, and used his other hand to grip the bottom of my thigh just above my knee.

"Agh!" I grunted as he lifted me off the ground, stumbling a bit while trying to find balance. It was the beginning of eighth grade and I'd just turned fourteen—I wasn't as small as I used to be.

My dad panted, slowly making his way to the car my mom had pulled up to the front of the parking lot.

Rafe ran to catch up with my dad, fast-walking on the side where my head was. He had this look of fear in his eyes, his eyebrows knitted together so tightly they almost touched. There was a large frown on his face, which, for some reason, hurt more than my leg.

"What happened?!" If I weren't squinting at the bright sun beating down on my face and could actually see, I'd think Rafe was crying.

"I must've hurt my leg when I tripped over my bag before the game," I lied. "But it wasn't this bad. I think it's just because the catcher tagged me where I hurt it." My mouth became dryer by the second, the fake words causing me to sweat.

My dad set me onto the cool leather seats of the car. I lay on my back and adjusted my position using my elbows and right foot to scoot myself back so I had more room for my legs.

"*But you were limping before the game even started—*" *Rafe didn't finish his sentence, the closing door interrupting him.*

I waved at Rafe through the window as the engine roared, my mom driving away. He didn't wave back, he simply looked at me, confused and worried.

My lips pursed, trying to silence the screams of pain aching to come out. I chewed on the corner of my lip, the small stinging momentarily distracting me from the real issue.

When we arrived, my mom parked as close to the entrance as she could. My dad opened the door and assisted me out, placing his arm under my left shoulder to help carry my weight. With the help of my dad, I limped into the waiting room where I took a seat in one of the numerous chairs while my parents went up to the front desk.

My parents hounded me with questions. I told them the same thing I'd told Rafe; I needed to be consistent.

My dad was completely unconvinced. He believed that the other team's catcher had been playing dirty, which wasn't the case, and I felt bad that I'd put some of the blame on him.

"Aspen Ace?" a nurse wearing magenta scrubs called. She didn't look up as she scribbled something on her clipboard.

"Wait here for a second." My mom tapped my shoulder gently, standing to confront the nurse and politely ask for a wheelchair.

She came back with one moments later. I placed my arms on the armrests of the plastic waiting chair, flexing my muscles to keep steady and using my right leg to stumble into the black cloth of the wheelchair.

She directed my parents to a room and told them to wait there while I got my leg X-rayed.

I sat on the grey edge of a long table, my leg resting on the shiny black material covering the center, a giant machine attached to the ceiling dropping down. She placed it in four different spots, taking several images each time. The nurse made sure that every portion of my leg was covered from my hip joint down to my foot.

When the X-ray tech finished, the nurse helped me back into the wheelchair and brought me to the room my parents were waiting in. I hoisted myself onto the dark-blue, almost turquoise bed in the corner and waited patiently for the doctor to come in.

Three knocks rang against the door before a woman with pitch-black hair poked her head into the room. "Hello!" She walked in and closed the door behind her, placing herself on a circular seat and swiveling toward me. "Hi, Aspen." She reached out her hand for me to shake. "I'm Dr. Miller, it's nice to meet you." She paused. "Well, the circumstances aren't exactly nice, but you get what I mean." She gave me a large, straight-toothed smile.

"I took a look at your x-rays, and you have a closed simple fracture on your left tibia." She turned the computer screen, showing my family an image of my X-ray. "As you can see here," she pointed to the break, "the lower part of the bone has been broken off of the top portion. It's a clean break. There aren't any splintered fragments, and thankfully it didn't breach the skin. I know that it hurts now, but if you wear a cast for six to twelve weeks, it'll heal quite nicely and your leg will be good as new." The doctor grinned, nodding while keeping eye contact.

"Could tripping over a bag cause something like this?" my dad asked, rubbing his stubbly chin.

"Depending on the way he fell, it's possible," the doctor explained.

I did fall. But not over a baseball bag.

My parents had gone on a date the previous night, leaving me alone with Alex. He didn't usually go this far... but as time had passed, he'd continued to get more and more physical. At that point, I was simply the personal punching bag he used to let off steam.

I'd been standing next to the fridge looking for something to eat when Alex walked up to me and closed the door. He placed himself between me and the silver appliance. When I took a step back, he smiled.

He just smiled.

And then he told me not to move, to stay completely still, and that I would "get it" if I dodged. The next thing I knew, Alex had stomped on my shin. The impact made me fall into the island in the middle, giving me a nasty bruise at the bottom of my rib cage in a long, thick horizontal line. The bruise was darker near where the table made contact with the bone, while the rest spanned out into pinks and yellows, with spiderwebs of purple protruding out.

I was lucky I didn't hurt my knee. That would've been much more difficult to recover from.

A year later and I still didn't understand what I'd done to deserve this... but in the end, it wasn't about what I understood. It was about how much I could take. The answer: not a lot more.

"What was it this time, Aspen?" His face was fuzzy and his voice blurred into the loud ringing in my head.

My breaths were labored and shallow. From the corners of my eyes, I saw the clear outline of the mask that covered my nose and mouth, aiding my attempt to breathe. There was a soft pillow under my head and curtains on both sides of the tall bed.

"Aspen! I need you to tell me what you took!" Dr. Amin shouted, trying to get my eyes to focus on him. But all I could see was the vague image of his curly black hair mixed into his dark skin, his white coat completely blending into the white curtain.

"Damnit!" he muttered as he lifted my eyelid and shined a bright light into it. I tried to close my eyes at the irritating handheld sun. "Aspen! I can't treat you if you don't tell me."

I opened my mouth, but the words didn't come out.

Did I want to tell him? Not really...

"Vicodin..." I whispered, my throat raspy and burning.

"And?" He knew me too well.

"Vodka..."

Dr. Amin left the room, returning and sticking a needle into my arm.

"How much?" He sighed. The clicking noise in the background from him adjusting the dosage of whatever he was giving me distracted me, prolonging the time before I answered.

"Five—maybe six. Possibly ten..."

"You're lucky you're still breathing right now! We had to pump your stomach! Again!"

Lucky wasn't the exact word I would've used...

"How did I get here?" I asked, looking at his seemingly clearer face.

"A druggie saw you popping pills and wanted to steal them, but then you collapsed and were lying unconscious on the ground, so he brought you here."

I was all too familiar with the clinic. It wasn't my first trip here—whenever I thought Alex had broken or sprained something, or if I made an attempt and it hadn't worked, I'd usually come here to get stitches or to make the pain disappear temporarily.

It was a free clinic that operated for people without healthcare. My family didn't know about it, and the doctors I saw here regularly only knew my first name. They couldn't do anything when I refused to give them more information.

The doctor sighed and placed a hand on my clothed arm. I wanted to flinch. It hurt. But he wouldn't be able to see why, although he probably knew, since he quickly retracted his hand.

"You've been coming in here with these same issues for the past two years. If you just tell me what's happening, I can help you. Seriously, Aspen. I can help." What he wanted was to involve my parents so that I could be admitted to a hospital. He couldn't do shit without *their permission, since I was still a minor. "You're only sixteen! You don't need to deal with everything by yourself."*

No, thank you.

Even if I needed it, I was not about to spend my time in a psych ward where I'd be monitored twenty-four seven. I knew that if I went, they'd take away the only things that still made me happy.

I wouldn't be able to play baseball.

I wouldn't get to talk to Rafe.

... Yeah, kind of a short list, I know.

I wouldn't have the privacy I needed to make myself feel... better...

I wouldn't be able to release the hurt...

And worst of all, it would mean telling people, my parents, what happened—and why...

That wasn't an option, and it never would be.

Even if I needed help, I didn't want it.

Chapter Six

Aspen

MY EYES BURST OPEN AS an agonizing wheeze escaped my throat while chilling cold sweats broke out across my body. Alex forced me out of the painful memory-filled dreams when he jumped on top of my stomach as if it was a trampoline.

He wore a sadistic smirk that made me blanch. When his body raised into the air, his floppy hair rose with it only to fall back down every time he landed on me, his heels cruelly digging into my left side just below my rib cage. My body seized, my torso involuntarily contracting toward my legs.

In my panic and confusion, I grabbed hold of one of Alex's legs and threw him to the ground. With a loud grunt, the back of his head collided with my desk.

I gasped, heaving for air, unable to catch my breath as I clutched my stomach and brought my legs to my chest, curling into a small, tight ball.

"Did you just *touch* me?" The seething voice had me averting my eyes, looking down and nowhere else.

Alex removed himself from the ground. With one knee on the floor and his other foot firmly planted, he used his hands to push off his propped leg. The floorboard under the carpet creaked with his angry strides. The second he had both feet on the ground, Alex lunged toward me, wrapping his hands around my neck and forcing my head back onto my pillow. "Who the fuck gave a disgusting piece of shit like you permission to put your hands on me?!"

My hands scraped at his hold, desperate to find release. I kicked and squirmed under Alex's vicelike grip. I tried to wedge my fingers between the skin of my neck and the flesh of his fingers, but he pressed so hard that all I was able to attain were numerous bloody scratches to my neck.

Blood rushed to my face and a tingling sensation spread through my fingertips. I thrust my hands into Alex's face to try and push him away, shoving at his cheeks and forcing his chin to rise into the air and his upper body to straighten.

There was a slight ease in strength from the two hands around my jugular. I wanted to breathe in all the oxygen my room contained, but the burning in my airway forced me to cough instead.

Realizing that his hold had loosened, Alex cocked his right arm back and brought it down onto my face.

He didn't stop until there was a loud cracking sound followed by a string of curse words. "You broke my hand!"

My hands ghosted lightly over the tender skin of my throat before I leaned to the side, coughing small bits of red liquid onto my blankets. My mouth tasted like iron and something dripped down the corner of my painfully split lips. My jaw hung open and the gooey substance of blood mixed with saliva dribbled out of my mouth and onto my sheets.

He clenched his jaw and turned his harsh glare to me, cradling his bruised, blood-covered knuckles. Alex's nostrils flared and his eyes were on fire—like he wanted me dead, and at some point, he might be willing to get the job done himself.

"All I wanted was to be a nice big brother and wake you up since you missed school. But I guess this is what I get for trying to help a fag," Alex snarled, slamming the door shut on his way out, the vibrations rattling through the walls.

I collapsed onto my bed. *So it didn't work, huh?*

My shaky breaths slowly became more controlled. My entire body trembled, which wasn't surprising. I was probably as pale as a sheet of paper, the color most likely completely drained from my lips. Sweat soaked through my clothes, creating a damp spot on the comforter beneath me.

I looked up at the strange texture of the white ceiling. Something about it drew me in—it was almost hypnotizing. I'd left my curtains open, not bothering to close them last night—scratch that, this morning. It looked to be around sunset by the tint of orange from the light filling my room.

I sighed. Disappointment dripped from the veins of my arms along with the blood.

Nothing ever went my way. All I wanted was to die, yet I'd gotten the shit beaten out of me instead. Wonderful.

Wasn't life ironic? I inflicted pain on myself to deal with the damage my brother dealt constantly. Double the agony. Didn't seem very fair, did it?

At first, my goal last night was to relieve some stress. I kept the cuts thin and short, my inner thighs now covered in ugly checkered marks. But the more I kept doing it, the more I couldn't keep the thoughts away.

I wanted to end it. So I did *everything* I could to make sure it happened. I should've tried to find stronger pills, but it wasn't always easy to get a hold of good shit on short notice.

I attempted to sit up, but pain jolted through my abdomen. I clutched my side over my plain, light-grey shirt. My eyes closed as tightly as they could, and I shuffled my body as high on my bed as possible before weakly lifting my black covers. I struggled to hold it up while I softly slid myself under the comfortable warmth. Once fully inside, I twisted to lie down on my right shoulder.

I reached out to grab my phone, happy to see I'd managed to plug a charger into it before I'd passed out. Three missed calls from Coach Gale. One text from Isa. And nothing from Rafe.

Of course not... Why would he want to talk to me? He was the one that should be mad; it was my fault after all. Everything he said to me on the field was true.

Since I was still alive, should I apologize? But he would demand an explanation. What kind of lie would work with something like this?

I unlocked my phone, and the first thing that popped up was Devin's story; the video was from last night.

"Yooo, Rafe!!" Jason shouted excitedly, holding a camera extremely close to Rafe's face. Rafe was slumped against the couch with a red cup in hand. His eyes drooped and tears streamed down his face.

"Tell us again why you're so upset to the point that you're getting shitfaced on a Tuesday night," Devin snickered, recording the whole ordeal.

"Amelia broke up with me." Rafe's words were quiet.

"And why did she do that?" Even though I couldn't see Devin in the video, I could tell he was smiling and getting a kick out of this.

"Fuck!" Rafe shouted. "I can't believe I just left him there by himself." Rafe peered up toward Devin's phone with a giant frown on his face. I couldn't help but think he looked cute. "What if he got lost?! He has a terrible sense of direction."

He's talking about me, isn't he?

"Why didn't you just call him, then?" Jamey asked, sitting next to Rafe on the small couch.

"I really fucking wanted to, but I dropped my phone off of Amelia's balcony and into her pool." He sniffled and took another swig of his drink. "I want to apologize so damn much! After I left Amelia's house, I drove back to the field, but I didn't see him on my way there or the way back..."

"That still doesn't explain why she broke up with you," Jason commented.

"We had a kind of deep conversation and she made me realize a lot of things. And because of those things, she said we couldn't be together," Rafe sighed. He seemed coherent enough to not be drunk, but the slightly out of character openness made me think he was at least a little buzzed.

"Shit, it must have been something big for her to break up with you," Jamey added.

"Yeah... Really fucking big." Rafe rubbed his temples as if the reason had given him a splitting headache.

"So," Jason drew his words out, "what was it?"

"Nothing, don't worry about it," Rafe waved him off.

"Wait, I'm confused. Are you sad because your girlfriend broke up with you or—"

Rafe cut Jamey off. "It was a mutual decision. We decided we'd better off as friends." He took a large gulp of the liquid in the solo cup.

"What does that have to do with Aspen?" Devin asked.

"Well, I'll just say that our conversation started off with Amelia telling me that all I talk about is Aspen and she thought I cared about him more than I do about her." Rafe didn't go into further detail. "So I told her that she was right."

"That's kinda gay." Devin's lighthearted tone concealed the passive aggressive words.

"Yeah, man," Jamey started with a disbelieving laugh, "why the hell would you say that to your *girlfriend?*"

"Of course Aspen is more important!" Rafe said adamantly. "I've been with him for fourteen years. *Fourteen*. That's a long time! I'd barely been dating her for *three weeks.*"

"Yeah, but one will get you laid, and the other is like the weird next-door neighbor your mom makes you spend time with." Jason's words stung.

I could've guessed that I didn't mean much to them, but still.

"*Jason.*" Devin's stern voice forced Jason to look at his camera.

He should've stopped recording at this point. Why did he post this? He knew I'd see it... *Oh.* He *wanted* me to see it. Devastation crept its way up my spine. My lack of surprise was replaced with instant understanding. I couldn't blame them—I wouldn't want to be friends with me either.

"Come on, man. You can't say that shit. Aspen's our friend." Jamey's brows were furrowed as he defended me.

Devin moved his phone back to Rafe whose jaw was visibly wired shut. Rafe scowled, "If I hear you say one more thing about him, I will fuck you up so bad that your own parents won't recognize you."

The room filled with silence before Devin abruptly ended the video.

Wow... okay.

A dreadful-yet-giddy feeling enveloped my mind and sent butterflies to my stomach.

He felt bad about ditching me... that thought made me feel a little better. But then again, did he care about me that much, or was it the alcohol talking?

I'd heard a lot of people say a drunk man's words were a sober man's thoughts. But I'd also heard the most bizarre and absurd things come out of Jamey's mouth when he was intoxicated. Like that one time when he tried to convince everyone he used to be best friends with a flying leprechaun named Mauricio. If I didn't know better, I'd think someone had slipped him something.

Maybe I should go ask Rafe what he meant... it couldn't hurt, right?

I sighed and carefully sat up in my bed, throwing my covers to the side and flinging my legs over the edge. I stared at the ground with my phone clutched tightly in my hand. The muscles in my abdomen contracted involuntarily, my body unsure of how to react and deal with the new injury; I should've known by now.

I built up my courage, using my arms to help push me off the mattress. I managed to get myself into a standing position. I huffed as I tried to take a step, ultimately stumbling forward. My palms landed on the desk just feet away from my bed, but the distance forced my legs into a strange lunging position.

"Ow! Shit!" I yelled, still trying to keep my voice somewhat quiet.

I could feel the strain on my inner thighs tearing the fresh scabs. I used the desk to pull myself back up, hissing with every movement.

What did I have left that *didn't hurt* at this point?

The bruises and lumps and skid marks and burns and pain, so much fucking pain, were adding up faster than I could heal. But Alex didn't care. He didn't give a single crap about anything and everything that hurt. And that long list now extended to my torso... from being jumped on. *Jumped on.*

Who the fuck would do that?

And I couldn't leave out the self-inflicted injuries, could I? No, of course not. My arms were still raw, my thighs freshly cut, and my body rejecting the stuff I tried to take last night. I'd sweated through my clothes and probably had a mild fever. Yay... how pleasant.

My only regret from last night was that I woke up.

Without a second thought, I rummaged through one drawer and pulled out a joint and a lighter, shoving them both into the pocket of my black sweatpants. I limped my way to my closet, rummaging through the many piles of clothes stacked on shelves until I clasped my hand around the neck of a bottle of Spirytus. I pulled it out and looked at the half-empty bottle. It tasted like shit, but it sure as hell did its job; I wouldn't be able to find a better-tasting drink with an alcohol concentration as high as this. I popped the small, circular cap off and took a hefty swig of the vodka. My face contorted, relishing the slight burning sensation filling my mouth and throat.

I wobbled to my closed door, my right hand not leaving the jolting pain in my rib cage. I slowly turned the knob. Being careful to not make any noise, I peeked through the small crack and peered into the hall. My brother's door was wide-open, which usually meant he wasn't in there.

My left hand trailed the wall as a means for stability until I got to the top of the staircase, where I checked left and right, leaning down as far as I could without falling. My eyes caught nothing and the only sound in the house was the buzzing of the air conditioner.

It took me forever to get down the stairs. I passed each step with extreme hesitancy, since the shifting of my weight and the uneven distribution needed to descend the staircase was proving to be more agonizing than I'd originally thought.

Once through the front door, I was met with Alex's vacant spot in the driveway. I presumed that he'd driven himself to the emergency room. Noting that I was in the clear, I began the awful journey to Rafe's house. It was already dark outside, but the night breeze created a nice medium between the hot air that still lingered from the scorching sun earlier in the day.

I think that was the first time Alex had ever gotten hurt doing that *stuff* to me. Although I wasn't thrilled about how it happened, a part of me enjoyed the pained expression on his face. The bastard deserved it.

I hated violence; I wouldn't have wished it upon anyone. *But my brother deserved it.* I knew he'd never go through the things I had, but he deserved to suffer. Even if it was just a little. Just a broken finger or knuckle. Just a fraction of what he'd done to me.

My thoughts kept me company on my prolonged walk to Rafe's house. I had some very detailed discussions with the voice in my head. Yes, it was my own voice, but it was one hell of a conversationalist. It made up scenarios that would only come true in my dreams, and for its favorite pastime, it liked to replay traumatic events. Tonight's cinematic showing focused on what Rafe had said about me to Jason and everything it could, but wouldn't, mean. I almost wished I hadn't heard those words. It was like he was giving me hope. *False hope.*

Standing in Rafe's driveway, I placed the alcohol next to a small shrub before approaching the Alvarezes' front door. Without removing my right hand from my abdomen, I lightly knocked.

"Just a minute," Teresa yelled from the other side.

Within seconds, pounding footsteps approached. The door unlocked and she flung the wood open. She wore patterned pants and a tight hot-pink shirt with a short, moss-green cloth wrapped around her neck that she used to dab sweat off her forehead.

"Oh, this?" Teresa gestured toward her getup. "I was following a Zumba video!" she shared excitedly before her smile dropped into a frown and a worried expression overtook her face. "Dios mío! Aspen, what happened to you?" She reached out her hand and cupped the side of my face, inspecting all the cuts and bruises.

"I was going downhill too fast and ended up falling off my bike." I flashed a cheeky smile followed by a soft chuckle. "It looks worse than it feels, so don't worry too much."

Teresa sighed in relief and retracted her hand.

"I actually came to talk to Rafe…" I glanced past her and into the quiet house.

"Oh, that's right! Rafe said he broke his phone, so I guess he couldn't tell you. He left a couple hours ago to listen in on one of Mateo's conferences.."

"So he's not here?" I bit the inside of my cheek, ignoring how it was already bloody from having been cut by my teeth when Alex punched me.

"No. He'll be back Monday afternoon. It'll last several days this time, so he'll miss school."

Mateo worked as a therapist and often traveled to different states to speak at conventions and such. Rafe had gone to a couple before, usually leaving for three days up to a week.

Looked like I needed to find another way to get to campus tomorrow. Walking... walking wasn't going to work. Not with the distance and the state of my ribs.

"Uhm, did he say why he's going?" We had a game this weekend. I didn't want to play, but if Rafe wasn't there, I had zero incentive to show up, especially not with the crippling pain that had me questioning how I was even still standing.

"Mateo didn't want to take him, and Coach Gale wasn't happy, but Rafe was unusually adamant about attending this one. He has a great deal of interest in psychology. He often goes to his father with questions about specific symptoms and treatments. His face is always buried in electronics, doing research."

I didn't know that. *Why don't I know that?*

Rafe used his dad as an opportunity to ditch all the time, always complaining about how boring psychology and sociology were when he got back. Rafe told me everything, but he'd never mentioned this.

"Oh!" The sudden noise startled me, my wide eyes jumping to hers. "He's so strange! Whenever Rafe looks something up, he tries to put on a very straight face. It's almost unnatural. I think he's trying to hide his interest in the subject. He's probably embarrassed that he likes something besides baseball when he used to rant about how that sport is the love of his life!" Teresa burst out into laughter and rubbed small tears from her eyes.

"I see," I nodded. "Well, it was nice to see you, Teresa."

"Yes! You're welcome any time. Even if Rafe isn't here, don't hesitate to come by for some food if you're hungry!"

I flashed a bright smile and pretended to laugh. "Thank you."

"Of course! You're practically my second son!"

I wish.

I parted from Rafe's house even more confused than when I got there, grabbing the much-needed high-ABV drink on the way. I'd received no answers.

I made my way to the park near my house, stumbling onto the playground. The streets were eerily quiet, the only noise coming from an occasional car passing by. Wednesday night left the area completely abandoned by its usual host of children, any kids that would've been playing probably tucked into bed. Streetlights illuminated the structure, flashing dim lights onto me and the hole-filled walkway I sat on. I leaned against a thick, blue pole bolted into the top of the slide.

I slumped against the metal, utterly exhausted. My whole body wailed in miserable pain. It was so overwhelming that the aches gave me a splitting headache.

I fished the pre-rolled joint out of my pocket, taking out my Zippo lighter and admiring the Joker card design. My life was one giant joke. I faked everything every day. Didn't that make me the ultimate Joker? I even kept a smile plastered on my face.

I flipped open the lid and rolled the metal spark wheel down with my thumb, lighting the tip of the joint and slowly rotating it with my fingers. I put the weed to my mouth, sucking it in and holding the drug-filled air in my lungs for several seconds before leisurely blowing it out. Smoke fell from my nose and ajar mouth. I took another hit and then another, feeling a little better. I wasn't so focused on the pain and my mind was able to briefly forget about the cause of my problems.

I felt content while I gazed at the full moon. It was so bright and beautiful. The stars occupying the sky captivated me. The crisp nighttime air numbed my fingers, and my nose twitched from the cold. I sat in a comfortable quiet while the sound of crickets filled my surroundings as I continuously went back and forth between smoking and taking large gulps of the bitter liquid.

I put my lips to the joint, breathing in more of the natural plant.

"Aspen?" The sudden voice startled me; I choked on the smoke and erupted into a coughing fit.

I looked down at the source of the female voice standing near the bottom of the slide. "Isa? What are you doing here?" I asked calmly; the alcohol and weed had not only made my mind foggy, but also mellowed me out.

"I was bored, so I decided to come here and maybe hang out on the swings. What about you?" Isa asked as she walked over to the mini rock wall that led to the platform I was on.

"Wanted to get out of the house and relax a bit." I gestured toward my joint.

She climbed up and placed herself at the opposite side of the top of the slide, just a couple of feet from where I had my legs stretched out. She scrunched her nose up, placing a hand over it and turning her face away from me. "Damn, Aspen, you *reek!* What the hell have you been drinking??"

I sluggishly turned the bottle resting next to my hip to show her the label.

"Want a hit?" I asked, holding the rolled joint out to her.

"Don't mind if I do." She quickly rubbed her hands together to warm them up before taking it to her lips.

She murmured along with her released puff, "This is *good* shit."

"Damn right it is."

Isa handed it back to me, and as she did, she caught sight of my face. "Holy shit, Aspen! What happened to you?!" Her eyes bulged and she suddenly sat up as straight as a board. "Is that why you're drinking something so strong?"

"Hmm?" I mumbled, taking yet another hit. It was probably the last one I was going to get tonight. "I guess you could say I got into a fight... although I'm the only one who looks like *this*..."

"Why would anyone do that to you?! You're literally the sweetest person I've ever met." Isabella's voice was soft and genuine. Her eyes drooped down at the ends, showing the utter disbelief and heartache she felt at seeing her friend like this. If I wasn't still so put off by what Jason had said about me, I might've been touched. "Who was it?"

The drugs might have made me high, and I was nowhere close to passing a BAC test, but the substances also gave me a sense of confidence and carelessness that I otherwise lacked in my sobriety.

"My brother," I slurred, placing the joint back on my mouth in hopes I could suck just a tiny bit more out. My eyes were half-closed, the alcohol making me drowsy and the weed making my eyes unnaturally red.

"What?! *Alex?* Why would he do that?!" she practically screamed.

Normally, I would've told her to be quiet since her voice was loud enough to wake up the entire neighborhood, but something in me simply didn't care anymore.

I was calm... Or maybe it was just the emptiness settling in for the night.

I'm so tired of this...

My voice came out monotone, as if I hadn't a care in the world. "Because I'm gay."

Chapter Seven

Aspen

WHAT DID I JUST DO?

The second those forbidden words spilled from my mouth, the joint fell from my fingers and dropped through a hole on the platform.

I averted my gaze from Isa, my body frozen and rigid with wide, startled eyes.

There was no way I just said that...

I slowly raised my eyes to gauge her reaction. She was the only other person I truly considered a friend besides Rafe.

Her brownish-pink upper lip pulled up, her eyebrows knitted, and nose wrinkled.

A look of disgust.

"Wait—" I reached my hand out in a panic, but she flinched away from my touch.

Isa paused for a second before rushing to her feet. She glanced at me one more time before she shook her head in disapproval and descended the structure.

Regret. A suffocating, all-consuming regret. Even in my drunken state, I recognized the unsettling feeling making its way into the back of my mind and the pit of my stomach.

Oh shit... *Oh shit!* What possessed me to think I could say that to someone who was openly homophobic?? *Dammit!*

I watched her body disappear down the street. I wanted to run after her and make up some lie. I wanted to pretend it was a joke or at least ask her to not tell anyone, but my energy was spent and I could barely move. She was too far away and walking too fast for me to catch up.

I let out a shaky breath. *Why did I do that? Why did I say that? Why would I... Fuck!* I'd spent years trying to keep my sexuality to myself. I let my brother fucking *torture* me... yet some measly alcohol messed everything up. *Years'* worth of nothing but pain and hurt, and I'd thrown it all away because I got drunk...

It wasn't even my first time, *so why?* Why now? Was it because I couldn't take it anymore? Because I'd hit my limit and was just so sick of keeping everything to myself?

Her silence afterward only made my discomfort spike. The uncertainty surrounding how she would handle that information tormented my mind.

I chewed on my torn-up lip, warm liquid spilling into my mouth and coating my teeth in a red film. *Was she going to tell everyone at school? Would she post about it on social media or send a text to our group chat? Or on the off chance, would Isa keep it to herself?* Probably not...

It was all utterly ridiculous, this whole situation. Why did the people here care so much about who I slept with? It had nothing to do with them and affected no one but myself. Was it because I couldn't have kids? The world was already overpopulated. If anything, I'd be doing people a favor. That and I didn't want any in the first place, which had nothing to do with who I'd like to share my bed with. Because it was *unnatural?* Who the hell decided that? What was unnatural about it? Because it was against their religion? Now that was a crap excuse. People who used their religion as an excuse to oppress, discriminate, and hate against others were worse than the very people they deemed sinners.

It was laughable. It was fucking *laughable.* I couldn't help the twisted smile that formed on my mouth. I began to snicker.

I was fucked.

And the reason was absolutely ludicrous.

"Fuck!" I smiled with a full-hearted laugh. I laughed so hard I started to wheeze and hiccup. Those hiccups were soon accompanied by sniffles. I couldn't breathe, and suddenly, warm liquid spilled down my cheeks. I lowered my head to look at my legs. They were bent in an uncomfortable position, but I couldn't move them. If it was because I was drunk and out of my mind, or if the cold had numbed me to the point where I physically couldn't feel the appendages, I wasn't sure. I simultaneously laughed and cried because there was nothing else I could do. I threw my head back, banging it on the cold, hard metal pole over and over again.

Why did I do that? Why did I do that? I want to take it back...

Maybe—maybe it wasn't too late. If I went home now and called her and told her I was kidding, then maybe...

I made up my mind, clasping one of the many bars behind me and hoisting myself up. I left the bottle and joint where they were. My walk home started off full of anxiety and trepidation, my slow pace giving me enough time to sober up.

I quickly stumbled through my front door, hanging on the doorknob as I struggled to close it. Shifting my weight, I allowed myself to lean against the door. I blew out a breath of air, exhausted from the trip home. My body hurt... my mind hurt... why did everything always hurt?

A sudden noise had me snapping my head up to the dining table. My heart dropped out of my chest and the air was sucked from my lungs. Sitting at the table next to the kitchen was none other than the person I'd accidentally told my secret. Isabella stared at me with a cup of tea in her hand.

The corners of her mouth dipped downward and she abruptly stood. "Mrs. Ace, Mr. Ace, thank you for the tea. I should head home now." She looked behind her toward the kitchen and slightly bowed her head. She stomped toward me, harshly knocking into my shoulder on her way out.

No. No, no, no, no, no. No way... *please...*

My eyes that had been glued to the table slowly shifted to the scowls of my parents leaning against the counter, keeping an uncomfortable distance from me—as if they would catch a *disease.*

I stopped allowing oxygen to flow through my chest. I held my breath, and even though I was aware of that, I couldn't stop. My thoughts paused, my mind no longer working. The room was suffocating with deafening silence, yet loud static filled my head.

The arm clutching my abdomen began to violently shake. I hastened it behind my back to hide the erratic movement, trying to ignore the increased pain with the absence of pressure.

"Wh-why are you home?" The whisper barely escaped my mouth.

My mom's blonde eyebrows furrowed, her arms wrapped tightly around herself, my dad's hand protectively holding her waist. "We finished earlier than planned. What happened to your face—" her words were cut off when my dad squeezed her side and shook his head.

My gaze darted to him, fear taking over. My skin paled and became cold to the touch, sweat trickling down the back of my neck despite the night's cold weather. My chest felt clogged and my eyes, stinging with tears, opened as large as they could to keep the water from spilling. I knew I shouldn't have, but I sucked my bottom lip into my mouth and bit it, chewing it harder than I ever had. The large scab fell off and I felt the rough, soggy dead flesh on my tongue. The taste of iron filled my senses. I didn't know if it was the biting that calmed me down, the taste of my own blood, or the slight jolts of pain being sent through the nerves around my mouth.

Both my parents were silent, blank looks on their faces.

"What," I had to pause, the lump in my throat making it difficult to speak. "What was Isabella doing here?"

My mother pursed her lips and turned her head up, her chin held high. "Your friend told us something... She came to us because she wants to *help* you. She wants you to get the help you *need*."

My lips quivered and my eyes darted around the room, eyelids blinking in a flurry, unable to focus on anything, my jaw trembling along with the rest of my body.

"We can *help* you, Aspen." She placed a hand delicately over her heart.

"Help?" my voice broke. "I-I don't need any *help*."

"You *do!* You *need help,* Aspen. *You're sick.* It isn't natural! It goes against *everything* we stand for." My mom's artificial curls bounced, her blonde hair swaying as she used her body to express herself.

My mouth parted, but no words came out.

"I know a friend," my mom started, looking straight at me, but I couldn't bring myself to raise my eyes to meet hers. "He runs a camp upstate. He helps people like you, Aspen. He can set you back on the right path. You have strayed from the direction God intended for you, but it's not too late." She nodded aggressively, not only trying to convince me, but herself as well.

"Madeline," my dad said sternly, causing her mouth to shut quickly.

I stared at my feet, my nails scratching uncontrollably at my arms behind my back.

"Madeline, you know therapy doesn't work. He's already parted from the path of God. He's already *chosen* what he wishes to be," the green-eyed man's voice boomed, echoing throughout the room.

"But—" I interjected, panic written on my face.

"Aspen, I will ask you one time," my dad interrupted. "Are you a homosexual?"

"N-no, I—" the front door slammed roughly into the same shoulder that Isabella had shoved earlier—the same one that still hadn't healed from weeks ago.

Alex pushed past me, closing the door and pausing in place right next to me, noticing the obvious tension in the room. He stood there, looking between me and our parents.

My dad cleared his throat, directing my mom's attention back to me. "Are. You. A. Homosexual?" he spit.

"Oh?" Alex chirped in surprise. "They finally found out? Did you tell them yourself?"

My head shot up, and I grabbed the bottom of his sleeve near his elbow with a shaky hand. "You... you *promised. You promised not to tell,*" my voice was broken, tears slowly falling down my face.

He ripped his arm away from me, my hand falling back to my side while my eyes begged him for help. He leaned in to whisper in my ear. "I kept my promise. I didn't tell anyone you're a faggot. But remember..." The tone lacing his voice was enough to make me abruptly aware of the vile smile I knew he was sporting. A chill went down my spine, his words like ice. "I also said I would *never* lie for you."

He pulled away and addressed our parents with a lighthearted voice. "You're home early." Alex grabbed a glass of water from the fridge. He leaned against the silver box and sipped his drink leisurely, waiting for things to unfold.

"I won't have a homosexual son."

"That's why we should send him to that camp—" my mom started to explain.

"No! I will not have a *bitch* for a child!"

The tips of my brows were raised and streams of water fell from my eyes. "But nothing's changed! *I* haven't changed! I'm the same as before, I'm still *me!*" I pleaded with a quavering voice.

With a contorted face, my dad's piercing eyes drilled holes into me. Green veins protruded from his increasingly red face and his jaw shook from its tight clenching. "Get out."

"What?" I asked breathlessly, unable to process.

"Get. Out," he repeated.

"Now hold on, Garret." My mom placed a hand on his shoulder. "Let's not rush things. He can still be cured—"

"Get out! GET OUT!" He threw his arm into the air, his index finger pointing at the front door. "I *will not* have a gay son. Get out of my house, you good-for-nothing piece of shit!!"

"Mom?" I croaked, panic rising.

She simply looked at me, shaking her head from side to side. *She can't help me...* Or maybe she *wouldn't.*

My jaw fell open, jutting out in an awkward position as the most painful pang coursed through my chest. I clutched at my heart, tears escaping my eyes; there was so much that they began to drip from my nose, making my entire face look wet and sweaty.

"S-so that's it?" I tilted my head. "You're-you're kicking me out..." I picked at my arms, feeling yet another scab fall off. Blood dripped down onto my hand, falling from the tips of my fingers.

"If you don't leave right now"—the fire in my dad's eyes emitted a different type of fear in me, one that even Alex hadn't invoked—"I will *make you* leave." It wasn't just a threat, it was a promise. A promise of affliction and anguish worse than anything I'd experienced. A promise to act on a level of hatred I couldn't comprehend.

I searched my family's faces for something, *anything*. My dad was cold, unattached, but he always had been. Alex smiled as if this was a long time coming. And my mom, she was neutral. She didn't seem to agree with my dad's decision, but she sure as hell wasn't against it.

I guess that's it, then.

The world slowed as I turned on my heels. I reached for the doorknob with a shaky hand, holding my breath as I twisted the metal. I didn't want them to see me break completely. I refused to give Alex the satisfaction.

I stepped into the brittle air, looking up at the shining stars lighting up the black sky. They were so bright, completely filling up the emptiness encasing the world above me.

What I would give for that... to feel empty. To *be* empty. To be *nothing*.

Everything. I would give it all.

I'd gladly give my life if it meant I could finally join the stars in their eternal peace. *Eternal nothingness.*

Chapter Eight

Aspen

I STOPPED PICKING AT MY wrists, my sleeves now stained with blood. My arms went slack as I continued to walk away from my house, my eyes not once leaving the night sky. The stars twinkled— they were dazzling. Even though they weren't living things, they looked to be filled with emotion. The vivid colors reminded me of nothing but joy. Happiness. A feeling I couldn't seem to recall.

And I didn't want to. I wanted this emptiness I felt, this never-ending despair, to take me. To pull me down to the very depths of the sea and drown me. Drag me down to a place where I would never get up, and eventually, wouldn't need to.

My dried tears made the skin around my eyes feel strained and tight.

Well... I'd lasted over five years.

I'd reached my limit.

I'd endured enough—*this* had gone on long enough.

There was no reason for me to keep going, and now I just wanted it all to stop. I just *needed* it all to end...

What was I even living for? Because of hope? What *bullshit.* What was I hoping for? That baseball would carry me out of all my issues? That a sport would somehow rescue me?

And Rafe... what was I trying to get out of him? What was I *hoping* for? That he'd magically accept me? Dare I say, even fall in love with me?

How unrealistic... I should've woken up from that dream a long time ago.

It had been stupid of me to believe that one day everything would be okay. That my life would suddenly become perfect... that I could miraculously become happy.

Reality wasn't that kind.

I continued to walk. Where I was going, I didn't know. I just kept on, the black hole in my heart forcing my legs to get me as far from hell as they could.

I had no sense of time, and with no phone on me, no way to tell.

My mind, normally a chaotic mess of self-pity, was now empty. It wasn't my first time experiencing something like this; whether it was mental peace or overwhelming numbness, I couldn't be sure. But I was okay with it. My mind didn't hurt, and that was okay.

Cars rushed past me on the street, my hair flying around in every direction. The sharp wind was somehow pleasant. Tranquil. The loose sleeves of my shirt flapped around, grazing the raw scars, but I welcomed the pain. It was just another distraction.

A car's horn knocked me out of my daze. I slowly turned my head around to see my mom's car.

Oh.

She parked it on the side of the road and dashed out. She opened the door to the back seat and pulled out a thick jacket, rushing over to me and throwing it on my shoulders. "It's cold out here, so first, put that on."

I stayed silent as I watched her go back to the car to grab more things. I didn't move to put the jacket on and it fell to the ground; I was still, with a glazed over expression on my face. Why bother faking it anymore? I had nothing to hide; there was no longer a reason to pretend to smile.

She yanked two bags out of her car, both landing on the sidewalk next to her. "I was able to grab your baseball bag, and I put some clothes in another. I wasn't able to get your backpack. I'm sorry." She went into the passenger side and pulled out my phone, wallet, and a charger out of the side of the door. She walked up to me and grabbed my icy hands, bringing them up and placing my items in them. "I'm sorry," she whispered with tears pricking her eyes. "I tried to convince your father, but he won't change his mind. He doesn't know I'm here... but I wanted you to know that I can help you. I can still get you to my friend's camp. He doesn't have to know."

My nose was red and the undersides of my eyes were bright pink.

"Mom..." I croaked, pulling her hands up higher. "Look into my eyes." My words were breathless, barely audible.

Her gaze slowly drifted to mine. She sucked in a breath when she looked into the dull, grey eyes that reflected a mere fragment of who her son used to be. "Can't you see it?"

"I—"

"I'm gay," I continued before she could finish. "It's not something that can be changed. It's not something that needs to be fixed. I didn't choose to be like this..." I dropped her hands and looked away. I wouldn't cry anymore. What was the point? "I wanted to be normal. You have no idea how much I wished I could be like everyone else. I tried, I did. But it isn't something that can be controlled. You made your choice... you choose to not accept me for who I am, and I knew you would. I knew that when you found out, this would happen. Although I'm not surprised, I can't deny that it hurts. But what can I do? I'm eighteen, right? I'm an adult. Even though I'm still in high school, technically you and dad don't have an obligation to look after me. I was hoping it wouldn't come to this, but it's fine—*It's okay...*

"So," my voice quivered, "it's time to *let me go...* Dad said it, right? That I'm not his son anymore. I'm not your child and you're not my mom. I'm just some random kid on the street." I put on a small, genuine smile. I could finally speak my mind. I was, in a way, *free.* "Please don't try to change me anymore. I've been pretending for so long—I'm *tired,* mom. I tried my best. I did my time. *So let me go.*"

Tears stained her cheeks, but my eyes were crystal clear. "Thanks for... this." I gestured toward the bag resting near my feet. "But this is," I took a deep breath, "*this is it.*"

"W-wait, Aspen! It-it doesn't have to be—"

"I hope we never see each other again. With every bone in my body, *I never want to see any of you again.*" I stepped past her, grabbing the bags and putting them over my shoulders.

My mom grabbed my arm with a sudden shout. "Wait! Take this!" She fished a wad of cash out of her wallet.

I didn't want to take it, but she gripped my hand, placing the money in it and folding my fingers over the green paper.

I clenched my jaw and turned back around, leaving her to stand in the cold by herself, watching my back as I faded into the distance. I planned on never looking back.

I studied the money. Three hundred dollars. *Am I supposed to consider this an early graduation gift?* I crumpled the cash into a ball and shoved it into my pocket.

What should I do now? Where should I go? A motel, maybe? If I could find one that was dirt-cheap, it could work.

I hoped that I'd randomly come across somewhere I could crash, and after several hours, I finally did. The motel was only one story, with three sides surrounding a large parking lot in the middle. A loud bell dinged as I walked into the main lobby, which was a small room near the entrance to the parking lot. At the desk was a scraggly guy with an unkempt grey-and-brown beard. His potbelly was covered by a blue flannel too small for his figure.

I hobbled up to him, waiting for him to notice I was there. When he finally looked up from his newspaper, I spoke, "Can I have a room, please."

"One person?" he asked in a raspy voice.

"Yeah."

"The rate's sixteen ninety-nine a night. How many nights you plan on stayin'?"

I opened my mouth to answer him, but in truth, I didn't know. I'd stay as long as I could with what money I had, but I needed to account for food, too.

The man sighed at my nonexistent response. "You can pay day-to-day. Your stay'll last twenty-four hours, so by this time tomorrow, if you haven't paid for another night, we'll kick you out."

I nodded, pulling the money out and shoving the change into my wallet.

"Your key." He handed me a small, rusty piece of scrap metal that vaguely resembled a key. "Room sixteen."

"Thanks," I muttered.

I headed toward my room, pleasantly surprised at the low rates. Well, low for California at least. I understood why the second I got to the tiny bedroom that had next to no walking space and a bathroom that could barely fit a sink, toilet, and small shower. The faded green wallpaper peeled off the cracked walls, revealing tufts of mold. The bed had a large, orange comforter on top that consisted of itchy and probably unwashed fabric. Underneath was a single white sheet with a large yellow stain near the bottom. A short desk placed under a mirror across from the bottom of the bed left only a foot's space between the two pieces of furniture, and the absence of windows left the single light in the middle of the ceiling to cascade the room in a dim, yellowish-orange hue.

I shrugged my stuff onto the ground and sat on the edge of the dirty bed, reaching for one of my bags and inspecting what my mom had placed inside of it: one sweatshirt, two long-sleeved shirts, a T-shirt, two pairs of pants, one pair of shorts, and some socks and underwear. I took the plain black sweatshirt and shrugged it on, pulling the hood over my head. I threw all the blankets off the bed and grabbed the T-shirt I knew I wouldn't be wearing and shoved the pillow inside of it to create a clean, makeshift pillowcase.

I extended my body onto the firm mattress, rolling onto my left side with my back facing the door, curling into a ball.

Did this count as escaping? Because I finally got out? I didn't think getting kicked out was necessarily an escape, but it had a similar feeling.

But what was I supposed to do now? Wait several more months for September to approach so I could move into Rowland's dorm? I had the money my mom had given me plus an extra forty bucks already in my wallet. I had a credit card, but knowing my dad, he'd probably already cut it off. No matter, I didn't even have enough to last me a month.

God, I wish I'd been born straight... but what was so wrong about liking men? What did I do that was so wrong?

I'd done nothing to deserve this.

If my parents were only going to love me conditionally, why did they even have me? I didn't want to be here in the first place. I didn't choose to be born. I didn't ask for any of this.

I pulled my sleeves over my hands, placing them near my face and ignoring how much my ribs hurt. What I would've given for some pain killers, and I wasn't talking about ibuprofen or Tylenol. I wanted—needed—something that would make it all stop hurting. Everything. All at once.

I stared blankly at the patterned wallpaper the entire night, my eyes burning a bright red from my lack of sleep. I didn't know how the time passed, but I knew it was morning by the small bits of sunlight peeking in through the cracks of the door. Hunger and thirst wracked my stomach and throat, but I didn't want to move. No, I *couldn't* move. It didn't really matter, though. Nothing did.

The ringing of my phone forced me to roll onto my other side for the first time in hours. My shoulder ached from the movement after bearing my weight all night. Glancing at the caller ID, I picked it up and put it on speaker.

"Aspen?" Coach Gale's voice echoed through the line.

"Hey, Coach." I tried to make my voice sound as normal as possible.

"Where've you been? You've missed practice twice now, and I heard you aren't at school today, either." He sounded worried.

"Sorry. I meant to call you earlier. I didn't go to practice 'cause I have a fever." The lie flew out of my mouth with ease.

"Are you okay?"

"I'm getting better," I replied, struggling to add emotion to my voice.

"That's good. Uhm..." The man suddenly sounded serious. "Since you missed practice, I can't start you in the game Saturday."

I sighed. "I don't think my fever will break by tomorrow, anyway. I'll probably miss the game."

"Really?" he huffed. "Winning will be tough tomorrow, especially since Rafe won't be there either."

"Yeah, good luck..." I trailed off.

"You'll be back to school by Monday, right?" he asked with a hopeful tone.

"I'm not sure. I'll go if I'm feeling better."

"Okay, okay. I'll let you get some rest. Feel better."

"Thanks, Coach." He hung up with my reply.

I wondered if Rafe *knew*. If Isa had told him, too. How would he react? Maybe he'd shun me, ignore me as if I'd never been there in the first place. It probably wouldn't be hard for him to do; we weren't talking to each other right now, anyway.

He'd broken up with Amelia and said those things about me. I hadn't gotten the chance to ask him yet, and I knew I shouldn't be hopeful, but I needed to know. I needed to tie up this one last loose end. I needed closure.

Skipping baseball felt natural for the time being. I wasn't exactly enjoying the sport at this point. It was a means to spend time with Rafe and a prospect for a chance to get out. There had been an ongoing debate in my head: Should I wait to kill myself and see how things would pan out in the future, or end it now and spare myself the pain? I constantly wavered between the two options, and whenever I made up my mind, the decision never seemed to stick.

My stomach growled and I pushed myself up into a sitting position, the pain in my ribs a hundred times worse than yesterday. I stood cautiously and limped to the bathroom. After taking a leak, I found myself staring into the mirror. Wow, I looked like total shit, and even though I was faking a fever, it appeared that I might not have been lying, after all. Gone was my normally gold-tinted skin tone; I was inhumanely pale, clearly sick, with colorless lips and dark circles under my eyes, revealing exactly how I felt on the inside. Light stubble ghosted my jaw and the area under my nose, but I had no razor to shave it. If I bought one, I'd take it apart and try to kill myself before I got a chance to say goodbye to Rafe, and he deserved at least that much.

I lifted my sweatshirt and long-sleeve past my pecs, inspecting the bruises. Unsurprisingly, my entire front side was covered in revolting blue-and-purple bruises. The darkest parts were concentrated near my hips and the lower part of my rib cage, which was where Alex's heel and the balls of his feet had been when he was standing on me. The entire area was a dark color that faded into various shades of green near my sides, with lines of purple flowing into lighter colors. For some reason, it reminded me of the black spiderwebs that coated Cranks' skin in *The Maze Runner*. It was gnarly and made me look as if I was on my deathbed—which I was, in a way.

I dropped my shirt and pulled down the fabric near my neck. The bruises from Alex strangling me were also darker, but rather than blues and purples, they were a deep pink with splotches of light purple here and there. The scratches just above those marks weren't as bad as I thought they'd be. If I was lucky, they wouldn't scar and would fade in another week.

I tottered out of the bathroom and grabbed my phone, wallet, and key. When I stepped out the door to go to the lobby, sunlight blinded me and I immediately broke out into a heavy sweat from the heat.

I opened the front door and was met with the familiar chiming of bells. I looked to the side and noticed a door on the opposite side of the room.

"Is that a convenience store?" I asked the same man that had been working last night.

"Yeah. If you want anything, bring it here. I'll ring you up."

With a single nod, I ducked into the store. The size resembled that of a large office cubicle with enough space for only the bare necessities. I grabbed a toothbrush, a bottle of water, and a cup of ramen. When I came across the razors, I froze, my vision unfocusing. I could—*I could* use it just to shave. Beards were itchy. I could use it without... I *could*. I took it off the shelf and held it in my hands along with the other items, exiting the room just smaller than the lobby and dumping the items onto the front desk.

"And another night, too," I added as I gave the man a little over thirty dollars.

He glanced up at my face and bluntly said, "You okay, kid? You look like shit."

"Thanks," I grumbled, snatching my stuff off the counter. "I feel like shit."

Chapter Nine

Aspen

ALTHOUGH IT WASN'T THE FIRST time Rafe had been away, it felt odd not seeing him. Just six days had me recognizing my unhealthy dependency, but I had no one else. I didn't really have any other friends, especially not now. I missed Rafe, and I craved a type of comfort from him I knew I'd never be able to get, even just as friends. I needed someone to tell me it'd all be okay; I wouldn't believe them, but hearing it would still be nice. But more than that, I needed to know where he stood. Was he still mad at me from after the game last Tuesday? What did he mean when he'd said those things on Devin's story? And what about the fact that I was gay? What would he do with that? He probably didn't know yet since his phone was broken and he'd left before I accidentally outed myself. I wondered how he was going to figure it out. Or who else knew. Just Isabella? The entire baseball team? The whole school, perhaps?

I switched into a different long-sleeved shirt; the white fabric was tighter than I would've preferred, but my options were limited. I pulled out grey sweatpants and slid on the black hoodie and Vans. I was counting on the dark wardrobe to conceal the nearly-as-dark bruises on my face.

I hadn't planned on going to school today, since my ribs had begun to feel worse over the past couple of days, but I received a call from the assistant coach this morning telling me that Coach Gale wanted to have a brief conversation with me. He sounded pessimistic and unhappy. Maybe I was in trouble for skipping three days' worth of classes last week and hadn't bothered showing up today either.

I didn't leave until the last block period had finished to avoid running into as many people as I could.

I paid the manager, adding another twenty-four hours to my stay. I was already low on cash between scattered and sparse meals on top of the motel cost.

It took over an hour to walk to school. I was awkwardly hunched over the entire time, wheezing with every breath.

Here we go.

I hobbled through the front double doors with my hood up and covering a large portion of my face. Expecting students to turn to me and peer in disgust, confusion swept over me when everyone kept their eyes down, most scurrying out the doors. It was a Monday after all, and those who didn't have after-school activities tended to leave as quickly as they could. I avoided the spot where my friends met up after classes, just to be safe.

Not sure if Coach Gale was on the baseball field or in his office, I decided to call him so I wouldn't have to walk the extra mile. I held my phone to my ear as I awkwardly leaned against a random student's locker before he finally picked up. "Coach Gale?"

"Ah, yes. Hi, Aspen. Could you come see me in my office? We need to talk about something." His voice was serious and caused a slight panic in my mind.

"Right... what's going on?"

"Let's discuss this matter in person." The line went dead.

I struggled to pull myself off the wall, my right hand firmly placed near the bottom of my rib cage and my back hunched. I stumbled a bit, trying to take my first step. The world was fuzzy and a little dark. I focused on the ground and shook my head back and forth in hopes that I wouldn't faint. I blew out a puff of air and plodded my way to the back of the gym. My pace was excruciatingly slow and anyone walking the same direction passed me.

"Aspen!" My head shot up when Amelia shouted my name.

"Heyyy," I drew my words out. I'd hoped I could avoid her.

"Have you talked to Rafe yet?" she asked. The way her soft waves framed her face complemented her large green eyes; she looked rather bright for someone who just went through a breakup.

Maybe they got back together...

"No... I haven't seen him since last week. He's out of town right now."

"Really?" Surprise was etched on her face and she rubbed a hand over the side of her neck. "There's something important he needs to tell you. I told him he should do it sooner rather than later."

I raised an eyebrow, clueless as to what she was talking about. I'd already gotten an apology from him, even though it was indirect.

"Well, I hope he builds up the courage to say it when he gets back." She gave me a tight-lipped, indifferent smile, as if she wasn't happy or upset regarding whatever she was talking about. I craned my head to watch her as she left. It didn't seem like she knew about me, *so what the fuck was that about?*

I shook the thoughts from my head. I already had a headache and didn't need more unanswered questions cluttering my mind. I shoved my hands into my pockets and attempted to walk through the empty hallways to Coach Gale's makeshift office.

"Have a seat." He gestured toward the chair in front of his desk. There were all kinds of sports equipment stacked behind him, partially blocking the large window that showed the outdoor pool. "Devin came to me this morning with an urgent piece of information. He told me you were hiding a serious injury, and that's why you haven't been playing."

"What?" I exclaimed. "That's ridiculous, I'm not injured!" I struggled to convince him on account of having to keep my head down and avert my gaze to better hide the bruises and cuts on my face and neck, which I knew was typical behavior you'd see in people when they lied, but I couldn't help it in these circumstances. And I may have been *slightly* injured, but I healed fast. Alex-related injuries rarely affected my ability to play baseball, and if they did, well... I hid pain well. This occasion was no different.

"I know you know how Devin is, Aspen. He told me because he's worried about you. And I won't sit here and see you develop a permanent injury that could potentially ruin your future and career." The look on his face made it seem like he was breaking news to an old lady that he'd accidentally run over her cat.

"I'm sorry, but I have to suspend you from playing until you can turn in a doctor's note stating you are in perfect health and at no risk of furthering any injury." He was austere, his mind made up with no room for negotiation.

"Okay," I muttered. I brushed my hand against my nose and sniffed, mentally preparing to stand. I gripped the armrests of the chair and tried to lift myself without wincing or cradling my stomach. I turned on my heels and walked as steadily as I could from the gym. There was no point in trying to convince Coach Gale that Devin lied. I had to assume Isa told Devin, and that was the reason he wanted me off the team. Regardless, I wouldn't be able to argue against an injury at the moment...

Just as I passed the locker rooms, I caught sight of Devin, Jason, and Jamey striding toward me with their baseball bags in hand. Devin was the first to notice me. He tapped Jason's shoulder and nodded in my direction. A cruel smile overtook his face; it reminded me of Alex. My body shuddered at the similarity.

"Aspen!" Jason shouted from across the hall as the three got closer. I took a step back when they were right in front of me. "Just the person we wanted to see!" He wrapped his arms roughly around my shoulder. "Let's have a quick chat."

They pushed me into the empty locker room, locking the door behind them. My heart thumped in my chest as they cornered me, forcing me backward until I collided with a row of blue lockers.

"So you just weren't going to tell us you're a fucking *homo?*" Devin seethed.

"Wh-what? No-no I—" my eyes jumped around the room, but no one was there.

"Shit, and we even changed in front of you!" Jason spat on the ground. "You thought you were so slick, didn't ya. Perving on guys while they changed."

"I *didn't!*" My throat went dry.

"Fucking disgusting. We can't just let this go, Aspen." Devin said with wide eyes.

"I never looked! I swear!" I sputtered in a shaky voice.

"I can't believe we've been friends with this motherfucker for years," Devin snarled, raising his fist.

Before I could comprehend what happened, a dull, painful ache exploded on my left cheekbone. My hands flew up to my now squinting eye. My mind paced frantically when my teammates crowded me.

"Jason," Devin said without turning his gaze away from me, "give me your bat."

Jason diverted his attention from me to look at the blonde with surprise. "What?"

"Your. Fucking. Bat." Devin held his hand out impatiently.

Jason glanced at Jamey, unsure of what to do, but he ultimately obeyed the captain and grabbed his bag, rummaging through it until he was able to pull his bat out smoothly. He tossed it around until the aluminum barrel rested in his right hand. Jason placed the handle into Devin's palm, who tightened his grip and twirled it around in his fingers, trying to find the perfect hold.

A bat? A Fucking *bat??* What was he going to do with a—

With two hands firmly placed around the grip just above the knob, Devin turned to me and took a full swing. I dropped to the ground as fast as I could. The bat slammed into the lockers behind me; the sound echoed throughout the room and could undoubtedly be heard from the other side.

My heart rate spiked as I stared up at Devin in disillusion. I had one hand spread out on the locker to keep my balance in the awkward squatting position. My fingers and toes tingled, an intense throbbing sensation radiating throughout my entire body, all stemming from my heart.

Trembling, I turned my head to look at the dent he had made with the bat.

That's where my head was.

Was he trying to fucking kill me?!

Holy shit! No way no way no way...

He was actually going to—

"Woah! Devin, what the hell!!" Jason shouted, nearly as startled as I was. Jason grabbed Devin's shoulder in an attempt to pull him away from me.

I panted in fear, unable to control my breathing.

"Get the fuck off!" Devin screamed, shoving Jason off him, the darker boy falling to the ground.

Devin threw his bat into the air and I cowered underneath him, tucking my head down while my arms formed an X over the top of my hood. I squeezed my eyes as tight as I could, waiting for the blow to strike.

But it didn't happen.

I opened my eyes hesitantly and peeked through my arms. Jamey stood before me with both of his hands holding the barrel of the bat as Devin struggled to force it downward. With Jason behind Devin, he tugged Devin's right shoulder back to prevent him from swinging at me.

"Devin! Stop it, man! I get it, but you can't *kill* him!" Jason screamed in alarm.

"Leave!" Jamey shouted. I didn't know who his words were directed at, so I stayed still, paralyzed by fear.

"Fuck! Aspen, hurry and *leave!!*" Jamey grunted as he struggled to keep Devin back.

I scurried to my feet and stumbled past the three boys, glancing back at their internal struggle. I was terrified, limping as fast as I could to the door. While my fingers fumbled with the lock, I turned to see how much longer I had.

Devin was stronger than the other two. A lot stronger. He threw the boys off him, his bat dropping to the ground. He made a beeline straight for me.

My quaking hand finally turned the metal lock to the left. *I got it!*

Just before I could open the door, Devin's fist came flying past my face. I barely saw it from my blurred peripheral vision, only able to move my head a single inch to the right to avoid it. His knuckles connected with the door and I jumped backward.

"You're fucking dead!" Devin fumed.

I looked behind me and Jason and Jamey were just starting to get off the ground.

Devin took a half-second to recover, his curled fingers probably hurting from hitting the door with full force. Startled, I let my reflexes take over and sent a punch into his right cheek.

He stumbled to the side, his hand catching the doorknob and accidentally turning it.

I saw an opportunity. I rammed myself into Devin's back, forcing the door to swing open. Devin fell to the ground with a heavy thump just outside of the locker room.

I jumped over his body and sprinted down the hallway, ignoring the other students giving me strange looks.

"Aspen! Get your ass back here!" Devin shouted. His voice sounded much closer than I would've liked.

I glanced back and saw Devin just feet behind me—so focused on the man on my tail, I didn't see when I slammed into a firm chest.

"Ugh," I grunted, craning my head to see who I ran into.

My eyes made contact with a confused-looking Rafe sporting a dark-grey moisture-wicking practice tee with his baseball bag slung over his shoulder.

He must've just gotten back.

"Aspen? What are you doing?"

I didn't reply, gaping at him and gasping for air. Rafe placed his hands on my shoulders to push my weight off him.

My head snapped to the side and I muttered a quick, "Sorry" to Rafe before running past him.

"Where the hell do you think you're going?"

I ignored the loud voice.

Devin tried to run after me, but Rafe placed his forearm on the blonde's chest and pushed him back. Rafe's black eyebrows furrowed as Jason and Jamey caught up, grabbing hold of Devin. Rafe was probably acting on instinct after seeing me running away.

The second I was out the front door, I rushed to the side of the building and my body folded in half, nearly toppling over. My entire being shook and I had no control over my twitching fingers. My legs locked in place and I couldn't get them to move.

I heaved, trying to breathe, but it was as if I was stuck in a chamber devoid of all oxygen.

What the fuck. *What the fuck??*

Devin wanted to smash my head in with a bat. *He tried to kill me. My friend tried to kill me...*

Was being gay such a bad thing? Was I so disgusting that people would rather see me dead than with another man?! *Fuck!*

Did that really just happen? The guy that had looked out for me since I met him four years ago was going to *murder* me. He was willing to commit a hate crime just to get rid of me...

My closest friends' reactions had resulted in me getting disowned and almost killed. If their reactions were that bad, did that mean Rafe's would be even worse? Two times? Or three, since I'd known him that much longer? Since I'd been hiding it from him for that much longer?

I *knew* Rafe... I'd known him nearly my entire life and I was sure he wouldn't be like Alex or Devin. He wouldn't hurt me... but then again, the topic of homosexuality wasn't something we'd ever discussed. I refused to bring it up, to even test the waters. Because I couldn't be sure that he wouldn't have a negative reaction, and Rafe was someone I never wanted to lose.

I wished I wasn't like this... I wished I hadn't been born different. Why *me?* Why did *I* have to go through this? What did I do to deserve it?

Nothing. I hadn't done anything.

I was so tired of always being hurt, of the constant pain...

My hands dropped to my knees and bile rose in my throat. I choked on my stomach's contents as they spilled out of my mouth. I coughed and gagged, continuing to spit up until there was nothing left.

Chapter Ten

Aspen

"Aspen?" A hand grasped my shoulder softly.

With wide eyes, I shoved the limb off and jumped back, startled. "Rafe," I sighed, sliding my arms across my mouth to try to clean up. There was now a thin line of yellow-and-clear saliva staining my dark sweatshirt. I rubbed my other hand over my eyes, flinching when I accidentally touched a raw cut on top of my cheekbone. I diverted my gaze to the ground in an attempt to hide my face.

"Are you okay?" His face scrunched up and he took a step closer. Rafe slid a hand onto the middle of my back and rubbed gentle circles, warmth spreading through my stomach. I couldn't tell if the motion was calming or upsetting my stomach even more.

"I'm fine," I mumbled.

"What was that about?"

"It was nothing." I pulled my arms closer to my body as I took a step away from him.

His hand dropped back to his side. "Really? Because it didn't seem like nothing. Why was Devin chasing after you?"

"I must've forgotten something in the locker room and he wanted to give it back," I muttered with a raspy voice, my throat on fire from the acidic aftertaste.

"Then why were you running away?" Concern laced his soft tone.

I bit my lip, not caring if I reopened the scab for the millionth time.

Rafe sighed, "Aspen, I actually really need to talk to you about something."

"Uhm," my voice cracked, "if it's about what happened after our last game, it's fine. I saw Devin's story, so..."

"I wanted to apologize for that, too, but no. There's something else I want to say." There was a long pause. "Why won't you look at me?" It was practically a whisper.

My heart felt like it was beating out of my chest and I picked at the skin around my fingernails.

Rafe bent his head down to see me, but I turned away, hoping that my hood covered enough.

"Do you have a black eye?! And your cheek's bleeding..."

I didn't respond.

He advanced farther in front of me to the point where I couldn't move and he could see my face, even when I turned away.

"Come on." He grabbed my hand, four of my fingers squished together between his.

He's holding my hand.

It feels so nice...

His hand bled warmth into my own, forcing my palm to clam up. But I didn't care, the feel of his skin against mine, of his fingers so close to intertwining with my own, it was electric.

"Where are we going?" Exhaustion dripped from my mouth; I didn't have the energy to resist, to keep Rafe from seeing how bad my face really looked with Alex's punch blooming into a deep red around my mouth and Devin's a deep purple on my eye.

"My house." Rafe's answer was brief and offered no explanation.

"But you have practice."

Rafe stopped in his tracks the second we were in front of his car and pursed his lips. "There are more important things than

THE SMILE HAS LEFT YOUR EYES

baseball."

He let go of my hand and climbed into the driver's seat. I looked down at my fingers; humid wind swept across the damp skin, prickles of cold tickling my hand. Tingles rippled through my nerves like something was missing, like the heat that had been encasing my hand was supposed to be there, like *Rafe's hand* was meant to be there.

I slid silently into the passenger's side, leaning my head against the window and letting my thoughts take over on the stiffly quiet ride, absent of music or radio.

Amelia's comment from before had my nerves reeling. What could he possibly want to talk about that was so important even his ex had approached me?

My eyes hopped from tree to tree as the brown and green plants flashed by. The sun shone in through the window, illuminating the tip of my nose and lips while my hood cast a dark shadow over my eyes. The concrete that made up the road was cracked and split, the yellow lines almost completely faded. The gravel reminded me of myself. Broken and nearing the end of its use if it couldn't be repaved. And just like the road, even when I covered things up, those cracks would always be there, hidden underneath.

"How did you get that cut on your eye?" Rafe broke the silence.

"I accidentally walked into the door when I was going to the bathroom last night. I was tired, so I didn't feel like opening my eyes."

I let myself believe Rafe took the bait, ignoring the low rumble of his voice saying, "The blood's fresh."

We pulled up to the side of the road in front of his house. Rafe left all the gear in his car and ushered me inside and toward the bathroom. He rushed past both of his parents, who had been watching a movie in the living room, not giving them a chance to say hello.

I threw him confused glances as we stood in the doorway to the cramped restroom. "You threw up, right?"

I nodded my head.

Rafe stepped past me and opened the bottom drawer under the sink, pulling out an unopened toothbrush package. "Here. Come into my room when you're done."

I looked into the mirror, watching Rafe's reflection walk down the hall. I wanted to talk to him, too. I had so many things to ask Rafe, but now that I was here, it felt like it'd be impossible to get the words out of my mouth.

I grabbed the opened toothpaste out of the cabinet on the wall next to the mirror, squirting some onto the white bristles and mindlessly running it under the sink water. I sluggishly moved my arm back and forth, the brush moving around in my mouth. My heart felt like it was beating so slowly, I could drop dead at any second.

What am I even doing here?

I should just kill myself and spare myself the pain of seeing Rafe reject me for being gay.

I wish I was dead. That would be better for everyone...

Why do the people in my life keep hurting me? I don't understand. I want to make it all stop.

I want to die. I want to kill myself. I should end it. Why do I have to keep enduring this shit? I should just kill myself.

I want to kill myself.

I want to die.

I want this to stop.

I want to die.

I need it to stop. I need everything to stop.

The best way to do that is to just fucking die.

In fact, I should already be dead.

And I needed this damn voice in my head to *stop.*

A burning sensation in my mouth shook me from my spiral. The minty toothpaste had been sitting on my tongue for too long and became uncomfortable. I spit the white foam into the sink and rinsed my mouth with water, setting the new toothbrush onto the counter so the bristles hung over the edge of the sink.

Limping out of the bathroom, I fiddled with my sleeves as I opened the door to Rafe's room. I awkwardly stood in the doorway, assuming that he'd be uncomfortable being in the same room alone with me.

"Why are you just standing there?" Rafe sat at the top of his bed facing the footboard with his legs in a criss-cross position. Well, the imaginary footboard, since his parents had to remove it when he'd turned sixteen so his feet could fit onto the bed. "And close the door."

I turned around hesitantly, grasping the handle and pushing it toward the frame until there was a subtle click.

"Have a seat." Rafe leaned forward and patted the bed space in front of him.

I placed myself on the small bed, barely a foot between the two of us. We sat in similar positions, but unlike Rafe, whose back was straight, leaning forward aiming to see my expression, I was hunched over, my neck craned so that my face was parallel with the top of his comforter.

Rafe twisted his body toward his nightstand and grabbed what looked like a first aid kit. He pulled a cotton pad out and poured a small amount of disinfectant onto it.

He looked at my face, but I kept my gaze away from him. He gently grabbed my chin and held my face while pressing the pad to my cheek, probably expecting me to hiss or wince at the sting from the alcoholic solution. But I didn't flinch. This was nothing compared to the things I was used to.

When he finished, Rafe tossed the white pad into his trash can and grabbed his nearly-empty box of band-aids and fished out a small one, pressing forward until his face was just inches from mine. I wanted to look, to see him up close. But I wouldn't dare.

He stuck the plaster onto my cheekbone. "There."

"Thanks," I muttered.

"So..."

"So..." I repeated.

"*What happened?*"

Realization struck me. *He doesn't know... he doesn't know I'm gay.*

Maybe I could play it off... maybe he wouldn't figure it out. If he didn't know, maybe we could stay friends.

I quickly dodged the subject. "I, uhm, I got kicked out of my house." I scratched the back of my head, trying to play down just how bad things were.

"Aspen," Rafe said sternly, "You can't make jokes about serious stuff like that with a straight face." I didn't know if there was a crack in my facade, but Rafe's face instantly screwed up. "You're not kidding?"

I shrugged. "Nah, but it's not actually that bad. My parents are on a business trip and Alex wanted the house to himself so he could have his girlfriend stay over without worrying about having someone else there." I kept my tone straight, willing it not to falter and give me away.

Sometimes it scared me how I felt no guilt lying—or embellishing the truth.

I knew Rafe was skeptical, but there was nothing I could do but keep going.

"When did he do that?"

"Thursday night."

"Where have you been staying?" His voice had risen slightly.

"At that motel downtown. The one at the corner of Weston and Remington." I had the urge to scratch at my arms, but I was too close to Rafe and knew he would notice if I tried to ease my anxiety.

"That's a really bad area, Aspen!"

I knew it was, but it was cheap, the cheapest I'd be able to find in Cedar Heights. "It's not that bad, don't exaggerate."

"Why didn't you just ask to stay here?! You know my parents would be fine with it!" He wasn't shouting, but the intensity of his delivery meant he didn't have to.

"It's fine. I'm doing okay on my own. It's only been a couple of days."

Rafe sighed. "Is that why you look like you got hit by a car? Your dark circles make you look like you're dying."

Hah, I wish.

"Don't worry about it, I'm just a little tired."

"Do you have enough money?"

"Yeah, I'm making it work..."

"Making it work?" Rafe repeated in a dumbfounded tone. "What about food?"

"I ate some food yesterday..." The truth was, I couldn't even tell if I was hungry or not. Pain was a stronger sensation than hunger, so whenever my stomach growled or hunger pains riddled my abdomen, the intense ache from my rib cage would take over, completely overwhelming the feeling. I was almost thankful that the pain was saving me money. *Almost.*

"And water?"

I had the plastic bottle that I'd bought on Friday, but I finished it that same day and never bothered to refill it. The sink water wasn't exactly clean.

I kept my mouth shut, giving Rafe the hint that it had been an unhealthy number of days.

"Do you want to die of dehydration?!" He jumped off the bed and I followed his movement, still avoiding his eyes that I knew were trying to look into mine.

Okay. I sighed internally. *I guess it's time.* If there was a chance I could still be friends with him—if there was a possibility that he wouldn't find out, that things wouldn't change between us—I had to take it.

I plastered on a fake smile, scrunching my eyes and letting out a small chuckle. I pulled my legs toward my chest as I tried to hide the amount of pain I was really in. "You believed that?" I laughed. "Of course I've eaten and drinken. Alex gave me a shit-ton of money. Honestly? I'm enjoying having a space for myself." As if I wasn't usually home alone, anyway. "And I'm only tired because I stayed up binge-watching a show last night," I explained without stuttering or pausing.

Rafe clenched his jaw. "What show?" he tested me.

"Supernatural." The lie slipped out with ease.

"And today? Have you eaten yet?"

"No, I slept in." I smiled, flashing my deceiving dimples.

Rafe let out a long exhale, running a hand through his hair. "Okay, I'll go grab something from the kitchen."

I tried to get some last words out, "You really don't have to—" but he'd already exited the room.

Several minutes later, he came back up with a plate and a bottle of water.

"Oh! You made eggs?" I faked my excitement. I actually couldn't eat eggs anymore. An instance with Alex, his foot, and my stomach had made me all too acquainted with the shape of a toilet bowl. The smell and taste of bile eggs and piss water... need I say more? But I couldn't say that out loud. Rafe went out of his way to do something nice for me, so I needed to accept it with a smile. Being friends with me was already hard enough. I didn't need to add being picky to the list. "Wow, breakfast in bed. Feels like my birthday! Thanks!" I chuckled, taking a sip of water.

I leaned even farther into my legs, slowly picking at and eating the food.

My best friend hadn't sat down yet. Instead, he loomed over me, staring intently and studying me. I fidgeted in place, trying to hide my discomfort. He suddenly bent down and leaned his face closer to mine. My head jolted up in surprise and Rafe's eyes narrowed in on my neck.

"What's wrong with your neck?" he asked grimly.

"My neck?" I furrowed my brows in confusion. *Oh.* He must've seen the bruise and scratches.

His jaw clenched tightly as he brought his hand to the hood of my sweatshirt. I flinched reflexively at the motion, and Rafe's eyes went wide. "What the hell was that?"

I tried to laugh it off. "I had the chills."

"You flinched!"

"I didn't, Rafe. Stop overreacting." I smiled and shook my head.

He brought his hand back up, and I made sure to stay still. His fingers grabbed the collar of my hoodie and tugged it lightly to the side. "Aspen..." It was a pained whisper.

"I got that from my gear. My new chest protector. It was too big so the top dug into my neck the whole game last week. It looks worse than it is," I spoke with utmost confidence.

"I've never seen catcher's gear leave shit like this. Can it really do something like that?" he questioned.

"Of course!" I chuckled. "It's just part of breaking in the equipment."

I adjusted my hoodie to make sure it covered the discolored skin as Rafe's eyes bored into me.

"Rafe," I started, deciding I should leave before he could get a better look at the well-defined purple fingerprints wrapped around my jugular and piece together what the bruise was really from. "Thanks for the food and everything, but I think I should get going. I have a lot of homework to catch up on."

I didn't want to go, but I just couldn't help pushing him away. I couldn't ask for help if the reason I needed help in the first place was because of a secret I'd have been willing to take to my grave.

"Don't go!" he shouted, just as I was about to stand. I froze in place, moving back into my sitting position.

"You're really not going to tell me?" Rafe placed himself in his desk chair, turning it around to face me. Rafe's legs were spread apart and his forearms rested on his thighs with his hands tightly clasped together, a serious look on his face.

"What are you talking about?" I opened my eyes wider than normal and innocently took another bite of food. It made me look more awake and overall happier.

"Stop!" he clamored. "Just stop it already! I'm so sick and tired of you faking it! Of you faking everything!"

The smile immediately dropped from my face. I turned my head away from him and focused my eyes on a random spot on his comforter, placing the fork on my plate and setting it on the ground along with the bottle of water.

My mouth twitched a bit before my smile was back on. "I don't know what you're talking about. You're not making any sense."

"Aspen! Stop lying for once!"

He hates me, doesn't he...

He must know I'm gay. Is he mad because I'd kept it a secret? Angry that I'd hid it from him?

"I can't fucking do this anymore," Rafe gasped, completely exasperated. "I gave you space, Aspen. Did you really think I didn't notice how you've changed? I gave you so much fucking space because I was scared that if I pried you would shut me out more than you already have!" His voice cracked at the last part.

Oh.

I stared into his distraught eyes. I tilted my head and curled the ends of my mouth upward, squinting slightly to get faint smile lines to form around my eyes. "Don't be ridiculous, Rafe. Wouldn't it be weirder if I didn't change over time?" I felt a lump forming in my throat. I'd been playing this game for years; I couldn't let all my hard work crumble, just like that.

"*Aspen,* what's with all these *lies?* They're just small things— simple white lies... but *everything* that comes out of your mouth is *fake!*"

"That's not true—"

He cut me off. "It is! And you know it! Aspen, stop smiling. Stop it!"

I bit the inside of my swollen cheek, even though it felt like there wasn't a lot of skin left. "Can you please stop yelling at me?" My voice came out in a soft whisper.

Rafe huffed, getting up from his seat.

There it was. Now he'd leave me too.

This was just like what happened on the field that day. Was this why he was acting like that? Because he knew? There was no reason for him to stay; I was a liar he'd put up with for long enough.

Rafe resumed his position at the top of his bed with his legs crossed like a pretzel.

"I'm sorry. I didn't mean to shout. I'm just so frustrated." Rafe's words were gentle and apologetic. The worry in his tone was evident and it made me feel strange. "I realized when it started—whatever it is, but every time I mentioned something, it's like you'd distance yourself from me. I knew that no matter how much I asked, you'd never tell me. And then the years kept passing... but shit, Aspen, *it's getting worse.* I can't just let it go anymore. I was scared that you would become completely closed off, but that happened anyway."

My jaw clamped shut, the muscles in my face flexing. I wouldn't cry... "I don't get what you mean. I'm perfectly fine. Don't tell me you're saying all of this because I'm clumsy and gave myself a couple of bruises?" I tried to make my voice sound light-hearted.

Rafe continued breathlessly, "Aspen. We've been friends since we were four. I know that you've been hiding behind that smile of yours. People are bewitched by it, but that's not the case for me." *Of course, it isn't. You aren't gay, I get it. But there's no need to rub it in my face.* "I can see it in your eyes... your smile never reaches your eyes."

The whites of my eyes were now tinted red; they burned from struggling to keep myself together, from not allowing myself to *let go.*

"Your eyes are so big and alluring, they pull you in, *force you* to focus on them... so did you really think I wouldn't notice? I can see right through you, Aspen Ace. I can see how dull your eyes have become... you can't hide anything from me, your eyes show it all."

Tears pooled in my eyes. *What does he know? Rafe doesn't have a clue.*

"Aspen, look at me," he demanded.

My gaze shifted slowly and with uncertainty. It bounced around the room, looking at anything but him.

"Aspen." His voice was so comforting, I couldn't help but bring my eyes level to his.

How long has it been since I looked Rafe in the eyes?

Ah. That's right... They're breathtaking—beautiful.

Was that why looking into them hurt so much more? Because I knew his brown eyes would never look at me the way mine looked at him?

"Can you please just tell me what's going on?" Rafe pleaded.

Then I felt it. Warm liquid cascaded down my cheeks. My brows were knitted so tightly that my forehead hurt. My right hand rested on my abdomen, clutching my rib cage.

"Why are you crying?" Rafe's voice sounded broken.

Why did he sound so hurt when I was the one in pain?

Rafe gradually lifted his hand toward my face. His thumb brushed across the bottom of my right eye, wiping my tears away.

I sucked in a breath; the wheeze sounded similar to a hiccup. I sniffled and tried to calm myself down, but I couldn't get the tears to stop.

No one had ever asked me if I was okay. No one had noticed how hurt I was inside—and I'd assumed Rafe was the same. But no, he knew. Which meant that I'd hid it all for nothing... I didn't *want* to hide how difficult things had been, but the reason for those hardships forced me to keep my pain a secret. But he knew... He knew and now he'd want to know *why*. It was only a matter of time before he found out, whether it be from my family, the people at school... *or myself.*

I want to die. I can't keep doing this anymore.

I want this all to end.

I'll do it for real this time. I won't hold back. This time, I'll make sure it works.

This time, I'll make sure to stay dead.

I want to die... But can't I have just one thing?

Is it okay for me to have this one thing before I do it? Before I kill myself?

Can I?

I'm going to die. Everything will end. I've never gotten anything I wanted—so is it really okay? Just this once, can I?

I searched Rafe's eyes one last time. My eyes jumped from his left to his right, over and over again. With every blink, salty water dripped into my mouth.

"I'm sorry, Rafe," I whispered. "Just this once." I sucked in a breath as I started to lean forward. "Just this once... and never again." I crashed my lips onto his, basking in the soft feel of his plump lips with my eyes screwed shut, not wanting to look into his wide, startled eyes as I waited for him to push me off or punch me back into reality.

Chapter Eleven

Rafe

I PRESSED THE DOORBELL *a single time, still fuming. I knew Aspen was keeping secrets from me, but sometimes it was too much. It was as if our friendship meant nothing. It'd been more than a decade, yet he became more closed off with every passing day. I couldn't help but worry.*

The handle turned, someone grasping it from inside the house. Amelia peeked through the opening. "Rafe? What are you doing here?" She opened the door wider, ushering me inside.

"I think I fucked up." I let out a breath as I followed her up the wooden staircase. "Or maybe not—I don't know."

We passed through the white door that led to her bedroom. I closed the door behind me and Amelia sat on her mint-colored comforter with her legs crossed. I paced in the center of the room, making my rounds from one end of the soft lavender rug to the other as I nibbled on my fingernails with my arms crossed tightly over my chest.

"Is this about Aspen?" Her voice was delicate, understanding.

I froze, my hand dropping from my mouth. "How'd you know?"

She gave me a faint smile. "Anytime you get worried or stressed out —it's undoubtedly about Aspen. So, tell me. Why do you look like your dog ran away from home?"

I chuckled, "You know I don't have a dog."

She waved me off. "Your expression says otherwise."

"Well," I huffed, "I got into a fight with Aspen. Kind of. He was acting super weird and wouldn't answer any of my questions... then I accidentally crossed a line I shouldn't have..." I covered my eyes with my hands, roughly rubbing them and seeing stars behind my closed lids. "And I—I got angry... so I left."

"Left him where?" My girlfriend asked me with a pointed look.

"At the field..."

"In Riverside? Let me get this straight; you're freaking out because you didn't give Aspen a ride home?"

"Yeah..." In a dumbed-down version.

"Then why don't you just call him?" She raised her eyebrows.

"I don't know... I guess I just needed to calm down a bit. He infuriates me, but at the same time, he makes me so—"

"Worried?" Amelia interrupted. "Yeah, that's a common theme I've noticed."

I meandered away from the brunette on her bed and toward the clear glass doors leading to the small balcony. A warm breeze rustled my hair. The sun was just beginning to set, illuminating the white rails with blinding light.

I pulled my phone out of my pocket and called Aspen, leaning against the metal fence. The call went straight to voicemail. I pursed my lips in annoyance, trying to call him again, but the phone didn't even ring. That asshole forgot to charge his phone again, didn't he?

If his phone was dead, did that mean he wouldn't be able to call anyone else to pick him up?

"Shit," I muttered.

"What's wrong?" Amelia yelled from inside her room, leaning to her right to peer at me.

"He's not going to pick up," I sighed, looking up at the orange sky and closing my eyes. I rested my forearms on top of the rail, jutting my legs out and leaning forward.

"I'm sure he'll be fine. Aspen's not a little kid."

"I know that. I'm just worried that he's going to get lost."

"Rafe," Amelia said in a quiet-yet-hard tone.

"Yeah?" I opened my eyes, craning my head to look at her.

She had a soft expression on her face. "I think we should break up."

My fingers went limp, my phone falling from my lax hands and crashing into the large pool below.

I didn't know what to react to first—Amelia, or my now drowning phone. So instead, I stood still, my body facing her backyard and my face staring into her green eyes.

I glanced back at the pool, knowing there was nothing I could do about it. I slowly removed myself from the rails.

Amelia lifted herself off the bed and sat in the middle of her fuzzy rug. "Come sit down."

I abided wordlessly and sat in front of her.

"This is something I've been thinking about doing for a while..." she started.

"A while?" I let out a humorless laugh. "We haven't even been dating for a month."

"No, I know. And I'm not breaking up with you because I don't like you."

"Then why?" I searched her eyes.

"At first, I was super happy when you asked me out. But then I started spending more time with you... and Aspen. I noticed some things and spent the past week really thinking about it, and I believe this is best for both of us."

"What are you talking about?" I furrowed my brows, not following her logic.

Amelia bit her pink bottom lip. She reached her hands out and took mine into hers. I peeled my eyes away from the small, delicate fingers embracing mine to meet her sparkling eyes.

"I'm going to talk about some stuff... and I want you to really think about what it means. And Rafe, I need you to keep an open mind." She spoke uncharacteristically seriously.

I nodded, clueless as to what she was getting at.

She dropped my hands but kept intense eye contact. *"Whenever we're together, our conversation somehow always shifts to Aspen. And don't get me wrong,"* she held up her hands in defense, *"I love Aspen. I think he's a sweetheart, but for some reason, I feel like he's the centerpiece in our relationship."*

"I don't get—" Amelia held up her finger, signaling me to stop talking.

"Just listen. I know he's an extremely important person in your life. Fourteen years of friendship is really powerful. Yet, even so, the way you talk about him—it just makes me wonder..."

"Wonder what?" I asked sternly, becoming increasingly anxious while wondering what role Aspen could have possibly played in the reason Amelia wanted to break up with me.

She cleared her throat and adjusted her position on the ground. With a straighter posture, she used her hands to express herself. *"Are you aware that you have a type?"*

"Uhm," I paused, *"I haven't given it much thought before."*

"Well, allow me to explain. In seventh grade, you dated Jenna Myram. She's white, has brown hair, and green eyes. Freshman year, you dated Sienna Hale. White, brown hair, green eyes. Sophomore year, Megan Clarke. She also has brown hair and green eyes. Then fast-forward to now. I have all of those things, too. At first, I assumed that you just had an alarmingly specific type, but then I realized that wasn't necessarily true."

"Okay—so what if I like white girls? What does that have to do with anything?" I was getting frustrated.

She glared at me, forcing me to close my mouth once again.

"Rafe." Her tone was sharp. "Don't you get it? Can't you see what I'm getting at?"

"No, I don't!" I didn't raise my voice, but anger seeped through my words. "I have no clue what you're going on about!"

"Think about it for a minute! Who's the person you never shut up about?! Who's the person you put before everyone else? Who exactly is the person always by your side, who just so happens to have all the exact same features as your exes?! Brown hair and green eyes." She took a breath.

My mouth slightly parted, beginning to sense the direction she was going in.

"Can you see it now, Rafe? You're only dating me because of my physical traits. You only dated all those girls because of their appearances... you've only dated girls that look like Aspen." She nodded, her eyes boring into mine, trying to convince me.

The color drained from my face.

"You dated me because I look like Aspen. It's not me you want to be with. I'm nothing more than a substitute for the person you truly love."

I gulped. My eyes broke away from hers, jumping from object to object around her room, ultimately unable to find something to focus on.

"You're in love with Aspen," Amelia pressed.

"B-but I'm not—" I couldn't finish the words, but Amelia understood what I was saying.

"Rafe, I want you to forget about gender for a second. Pretend that gender and sex aren't a thing, as if they simply don't exist. Let's say I had no breasts and nothing down below. And that Aspen also had nothing underneath his pants. If we took away the things that defined us as female and male—would you still pick me?"

I whispered, "No."

"And that's okay." She offered me a small smile. "It's okay for you to like Aspen."

My mind was a whirlwind, my thoughts frozen but going into overdrive at the same time.

"I was hesitant to talk to you about this because I've heard the way some of your friends talk about the LGBT *community. But I want you to know, there's nothing wrong with liking another man. It's not strange or gross. It's okay. It's okay, Rafe. You can be in love with Aspen."*

I swallowed hard. "I'm not gay... I like sleeping with girls, I'm not gay." I repeated the words like I was trying to reassure myself; I could tell the attempt was failing.

"I never said you were gay. It's not as if liking someone of the same sex automatically makes you gay. Sexuality is a spectrum. You can like girls and boys at the same time. You can like anyone you want to," Amelia spoke in a calming tone.

"So you're breaking up with me—because you think I'm in love with my best friend?"

"Rafe, look into my eyes." I raised my head to meet her piercing gaze. "Look into my eyes and tell me that you aren't in love with Aspen. Tell me that I'm wrong. That you don't want to be by his side for the rest of your life. That you don't think he is more important than your other friends. Tell me you can't imagine yourself holding hands with Aspen, kissing him—and liking it. If you tell me that I have it all wrong, then I'll take it back. But Rafe, can you seriously look me in the eyes and say you aren't in love with him—not in a brotherly way, but romantically?"

The room fell into silence. I kept my eyes on Amelia, but the image in my head wasn't her.

It was Aspen.

I let out a deep, trembling breath of air. My eyes concentrated on the beige dirt stains on my white baseball pants.

Liking another man—liking Aspen—being in love with my best friend—was I really allowed to do that? And if I actually did like

Aspen, then why hadn't I realized it before? It didn't make sense.

But then again, it did. I knew I saw him... differently, but it always stopped there. I hadn't let myself think about what that meant.

I'd heard derogatory slurs every day and grown up surrounded by family and friends that frowned upon same-sex relationships. It was so normal for queer people to be condemned around here. So, maybe... maybe I was pushing it down subconsciously.

But it made sense.

Everything Amelia said made sense.

There was a reason Aspen was always on my mind, and it wasn't just because he was my best friend...

"I know this is probably a lot to take in, and I'm not trying to force this on you. It's simply what I observed, and I felt that it was important for me to talk to you about this. I don't want to make you uncomfortable."

Uncomfortable?

I wasn't uncomfortable at all—which was exactly why I couldn't deny it.

"Theoretically speaking, if I did, in fact, like Aspen in that way, I should keep it to myself, right? I shouldn't tell others?"

"It's up to you. I won't say anything to anyone. You're taking this a lot better than I thought you would."

"Well, it's not like I have anything against gay people. It's kind of weird and a little awkward to think about. I've never questioned my sexual orientation before, but if it's Aspen... Do you think he'll hate me if he finds out?" *My lips formed a thin line.*

"From what I've seen, Rafe," *Amelia looked me straight in the eyes,* "you should tell him how you feel."

I frowned. "I don't think that'll go very well. Like you said, the people I'm friends with aren't exactly okay with this sort of thing."

Amelia stood and placed herself on her bed, resting on her side and propping her head up with her hand. I twisted my body around, uncrossing my legs and stretching them out on the floor. My elbows locked with my arms extended behind my back, holding my torso's weight.

I wasn't sad she wanted to break up with me, but rather, was surprised by the revelations her reasoning brought. However, I wasn't disgusted—slightly anxious, maybe. But Amelia's acceptance and openness somehow gave off the feeling of us being close friends rather than, well, exes.

"I've always been a pretty observant person." Amelia's voice was nothing less than soothing. "Whenever I heard your friends calling things gay as if it was an insult—which it isn't, by the way—I noticed how you wouldn't really go along with what they were saying. You never agreed with it, but you also never spoke out against it."

"Aspen always agrees with them." I moved one of my legs up so that it was bent and I could rest my elbow on my knee. I leaned into my hand and brushed my fingers through the side of my hair, stressed and deep in thought.

"I noticed that too. But it's different than what you're thinking. Whenever they say those types of things, Aspen always gets extremely nervous. He agrees with them, but reluctantly. To people like me, it's obvious he's faking it."

"What do you mean?"

"Honestly, I think Aspen likes you too."

"How can you be so sure?" I bit my lip, my brain a muddled mess. I listened to what she was saying, but it was processing slowly.

"It's just a gut feeling."

"That's not a lot to go off of."

"Just trust me. If you confess to Aspen, I have a feeling that everything will work out in the end."

Chapter Twelve

Rafe

THERE WAS SUDDENLY A CLOSED pair of lips attached to my mouth. I froze in shock, staring wide-eyed at the boy in front of me. His eyes were screwed shut and his tears slipped into my mouth.

Aspen's lips were warm and smooth. *This is it. This* was how it was supposed to be. *I definitely love him.* The feel of Aspen on my mouth, it was unlike any kiss I'd ever experienced. It felt like all the oxygen in my lungs had been sucked out, my whole body tingling and my mind fuzzy.

I'd been questioning everything for the past six days, reanalyzing every part of my life that involved Aspen. The big question: was my love for him platonic, or so, so much more? I'd come to the same conclusion Amelia had reached: Deep down, I'd never truly seen Aspen as my best friend. Because even though that was what we were and what we would always be, I couldn't help but want more. I was in love with my best friend, and as his closed mouth pressed against mine, I started to believe that he felt the same.

I *wanted* him to feel the same... but why was he crying? I had an itching need to understand why Aspen was having such a hard time, and I was doing everything I could to figure it out. I thought the trip with my dad would give me time to sort my thoughts, figure out how I'd handle things and how I could help Aspen. But now he was kissing me and it felt as if everything had fallen into the open, blowing my planned confession out the window.

The hinges of my door subtly squeaked and my mom came barging into my room. "Boys, would you like some—" the plate of fruit fell from her hands, smashing to the floor and leaving bits of painted ceramic scattered on the wood below.

Aspen jumped off me and averted his gaze, turning his head away from my mom and toward the window next to the side of my bed. I looked at my friend, who furiously rubbed at his face in an attempt to dry himself.

"Rafe. Living room. *Now,*" my mom demanded.

Oh, crap.

I hesitated as I slid my legs slowly over the bed. "Wait here. I'll be right back," I whispered.

He gave me no reaction. No movement, or words to acknowledge what I said.

My mom stomped out of the room and I followed closely behind, closing the door so Aspen wouldn't hear whatever my parents were about to say.

My dad was slumped in the recliner next to the couch. I hovered in the entryway and my mom paced around the center of the living room.

He leisurely set down the book in his hands, his legs propped up on the footrest. "What's going on?"

"I"—my mom was fuming—"caught our son *kissing* another boy!"

"A boy?" My dad raised a brow.

"Explain yourself." My mom pointed a finger at me hastily with her other arm placed on her hip. She reminded me of those cartoons where the angry character's face turned red and literal steam came out of their ears.

I didn't want to waste my time playing a roundabout game with my parents; I had more important things to do. I couldn't keep watching Aspen fall further and further into the dark space surrounding him. And I needed to know how he felt about me—I needed to hear the words come out of his mouth.

I sighed and scratched the back of my head, telling myself to just *fuck it.* "I'm bi."

My mom roared, "Bisexual?"

"Hmm, that's surprising." My dad seemed unfazed.

"Y-y-you-you," she couldn't stop stuttering. My mom's eyes fluttered uncontrollably, and it felt like I could physically see her blood pressure rising.

"Come on, Teresa," my dad began. "What're you so worked up about? So what if he likes men?"

His nonchalant perspective was unexpected—startling, even.

"You're telling me you're okay with this?" she cried out.

"It's his life. It's not my place to dictate who he likes." He adjusted his reading glasses and grabbed his book, putting an end to the conversation.

"You still like girls, yes?" My mom's pleading eyes locked on mine.

"I like girls too, yeah…"

"Th-then you can still date a girl! You can still get married and have children!"

I rolled my eyes. "*Mom.*"

Without looking up from his page, my dad said, "Let the kid date who he wants, Teresa. I know you come from a more conservative and traditional family, but in this day and age, this sort of thing is perfectly normal."

"*Mateo,*" my mom's harsh voice was joined with a steep glare directed at my dad.

"*Teresa,*" my dad repeated back. He shifted in his seat, placing his feet on the ground and leaning forward. "What would you have him do, then? Hmm? Tell me."

My mom said nothing, falling down onto the couch and placing her hand over her eyes, probably having an internal breakdown.

"See. There's nothing you can do. And even if you tried, all you're going to do is push Rafe away. He's perfectly normal, just accept him for who he is. It's really not that hard."

"Thanks, Dad." I shot him a small smile.

"So, who's the boy in your room, then?" He prodded, trying to tease me.

I glanced at both of my parents to gauge their reactions. "Aspen..."

"I didn't know he was gay," my father hummed.

"I actually don't know if he is. Is it cool if I leave now? I have some stuff I need to talk to him about."

I didn't wait for a reply before I turned on my heel and rushed back into my room, just to be met with the humid breeze from my open window.

"Shit!" I muttered as I ran up to my bed. I craned my head out the window and looked to my left and right. He wasn't there.

And then I saw it: a small post-it note on my pillow. I picked up the yellow square and couldn't help but chew on my fingernails as I read the disturbing words.

"*My life is already fucked. I didn't mean to drag you into this too. I thought I could have one last thing, but I just made your parents misunderstand. I'm not really sure what to write... I'm sorry for always lying to you. I'm sorry for making you angry. I'm sorry that you had to skip out on stuff with your friends because of me. I hope that you'll be able to go back to how things used to be. Your life can be better without me in it... I'm sorry, I should never have kissed you...*"

Why did this sound like a goodbye?"

My mouth went dry as I reread the small note over and over again. I let out a shaky breath, my brain trying to piece together what his words really meant. In a panic, I crumpled up the post-it, the paper falling to the floor. In one leap, I was grabbing my keys off my desk and bounding out the door. I sprinted to my car and threw myself into the seat.

I didn't bother looking over my shoulder for oncoming cars as I pulled into the street, my mind too occupied to think clearly. My foot pressed against the gas pedal harder than it ever had, the tapping of my left foot drowned out by my anxiety.

I knew the general area where Aspen was staying. And although I didn't understand why he had to go to such lengths just for his brother, I also couldn't guarantee a shitty motel was where he went, but I had nothing else to go off of.

It felt like I was holding my breath the entire drive. I ran several red lights, lucky that there were no cops around.

Approaching the gas station Aspen had mentioned earlier, I quickly realized that there was a string of motels lining the surrounding streets. He didn't tell me which one...

"Shit!" I cursed, hitting the top of my steering wheel.

I could ask his brother. I hadn't talked to Alex in years; Aspen always made sure we never crossed paths. That started around the same time Aspen began to change...

Deep down, I knew what that note meant. The gut feeling it gave me was all-consuming. *There is no doubt in my mind.*

I made an abrupt U-turn, ignoring the flashing red lights hanging above. The momentum threw me toward the middle of my car, my tires screeching in the process.

I hadn't planned for backtracking. I was wasting time. Turn after turn, I rushed through yellows and swerved haphazardly between cars. My heart was beating out of my chest. I didn't remember Aspen's house being so far away from the outskirts of the city.

I pulled up next to Aspen's house, my car pointed at an awkward angle near the street. I didn't bother turning off my car as I sprinted toward the front door, ringing the bell several times until someone came to the door.

"You're so damn loud." I was met with a slightly shorter brunette male. Alex.

"Do you know where Aspen's staying?" The words rushed out. I didn't bother with formalities like saying hello.

He had a strange smirk. "It's nice to see you, too. And no. I don't give a fuck where that little shit goes, it's not my problem."

I didn't remember Alex being like this...

"Honey, who's at the door?" Familiar blonde curls came into view. She carried a rag to wipe her hands, wearing a vintage, pale off-white dress and pearls wrapped around her neck. The bright smile fell from her face. "Oh... Rafe."

Why was his mom home? He said his parents were on a trip.

He was lying again... I should've known that.

But if his parents were here, then why wasn't Aspen staying at his house?

"He was asking where Aspen is," Alex snarked.

She pursed her lips and hesitated before speaking, glancing around the room for someone. The blonde woman leaned toward me and whispered, keeping her words out of earshot from Alex, "I think he's been staying at the Garver Motel."

I clenched my teeth. "Why?"

"I think you should go." She straightened her back. "You shouldn't come here again." With that, the woman ushered her son away from the door and closed it in my face.

I stood there, stunned and unable to move. I tore my eyes away from the door and moved stiffly to my car.

What the hell?

Yet another thing I needed to add to my never-ending list of things I needed to bring up with Aspen.

I tried to shake the thoughts from my head, needing to focus on the issue at hand. It was already getting dark out.

I reached the Garver Motel at the peak of dusk. The sky was no longer orange, but a deep purple that spread between clouds. I quickly parked in the middle of the large lot, jumping out of my car and spinning around. *What room? What room was it?*

I turned to the side, peering through a large window. A hefty man sat on a stool behind a desk. I didn't think, I just ran. I burst through the entrance, ignoring the loud chiming noise as the door swung back and forth.

Startled, the man's head shot up with an angry-looking expression.

"Is someone named Aspen Ace staying here?" I asked urgently.

"Tall brunette boy?" The man questioned, setting down the Monster he was holding.

I nodded vigorously.

"He is. Why?" He looked ready to call the cops on me, assuming I was looking for trouble.

"What room?" I felt out of breath, the sound of my heart taking over my ears.

He didn't answer, eyeing me suspiciously.

Huffing, I ran my fingers through my hair, trying to calm my panic.

"Geez, kid. Calm down a bit." I think he could tell something was wrong. "Sixteen."

I hit the top of the counter and burst out of the small office with a kick in my step. I sprinted until I got to a room with a small plaque on the door. Room sixteen.

I knocked on the door, softly at first. "Aspen?"

There was no reply, so I hit the door harder, yelled a little louder. "Aspen?! Come on, open the door."

Nothing indicated he was here, but I'd already passed all the places Aspen usually hung out when I was driving to and from his house. If he wasn't there, this was the only other place I could think of.

"Fuck!" I shouted. A pit formed at the bottom of my stomach. I took a step back from the door. A twisted feeling took over my body and my arms began to shake.

"Stop being so loud, you'll disturb the other guests." The man from the desk leisurely approached. "I brought a key." He waved a small piece of metal in the air.

Maybe he sensed my urgency, but he quickly stuck the key into the aged knob. The second I heard a click, I rushed past him, shouting Aspen's name as I came face-to-face with an empty room.

The door to my right was ajar.

A chilling sensation brushed down my spine.

One step after another, I slowly approached the door. I nudged the stained wood, giving way to a loud creaking noise.

"Aspen?" I choked on my words as I looked at the ground.

I found Aspen... in a puddle of his own blood.

Chapter Thirteen

Rafe

ASPEN'S WHITE LONG-SLEEVE WAS DRENCHED in red. His skin, now a ghostly pale, no longer matched the golden bandaid I'd placed on his cheek. The wall behind him kept his head upright while his body lay motionless on the floor. His eyes were half-open, the dull green barely peeking through.

In his limp hand was a razor dirtied with a deep shade of crimson. There was a single bottle loose on the floor, its cap nowhere to be seen. Thick tablet pills surrounded the unlabeled white container, too few for a bottle of that size.

I wanted to throw up. I trembled in place, my heart beating through my throat.

I fell to the ground, unable to feel my legs. I pushed myself toward Aspen, feeling the now-cold, dark liquid against my knees. With a shaky arm, I moved my hand toward his face. "As-Aspen," I gasped as my fingers brushed across his cheek.

I began to hyperventilate. "Aspen, wh-why are you, why are—" I couldn't *breathe*. I could barely even see the lifeless boy in front of me; the tears streaming down my face completely overtook my vision. I grabbed his shoulders, moving him so that his head rested on my legs rather than against the hard wall. Looking down at the boy, I hesitantly moved my hand toward his neck, just below his jawline. I noticed a small cut dripping a little blood; it looked different from the bruises and scratches I'd seen earlier. I pressed two fingers to his neck, letting out a sob when I felt no pulse.

"What's with all the noise—" keys clattered to the ground behind me. I turned back to the rough-looking man with tears and clear mucus covering my face to see his hand clasped firmly over his mouth.

"He-he's, he's n-not breathing." I struggled to get the words out.

"I'll call an ambulance." The man suddenly jumped into action.

In less than two minutes, wailing sirens echoed outside of the room.

Paramedics burst into the bathroom, one of them grabbing my shoulder and asking me to move out of the way. I stood next to the grimy shower, watching them rush around frantically, one person doing CPR, another getting a defibrillator reader, and more rushing in with other gear. The EMT stopped pressing on his chest as the other placed the paddles on Aspen's chest, causing the boy to jolt. They did it again. And then one more time.

"I've got a pulse!"

They slid him on top of a yellow platform, hauling him up and carrying him out.

I lifted my hands and looked at my palms, sobs wracking my body. They were drenched in a thick red liquid. *Aspen's blood.*

And then I looked at the mirror. *It isn't just my hands covered in my best friend's blood.*

My cries got caught in my throat, adding to the unbearable pain in my chest.

"What's your relationship to that man?" I was jolted from my thoughts as a paramedic's hand touched my shoulder.

I jumped to look at the person. "We're f-friends," I hiccuped.

"Okay, then. You can ride with us." The paramedic grabbed my arm and dragged me away from the bathroom's bloodstained tiles.

We passed the distraught manager and settled into the back of the ambulance. I sat on the seat near Aspen's legs, completely zoned out as the medics talked about things I couldn't comprehend. There was an oxygen mask on Aspen's face, and his arms fell off the sides of the gurney. I wanted to hold his hand, but I couldn't move a muscle despite the constant trembling of my hands and uneven breaths.

Sirens rang in the back of my mind, the vehicle coming to an abrupt stop. The doors flung open, giving way to the hospital's ambulance bay. Doctors rushed out as they lowered Aspen to the ground; I followed closely behind.

"What happened?" A doctor with a loose ponytail and strands of hair falling in her face asked, grabbing hold of the side of the gurney as they began pushing him inside.

"Attempted suicide," a paramedic shot back. "Lacerations to the..." I tuned them out.

Once inside, the gurney rolled much easier and the pace increased. Another doctor jogged up to the bed, tugging on a pair of blue gloves over his hands. "Aspen?" He seemed shocked.

They wheeled him through two automatic doors with a large illuminated sign labeled "SURGERY" above.

The doctor stayed behind as the team of people rushed through.

"Are you the one that found him?" The doctor asked. I could only nod.

"I'm Dr. Amin."

"Rafe," I croaked, my eyes not leaving the closed doors.

"Do you know what he took?" I glanced up at him.

How does he know Aspen took something?

I shook my head, struggling to get the words out.

He let out a frustrated sigh. "That's alright. I think I have an idea." He didn't elaborate before disappearing behind the doors to the operating room.

I felt like I was going to collapse.

"Hi, hun. Would you like me to show you to the waiting room?" A nurse approached.

I quietly followed her to a room full of blue-cushioned chairs. There were several other people in the room, all of whom stared at me in bewilderment. I was covered head-to-toe in blood; my hands and knees looked like someone had poured a bucket of red paint on them.

The nurse dropped into the chair next to me with a clipboard and pen in her hands. "Is it okay if I ask you some questions about the young man you came in with?"

I nodded. My tears had just started to dry, but I was anything *but* calm.

"Good, good," she hummed, trying to speak calmingly. "Could you tell me his name?"

"Aspen Ace."

"His Age?"

"Eighteen."

"Do you know him personally?" she asked compassionately.

I dipped my head in a nod.

"Then do you know if there's someone we can call? Family that would be listed as a guardian or emergency contact?"

"Probably his parents," I whispered.

"Hmm, okay. I'll be right back." I spent the next five minutes staring blankly at a wall before the woman returned. "So we weren't able to get in contact with anyone, which means that all medical decisions will be left to the medical staff in charge," she explained. "Is he your friend?"

"Yeah." A tingling sensation burned in my nose.

"How long have you two known each other?" She set down the paperwork. I think she was trying to distract me.

"Since we were four..."

"Wow... so he must be pretty important to you, huh?"

I bit my lips, nodding my head as salty water pooled in my eyes.

"Then, would you happen to know if he has any pre-existing or underlying medical conditions?"

"I'm not sure."

"That's alright. You should call someone. At times like these, it's good to talk to another person." She got up from the seat and left me to my lonesome.

Why did she say it like that?

I pulled my phone from my pocket, slowly dialing my dad's number. I held it up to my ear, my hand quaking with barely enough strength to grip the device.

"D-dad?" I sniffled.

"Rafe? What's wrong?" He immediately detected the weird tone in my voice.

"Y-y'know how I've been asking you all those questions the past couple of years? What it meant if someone started talking less. Losing interest in things they used to like. If they randomly show up with weird bruises and injuries. If they flinch whenever someone gets too close. If they stopped wanting to hang out with friends. Always seeming tired and spaced-out... *th-they weren't just random things I was thinking about...*" my voice cracked.

"What do you mean? Are you okay?" I heard rustling from the other end of the line, concern lacing my dad's voice.

"I'm at the hospital right now."

An engine revved in the background. "Rafe, what's wrong? You're scaring me."

"It's not me," I practically whispered. "It's Aspen."

There was a long silence, but I could tell my dad was driving.

"I-I should have done something sooner. I knew something was wrong. I've known for so long! If—if I had done something sooner, then maybe..."

"Rafe, hold on. I'll be there soon." He hung up.

Holding my phone, my hands dropped between my legs. I let my head fall and cried silently, trying to not disturb the other people.

When my dad got there, he quickly claimed the seat beside me.

"What if he dies?" I was breathless, my words sluggish. My energy had been completely drained, physically and emotionally. "*I knew he was depressed. I knew* that something was going on, but he wouldn't tell me. He would always change the subject or lie about it... and I just *let him.* I thought that giving him space would help—he just seemed so anxious and nervous all the time. He was trying to hide things, and it felt like it got worse whenever I tried to pry. So I gave him space... *I shouldn't have.* I should've confronted him sooner. I should've helped him more. *I didn't know it was this bad.* If I—If I had just—" I broke down again, my blood-covered body shaking uncontrollably.

My dad stiffened. "So Aspen, he..."

"*He tried to kill himself.*"

If only I had done something more. Why *didn't* I do something? *Why?*

Fucking why?!

I should've just—

If only I—

Why did he do it?

If I'd done something sooner, I could've helped him! I could've stopped this from happening, right?

"And he's being treated now?"

"In surgery," I mumbled.

My dad glanced at my hands.

"It's his," I replied, knowing what he was thinking.

"I'm going to go call his parents." My dad stood to find a less crowded space, coming back in less than a minute to tell me that neither of them had picked up. I could've told him that would happen.

"You should go clean up a bit while we wait," my dad told me.

My nose twitched; I was sure the skin was bright red by now.

I caught my reflection the second I was in the restroom. *Some of Aspen's blood is smeared around my face.*

It makes me sick.

I placed my hands under the faucet, turning the water on and aggressively scrubbing the blood off my hands. My face contorted as I tried to keep myself together. My emotions were unstable and I still felt like I was about to break down.

I grabbed some paper towels and got them wet. I wiped down my legs, but the small amounts of blood splattered on my clothes wouldn't come out with just a little water.

I walked out, rubbing my face. On the way, I stumbled into my dad, marching alongside the same doctor from earlier. Dr. Amin, I believed.

"Rafe, good. The doctor here says that Aspen's out of surgery!" His cheerfulness did wonders to soothe the storm in my head.

My eyes went wide and the tension in my shoulders released. "S-so he's not dead? He-he's okay?"

"I wouldn't say *okay,* but he pulled through. We just moved him to the ICU."

"He's not awake?" I questioned.

"Let me take you to see him." The doctor offered me a small, tired smile.

We walked down mazes of hallways that I'd never have been able to navigate on my own until we were face-to-face with thick glass.

"In there." He pointed to the third bed on the right. "I can't let you in there because he's not in the clear quite yet."

There was a tube shoved down his throat; it was the only thing keeping him breathing. He was dressed in a standard short-sleeved hospital gown, white with blue details here and there. A thin blue cotton blanket covered him from his chest to below his feet, his arms placed at his sides, above the cover, wrapped in bandages from his thumb to under the sleeve. There was a smaller bandage on the cut I'd seen on his neck, and if there were more, I couldn't see them.

The doctor noticed where my gaze lingered. "If Aspen had cut even a millimeter deeper, he could've cut a tendon or suffered permanent nerve damage. If that had happened, he would never be able to play baseball again. He'd be lucky if he could even grip a ball."

I bit my lip, listening to him talk.

"That wasn't the only issue."

I glanced at him. The doctor occupied both mine and my dad's attention as he stared at Aspen with a deflated expression.

"We had to pump his stomach. It's good that Aspen is a habitual person; it makes him easier to treat." Dr. Amin shook his head and crossed his arms.

I furrowed my brows. "What do you mean 'habitual?'"

He sighed and rubbed his temples. "I spend a majority of my shifts at a clinic associated with this hospital. Most of the regulars we get are homeless, low-income families without healthcare, and junkies. And Aspen... he's no exception. Suicide attempts. Self-harm. Breaks, fractures, sprains, and bruises. Drug and alcohol abuse," the doctor listed. "I've lost count of the number of times I've seen Aspen for these things the past four years."

"*Four years...*" I whispered back, dumbfounded.

He'd been doing this since he was *fourteen*. Four fucking years—and I had no clue. I did nothing to help him... I didn't even *know*.

This was why he was always hiding his arms. This was why I hadn't seen him wear a T-shirt since seventh grade. Because he'd been cutting himself all this time. The bloody bandages I found in trash cans on more than one occasion and going through boxes of band-aids as if they were packs of Tic Tacs—it was all to hide this. To hide how much he was hurting on the inside.

"I wanted him to be admitted so he could get help, but the clinic is part of a program to help those who don't have the insurance or money to cover the cost of treatment, and Aspen refused to give out any personal information, so I had no way to get in contact with his legal guardians."

Like the nurse, my dad still couldn't get in touch with Aspen's family. I had an inkling they were doing that on purpose.

"While we were checking his body for any additional cuts and lacerations he could have inflicted on himself, we found a bump near his left shoulder blade. We decided to look into it, and we found a large shard of glass lodged between his muscles. The surrounding skin had completely healed as scar tissue; it had to have been there for years. I can't even imagine the pain it would have caused."

I grimaced.

"And it isn't my first time having this thought, but I have reason to believe he's being abused."

I sucked in a breath. *What?*

"Why do you think that?" I choked the words out, my eyes burning, a lump in the back of my throat.

"I know Aspen plays very competitive baseball, but the injuries he receives just don't fit the sport. Right now, his body is covered in bruises from head to toe. Some fading, and some brand new. Did you know his rib cage is broken?"

"Broken?" I echoed, recalling the way he'd been walking and sitting earlier, curled over as if he would collapse at any second.

How... how could I have missed something like that? There was no way, *no way* I wouldn't have seen it. I was by his side all the time, how could I—

Who would want to hurt him?? Aspen was the sweetest, most genuine person I'd ever met. Regardless of my bias, Aspen was better than *everybody*. He deserved the world, and I'd been stupid enough to think everyone else thought the same.

Hours passed, and soon enough, I was bent over an unconscious Aspen's hospital bed—or rather than unconscious, it was more of a deep sleep. My head rested on top of my crossed arms laying on the side of his bed near his waist.

They decided he was stable and moved him into a separate recovery room overnight and my dad left to get me a change of clothes. I didn't want to—couldn't—leave.

For several hours, Dr. Amin continuously came in to check on Aspen's vitals. He asked me to try and convince Aspen to admit himself to the hospital—not for his physical injuries, but for his mental health.

Since Aspen was suicidal, my dad agreed it was a good idea and it'd be best for him. But the issue arose where Aspen was an adult, meaning he had to be willing to do so. After realizing how hard he'd tried to keep all this to himself, I couldn't imagine him caving so easily.

I was stressed and upset. Angry that Aspen did this to himself. Angry that he felt the need to go this far. And even angrier at what pushed him to feel like this was the only option.

It all left me with the same question that had been on the back of my mind for years: Why?

I hadn't gotten the chance to tell him how I felt, or learn how *he* felt.

Why did he kiss me?

Did he like me too? In *that* way?

He must, right? *He* kissed *me*. Did that count as coming out? Coming out and a confession?

The early morning sun hadn't risen yet, the room still dark and illuminated by the glow of the machines hooked up to my best friend.

I felt like crying, but I'd already exhausted all the liquid in my body; there were no tears left in me to shed. Instead, I was left with an unpleasant cork in my throat that strained whenever I tried to talk, and a wrenching pit in my stomach that made me feel like I needed to throw up and pass out at the same time. I'd never felt this kind of pain before, and I wasn't even the one lying in the hospital with a needle in my arm.

Just like the past several years, I felt clueless.

I rested my head on my forearms, my face pointed toward Aspen's. He was too beautiful to have bruises on his face. I wished he'd never had them in the first place. That he didn't have to go through the pain of receiving them. I wished I could take his pain, stop his suffering. I wanted him to be happy. I always had, even when I thought he was nothing more than a friend.

I'd always loved him, just not in the same way I expected to.

Chapter Fourteen

Aspen

WHEN I PRIED MY EYES open, they were glossed over. I tried to take in my surroundings, but confusion and blurry vision swept over me.

Where am I?

My nose twitched and I breathed in the air. I recognized the familiar scent of disinfectant immediately.

Damn, why is it so fucking hard to die? How much further do I need to go?

I shouldn't have hesitated. I should've just done it. I remembered pressing the cheap blade against my throat. A shallow slice in the right place would guarantee death. I'd thought about it. I'd wanted to do it. And I'd started, but the brain worked in annoying ways. A person could bite their finger off as easily as they bit into a carrot, but your brain would stop you. That was why it was so hard to kill yourself. Because no matter how much you wanted to, the subconscious part of your mind did everything it could to survive.

"Aspen?" a deep voice whispered.

I turned my head to the right, instantly groaning and moving my head back to a straight position. My left arm was slung inside a dark-blue brace hanging from my right shoulder, laying across my stomach. I was too tired to even question why my shoulder hurt.

"Aspen?" Rafe's soft voice tried to get my attention.

My mind was hazy. Was I still dreaming? I'd never woken up in a hospital bed next to someone I knew—I must've still been asleep.

Even if it wasn't real, I couldn't help but want to apologize. I messed up, and I knew how monumental that screw-up was the second Rafe's mom walked in. If his parents reacted the same way mine did, then I'd completely fucked him over. And all for nothing. Just like always, I brought needless trouble to everyone around me.

"I'm sorry..." I rasped.

"Why would you be sorry?" he chuckled, hoping to lighten the mood. "You didn't do anything wrong."

"I kissed you..." My voice faded at the end, almost inaudible. If I was dreaming, it was okay to say it, right? It wasn't real, which meant there wouldn't be consequences for putting my feelings out in the open, right?

"You don't have to be sorry for kissing me." He hesitated, red-tinted skin surrounding his eyes, looking at me with distraught before leaning forward. My eyes fluttered shut, expecting his fist to follow, but instead, I was met with the softest press of lips against my forehead. Light and delicate, as if the touch was meant to convey a thousand words, a thousand feelings. *You're safe. You're okay now. I'm here.*

With a shuddering breath, I asked, "*Why?* Why aren't you hitting me? Why aren't you swearing and calling me disgusting?"

Rafe pulled away to meet me with an expression of adoration and helplessness. "I'd never hit you. *Ever.*" He reached out, his fingers brushing through my hair; I let out an involuntary sigh. "I hate this," he mumbled. "I hate seeing you like this, hurting. I can't—I *can't.* I don't want you to be in pain, I don't want you to hurt or cry or be *here.* And I want to hug you and kiss you and tell you everything's going to be alright, but I can't, because you're *not alright.* You're already hurting, and a kiss won't magically take your pain."

"I don't understand, why would you want to..."

"Later," Rafe whispered. "We'll talk about it later. Right now, I just want you to be okay."

My head swam with the implications. If this was what death was going to be like, affirmations of affection and love spilling from his eyes, not endless nothingness like I'd thought, then dying didn't seem all that scary. If anything, it just confirmed what I'd always believed: Dying was better than living. And even if I wasn't dead, if this was a dream, I never wanted to wake up. If things could continue like this, I'd be willing to spend an eternity in a coma, trapped in my own mind. If it could be like this...

His hand slipped under my right palm, looping his fingers around mine while avoiding the IV and the pulse oximeter clipped onto the tip of my index finger while his left thumb brushed over my cheekbone.

If I could be with Rafe like this, I wouldn't mind staying in this place between life and death. I didn't want to wake up, but if it could be like this... I didn't want to die either. I was overwhelmed with a sense of giddiness and dejection, knowing I'd never have this in real life. So why did this feel so real? Why did this not feel like a dream? Was I *high*?

My eyes narrowed in on the way his fingers wrapped around mine, avoiding the wires. "Fuck," a humorless laugh fell from my mouth. "This is the best trip I've ever had. I don't want it to end. Maybe I should ask the doctor what they gave me so I can try it again later," I hummed to myself.

"You're not high, though," Rafe laughed stiffly. "Or dreaming, or anything else."

I searched his eyes. "No... I think I am. This isn't real. You wouldn't want to kiss me in real life."

"Somehow, I don't think you'd believe me even if I pecked you on the lips right now." He flashed a tired smile.

I swallowed hard and then turned my face parallel to the ceiling. Rafe didn't let go of my hand, not even when Dr. Amin entered the room wearing royal-blue scrubs with a spotless white coat over top, flicking on the blinding lights. Of course, it was him. It always seemed to be him.

"Good morning." He picked up a clipboard attached to the bottom of the hospital bed and flipped through the pages.

"Did you give me something that could make me hallucinate?" I asked straightforwardly. The doctor stopped what he was doing and looked up in surprise. "Because I tried LSD once, and the trip was nice, but I can't taste color right now and this one's overly realistic. Although I'm not complaining."

"Aspen, the only things you're on right now are some painkillers and IV fluids. And the painkillers aren't even strong. I'm not stupid enough to give you fentanyl or, god forbid, more hydrocodone."

"Aww, come on, doc. What harm could some good old Vicodin do?"

Dr. Amin glared at me. "I'm not replying to that. Either way, you're neither high nor tripping. I have no clue what would give you that idea."

The faint smile dropped from my face. My gaze slowly drifted to the hand clutching mine. My eyes shot to Rafe, a sudden overload in my head. My mind tried to process, but couldn't connect the dots. My breathing halted. I opened my mouth, trying to suck air into my lungs, but instead, I felt like I was choking. My right hand twitched and I clenched it, flinging it from Rafe's grip and bringing it to my chest, grasping at the area over my heart, scratching and tugging at the skin.

Dr. Amin's hand froze, holding a page up. His attention transferred to the screen emitting an increasingly fast beeping noise.

I hit my chest.

No. That's not right. This has to be a hallucination or a dream.

This isn't real.

It can't be.

I was supposed to die.

Rafe was never supposed to know about what happened—I was never supposed to see him again.

I started pounding on my chest.

He knows. He knows I like him...

A firm hand wrapped itself around my knuckles, another pressed against my chest to cushion me from the punches.

Why did he kiss me? Why is he holding my hand? This can't be real, it can't. It's impossible.

"Aspen?" The voice was a distant echo my brain chose to ignore, my anxious thoughts consuming me.

"Aspen." It was a different voice. It shook me—made me shiver. Rafe was squeezing my hand, trying to get my attention. "Stop—please stop hitting yourself."

My hand froze a couple of inches from my chest. I looked down wide-eyed at the tightly wound fist cupped in Rafe's hands. I let out a shaky breath, entranced by the warm, dark skin enveloping my fingers.

"Maybe you should have something to eat. It might help settle you down a bit," Dr. Amin commented, visibly on edge.

I gulped, returning my gaze to the smooth white surface above me.

He pulled a pen out of his pocket. "I'm going to shine this into your eyes, okay?" The light burned and I felt the urge to squeeze my eyes shut. "Your pupils aren't dilated, that's good. Here." He picked up a small remote attached to the side of the bed and handed it to me. "You can move a bit, but be careful—your chest and abdomen will be sore."

"Hmm," I mumbled, unsurprised.

"I need to talk to you about your injuries and further treatment. You may need someone to help you while recovering and it'd be best if that person is in the room with you during this so they are aware as well." He set the clipboard down.

I pressed the button and winced as the back of the bed rose slowly. I didn't put it at a ninety-degree angle, but it was high enough that I could sit up.

"Is your friend okay?" He gestured toward Rafe.

I dipped my head in reluctant agreement. I didn't want to let go of Rafe's hand. I knew I might never get the chance again.

Was he doing it out of pity? Caving in because he felt bad that I'd tried to kill myself?

"We removed some glass that had been lodged in your back. You'll need to wear the sling for a week and the stitches will be removed at a later time along with the ones in your left wrist."

I kept my eyes trained on the wall ahead of me, unprepared for him to go into such detail. These were things I didn't want Rafe to know about. Things I never wanted *anyone* to know about.

"You have four broken ribs. And, thankfully, no punctured organs. They'll heal on their own in three to six weeks. In the meantime, don't do any strenuous exercise that could cause pain, like weightlifting. If you feel any pain or discomfort, stop what you're doing. Your ribs are wrapped right now, but you can take that off after you're discharged."

It was a lot of information to take in. "Okay," I replied.

"Switch the bandages on your left shoulder and wrists every day to prevent infection until the areas around the stitches are no longer red or inflamed."

He didn't need to explain this part to me. I was well-aware of the process. I'd just do what worked for me in the past, anyway. There was no need to go the extra mile; basic disinfecting was more than enough.

"I also still firmly believe that you should admit yourself." He didn't go into further detail. I knew exactly what he was talking about.

I glared at the man. "You already know my answer."

"But Aspen," he sighed, "at this rate, you'll never get better. You have a whole life ahead of you. You can overcome this, but you need extra help."

"I'm fine. I don't need it."

I didn't look at Rafe. I wished he wasn't here.

"Do you not understand how serious this is?" His anger began to rise. "You were this close"—he held up his index finger and thumb, creating a small space between the two—"to never being able to use your left hand again, let alone play baseball."

"I won't do it again."

"Don't lie to me, Aspen. We both know that isn't true. You've said that exact same thing more times than I can count."

"I'm not going to waste my time rotting in some boring psychiatric facility."

"You're already rotting away, aren't you?" The doctor spat back. He was being unprofessional, but it just showed the past four years' worth of built-up frustration. Even if he was worried, I didn't care. It simply wasn't the right decision for me.

I laughed, "So what if I am? Either way, I don't have jack shit to pay for a stay in the psych ward. Hell, I don't even have the money to pay for *this*. In case you haven't noticed, I don't have fucking health insurance. Plus, I already have enough grippy socks. Got a new pair on right now."

I hated that Rafe was listening in. I knew he was grasping onto pieces of information and trying to place them into a puzzle.

"Okay. I understand. You can be discharged this afternoon. I'd like to make sure no other complications pop up. A nurse will provide you with disinfectant and bandages. Aspen," he halted in the doorway on his way out, "please think about it again."

Chapter Fifteen

Aspen

I TRIED MY BEST TO muffle the grunts dying to escape my mouth to appear as if I wasn't exhausted and in immense pain.

Keep it together, Aspen.

Rafe hovered behind me, off to the right, ready to catch me if I were to trip or pass out.

Once we passed through the clear, automatic doors, we were met with Rafe's dad's car pulled up to the pickup zone at the front of the hospital. Mateo glanced at the two of us through his rearview mirror while Rafe opened the door to the back seat. I slid in, grabbing the seatbelt and pulling it over my left shoulder, buckling it near my right hip. Rafe crawled in after me, reconnecting our hands and holding them on the narrow middle seat, rubbing small circles with his thumb on top of my dry skin.

I wanted to yank my hand away and yell at him. *What are you doing? What if your dad sees?*

The silence was killing me. No one asked for an explanation; all I got were worry-filled glances. I had the urge to scratch my arms, overwhelmed by anxiety.

It was *suffocating.*

My fingers twitched in Rafe's hand, wanting to not only pull my arm back, but to rip off the bandages and tear out the stitches.

Why are they pretending like everything's okay?

I winced when the car came to a stop. Rafe leaned over me, pushing the door open. He loosened his grip on my hand reluctantly, allowing me to get out.

Mateo's keys clinked together as he stuck one into the gold keyhole. "Aspen," he began, "why don't you take a seat on the couch first."

I simply nodded. My throat burned even more now than earlier—apparently, I'd had a tube shoved down my throat the night before.

I huffed, gently lowering myself onto the grey, slightly scratchy sofa. Rafe sat next to me, leaning back against the fabric and turning his head toward me. He searched my face, but I didn't dare look back.

I placed my hand in my lap and nervously picked at the corners of my fingernails, trying to ignore my best friend's sad gaze.

Rafe's parents both walked out of the kitchen and into the living room, whispering frantically amongst themselves. Mateo took the recliner with an uneasy expression. His wife seemed upset, sitting on the smaller, two-seat couch to the left of the television.

"Can you tell us what happened?" Rafe's dad crossed one leg over the other. "I called both of your parents, neither picked up. I also went to your house, but no one answered the door."

I ignored the uptick of my heart, clearing my throat, wanting to appear at least somewhat okay. "I-uhm, I got kicked out of my house." My voice was quiet and I looked everywhere except at the faces surrounding me.

"Why would your parents do that?" Teresa gasped.

I gulped. I should just say it, right? I could easily make up some lie... but then again, what was the point? She'd already seen me kiss Rafe.

"They, uhm... they found out I'm gay..." My voice sounded foreign to my ears.

"Your mother was okay with this? I can't imagine Madeline going along with such a thing." Rafe's mom furrowed her brows.

"She didn't really want to kick me out. It was my dad. My mom wanted to send me to conversion therapy." My volume faded with each passing word.

She hummed in thought. "Conversion therapy, it would've been a good way to fix—"

"Mamá! What's wrong with you?! ¿Cómo puedes decir algo así?" Rafe shouted at her, the most upset I'd seen him since I woke up in the hospital.

"¿Qué?" She raised her eyebrows, confused.

"Teresa, you can't say that kind of thing!" Mateo interjected.

I hated being in the middle of this. I didn't want to be the reason they fought.

"Do you even know what kinds of things they do to people in conversion therapy?" Rafe spat.

"They help you reconnect with religion, no?"

"No, not at all. I've had several patients that were forced to go through conversion therapy, and you know what we call them? *Victims.* Some of them are beaten and raped until they can convince people they no longer have an attraction to the same gender or they break under the trauma. I know we have different views, but I also know you well enough to understand you wouldn't support that kind of thing."

Her face dropped, looking between the three men in the room. "I'm so, *so* sorry, Aspen." A look of horror overtook her. "I didn't know that. I've only heard about it in passing conversations. I didn't know they did such things."

"It's alright," I whispered.

"Is that why you did it?" Teresa appeared downcast, ridden with guilt.

"Let's talk about this later, yeah?" Rafe interrupted.

I think he could tell I didn't want to talk about it. If it were so easy to say out loud, he knew I would've told him long ago.

"Sure. Yes. Let's do that." Mateo said as Rafe grabbed my hand and helped me up, guiding us toward his room.

I paused, turning my head around with my back still facing his parents. "Uhm, I don't have any money to pay you back for the hospital bills..."

In a soft tone, she said, "Don't worry about that right now. It's fine. If you really want to pay us back, you can do it when you make it big in the baseball world." The black-haired woman gave me an encouraging smile that I struggled to return.

"And Aspen, you're welcome to stay here as long as you need," Mateo told me.

"Thank you." I didn't really want to stay. I'd just make things harder for them—for Rafe—again.

"And boys, keep the door open," I heard Teresa say.

Rafe closed his door anyway. He dropped my hand and moved to the top of his bed, grabbing his pillow and setting it up against the headboard. "You should probably sit down."

I walked wordlessly over and settled myself onto his bed, adjusting myself with my right arm since I wasn't supposed to move my left to not tear the stitches.

I wore a maroon short-sleeved shirt as well as a pair of black shorts, courtesy of Rafe's dad. Rafe's clothes fit the exact same as mine, although I couldn't lie and say that it didn't feel strange wearing a T-shirt. I hadn't worn one in years. A nurse had helped me change earlier; it was a lot harder than I thought it would've been. They should've just left the glass in my back. It didn't even hurt that badly...

Rafe settled down on the other end of the bed near the bottom of my legs that were spread out into a V-shape.

We sat kind of like this when I kissed him. On his bed. *Close.*

"How are you feeling?" he asked.

"Okay," I mumbled.

He took a deep breath before speaking in a low voice. "Y'know, when you kissed me yesterday, I never got the chance to say anything." He was trying to look into my eyes again. *Why does he always do that?*

"I don't really want to talk about it." I rasped, hoping we could pretend it never happened. Maybe—maybe he would still be my friend. Just maybe.

"So you don't want to know about how much I want to kiss you?" He tilted his head to the side, leaning in.

I turned my face away and kept my mouth shut. The thought of knowing the truth *scared me.*

"Do you want to know why I broke up with Amelia?"

Yes. Of course, I want to know.

Why did you break up with her?

Why did you keep holding my hand?

Why did you *kiss* me?

"I wasn't dating Amelia because I liked her... I dated her because she reminds me of you."

I sucked in a breath, my eyes snapping to Rafe's. Did that mean...

"Everyone I've dated looked like the girl version of you, and in the end, I broke it off with all of them because no matter how much of a resemblance there was, they never measured up. Because they weren't you. I didn't understand how I could like my best friend, but then I realized, it's *because* you're my best friend. Because it's *you.* It's always been you."

I tried not to chew on the inside of my cheek.

"I was always worried about you." He let out a bitter laugh. "Every little thing you did, I noted it, placing it in the front of my mind. The way you laughed... the way you hurt. I tried to be there as much as I could. I didn't want you to be alone. I knew something was wrong, but a part of me was too scared to ask. And then you kissed me, and it felt like I finally understood. Aspen," I stared into his serious, sorrowful eyes, rubbing my fingers together with a painful amount of pressure. If my hands weren't sweating, it felt as if I could've torn my skin. "Did you do this because you're gay?" Rafe's voice was breathless, tears stinging his eyes. His eyes were too beautiful; he shouldn't cry. Especially not over someone like me.

"Do you hate me?" I whispered, my lips quivering.

"*I love you, Aspen.* I could never hate you. *Ever.*"

"As a brother? Or as your friend?"

"As my best friend"—my heart clenched—"and as someone so much more."

I struggled to swallow the lump in my throat. "I don't understand what you mean."

"When you kissed me—that was your way of saying goodbye, *and* your way of confessing to me, right?"

I nodded tentatively.

"I wanted to kiss you back and tell you how much I love you, but you were gone. So now I'm telling you, I feel the same." The corners of his lips turned up. He was smiling, but why did he look so sad?

I felt strange. Was I happy? No. Happiness was too strong of an emotion. But then, what was this? My chest hurt, but at the same time, it felt incredibly warm.

"So you like me... in the same way I like you." I tried to grasp the idea. It was such a foreign concept, something I hadn't hoped of having in real life.

"Not just as friends, but romantically," he clarified.

"Do your parents know?"

"I told them after my mom saw us kissing."

"And they're okay with it?"

"My dad doesn't care. My mom doesn't like the idea, but she'll get there, eventually."

"Oh. You have really great parents, huh?" A pang of jealousy shot through me, followed by splinters of guilt. I shouldn't feel that way, yet even so, I wondered how different my life could've been if my family was like Rafe's.

"I'm lucky."

"Yeah," I rasped, looking away.

"Are you—" Rafe's voice broke. "Are you going to do that again?"

I knew what he was referring to. My brain wanted me to lie. Out of habit, or maybe to protect myself. But there wasn't a reason for me to do that. He said he knew. He'd *known*. And now he'd *seen*.

"I—" I bit my tongue. "I don't know," I sighed.

Things were different now. He knew I was gay and accepted me. He knew I was suicidal, and he hadn't left. I had nowhere to go, and he gave me a place—a reason—to stay. Every awful scenario I'd ever played in my head about how my life would pan out came true. Everything I'd feared the most already happened. Things couldn't get worse, so it was impossible for me to know if my mind would follow the trend.

"Will you tell me about it?" He pleaded softly, conveying that if I still didn't want to talk, he was okay with that. He'd waited all this time to ask, so waiting a bit longer was okay.

"It's complicated..."

"Does it have to do with you being gay?"

"Yeah," I croaked. "It has everything to do with me being gay."

"Because of your parents?" He led the conversation.

"They played a big part, yeah. But it was mostly something else." The tendons in my wrist and forearm became sore as I fiddled with my fingers and hand.

"Were you scared of people finding out?"

"That, too... but it's because of someone that's known for a while." My voice quaked. "When I started to realize I had feelings for you, in seventh grade, I actually came out to Alex. He, uhm, he reacted *badly*."

Rafe's eyebrows tightly knit together as I slowly spoke, letting out small pieces of information here and there. "When you say badly?"

"He got kind of aggressive with me... but there was nothing I could do... and I don't regret it." I pursed my lips. "Not really. Otherwise, my parents would've found out sooner. I—I think this way was probably better."

"Aspen." I looked up at the cracked words of Rafe's voice. His mouth quivered and a tear escaped his eye. "Does—" he took a second to compose himself. *"Did Alex abuse you?"*

The tips of my eyebrows dipped inward. My nose scrunched up and I sucked my lower lip into my mouth. My throat began to close, making it increasingly difficult to breathe. My chest heaved painfully. I bowed my head as the salty liquid cascaded uncontrollably down my cheeks.

It hurt.

God, it hurt so much.

Everything Alex did to me, it *hurt.*

And it still did... on my body. In my mind. *Everywhere.*

The bed creaked. Rafe got up onto his knees and wobbled toward me. He silently wrapped his warm, muscular arms around me, one ghosting over my back and the other wrapping tightly in my hair.

I let my head fall forward, my forehead resting on his abdomen. For the first time, I truly let myself cry.

I let it all out.

Everything.

All the pain I'd kept to myself.

For all the times I'd felt alone and broken.

And all the times my emotions had been so overwhelming I thought it'd be better to just feel nothing at all.

For everything, I let it out.

My right hand clutched onto the fabric of Rafe's shirt as if I would lose him if I let go.

Rafe sniffled above me. His hand left my back and went to wipe his face before he lowered himself so he was sitting on the backs of his heels. He pulled away from me, not removing the fingers that stroked my head calmingly.

His nose was red with his eyes matching the pink tint. My face was soaked, wet and messy from the excess tears that collected in my tear ducts and escaped through my stuffy nose.

Rafe bent down, placing his lips on my forehead, where they stayed for several seconds. "It's okay now," he murmured against my skin. "No one's going to hurt you here."

I let out a deep, unsteady breath. "I know."

Rafe kissed my cheek just under my eye and then on the corner of my mouth. He looked blurry in my tear-stricken eyes, and I probably looked similar in his. His lips connected with my damp ones. I closed my eyes, basking in the cozy feeling of his lips against mine. The temperature of his mouth made me feel pleasant, warmth spreading through my body. Rafe radiated heat.

The kiss wasn't intense, but it was the most intimate moment I'd ever experienced with someone.

Despite wearing fewer layers than usual, the summer heat mixed with the feeling of Rafe against me made me hot. Too hot. Sweat collected at the back of my neck from my damp hair, falling down my sweaty back. I retracted my mouth from the boy in front of me, and with a grunt, I lifted my right hand back to scratch myself. The sweat mixed with the tight fabric wound around my torso created an unbearable itch, but with my ribs in the condition they were, I couldn't move enough to reach my back.

"What are you doing?" Rafe's voice was hoarse from crying.

"It's itchy," I mumbled.

"Oh, right. Dr. Amin said you could take it off when you got home."

"Mhmm." I winced.

"Here." Rafe moved outside of my legs. "I'll help you take it off."

He reached toward my left shoulder, gently slipping the strap off my arm. The pain from moving around wasn't an issue, it didn't bother me, but I had to be careful because of the stitches. I slid my arm out of the sling; Rafe took the fabric and placed it on the side of the bed.

"Are you okay if I take your shirt off?"

I liked that he asked.

I wanted to say no, but I didn't. "Yeah, it's fine."

"Can you lift your right arm up?"

I straightened the limb above my head. Rafe gripped the hem of the shirt tenderly and pulled it up; I moved my right arm so it slipped through the sleeve. He tugged it over my head and brought it down so he could remove it from my left arm without me having to move it.

The tan bandage covered my torso from just under my chest to the tops of my shorts. Rafe studied the wrapping, making me thankful it covered the self-harm scars on my abdomen.

"I think it's hooked in the back. Can you turn around?"

"Sure." I pushed myself up with my right hand and tried to turn around without twisting my waist. Easier said than done.

I crisscrossed my legs, facing Rafe's headboard with my feet just below his pillow. I squirmed when his feverish hands came into contact with my skin. Rafe worked carefully to unhook the small metal clips that held it on my body. I soon felt one end fall to the side. Rafe got on his knees again and leaned his head over my shoulder. He wrapped his arms around my waist, trading the end of the fabric from one hand to the other as he unwound the layers bundling me.

When there was nothing left on my skin, Rafe dragged in a long puff of air. "Aspen, you—"

"It's not as bad as it looks."

Rafe slumped behind me. "If I ask, will you tell me?" he asked with a hushed voice.

I answered hesitantly. "If you really want to know."

The bed creaked as Rafe shifted his position to sit comfortably with his legs sticking out on each side of me. My arms lay limply in my lap, my eyes trained on my feet.

The tips of his fingernails grazed my skin. My body shuddered as he dragged his hand lightly toward the outside of my right shoulder blade. "This one?"

I swallowed hard, trying to keep my emotions in check. My heart hammered in my chest; I wasn't sure if it was from crying or because *Rafe was touching my bare skin.* "You'll have to describe it. I can't see it, so it's hard to remember."

He tapped my back several times, each touch keeping to a confined cluster. "They're circular, kind of small, and a deep pink."

"Oh, those... when Alex was still in high school, he thought smoking cigarettes was cool so..."

Rafe's hands tensed before traveling farther down my right side, settling between the muscle and spine. "Two dots. It kind of looks like a vampire bite."

"He wanted to test out his friend's taser."

"A taser?" Rafe repeated in a low voice.

"He probably would've done it a couple more times if I hadn't passed out," I exhaled.

"Was—was Alex doing this kind of stuff to you until you were unconscious normal??" Rafe stuttered.

"It happened often," I admitted.

"And the glass that was removed?"

"He pushed me onto a glass table the day he found out."

Rafe's hand jumped up to the area where my neck met my back. He traveled a gentle finger all the way down my spine, causing me to shiver. "You have bruises on each vertebra..."

"Hmm, those haven't faded yet? I'm not really sure when they showed up. Maybe when he threw me down the stairs. Or another time when he dragged me up..."

The words were barely a whisper. "Why didn't you fight back?"

"It's not that easy. If I did anything, he would've told my parents. That would've meant no support and no money, which meant no baseball. Without baseball, I wouldn't be able to afford college. Without my parent's support, I would've hit a dead-end before I even got to high school. If anything, I'm lucky that they didn't find out until after I already got into Rowland," I spoke sluggishly, worn out.

"I see." Rafe didn't like my logic, but he understood it. "I get that you were scared of your parents finding out, but why—*why* didn't you tell me? We've been best friends for so long... did you think you couldn't trust me?"

"It's not about trust. You've seen it for yourself, how people around here view that kind of thing. I didn't think you'd hate me, but I also couldn't be sure. I was worried about how everyone would react, and rightfully so. It's not like my family are the only people that have responded poorly to finding out I like guys."

"What do you mean? Do other people know? Wait," I could sense the agitation in his voice, "is that why you were arguing with Devin?"

"I wouldn't say we were arguing," I mumbled, "more like running for my life. Literally. He—Devin, he was swinging a bat at my head."

"What?!" He shouted right in my ear, making me wince.

"The only reason I was at school today was because Devin told Coach I was hurt and hiding an injury. He didn't know that I broke my ribs, so he probably did that to get me off the team..."

"Wait, no, Aspen, you said he was swinging a bat at you! What—"

"I don't know... I think Jamey, Jason, and Devin wanted to beat me up, but they freaked when Devin decided to pull a bat out of his ass."

"How did he even find out?" Rafe was struggling to keep himself calm.

"Well, I got wasted and let it slip to Isa... I don't know who else she told, but my parents found out, and so did the guys." I couldn't remember the last time I could talk like this—open and freely, not caring if I spilled my secrets. After all, they weren't secrets anymore.

"Hey, Rafe," I started, my voice slightly cracking.

"Yeah?"

"I was talking to Amelia on Friday, she seemed to know that you..."

"Oh, yeah. She was the one that made me realize I liked you. I guess she could sense that something was missing in our relationship—*emotionally,* and somehow put it together."

"So you liked me, but didn't know?" In all honesty, I didn't understand it. Not one bit.

"I think my issue was more of not being able to discern what kind of love it was. I never bothered to think that it was anything more than platonic love, but when she pointed out that it could be, I couldn't deny it."

"Are you gay?" I whispered.

"I don't think so, no."

"Bi?"

"Probably."

"When you say you like me..."

"You don't believe me?" There was an ounce of hurt in his voice. But no matter how many times he said it, I couldn't help but doubt.

"It's just—" I stopped, unsure of what to say.

"I didn't think you liked me either, but Amelia argued otherwise. She said she could tell by the way you looked at me. She was right about my feelings for you, so I hoped that what she said about you was true, too. I was going to confess as soon as I got back, although things didn't go as expected."

You mean you didn't expect to get dragged into the mess that is my fucked-up mind.

"So what does this mean... for us?" Was it okay for me to say it like that? *Us?*

"Since we like each other, shouldn't we..." he asked awkwardly without actually saying the words.

"Date?" I finished the sentence for him.

"Yeah."

"You know what it means for you if you date me, right?"

"Hmm?"

"Being a straight couple is different from being in a gay relationship. If people find out, they'll say and do *things...*"

"I know," he breathed.

"I can't—*we* can't—be open about it. Or do shit in public. Especially around here."

"I know."

"And being with me... I can't guarantee," *I can't guarantee I won't kill myself* is what I wanted to tell him. I might not be able to make him happy. I was fucked-up and I couldn't see myself getting better. I had bad habits that would put him off. My emotions were all over the place; they radiated off me and could be too much for him to handle at times. And above all, I had a dick. I wasn't like the girls he'd been with. I wasn't short with a small waist; my chest was muscular and hard, not soft and squishy. If he was with me, in a *gay relationship* with me, his life would become a lot harder. But I didn't know how to tell him all that. I didn't know if he truly understood what it would mean to be with someone like me. I was having a hard time, and being with me would be hard.

There was this part of me that wanted to believe Rafe liked me, but there was so much doubt in my mind. Did he really like me? Was that actually possible? And then came the fear. What would happen when he realized I wasn't what he wanted? Would he abandon me, too?

"It's okay. You don't have to explain it. I know. But it's okay. Because it's you, it'll all be okay." He leaned forward and rested his chin on my right shoulder. He scooted forward so his chest pressed against my back, snaking his arms under my own and around my waist.

My heart rate picked up, a nervous feeling spreading through my entire body. I could feel his eyes staring at the side of my face as his hands crept closer and closer to the bare skin of my stomach. Right as they made contact, I grabbed his hands, trying to stealthily pull them away.

It didn't work. His thumb stroked my skin, grazing over the bumpy lines.

His gaze left my face and he peered over my shoulder to look down at the textured skin. "Here too?"

I nodded in return, my body rigid.

My mind clouded. All these things on my body—the scars and bruises—that I'd struggled to hide for so long were suddenly thrust out in the open for Rafe to see with no warning or time to prepare. I felt exposed and vulnerable. I didn't like it.

Rafe noticed how uncomfortable I was, but he didn't remove his hands. Instead, he bent his head down and placed a soft kiss on the skin between my shoulder and neck. I let out a shuddering breath at the feeling.

He flattened his hands against my stomach, speaking between soft pecks. "I never thought I'd be in this kind of a position with you, but now that I'm here, I really fucking like it."

Chapter Sixteen

Rafe

I SIGHED, STARING AT ASPEN'S sleeping figure. He curled up into a ball as soon as I got out of bed. His hands were cradled near his face, which was half-covered by his shaggy hair. In his sleeping state, Aspen was vulnerable, relaxed. He wasn't constantly trying to hide how he felt. His expression, for once, truly represented how he felt on the inside. The corners of his mouth pointed down, his dimples nowhere to be seen. Aspen's closed eyelids seemed to droop more than normal, deep bags draped underneath. He looked utterly defeated.

I shrugged my backpack over my shoulders, walking blindly through my unlit room. I glanced at my baseball bag before ignoring the gear and slipping through my door, shutting it behind me as quietly as I could to not wake the boy sleeping in my bed.

I rubbed my face harshly as I made my way into the kitchen. My mom and dad were seated at the small table eating what looked like eggs.

"Buenos días," I mumbled, grabbing a plate from the cabinet above the stove.

"¿Cómo has dormido?" My dad took a sip of his coffee.

"I slept okay, I guess." I didn't.

When Aspen slept, he had these nightmares... he would kick and cry silently, and sometimes it seemed as if he couldn't breathe. I'd try to let him sleep through it, hugging him until he calmed down, but there were times it was so bad I needed to wake him up. He'd bolt upright in an instant, his eyes roaming over the room, lost. He'd take a bit to get his bearings, and then I'd help lull him back to sleep, hoping my arms could provide some form of comfort and safety.

"And Aspen?" my mom asked eagerly.

I took half of the remaining scrambled eggs from the pan, saving the rest for when Aspen woke up. She didn't understand what was going on, the whole same-sex attraction thing. I wouldn't say she was okay with it, or with us staying in the same room and bed for that matter, but my mom felt guilty for the things she said the other day. Aspen had been in our lives for over a decade and that meant something to her. Aspen was an important person to my mom, and the last thing she wanted was for him to be in this position.

"He's still asleep." I leaned against the counter and shoveled food into my mouth.

"Should I take the day off so he isn't home alone?" she asked.

Honestly, I wasn't sure. On one hand, I was scared Aspen might do something, but on the other, I didn't want him to feel uncomfortable. "If you do, give him space. Let him know you're home, but y'know..."

"Okay, I'll do that."

I washed the now-empty plate. "I'm going to pick up some stuff for Aspen after school. Is there anything you need from the store?"

"No, I made a run last week, so we have everything we need for now," my dad chimed in.

"Okay." I swiped my tongue over my lips, trying to not let the stress get to me. "I'll see you later, then. Que tengan un buen día." I rushed out the door, wanting to avoid the awkward mood.

I slid into my car and took a deep breath, throwing my backpack in the passenger seat and turning the air conditioning to high. I got lost in my mind, staring at my hands as they gripped the wheel roughly. So much had happened so fast, and I couldn't help the crushing sensation telling me a lot of it was my fault.

All I had to do was ask him about what was going on. I could've helped him so much sooner. Maybe then Aspen wouldn't have had to deal with Alex for so long... maybe then, he wouldn't have tortured himself for liking someone he didn't think would like him back. There was so much I could've done to help him, but like the fool I was, I'd stood back and watched.

I watched him fall apart.

I drove to school distractedly. I hated going without Aspen, but there were only a couple of weeks left before we graduated, the seniors finishing a week before the other grades, and with him in his current state, it'd be better if he didn't go.

I shifted my car into park and grabbed my bag roughly, slamming the door shut. School was the last location on my list of places I needed to be.

"Rafe!" A smiling Amelia ran up to me and grasped my arm, her tight ponytail tied with a mint scrunchie, swaying along with her strut. "So," she linked her arm around mine and dragged me into the halls and toward our first-period classes, "how did it go?" Her head tilted upward with wide eyes, twinkling in anticipation.

She seemed so happy to see me, but I couldn't return the smile.

Her hands dropped from mine and she stopped dead in her tracks. "Oh no. Was I wrong? Did I—did I screw things up between you two?"

I glanced around before settling my gaze back on Amelia. "No, no. You were right."

"That's fucking great!" she yelled, slapping me across the shoulder with a blinding smile.

My expression deflated even further and turned into a grimace.

Her smile tweaked and then fell upon sensing my mood. "What's wrong?"

"Nothing, I just had a bit of a rough weekend." It wasn't me that had a bad weekend, it was Aspen. But it wasn't my place to share that.

"Bullshit." She raised a brow and gave me a pointed look.

"No, seriously, it's nothing."

"Did you get rejected?"

"I didn't."

"So you two are dating, then?" Amelia perked up a bit.

"We are."

"Then why do you look like me after I found out my boyfriend was in love with his best friend?"

Ouch. My bad...

I sighed and ran my hands through my hair. "Some shit's been happening and it's not my place to talk about it. But, uhm," I hesitated, "it's bad. Things are really fucked right now."

"Between the two of you?"

"No, it's not us. It's something else. I really can't tell you though."

"That's okay. One of the reasons I liked you so much was because you respected boundaries. Even if we aren't together like that anymore, it's still a great quality to have in a friend."

"Thanks for not pushing it."

The brunette slipped through the door to her classroom. With a deep exhale, I made my way toward my own, taking my seat just as the bell rang. I threw my backpack off my shoulders and placed my head in my hands. I didn't listen to a single word my teacher said; I was zoned out throughout the entirety of all my classes, spending the day wrapped in my mind, a heavy weight pushing on my heart and shoulders.

When the last bell blared with a static echo through the speakers, I waited several minutes to lift my head from my arms, the sudden light giving me a headache. I took a deep breath and surveyed the room; the only other people still here were the teacher and a student asking a question. I got up, rubbing my eyes as I walked into the halls. Kids rushed out the doors, done with school, and eager for summer vacation to start, even though finals week was still a ways off.

I trudged through the gym and toward Coach Gale's office, knocking on the blue-painted wooden door and looking through the square window to see him wave me in.

"Welcome back, Alvarez. Hope you had some fun while you were away," he said while sifting through a pile of papers.

"Hi," I responded, settling into the cheap, cracked grey chair on the other side of his desk.

"So," he finally looked up at me, "what can I do for you?"

"I just wanted to let you know that—" I cleared my throat to speak in a stronger voice. "I'm not going to be able to play in any of the remaining games. And I won't be going to practices either."

"W-what!?" he sputtered. "Why?"

"Some players on your team made a decision, and it's not something I can stand by. The things they did, I refuse to be around those kinds of people."

"Is this because of Ace's suspension? Because between hiding an injury and getting in trouble with the school for what he did to Devin, my hands are tied!"

I clenched my jaw. "What do you mean, 'what he did to Devin?'"

He rubbed his fingers along the stubble of his jawline. "That's not why you're here? I thought you would've heard by now. Aspen's been suspended for attacking Devin. Apparently, after he found out that Devin snitched about his injuries, he attacked him in the locker room."

I gaped, utterly dumbfounded. "You don't actually believe that, do you?" I scoffed. "You *know* Aspen, do you seriously think he would do something like that?!"

Coach Gale massaged his temples. "No. I don't. I mean, I *didn't.* But I was told there was evidence. There's nothing I can do."

My jaw dropped. "It was the other way around. Aspen was the one that was assaulted! And you're telling me he was suspended and kicked off the team without anyone even hearing his side of the story?!"

"I know! I know, but when they looked at motive, Aspen was the only one who had any! Not only that, but there were witnesses. Aspen hasn't been showing up at school either; there was no option but to believe Devin."

"Let me guess, the witnesses were Jamey and Jason," I spat their names out with disgust.

Coach Gale pursed his lips, his silence answering my question.

I stood abruptly from the chair, the piece of furniture falling backward from the sudden movement. "Screw this. I was already planning on quitting," I snarled.

"Wait, Rafe!" he shouted after me as I clutched the door handle. "We already lost Aspen. If you quit now, we're never going to make it past States!"

"Fuck Nationals, fuck States, and fuck you. *I hope they fucking lose.*" I slammed the door behind me, the frame rattling on the walls.

I stormed out of the gym, and to my luck, I passed my old friends.

"Rafe!" Jason called me over.

I had to bite my tongue not to lash out right here and now. "What?" I gritted my teeth.

"I don't have your new phone number, so I just wanted to make sure you heard about Aspen," Jason spoke as if he was doing me a favor. "I know you've known him since you were kids, so I feel kinda bad being the one to break the news to you. But Aspen, he's a dirty fag—"

I grabbed his collar and slammed him against the lockers. "Say one more word about him and you're dead," I spit venom, a growling whisper in his ear.

Jason grabbed my arm and tried to move it, but I was stronger than him. As was Aspen. But the main difference between us was that I wouldn't let him trample all over me, and I'd never let it happen to Aspen again, either.

"Rafe, what the hell!" Jamey came running over, grabbing my right shoulder and pushing me away from his other friend.

"You two have no idea what you've done, do you?" I laughed humorlessly. "You call him *disgusting. Telling him he shouldn't even be alive.* Well? What about you two? What makes you think you deserve to live after what you did to Aspen? Who gave you the fucking right to decide someone else's worth?! He was your friend! You did that to *your friend.*" I let out an exasperated cry, tears stinging the corners of my eyes. "Even if you don't like him, all he wanted was to live in peace. He never bothered anyone! He never did anything to you! So how could you—" I choked on my words, "how could you try to kill him when all he was trying to do was *live?*"

They were taken aback by my outburst. Numerous people in the halls stopped to see what was going on.

Jamey opened his mouth and closed it again. "It's God's will. He didn't create man and woman just so they could be gay—"

"You have no idea what you've done," I whispered, my voice breaking. "And you'll never be able to fix what you've broken. People like you—who use their religion to spread hate—you're the real scum. You use your bible to say that people can't love someone of the same sex, well, does that bible also say that you can physically hurt them? Does your fucking religion excuse murder?"

Silence.

"No. I didn't think so."

"But Rafe, Aspen can't just—"

"No." I cut him off. "Don't talk to me like we're still friends. *I'm not part of your fucking religious cult,* and Aspen isn't the problem! It's people like you! You're the issue. And you're lucky Aspen hates violence more than anything in the world, because if he didn't ask me not to, it'd be you two with a bat being swung at your heads," I seethed. "Devin and the two of you—*I hope you all burn in hell.*"

I didn't bother letting them reply. I knew I had to get out of the ever-shrinking hall before I lost it. I imagined what Aspen's face would look like if I came home with bloodied knuckles—he'd probably be horrified, maybe even scared, and that was the last thing I wanted.

Once seated in my car, I noticed my hands shaking in anger. Why did they get to go about their lives as if nothing happened, as if they did nothing wrong, while Aspen suffered? Why did Aspen have to go through this? It wasn't fair, and I hated that there was absolutely nothing I could do to change that.

I couldn't help him before, and I didn't know if I could help him now. I hated that people treated him like this—and I hated myself for letting it happen.

With a knot in my throat and a tightly clenched jaw, I shifted the gear and drove to the closest convenience store. I didn't bother putting music on; my head was too muddled, allowing the radio to blast the same five songs that were constantly playing in an endless loop. I blew out a puff of air as I parked. Bells dinged when I pulled the door open. I went directly to the men's hygiene section, scanning the shelves for things Aspen might need.

Shampoo, conditioner, body wash, toothpaste, an extra toothbrush, I listed off in my head. *We have enough at home.*

I had face wash and other things he could use; the only thing we couldn't share was a razor... my body stiffened in front of the different blades. I scrunched my nose up and turned away from the product. I knew he needed to shave—that he didn't like when his beard got stubbly—but I couldn't bring myself to pick it up.

I saw what Aspen did with his razor at the motel. With the way it was taken apart, it didn't seem like that was the first, and I didn't want to let there be another.

I looked farther to my left, noticing an electric razor. He wouldn't take something like that apart, right? It was a lot more expensive, but it was a safer bet.

I grabbed two, deciding I should throw my razor out as well. My mind drifted to the different ways Aspen might hurt himself, but I quickly realized that doing things like hiding kitchen knives would be going too far. I shouldn't kiddy-proof the house—taking away the things no one would notice missing, like a razor, would be enough. Or at least I hoped so.

Chapter Seventeen

Rafe

I STOOD OUTSIDE THE CLOSED door to my room. A flashback to when I found Aspen unconscious and covered in blood in the motel blared through my head like a fire alarm. The vivid images sent tremors through my fingers as they hovered over the rusty knob.

I encased the cool metal hesitantly, turning it more slowly than I ever had before, scared of what I might find on the other side.

The second the door cracked open, I was hit with a powerful gust of humid wind. I paced into my room, setting the bag of things I'd bought on my desk. Aspen slouched on my bed facing the open window, his ash-brown hair blowing all over the place and his hand lax in his lap. My eyes traveled up to his face; he didn't speak and his expression was unchanging. Aspen's eyes were closed, his chin tilted slightly upward as he basked in the breeze. He looked surreal, yet it was so obvious in his face that he wasn't okay.

His long lashes lay atop his cheekbones that seemed to protrude more than normal, the dark circles around his eyes consuming his face.

I stood in silence, just staring at the boy.

When he finally opened his eyes, all he did was blink. But not the normal kind; it felt as if his eyes were closing in slow-motion, his eyelids resting just a second longer than they should have.

A small smile appeared on his face—the one I hated so much. He turned his head to look at me. His eyes... god, they looked so empty. "I lost my scholarship," he whispered, barely loud enough for me to hear.

"What?" I exhaled.

He let out a laugh. He *laughed*.

"They took it back." Aspen leaned his head against the window frame, peering into the backyard. "The Dean of Admissions emailed me. It was about their zero violence policy."

I sucked in a breath. "Devin..."

"Hmm." Aspen nodded his head. "Rafe?" he croaked, his gaze shifting to mine with tears pooling in his eyes. "Why does it feel like the entire world is against me?"

I felt my nose start to burn and my eyes begin to blur. I wanted to give him an answer. I wanted to tell Aspen that he was wrong, that it wasn't like that. But the things keep piling on. Why did things keep getting worse? Why did it seem like nothing was going right in his life?

He sniffled, his smile unshaking. It was so rehearsed, so practiced that he could keep it on his face even when he felt like the whole world was crumbling before him.

I took a step forward. Then another, and another, until I was kneeling on the mattress and wrapping my arms around him. My chest pressed into his back and I expected him to break down like he did last time, but he didn't. Tears streamed silently down his face as he sat unmoving in my arms, watching the peach-colored petals falling from the tree getting caught and swept away by the wind.

"What am I supposed to do now? How am I supposed to get out of this fucking town when..." his voice trailed off.

I traced his gaze; his eyes followed a petal that looked different than the others. The light-pink contrasted the orange flower it fell from. Surrounded by lively and ripe colors, the pink was faded, washed out by the decaying ends that seemed to have been eaten away. It continued to get pushed around until it fell—right into a small puddle, the petal deflating and quickly sinking to the bottom.

"I thought about it," Aspen started. "I went through all my options... but there was nothing. If I still go to college, if I want to play baseball, I'd have to try out. I would never get a chance to play in games without having a scholarship position. I'd be pushed to second string without a second thought. But I wouldn't even be able to play on a team in the first place because I'd need to be working a job to pay for everything. Tuition, rent, food... and without a sports scholarship, I would need to get into a school with my grades, but that ship's already sailed. And if I somehow managed to get in and find a place on a D3 second-string team, it would be impossible for me to work a job, play baseball, and keep my grades high enough to not get kicked out. There's only so much time in a day—in a week. I can't do it all," he ranted, his expression hard and still.

I gulped, wracking my brain for something. Anything. "Aspen, just relax for a minute. You're upset and stressed out, so you're overthinking things."

A confused and pained expression overtook his face. "It's already the end of May, Rafe. Time's up. Colleges aren't accepting applications anymore."

I peered into his unexpectant eyes. "It doesn't have to be this year. You can always wait until next year."

He rolled his eyes. "I already told you, I don't want to play on some third-rate team that—"

"Aspen," I interrupted. "Send an email to a couple of the scouts from other schools that offered you scholarships. I *guarantee* they will offer you a spot. Maybe not this season, but the next."

Aspen tilted his head to the side and sniffled, seemingly calming down at my reasonable words, but the frown didn't leave his face.

"Let's say that did work, hypothetically. That I could still get my hands on a scholarship for next year. But what about this year? I can't go an entire year without playing in a competitive environment. My skill level will drop well below what they'd be paying for me to attend on scholarship. And I can't just stay here for a year, having your parents pay for my shit while you're off playing at college."

"You could always work. You could get a temp job for a year if you wanted."

"Yeah, but what would I do? You know better than anyone that all I have is baseball. I'm not good at anything else."

"Aspen, you're good at a ton of things."

"But I'm a *great* baseball player."

"Then can't you just play baseball?" I murmured, burying my face into the back of his neck. "Just because playing baseball in college is the normal gateway to the Major Leagues and leads to drafting and all, that doesn't mean it's the only way." The sudden idea spilled out of my mouth.

Aspen craned his head to look at me. I loosened my arms around him and lifted my face to meet his.

"You mean open tryouts?" he asked, tears drying on his face.

"Yeah."

"Are they even still doing those? I thought they were cutting it."

"The MLB Scouting Bureau did, but there are still some individual teams here and there that hold camps."

"The chances of getting picked through that are next to none. The MLBSB stopped doing them for a reason; most teams didn't take it seriously since all the talented players got directly scouted or drafted."

"Y'know you're one of those players too, right? You would've gotten drafted," I tried to convince him. "I think your chances of getting noticed are much higher than you think."

"But—"

"No, seriously. Think about it. You don't have anything to lose from trying out. If you don't try out, you'll get some part-time job and play in a just-for-fun league on the side. If you do try out and fail, you can still do that, wait a year, then go to a college and get drafted the normal route. But if you try out, you could get signed to a Minor League team and have that be your job. You could skip the college step and start making money right away."

"You make it sound so nice, but if it was that easy, then there wouldn't be so many people choosing college baseball over the Majors."

"It wouldn't hurt to try, though."

"I guess."

Aspen shifted his body. I moved my arms away from him and watched as he turned to face me. He looked up into my eyes and chewed on his lip. I should tell him to stop that. Our kisses always faintly tasted of blood.

Aspen hesitated to speak. "Can I hug you?"

I laughed. "You don't have to ask. I'm your best friend. Hell, I'm your boyfriend. You can hug me whenever you want."

"I'm just not used to being all touchy-feely with other people." He pouted his lips.

I opened my arms wide and a faint smile made its way onto Aspen's mouth. It wasn't fake.

My face was suddenly covered in an enormous grin for the first time in days. Aspen leaned forward and buried his head in my chest, enclosing his arm around my waist. Before I got the chance to do the same, Aspen continued to lean his weight on me until I fell backward and the two of us were lying down, my head somewhere near my pillow.

I chuckled and placed my hands on his back, struggling to resist the urge to squeeze him tight. "Are you comfortable?"

"Very." Aspen's words were muffled. Our legs were intertwined, his arm tucked tightly between my back and the bed. "Aren't I heavy?"

"You are."

"Is it uncomfortable?"

"Not at all." I smiled into the top of his head while giving it a quick peck.

I could feel Aspen smile into my shirt.

"Your exes were all a lot smaller than me… so I was curious."

He was finally starting to tell me the things going through that pretty little head of his; it made me feel like my heart was going to burst from love and adoration because even with all the bad things going on, somehow, it still felt like a step in the right direction. A small step, but a step nonetheless.

"They were lighter, sure, but picture yourself like a weighted blanket. Normal blankets are nice, yeah. But weighted blankets give that extra sense of comfort. They're heavier, but in a good way."

"Hmm, fair enough." He was whole-heartedly content with my answer.

"How's your shoulder feeling?" I peered down at Aspen who then turned his head to the left so his right cheek was squished against my collarbone, his hair tickling my chin.

"It doesn't hurt at all."

"And your ribs?"

"Not too bad. Just a dull ache."

"Good. What about your arms and wrists?" I asked cautiously.

Aspen was silent for a moment, making me regret the question. It was too soon; he wasn't comfortable enough talking about it—

"… itchy?"

"Is that it? They don't… hurt?" I furrowed my brows, despondent just thinking about it.

"It's nothing I'm not used to. They're scabbing right now, so if they're uncomfortable, that'd be why."

The way he spoke, as if it was nothing, filled me with rage. Damnit, it made me so upset—not at Aspen, but at everyone and everything that was part of the reason he did that to himself in the first place.

"Have you changed your bandages today yet?"

"... no. But in my defense, I've only been up for a couple of hours."

"We should change them, it'd be bad if they got infected."

"Not changing them for a couple of days won't kill me."

"Come on, get up," I grunted, rolling over so Aspen was lying on the bed instead of me. "We're going to listen to the doctor and change them." I grabbed the large plastic bag containing everything the hospital had sent home with Aspen.

Aspen groaned, rolling his eyes as he sat up awkwardly, trying to avoid moving his torso. I plopped down next to him and laid the bag beside me. One by one, I fished everything out. The white gauze, tape, cotton pads, Q-Tips, and disinfectant.

Aspen unclipped the sling with his right hand, pulling the strap over his head and sliding his left arm out. He stilled when he looked at me.

"Oh... did you want me to leave?"

"I guess not? It'd be hard to do the ones on my right arm by myself..."

"Okay. So you're okay if I take the bandages off?"

Aspen nodded reluctantly.

I flipped up the edge of the tape keeping the bandage stuck to his arm, peeling the film down from the pit of his elbow to the base of his palm, repeating the action with the other bandage on his left forearm. With the way he held his arms for me to remove the covering, I got a full view of the damage for the first time.

I held my breath, trying to keep any reaction to myself. There was barely any skin left that wasn't silver, pink, red, or covered in lined scabs. I attempted to keep my face straight, but I wasn't like Aspen. I didn't know how to hide my emotions like he did.

"It's not as bad as it looks," he mumbled.

No. It was. It looked this bad because it *was that bad.*

I poured some of the disinfectant onto a circular cotton pad and touched it gently to his skin. Aspen didn't even flinch. There was no wince or drawback like I would've expected when the alcoholic substance made contact with his raw skin.

"Is this why you never change in front of people?" I asked.

"Part of it. I also didn't want anyone to see the bruises... but Rafe," Aspen averted his eyes from the new gauze being taped to the tops of his arms, "shouldn't you be at practice right now?"

"No. I quit."

"Why?"

"Isn't it obvious? I don't want to play on the same team as those assholes. I don't want to help them win something they don't deserve."

"But you love to play baseball."

"I love you more than baseball, though." I cracked a smile at how Aspen's cheeks turned red.

"Cheesy," he muttered.

A smug smirk formed on my lips. "I know you like it."

"... maybe."

I shook my head with a dopey smile. I neatly rebagged the materials, leaving it on the floor near the foot of my bed.

Aspen's grin fell when he asked, "When you were at school today, did you see any of the guys?"

"I did."

"And?" He urged me to continue.

"I was going to avoid them, but Jason pulled me into a conversation."

A concerned expression made its way onto Aspen's face.

"Don't worry, though, I didn't hit anyone, I just told them off."

He visibly relaxed. "Did it seem like people knew about..." he picked at the cuticle of his nails.

"I don't think so. I talked to Amelia, and she didn't mention anything about that. She didn't know."

"That's a little surprising. I was sure they would've made a bigger deal out of it." Aspen frowned before letting out a hefty sigh. "Well, it's fine either way. I won't expect them to keep it to themselves, although it'd be easier if they did. Even if they do end up telling people at school that I'm gay, it doesn't really matter anymore since I got suspended. I guess there's at least one pro to all of this: Now I have an excuse to never go back or face any of them."

"Some bright side," I snarked, rolling my eyes.

"I'll take what I can get."

I tried to hide my sad smile, checking my phone for the time. It was around five p.m. "Did you eat lunch yet?"

"Yeah. Your mom came in a little after I woke up and gave me this tomato soup stuff. It was damn good." Aspen licked his lips, reminiscing.

"Was it cold?" I asked.

"Yeah."

"It wasn't tomato soup, it was gazpacho," I laughed.

He nodded his head.

"Do you think you'll be hungry again soon? Do you want to eat dinner earlier or later?"

"I'm always hungry. And yes. I want to eat earlier and later."

"Want to order pizza?" I pulled out my new phone.

"Hell yes."

"M'kay." I pulled up the website of our go-to place. One deep-dish pizza with cheese, black olives, and ham on one half, and cheese, spinach, pepperoni, and bacon on the other. "The wait's about forty-five minutes. Is there anything you want to do in the meantime?"

He fell silent, a thick wave of tension filling the room. Aspen scratched the back of his neck in a coy yet confident manner. "I could think of a couple of things."

"Oh?" I perked up. "And what might those *things* be?"

Chapter Eighteen

Rafe

"YOU HAVE AN ACTIVE IMAGINATION, I'm sure you can come up with a few ideas." Aspen bit his lower lip, looking at me with an excited gaze.

Oh, damn.

"Are you sure?" I asked skeptically. "We've only been together for a couple of days, I don't want you to feel like we're rushing into anything."

"Shut up. I've been wanting to do something like this since middle school. If anything, I'd be the one pressuring you into it."

"I don't feel pressured at all," I laughed.

Aspen stalked toward me on his knees. He looked into my eyes—goddamn, his eyes were so pretty—and gripped my shoulders, hustling me back against the bed. My legs hung off the side and Aspen hovered over me, his arms caging me in. He licked his lips and dove down, crashing our mouths together. He wasted no time in parting his mouth, egging me on to do the same. Aspen hummed as he tugged on my lower lip with his teeth, his tongue soon sliding into my mouth, forcing a low moan out of me.

Aspen shuddered, but it was impossible that he felt cold—no, the trembling and shaky breath stemmed from his mind. The contact sent sparks through his touch-starved body, wracking through him like a blizzard.

I threw my hands in his hair, loving the way his soft locks felt between my fingers. *Ah, shit. I love this so much.*

That was, until Aspen grunted in pain.

"What was that?" I asked as he removed his mouth from mine.

"My ribs are still a little sore. It's fine, though."

"It's most definitely *not* fine. Have you taken anything for the pain?"

He paused before replying. "No. I'm not supposed to."

I furrowed my brows. "Why?"

Aspen sighed. "Things like ibuprofen and Tylenol aren't going to cut it. I've built up a bit of a resistance."

"Oh." I frowned, suddenly remembering how long Aspen had been dealing with constant pain.

"So what? Are you going to tell me to stop just because of that? It doesn't even hurt that much," he huffed, still towering above me.

"Who said anything about stopping?" I smirked, lightly pushing on his chest until he was off me, allowing me to put him on his back. Aspen's head rested on the pillow and I climbed between his legs, not wasting a second before reconnecting our lips.

I planked over Aspen, my weight resting on my forearms to avoid putting pressure on his torso. He was rushing before, as if this was his only chance to be with me and if he didn't take advantage of it fast enough, it'd slip away. But that wasn't the case. I'd set the pace. I'd take it slower, so slow that it'd give Aspen enough time to understand that I wasn't going anywhere, and this wouldn't be his one and only chance to kiss me, to physically show me how much I meant to him.

His body was flush with mine, and everything that could be touching, was. Forceful heat coursed through me, sweat soaking through the back of my shirt. But Aspen didn't look like he was melting—it looked like he was feeling warmth for the first time in his life, like he'd spent an eternity in the cold by himself, frostbite chipping away at him bit by bit, counting down the clock until he froze to death.

I craned my neck, pushing my lips slowly toward his. I kept my eyes open, as did Aspen. I needed him to understand that this was real. That I was here and *seeing him*. I was with Aspen, and I was kissing *him*.

His mouth parted before our lips even touched. Impatient, wanting, and inviting. I didn't allow my eyes to flutter shut until Aspen's eyes were covered by his pale lids. My mouth worked against his in slow motions, the only noise filling the room were the small breaths shared between us. My hand slipped under his shirt, pushing the fabric up and allowing me to truly *touch*. But I wasn't touching him, I was *feeling*. Taking in the smooth skin, the bumps and scars. I rubbed tender circles near his hip, basking in the closeness I didn't know I yearned for.

Our bodies were still, but touches of fingers and wandering lips conveyed everything we needed. A peck at first. An open-mouthed kiss, slow and long, filled with sincerity, affection, and love.

I loved him. I loved him so fucking much and I'd do everything I could to reassure him.

Aspen could keep me in his embrace for eternity. I'd be okay freezing with him if it meant I never had to let go.

With my lips on his neck and his head tilted upward, pupils blown wide, my fingers played with the hem of his shorts, itching to slip underneath.

Aspen's hand caught mine, pausing all movements. "You don't have to..."

"And if I want to?" I dragged the pad of my thumb across the band of his briefs, caressing the flesh just above his hip bone.

Aspen hesitated to answer.

"Only if you want to, though," I clarified, making sure I didn't force anything on him if he wasn't ready.

"No, no. I want to. It's just that—you know..." his voice faded out.

"Know what?"

"Know what's underneath..."

I chuckled, "As in your dick? Yes, I'm well-aware."

"Exactly. It's a *dick,* Rafe."

"It's *your* dick, Aspen."

He rubbed roughly at the side of his face; the anxiety radiating off him was practically tangible. I immediately backed off.

I rolled to the side, claiming the thin space between Aspen and the wall. He lifted his head to make room for me, allowing my arm to slide under his neck so his head rested on my bicep. Ignoring the awkward angle, I bent my arms and threaded my fingers through his hair, hoping it'd release whatever tension his mind had created. "We don't need to rush this. I told you I wasn't going anywhere, and I meant it. I get that you've spent a long time thinking you'd be alone forever, that the two of us being together was impossible, but it's not. And I need you to understand that this isn't a sudden development that came out of nowhere. My feelings for you aren't something that popped up overnight. It wasn't like I woke up one day and decided, *yeah, I think I do like my best friend.* Because that's not what happened. My feelings for you, my *attraction* toward you, *it's always been there.* Even if I couldn't recognize what it was, it was there. And it's not going to go away, especially not because you're a guy, alright?"

Aspen hummed a nonverbal reply, his brows deeply furrowed as if his mind was fighting the idea but wanted nothing more than to accept it. I could tell it'd take him a while to wrap his head around the idea, but that was fine. He could take as long as he needed, because the way I felt about him was never going to change.

Chapter Nineteen

Aspen

INSECURITY WAS A BIZARRE THING for me. My dreams used to be plagued by scenarios that'd leave me in tears after waking up because everything was fake and I'd never have something like that in real life. But now that this was my *actual* reality, not another drug-induced lucid dream, it was hard to separate myself from all the emotions of past hopes and harsh truths—that apparently weren't so set in stone, courtesy of the boy cuddling me like it was the highlight of his week.

After we got back from the hospital, every little thing Rafe did assured me that this was, in fact, not a dream. He really did like me —*love me.*

One by one, my doubts were tossed out the window. He hadn't treated me any different since finding out I was gay, and he hadn't accepted me out of pity. I thought he'd be put off by my very-much-so-existent dick, but now that *I* was the one who wasn't ready to go there, it seemed laughable. It made me feel giddy inside, the butterflies reminiscent of the first time Rafe and I won a tournament.

The doorbell rang and I glanced up at Rafe, falling out of the calm daze he'd lulled me into and meeting his eyes. "It's probably the pizza. Where's your wallet?"

"Next to the bag." He nodded toward the cloudy white grocery bag where his keys and wallet were stacked.

I grabbed the black leather pouch and slipped out of Rafe's room. Striding into the entryway, I answered the door with Rafe's wallet in hand. My good mood instantly deflated when I was met with a familiar delivery boy wearing a disgustingly bright red shirt with black slacks, a large pizza box balanced on the palm of his hand. Noah, one of the few sophomores on varsity.

"Aspen?" The platinum blonde-haired boy's cap covered his icy blue eyes, but I could tell he was surprised to see me. "Is this your house?" He took a step back to look at the address.

I frowned. "It's Rafe's..."

"Ahh, somehow that doesn't surprise me."

"How much is it?" I asked, not wanting to drag out a conversation that had the potential to spiral downhill at any second.

"Eleven ninety-eight."

I pursed my lips as I fished out the cash. "So, you picked up a new part-time?"

"Yeah, my shift at my last gig overlapped with the new schedule for States."

"It's good that you found something this quick." Even though Noah didn't need the money, he liked to have a little extra pocket cash for fun. I found it somewhat admirable.

"I heard that you're not going to play in the rest of the games this season." Noah's frustration and kicked-puppy look sent a shrivel of confusion through me. "We're not going to win anything without you..."

Did the guys keep it from the rest of the team, too? It seemed like they really didn't tell anyone. At this point, my best guess was that they didn't want others to know they associated with a gay person, as ridiculous as it sounded.

"Some things happened. It was out of my control. But I'm sure you'll manage just fine without me," I tried to reassure him as I traded the money, taking the pizza from his hands.

He rubbed the back of his neck shyly. "I'm not half the catcher you are. And now with Rafe gone, too, things aren't looking too hot."

"All you can do is give it your best." I wasn't the best at dishing out encouragement; there was a reason I was never even considered for the captain position.

He pulled out a small black bag with a zipper, shoving the money inside and grabbing two pennies as change. I slipped Noah an extra three dollars as a tip, struggling to juggle Rafe's wallet and the pizza.

"But Aspen, are you okay?" He studied me from head to toe. Although I was better, my black eye was still prominent, my lip still split, fingerprints littering my neck in a light-pink hue, bruises on my legs, and bandages covering the undersides of my arms.

"As I said, some things happened," I said, putting an end to the conversation.

"Oh, uhm... Well, get better soon." Noah gave me an innocent smile.

"Thanks for the food, and good luck at your next game," I called as he backed off the porch.

I closed the door, sighing. Noah was a good kid. He was decent at baseball and, overall, a kind person. I wanted the team to lose in a complete shut-out, but there were some guys on the team, like Noah, that made me want them to win.

Not that much, though.

Noah had another two years in high school; that was plenty of time to secure a championship trophy. It didn't have to be this year with that exact team.

I went back to Rafe's room, opening the door and asking, "Do you want to eat in the living room so we can watch TV?"

"Yeah, let's do that." He got up from the bed and unplugged his laptop, following me out.

I placed the pizza on the small coffee table just feet away from the couch, ignoring the throbbing pain in the back of my head and eyes. Rafe set his computer next to the food and handed me the remote. I slumped against the cool grey fabric, flipping through channels until I found one playing *Supernatural* reruns.

"Why do you like this show so much?" Rafe questioned while he opened the box and took out a slice with an assortment of meats. He took a large bite, leaning over the table to not get crumbs on the carpet and furniture.

My answer was brief. "Jensen Ackles."

Rafe gave me a sideways glare.

"And the plot, of course." I reached for a slice from my half of the pizza, humming in satisfaction at the taste, focusing my eyes on the screen, and enjoying watching the young and inexperienced season one Sam and Dean.

Rafe opened his computer and I glanced at the screen. "You're already looking up open tryouts?"

"Well, yeah. We missed anything that happened in March, but there should still be a fair number of teams hosting tryouts in June and July. Summer's coming up soon so I thought it'd be better to start looking into it sooner rather than later."

"I guess..." I watched him flip through information on nearly all the Major League team associations and their Minor League affiliate tryouts.

The box of food had been emptied into our stomachs, leaving me sleepily watching yet another episode on the couch with my head resting comfortably against Rafe's shoulder.

"Okay, I think I figured it out," Rafe announced, cracking his knuckles.

"Figured what out?" I murmured.

He showed me a proud grin. "Which teams you should try out for."

"Already? Nah, no way. You couldn't have narrowed it down that fast with all the stuff to consider."

"It's 'cause there aren't a lot of Triple-A teams holding open tryouts, let alone during summer; most do it before Spring Training."

"So you basically just found all the teams still holding tryouts? That's it?" I snorted.

Rafe scoffed. "Who do you take me for? You're a lucky bastard, y'know that? Your amazing boyfriend here has been keeping tabs on the Major League teams we'd best squeeze into as a pitcher and catcher, so I only needed to do a little bit of research on the Minor League teams."

"Every single level? *Sure.*" I shook my head, calling his fib.

"Well... no. Not all of them. Only Triple-A."

"But if I'm trying to enter through open tryouts instead of being scouted or drafted, it's practically guaranteed that I'll start at Rookie, or Low-A if I'm lucky."

"You're way too humble," Rafe groaned. "I know, Coach Gale knows, hell, even the University of Rowland's scouts and baseball team know that you're a fucking amazing catcher. You didn't get offers from twenty-seven—*twenty-seven* different D1 schools that sought *you* out specifically—because you *might* be good enough to play Low-A or High-A."

"But it's better if I aim low and don't get my hopes up so I'm not disappointed if—"

Rafe cut me off. "If you try out, you *will* make it to Double-A— no, Triple-A. The coaches there aren't blind, they'll be able to tell that you don't belong in the low levels."

"Okay, fine," I gave in. "Let's say I do try out. Don't you think they'll automatically exclude me from the get-go since I'll be fresh out of high school? Most players have a *minimum* of four years' worth of experience on me, at least."

"You and I both know that there have been teenagers in the Majors before. You won't be the first."

There was a pregnant pause, Rafe's eyes filling with a gleam of hope.

"You'll at least give it a shot, right?"

"... yeah." Except all that would accomplish was giving me something to do; a Minor Leaguer's paycheck was pitiful, borderline illegal. But then again, I'd be able to peel off that leech status I'd procured by crashing at my best friend's—scratch that, boyfriend's house.

"Okay, so I was thinking of the Jackals, Hawks, Armada, and Knights," Rafe listed off the teams.

"Oh hell no, I'm not trying out for the Jackals," I stated adamantly.

"Why?"

"All it does in Varm is snow. All. The. Fucking. Time."

"Yeah, that's technically true, but they're in dire need of a catcher. They've sucked so badly the last three seasons since Willson is total trash. It won't hurt to just try it. You can always decline if they make an offer."

"It'd cost a lot of money to fly out to New York."

"Let's not talk about money right now," Rafe brushed it off. "The Jackals' Triple-A team has a catcher with potential and I bet they'll bring him up soon. There's no notable competition other than him."

"I don't like snow."

"Okay," Rafe dragged the word out. "Moving on. The Hawks. They're at the bottom of the totem pole and in desperate need of talent wherever they can get it. I'd bet they'd take you straight to the Majors."

"They're even worse than the Jackals," I groaned. "The Hawks are in last place. They won thirty-nine games last season, Rafe. *Thirty-nine* games out of a hundred and sixty-two!"

"Armada—"

"Ha, real funny." I let out a humorless laugh. "*No.* Armada's won the World Series seven times in the past decade. I'd have a better chance of getting on the field if I pulled a pitch invasion and rushed it. And isn't Armada's catcher ranked in the top three worldwide?"

"Exactly! They've been a top-tier team for years with Zander Sheb being their catcher and all, but if you look at their records when their secondary and backup catchers play, the results are subpar. Meaning that they're in the run for another extremely talented catcher. One isn't enough and everyone knows it; Sheb can't carry them forever. And even though their Triple-A catcher is good, he's not good enough to be brought up to the Majors and he's getting old."

"Fine. Let's pretend Armada is a realistic option for a moment. The bigger issue is money. It costs what for a flight to Varm? Two hundred bucks? Three hundred? And what about gas? The Knights play in Las Manos, that's over eight hundred miles from here. Flights would be just as expensive, and paying for gas would be a nightmare. And that's not including food and board expenses. I have no money, Rafe. I can't afford it."

"Let me take care of it. If you really want to, you can pay me back after you make some money. Until then, just think of it as borrowing."

"But—"

"Nope," Rafe shushed me, placing a finger against my lips. "I can do at least this much." There was a hint of something in his eyes, unrecognizable to me. Based on his tone, it might've sounded similar to guilt.

"Okay," I caved, knowing that Rafe wouldn't take no for an answer.

"So, here's the plan," Rafe started, leaning back against the couch and training his eyes on the wall while he focused his thoughts. "We'll head down to Las Manos since the Knights have their tryouts first, in late June. And then on the last day, we'll head up to Newhalm—"

"You're joking, right? We're going to go to Arizona, coming back to California—"

"And then we'll head east for the Jackals, and back central for the Hawks. We'll have time in between; the Jackals' and Hawks' tryouts are in late July. Think of this as our graduation trip."

"So, late June?" I huffed. "I can make that work... I can heal by then."

"If your ribs are still hurting, you can pass up on the first pair of tryouts and take an extra two weeks to make sure you're one hundred percent better."

"I'm sure I'll be fine. I've been resting for days and I'm already feeling a lot better."

"I know, but if you aren't, that's okay too."

His words struck a chord. The only time I'd ever not played because of an injury had been when it was visible, like a cast or a concussion. A month was more than enough time for me to get back on the wagon. Pain had never been an issue before, and I certainly wouldn't let it become one now.

I yawned, massaging my eyes with my right thumb and index finger. "I have a headache. I should probably get into bed."

Rafe checked the time. I knew it wasn't that late yet, but it was dark outside and that was good enough for me.

I'd been pushing myself all day. Well, not just today. The past couple of days had been extremely difficult for me, a different kind of difficulty than that of what I was used to. Being with Rafe all the time gave me no space and no room to fix the urges sporadically popping up and consuming my mind.

I couldn't cut—there was no razor.

I couldn't smoke pot—Rafe didn't have any, and it wasn't like I could ask him to buy it for me. He wouldn't do that, knowing the state I was in mentally and physically.

I wanted to pick at my arms, peel the new scabs away—but Rafe would notice.

I couldn't take anything from the Alvarez's liquor stash—they'd know if something went missing.

And I desperately craved the painkillers I'd become reliant on—but I had none, and it was killing me.

Chapter Twenty

Aspen

I SLID THE SHIRT OFF my body with shaky hands. No matter how hard I tried, I couldn't get them to stop trembling. My entire body was jittery and I was filled with anxiety, but not the crippling kind I was used to; it was different, familiar, but even more unpleasant. It had started the day I got back from the hospital and hadn't let up since.

My heart thumped in my chest. Faster and faster. It wasn't normal.

It wasn't a panic attack. And it wasn't an anxiety attack. I would know; I was no stranger to either.

But this... this was different.

The ever-quickening pace made it feel as if my heart was going to explode. As if a ticking time bomb had replaced the organ.

And it wasn't just the tremors and my racing heart. Of course not, because two things were too little for someone like me. The on-and-off headaches were killer and the random waves of nausea constantly threatened me with acidic bile rising in my throat, just to sink right back down.

The yellow lights from above lit Rafe's room as I changed into a fresh pair of clothes to sleep in. Rafe was in the bathroom and I wanted to change as fast as I could to hop into bed and hide the symptoms that weren't hard to miss. He was already worried enough; I didn't need to trouble him with yet another issue. Plus, I should be better in a couple of days. This wasn't the first time. And I didn't know if it'd be the last. All I could do was try, but even then...

I pulled a dark-blue T-shirt over my head, grabbing a pair of underwear and shorts out of Rafe's dresser.

Rafe knocked on the door before peeking his head in. I glanced up and offered a small smile. The corners of his mouth dipped down, but he said nothing as he walked into the room, closing the door behind him.

I moved to sit on the bed, pulling his covers up to my waist, crossing my legs, and clasping my hands in my lap in an attempt to hide the tremors. "You don't have to go to bed just because I am. It's still pretty early."

Rafe sighed as he bent down next to his nightstand, plugging his phone into the charger. "I know, but I'm tired too. It's been a long day."

A long couple of days. Or years...

"Oh, by the way," Rafe started, "I bought you a razor while I was out."

"Thanks," I replied, kind of surprised he thought of it. He must've seen me scratching my face.

"Uhm, I'm not sure if you've ever used an electric before, but it should be pretty straightforward."

I ducked my head down, nodding, and focusing my eyes on my fidgeting fingers. An electric shaver... he didn't get me a normal one and instead spent the extra money to make sure I wouldn't have the chance to... *Damnit. Why do I have to make everything so much harder than it has to be?*

"Anyway," Rafe cleared his throat, trying to overlook my mood, "if you're awake before I leave, I can help you with it tomorrow morning."

"Okay."

Just as Rafe was about to get in bed next to me, he paused. "Why aren't you wearing the brace?"

My face scrunched up, accompanied by a frown. "It's uncomfortable. I can't sleep with it on."

"Being uncomfortable is better than tearing the stitches, having to get them redone, and not getting them out until much later," Rafe scolded.

Sometimes he treated me like a child and it pissed me off. He acted like I couldn't take care of myself—well, in some ways I couldn't... but it was like he forgot we were the same age.

I rolled my eyes. "Stop nagging, will you?"

"I will if you just listen to what the doctor says," he shot back.

Rafe glanced around his room for a second before he spotted the sling on the floor next to his closet. He let out a heavy sigh and picked it up. He sat next to me and gently grabbed my left arm, sliding it into the blue sling and placing the strap over my head so that it rested on my right shoulder.

"You only need to wear it for another week and then you'll get your stitches out and be free to move as you wish, but until then, can you please just wear it?" Rafe begged as he gave me these adorable, sparkling puppy-dog eyes.

How could I say no to that face?

"Fine..." I let out a sigh of defeat.

I slumped down, pulling the covers up to my chest with my right hand as I lay flat on my back. Rafe turned off the lights and then crawled in next to me. It was nearly impossible to sleep with the sling on. Laying on my left side was a no-go because my shoulder was still sore, and I couldn't sleep on my right side because my arm would slide out of the brace. My only option was to stay on my back.

Rafe snuggled up next to me, burying his face into the crook of my neck with his arm draped over my stomach and left leg resting on top of mine like I was his personal body pillow. I stared at the darkness of the ceiling, listening to Rafe's breath slow down. His exhale fanned across my neck, causing my skin to erupt in goosebumps. The only thing that circled my mind was how warm I felt. Rafe was always so warm. Despite the discomfort of my rapidly beating heart, Rafe calmed me. The sound of his breathing slowly lulled me into a quiet sleep.

It was nice being next to Rafe at night; he acted as some sort of dream catcher. When I was with him, I wasn't overwhelmed by nightmares. I didn't have to dread going to sleep, closing my eyes, scared of what I'd have to see—relive—when the black screen of my eyelids provided my memories with a blank canvas to paint as they saw fit.

He clung to me throughout the night, and the only reason I knew that was because when I woke up, Rafe was in the exact same position he'd fallen asleep in. The only difference was that his forehead was pressed against my shoulder, giving him more room to breathe.

His room was slightly illuminated from the Tuesday morning sun seeping through the thin layer of Rafe's blinds. It created a soft light, making it easy to adjust when waking up.

It was day four now. The first three were always the hardest, but once I got over that hurdle, the withdrawal symptoms typically started to die down. And if that didn't happen today, then it would tomorrow.

I looked down at Rafe, only able to see the messy mop of black hair atop his head.

Something about this always felt off. *Wrong.*

It made me question if I was in a coma, dreaming. Or if I was hallucinating the life I wished I had, still bleeding out on the grimy floor of that motel bathroom. I wanted to believe it was real. Hell, I *knew* it was. But this thing in my head kept telling me it was impossible. That there was no way.

How could Rafe like me? *What was there to like?*

He constantly stated how much he hated my smile, although I could understand that one. When he looked at my face, I was sure all he could see was the fakeness. The countless lies it had spewed out of a grin, a fake smirk, fake happiness, fake everything.

Not to mention how my body was covered in... yeah.

Rafe's eyes always look sad when he thought about me. You weren't supposed to make people sad just by existing, and knowing that I was the reason he couldn't smile, that he couldn't be as happy as he should've been, suffocated me.

Personality, maybe?

I exhaled a short puff of air through my nose at the thought, trying to stifle my dry laugh.

What personality? The one where I didn't talk and barely responded to others? The one where I spent all my time wallowing in self-pity, watching TV, and keeping to myself?

A common interest? Baseball... that wasn't enough.

Was it really *me* he was in love with? Was Rafe actually in love with the current me—the Aspen that had nothing to offer in any way—or was he stuck in the past? Was Rafe still clinging onto a version of me that *did* exist—but died a long time ago?

Was he doing this because he hoped that if things in my head got better, maybe I'd go back to how I used to be? *Could I go back to how I used to be?*

What was I like? *I couldn't remember.*

A thumb suddenly pressed into my forehead, gently massaging the area between my eyebrows. "What's got you thinkin' so hard this early in the morning?" Rafe mumbled, his drowsy eyes gazing up at me.

The tension in my face eased and Rafe stopped rubbing out the lines I'd created in my skin from the scowl I didn't know I was sporting.

"Did I wake you up?" I asked.

"No, the light did."

I looked to my right, noticing it had gotten even brighter out.

"How'd you sleep?"

"Not bad…" Rafe trailed off, seemingly trying to decide if he should say more.

"What is it?"

He sighed, "It's just… did you have another nightmare last night?"

"I didn't." I gave him a soft smile.

He relaxed a little, but confusion and question were quickly rewritten on his face. "If it wasn't from a dream, then why was your heart beating so fast? I was getting nervous. I even thought about waking you up or taking you to the emergency room."

I placed my hand on my heart. It thumped slightly faster than it should've for someone who just woke up. An uncomfortable feeling still radiated throughout my chest, but even so, it was better than yesterday.

"Don't worry about it, I'll be fine in a couple of days," I tried to reassure him, not wanting to explain.

But Rafe always demanded an explanation. He had *always* been like this. Suspicious and concerned.

He sat up abruptly. "What would you need a couple of days to recover from?"

I raked my hand over my face. I didn't want him to know. I already seemed like enough of a fuckup, so why add this on top of it? "I'm fine. Seriously."

"If you're fine, then it'd be easy to just tell me, wouldn't it?"

Rafe was tired of me keeping secrets from him, secrets like this. But what did I have to gain from telling him that sometimes I became extremely dependent on drugs, and when I didn't have any, I'd go through withdrawals like an addict? What would he gain from knowing? More things to worry about, that's what. And that wasn't fair to Rafe. It wasn't fair for me to dump all my problems on him.

I pursed my lips, keeping my mouth shut.

Rafe ran a hand through his hair and over his face, kneading the sleep from his eyes. "You can tell me anything, y'know. I'm not going to judge you—for anything."

I glanced up at him, quickly averting my gaze when our eyes made direct contact.

"Come on, Aspen. Look me in the eyes and tell me what's wrong. No matter what it is, nothing's going to change between us or how I see you," Rafe tried to convince me.

Knowing he wouldn't let off, I let it slip. Another one of my secrets.

I stared into his eyes. The brown was dark, nearly black from the lack of light reflecting off them. "You know how Alex did all that stuff to me..."

Rafe hummed in response.

"Well, sometimes over-the-counter painkillers weren't strong enough... so I tried something stronger. I-uhm, I got into my dad's old stash of hydrocodone pills from a surgery he had. He never finished the bottle, he only took a couple. And at first, I just wanted to try it... to see if it'd make the pain go away," my voice caught in my throat. "And it did," I whispered breathlessly. "It made everything go away."

"So you kept taking them," Rafe finished for me.

I nodded weakly. "I don't know when it happened, but after a while, I wasn't just taking them when I got hurt..."

Rafe scowled at my words, the expression appearing too frequently as of late. "When did it start?"

"Freshman year? Maybe eighth grade?"

"And you've been taking hydrocodone this whole time?"

"On and off. It depended on when I could get a hold of some..."

"So right now you're going through—"

"Withdrawal."

"How did you even get stuff like that?"

"I know a guy..."

"Oh."

"Yeah."

"So you've been through—*this,* before?" His voice held no judgment. No scrutiny.

"Yeah..." I hadn't broken eye contact once.

Rafe's eyes seemed glazed over, wet. "Fuck," he let out a shaky breath.

"Yeah..." I didn't know how to respond.

"It's okay, though," he whispered, his voice cracking slightly. "I understand why. It makes sense why you'd do that." Rafe nodded, genuine words spilling from his lips.

He reached his arm over my head and grabbed my right shoulder, pulling me into a half-sitting, half-lying position, my body now slumped against his as Rafe leaned against the headboard. My head and upper back pressed against Rafe's chest, my lower back on top of his lap. He brought his fingers to my hair and lightly brushed through my tangled locks. I closed my eyes in appreciation.

"I wish I knew sooner. I wish I could've helped you. Maybe if I was there for you, things wouldn't have turned out like this— maybe things wouldn't have gotten so bad..." he murmured.

"But you're here now. That's more than enough for me."

Chapter Twenty-One

Aspen

"I HATE THIS PLACE," I muttered, looking at the disgustingly clean white walls surrounding me.

"We're just here to get your stitches removed. We'll be in and out in less than an hour," Rafe told me.

It was times like this I was almost grateful for my lack of insurance. They wouldn't admit me without it. No money, no service, no buff nurses willing to tackle me to the ground and inject their sleepy-juice sedatives into my neck.

Screw that. I'd have rather died than be stuck in some—well, I'd just have rather died in general.

My legs dangled over the edge of the beige hospital bed at the clinic, the disposable paper rustling every time I so much as moved a finger. Rafe sat in one of the two chairs lining the wall opposite the computer attached to the wall on my left.

Just then, there was a knock at the door. Dr. Amin came into the room, squirting hand sanitizer into his palms as he fell onto the small circular chair, rolling it toward the foot of the bed.

"Hello, Aspen." He pulled a white latex glove over his hand.

"Hi," I responded, fidgeting nervously in my seat.

"I'll be checking your stitches today, and if everything's looking good, we can go forward and remove them."

"Okay."

"Alright. First, I'm going to take a look at your back. Could you please remove your shirt?"

I bit the inside of my cheek, unclipping the brace and pulling it off, then slipping my right arm inside the long-sleeve and pulling it the rest of the way off.

The doctor stood from his seat and walked around me. I felt his cold fingers touch my back, poking and pulling lightly at the area around the stitches near my left shoulder blade.

"This is healing quite nicely."

"I've been making sure he wears the sling. He kept trying to take it off," Rafe said.

I shot him a glare, not appreciating his honesty.

"It's good that you wore it, Aspen. It made the healing process much faster. If you had slacked off, you might've had to wait another couple weeks before they could be removed."

I pursed my lips.

"Could you lie down on your stomach, please?" The man grabbed his small swivel chair and pulled it toward the left side of the bed.

I adjusted myself so my head was turned to the right, the left side of my face flush against the paper covering the small-yet-useless headrest.

"Could you lay your left arm next to your side? Just keep it relaxed," he instructed. "You'll feel a small tug or maybe even a small pinch. If something hurts too much, let me know and we can take a little break."

"Okay."

He went to work. The slight tug on the outside and inside of my skin was strange, more uncomfortable than anything else.

The room was silent for minutes before Dr. Amin spoke again. "Aspen," he approached hesitantly, "have you ever thought about pressing charges against the person who did this to you?" He was referring not only to the glass he'd removed from my back, but the countless other marks scarring my body.

I clenched my jaw.

I *had* thought about it. I'd thought about it *a lot*. But in the end, I didn't want their money. I didn't want to have to see Alex again. To me, the compensation wasn't important. It wasn't worth it.

"I'm not going to."

The doctor huffed, responding with a simple, "I understand," ending the conversation peacefully.

I couldn't see Rafe from where I was lying down, but I knew he'd probably want to talk to me about it more later.

"And that was the last one." Dr. Amin gave a professional smile.

I went to sit up, thankful that I could now move my arm as I pleased.

He wheeled the chair so he was seated in front of my legs. "Can I see your wrist?"

I put my arm out in front of me, my forearm to the ceiling.

A surprised expression filled his face. "It looks a lot better than I thought. Much better than the last time." He nodded in approval.

I looked at Rafe coyly. He berated me whenever I tried to skip cleaning or taking care of the cuts.

I watched in a dazed trance as Dr. Amin removed the stitches. One by one, he'd cut a small part, using a mix of his fingers and a metal tool to thread it out of my skin. There weren't a lot in my wrist—just enough stitches to line a couple of the large gashes.

"You're going to be graduating soon, right?" He started some small talk while continuing to take out the black threads. "I have a niece that goes to Cedar Heights. I believe I heard her complaining about how unfair it was that the seniors got to finish a week before the rest of the grades," he chuckled at the memory.

"Yeah," I responded. "Graduation is next week, I think."

He raised an eyebrow. "You think?"

"Well, I'm not going, so..."

He frowned. "After spending four years of your life there, you don't want to celebrate? Graduation is a pretty big coming-of-age ceremony."

"Oh, uhm, I'm actually not allowed to go. I got suspended for two weeks, and it goes through the end of school."

"You were suspended?"

"Yeah, it was just a small fight. Is what it is."

"And how about your friend over there, Rafe, was it?"

"Yeah, it's Rafe. I'm going, but after I get my diploma and my parents take some pictures, I'll leave. I don't plan on sticking around." The conversation deflated, bordering on awkward since both Rafe and I were unsure of how much detail Dr. Amin was looking to get.

"Not going to any graduation parties?"

I glanced at Rafe, waiting for him to answer, also curious.

"No. I'm not really on good terms with most of the people I used to hang out with. I'll probably just stay in with Aspen." He offered a content smile.

"Nothing wrong with a good ol' movie night with a small group of friends. I did something similar when I graduated high school."

We chatted idly through the rest of the appointment until Dr. Amin stated he was finished, removed his gloves, and threw them in the trash can.

"Thank you, doc." I gave a curt smile as I stood up, rubbing my newly freed upper limb.

With one step, Rafe stood before me and grabbed my hand. "Don't rub it. The scabs will fall off," he whispered.

"Of course, Aspen. And I wanted to talk to you about one more thing."

I turned and looked at the white-coated male, the three of us standing there awkwardly.

"I know I've mentioned this a million times, so I won't push it anymore, but can you please at least consider seeing a therapist? I'm not asking you to spend weeks or months in a place you feel trapped, but I think you would really benefit from talking to someone."

His words reminded me of a conversation I'd had with Rafe and his dad. Mateo had been adamant about me seeing someone. He couldn't do it himself because of a conflict of interest, as in me dating his son and him knowing me on a personal level, so he instead suggested a couple of his colleagues and trusted therapist and psychologist friends.

I refused his offer. Not only because I had no health insurance.

And I'd refuse Dr. Amin's as well.

"Sorry, but I can't. I'm fine."

My mind was a tricky thing. I wanted to feel better, but at the same time, I couldn't imagine what better would be like—and that scared me.

My brother couldn't hurt me anymore—hell, I was dating the guy I'd been in love with my entire life—and that was enough for me. It was more than I ever could've asked for, so I wouldn't ask for any more.

The doctor sighed reluctantly. "Alright."

Rafe studied my face as if he wanted to find a different answer dancing in my eyes.

I quickly made my way out the door, wanting to end the conversation before I could be questioned further. Rafe scurried after me, thanking the doctor. His hand brushed over mine, our shoulders bumping as we strolled down the hallway, knowing that we couldn't hold hands in public. Some things were better left for the privacy of one's own home.

But shit, *I wanted to hold his hand.* Even just the light touches of the tips of his fingers made me warm.

I picked up my pace, walking faster and faster. Rafe gave me a confused glance as he tried to keep up.

Loud tapping noises encased my ears as my feet made harsh contact with the white-tiled floor. I bit my lip when I finally made it through those familiar automatic doors, just to be met with blinding sunlight, instantly making me sweat. My feet burned as we made our way across the blazing concrete.

The second we were in Rafe's car, he asked, "What was that about? Why were you in such a rush?"

I gulped, turning my eyes toward his. *That's right. I can do that now.* I slowly lifted my left hand, grabbing Rafe's and intertwining our fingers. Once my hand was tightly clutched in his, I sighed in contentment. I turned to face the front windshield, my eyes briefly grazing over the numerous people walking through the lot.

A grin made its way onto my face and I cuddled into the seat, wholeheartedly comfortable.

Rafe let out a laugh. "This is what had you speeding outside? I thought something was wrong." He shook his head in amusement.

"Can you blame me? Even if I want to hold your hand in public, I can't."

He glowered. "I know."

I hummed in response as Rafe changed the gear of his car, my hand still fitted in his. I squeezed his hand tighter, almost as if loosening my grip would somehow result in Rafe slipping away. But Rafe squeezed back just as hard, making me believe the same insecurities were whirling through his head.

Chapter Twenty-Two

Aspen

"How would you feel if Amelia came over?" The question had me snapping my head toward Rafe.

"It's fine, I guess," I mumbled.

Rafe gave me a pointed look, knowing I had more to say. "We're just friends."

"If you want to..." My voice was small and timid.

Rafe sighed. "Seriously, there's nothing between us anymore. We only dated for a couple of weeks, anyway. That can barely even be considered dating."

"*We've* only been dating for a couple weeks," I pointed out with a heavy frown.

"But this is different."

"How?" I bit out, my frustration rising.

"Because it *is* different. Our whole relationship is *different.*"

"Because I'm a guy?" I accused with a sharp tone.

"No, because I'm in love with you!"

I clamped my mouth shut, my anger immediately subsiding.

"Sure, the type of love has changed over time, but I've *always* loved you," Rafe expressed with a soft-yet-serious look.

Tingles spread throughout my body and a small blush crept up my neck, my ears now a bright pink. Doubt and annoyance fizzled out, understanding settling in.

I'd heard the words fall from Rafe's mouth on more than one occasion. He wasn't shy, not at all. Those words were natural. Hell, he'd said them to me before he even realized he was bi. I ended up crying myself to sleep the first time that happened because I didn't think his "love" could ever be the same as mine. I was wrong.

"Still upset?" he prodded, a small smirk gracing his lips as he noticed my abnormally pink ears.

"No."

Rafe opened his arms wide. "Come 'ere."

Without a second thought, I walked the few feet from where I'd been standing to where Rafe sat on the couch. I moved my arms from my side and gracefully wrapped them around his neck, placing myself on his lap with my legs on either side of his. Rafe chuckled at my willingness to cuddle and enclosed his arms loosely around my lower back.

"You're like a koala." He nuzzled into my neck.

"I would call you the tree, but you're too short for that."

"I'm not short!" he defended. "We're quite literally the exact same height!"

I lifted my chest off him and gazed into his eyes. "Can you really say that when I'm *quite literally* looking down at you?" I quipped.

"Fuck you."

"Only in your dreams," I teased.

Rafe raised an eyebrow. "*Only* in my dreams?" An enormous smile broke out onto his face, showcasing his perfect teeth.

"Hmm," I smirked. "Maybe in my dreams too."

"Oh?"

"*Oh?*" I mocked, leaning down so my mouth was right next to his ear. In a breathy whisper, "But in my dreams, I'm fucking you, too."

"Oh," his voice cracked.

I chuckled, dropping my forehead to his shoulder, feeling his quickening heartbeat against my chest.

I shifted in my spot to get more comfortable and then felt something soft poking my stomach. I tried to hold in a snort. "Are— are you seriously turned on right now?"

"Hey! It's your fault I'm thinking about sex in the first place!"

"Is it now?" I grinned cheekily, gently placing my lips on Rafe's neck.

He tried to stifle a groan as I opened my mouth against his skin, my teeth lightly scraping the area just below his jaw.

Rafe seemed out of breath as I continued to suck on his neck. "Aspen, my parents are in the kitchen... they... they could see..."

His hands slid down my back until he grasped my butt firmly with both hands.

"You don't seem too worried about that," I laughed. I started moving my kisses from his neck to his jaw and then slowly connecting my lips with his.

He moaned into my mouth as my tongue slid in. "Fuck..."

"Fuck is right." The voice had me jumping off Rafe.

I looked up, wiping my mouth, to see Mateo. Rafe craned his head to look behind the couch at his dad who'd just come out of the kitchen with a mug of coffee in his hand.

Mateo's face was scrunched up in discomfort. "I know that you two are dating now and that you're both full-grown adults, but Rafe, you're aware that just down the hall," he slowly extended his arm to point, "is your very own, personal room. A room that does, in fact, have a door. One that very much so *closes.*"

With wide eyes, Rafe cleared his throat. "Right. Yeah, of course..."

Mateo's lips formed a thin line and nodded at us, awkwardly making his way down the hall and to a separate room.

"So, you're fine if Amelia comes over?" He immediately changed the subject.

"Yeah."

"Y'know, she misses you. She thought you'd at least show up at graduation. I thought she was going to cry when I told her you requested to get your diploma in the mail."

"Why would she miss me? It's not like I was the one she was dating," I grumbled.

I had trouble understanding why people would want to be around me. It was hard for me to grasp the idea—there wasn't a whole lot to me. I added nothing to friendships; my main personality trait was depression. And even then, I didn't know if I could say that since I didn't talk about my feelings in the first place. Leading me to the conclusion that I had no personality. Which meant I was boring and dry, and in turn, no one would willingly want to be my friend.

"Amelia's always thought of you as a friend. That didn't change when we broke up. She wasn't just hanging around you because we were together, she cares about you."

"But she knows that I'm gay..."

"Aspen," Rafe's eyes went wide. "You don't think everyone is going to hate you because you're gay, do you?"

"What? No! I mean, I don't know. Maybe?"

"Fucking hell, how long have you been thinking like that?!"

"No, I just—it's not like... look, you need to understand that I've spent my whole life hating myself and thinking everyone else would too. And I wasn't wrong—people do hate me for it. The number of bad experiences I've had with people when they find out I'm not straight completely overwhelms the number of okay ones."

"Aspen, I want you to look at my eyes when I tell you this." Rafe's hard voice forced me to turn my head toward him. He grasped the sides of my face, his hands splayed flatly on my cheeks, holding me in place and moving his face so it was just inches from mine. "Not. Everyone. Will. Hate. You. For. Being. Gay. There are so many people in the world who don't give a shit about other people's sexualities. Cedar Heights is just one town—that just so happens to be full of homophobic pricks."

I scoffed at his words. Not that I didn't think he was right, just because the idea seemed so out of reach. "I know, I know." I brushed it off, not wanting to talk about it. Cedar Heights wasn't one-of-a-kind in its way of thinking. Other cities were similar, if not worse, although I knew it wasn't like that everywhere. "Just call Amelia and have her come over. We can watch a movie or something."

Rafe grabbed his phone and glanced at me, acknowledging how I'd shut the conversation down while also respecting my boundaries. I thought he understood that although I was more open than before, it was still hard for me. Even though I knew I was okay here, part of my subconscious would always be wary.

Within minutes, there was a small knock at the door.

"I'll get it," Rafe said as he jumped off the couch.

I heard a small, enthusiastic "Hi," from Amelia. I looked over at the doorway as the two embraced in a small hug. With her arms wrapped around Rafe, Amelia glanced up and made eye contact with me. Her hazel eyes lit up and a giant smile climbed onto her face. Her arms dropped from my boyfriend and she came scrambling toward me. I raised myself from the couch just in time for her to fling herself over me, her forearms folding around my neck.

She let out a heavy sigh as her grip on me tightened, her smaller frame slightly swaying left and right.

"Uhm, hi," I greeted her awkwardly.

She let go and grabbed my face, squishing my cheeks between her hands. My lips formed a tight smile, my dimples popping out as she held me still and inspected my face.

"What are you doing?" My words were slurred from the new shape of my lips Amelia had formed with pressure.

"Would it kill you to at least look at your phone?! Rafe told me something happened but then I couldn't see you and it took weeks to even get the okay to come here and—Aspen, you have bruises and cuts on your face!" She tried to get out as many of her thoughts as possible, but they seemed clustered and she couldn't get the words out quite right.

The bruises she was referring to were mostly yellow and faded. My split lip had healed and any other cut that was visible on my face was a red, angry line, a remnant from scabs that had recently disappeared.

"Aspen, what happened?" Her brows furrowed and the corners of her mouth turned down.

I grabbed her wrists and gently pulled them from my face. "I thought you knew already."

"Rafe wouldn't tell me. I've heard some rumors but—"

"What rumors?" Nerves pushed the words out of my mouth before I could hear more.

"Just that you got into a big fight with some guys on the baseball team. Big enough that you decided to quit." Amelia scratched the side of her head, avoiding the hair that was tied into two long dutch braids.

"Well, that's basically true. It was a pretty one-sided fight, though."

"Will you tell me about it?"

I hesitated before answering. I looked at Rafe and he simply gave me an encouraging smile.

"If you really want to know, I guess I could... but are you sure? It's a little more unpleasant than you'd expect."

"I'm your friend, Aspen. I don't want you to feel like you have to go through everything by yourself. If you're willing to share, I'd love to listen."

If I'd been straight, I think I'd have fallen in love with her.

"Okay."

"Should we go in my room so there's a bit more privacy?" Rafe threw the idea out.

"I thought that maybe Aspen and I could go to a coffee shop or cafe?" Amelia asked.

"Just you two?"

Amelia turned to look at her ex. "Oh, come on, Rafe. Don't get pissy 'cause I want to spend time with your boyfriend instead of you. I saw you at school every day. I haven't seen Aspen in weeks."

Rafe blushed at her words.

"So, Aspen, what do you say? You're looking a little pale from being inside so much. Want to get some sunshine?" She gave me one of her charming smiles.

"Uhm, sure," I responded, glad I was already wearing a long-sleeved shirt and didn't need to explain why I'd need to change out of a tee.

"I'll drive," the brunette said perkily, holding up her keys and prancing out of the house.

"Ask Amelia to text me if you need anything." Rafe waved before closing the front door.

I ducked my head as I stepped into her small SUV, slightly uncomfortable in the unfamiliar territory.

Amelia placed both hands on the wheel and smoothly made a U-turn. "Karamelle's okay?"

"Sure."

The car ride was spent with Amelia playing music I'd never heard. It wasn't exactly my taste, but it was halfway decent.

We were met with the light-blue sign in the shape of a cloud when we pulled into the small cafe lot. Bells chimed when we walked inside, Amelia's eyes sparkling, reflecting the varying cakes in the display case.

With her eyes trained on the chalk menu behind the ordering counter, she said, "I think I'm going to get some coffee cake. You want chocolate ice cream, right?"

My eyes widened. "How'd you know?"

A devilish smile appeared on her face as she patted my shoulder, brushing me off.

"Go sit down, I'll order." She nodded toward a short booth near the storefront window.

I gave her a questioning glance as I slid onto the smooth white leather. I perched my head on my hand and looked out the window, watching as people walked by. There was this one large group of younger kids that passed by, probably middle schoolers. It was a giant herd of people, all laughing and having fun. It made me think about what I was like in middle school—I had a lot of friends at first, from both school and baseball, but after I came out to Alex, a lot of those friendships ended. They didn't know I was gay, so it was hard for me to understand why I was drifting apart from everyone. And then I realized it was because I was pushing them away. I was completely aware that I'd stopped responding to texts from my friends, always telling them I was too busy to hang out when they'd asked.

I blamed it on having a shy and quiet personality, but the truth was, I was scared of them finding out I was gay. I was scared of rejection, so I made it impossible for them to do so in the first place. But it wasn't just the fear of knowing none of them would like me if they knew who I truly was. It was the self-hate, the self-loathing that made me think I didn't deserve to have friends.

And I was tired. I was so tired of everything that it was easy to step away from others. *Too easy.*

"Here you go." The voice pulled my eyes from the smiling kids.

Amelia set down the cup with two scoops inside, handing me a spoon and a napkin as she sat on the opposite side with a slice of cake, taking a large bite before she finished settling in her seat.

"How'd you know I like chocolate?" I asked, smiling on the inside as I scooped some of the ice cream into my mouth.

Amelia grinned at me. "The same way I know that you always get two scoops and don't like cones."

"Rafe?" I guessed.

"Yep." If Amelia had a tail, I was sure it'd be wagging right now. "Do you want a bite? It's really good."

"Sure." I reached over the table and used my spoon to take a bite. I didn't usually like cake, but she was right: It was sugary bliss. As I chewed, I picked up my cup and held it toward her. She gave me a nod and used her fork, attempting to rake some onto it.

"You really don't hate me?"

Her eyes bulged. "What would make you think that?!" She set her fork down to look me dead in the eyes.

"Because Rafe and I..."

The shock wore off and she snorted. "Please, Aspen. Rafe told you what happened when we broke up, right?"

"Not really."

"I actually really liked Rafe." I shifted in my seat, somehow feeling like a homewrecker. "He's hot and has this hidden cute side, not to mention how kind and considerate he is. So when he asked me out, of course I said yes. But let me tell you," she chuckled, Amelia being the only person who felt this was a light-hearted conversation, "my fantasy of dating the guy was shattered real quick."

"What happened?" I asked tentatively.

"Well, for starters, he was annoying as shit. In the cute, lovestruck puppy kind of way. Well, a kicked, lovestruck puppy."

"I'm not following..."

"From the very beginning, it was obvious that he was head over heels—*for you.* He never shut up about you. He'd go on and on for hours. Honestly, I probably know more about you than I do about Rafe. That's how much he talked about you."

"So that's why you knew what I'd want to get."

"Mhmm." She shoved another bite into her mouth. "I saw our breakup coming from a mile away. And when I noticed that the way you looked at Rafe was the same way he looked at you, I realized where I stood and decided to push Rafe to take the first step. He was surprised when I brought up the idea of him being in love with you, but he knew I was right and took it rather well."

I was rendered speechless. I knew Amelia was okay with Rafe being bi, but I didn't know she was the reason we'd gotten together. "You aren't mad at him? Or me?"

"I only dated Rafe for half a month. We went on one date. *One.* We were practically still in the friendship/get-to-know-you phase. Anyway, this isn't exactly why I wanted to talk to you, but I thought it'd be good if you understood how different our relationships with Rafe are. We were at a point where we could still be just friends, but the two of you—I don't think you two could ever be *just* friends."

I cleared my throat. "Right, yeah."

"But Aspen, I know a lot's happened recently. And I've always thought of you as a friend, and I'm happy that things with Rafe are going well, but I'm still worried about you. I just want to know that you're okay." The mood took a sudden nosedive. I was thankful the cafe she'd chosen looked like it was made of cotton candy, or this topic could've been too much for me.

"I don't think going into detail would be a good idea... it'd be a pretty heavy conversation and I already kinda tend to bring people down when I'm around them; this would probably just make that even worse." I tugged at the loose white sleeve around my wrist.

"Please."

"Right... so you know how I'm gay and everything?" She nodded, not wanting to interrupt anything. "Well, my brother had a bad reaction when I came out—he said and did some pretty awful things to me. I started having a really hard time after that... and so I got into some bad stuff..."

"Drugs?"

"Habits... but yeah. Alcohol, weed—*and some other things*. I'm uhm, I'm not exactly *'mentally stable,'* in a sense." I struggled to find the words. "One time I was high and drunk on some strong shit and I accidentally told Isabella I was gay. She told Devin, Jason, Jamey, and my parents. So that night I got kicked out, and I stayed in a motel for a bit until Rafe... found? Me."

"When you say *found*..."

I ignored the comment, not wanting to divulge further. "Then my scholarship was revoked because of that fight, so I'm just gonna start trying to play professionally a little earlier than planned. But Rafe and I started dating, and he's letting me crash at his. His parents are cool with it, too, so that's nice. And everything... everything's good. Yeah, things are better now, so..."

"Can I give you a hug?"

"If you want to?"

She stood from her seat and placed herself next to me, throwing her arms around my neck and holding me tight. I patted her shoulder awkwardly, trying to comfort her. She didn't say anything. She didn't ask me to go into more detail or for specifics. I appreciated it.

Once Amelia calmed down, she lifted her head and sniffled. "So, what's this about playing professional baseball?"

I smiled, happy the discussion had shifted. "Well, since I lost my scholarship and the time to accept other offers has already passed, I'd have to wait until next year to play. I'm broke and have no money, literally. Even my phone plan was cut off. But if I work a job, I'll get super rusty, so Rafe thought of the idea that I could start my Minors career a bit early."

"So you're going to try out for the Majors?? That's so fucking exciting! When's this happening?!"

A smile grew on my face, a nervous excitement exploding in my stomach, butterflies and tingles spreading through my body. "Starts next week."

Chapter Twenty-Three

Aspen

"I SWEAR, I'M FINE! I even got the all-clear from Dr. Amin," I argued. "You can't expect me to go to tryouts in a few days and still make the team after not even touching a ball the past month and a half."

"I know, I know, I'm just worried about your ribs."

"I told you, I went to the clinic and got them X-rayed. I'm good to go. Now, stop being a mother hen and play catch with me."

"Alright," Rafe gave up with a sigh. "I've been itching to play, too."

A large smile broke out onto my face. *Finally.* "I'll go grab our gloves! Meet you out back?"

I waited for Rafe to respond when he suddenly stuck his finger out, the tip digging into my cheek.

"What are you doing?" I asked with a chuckle.

Rafe's brown eyes danced with delight. "Your dimples are showing."

"I've had dimples my entire life, Rafe. This isn't new."

"No, but the dimples accompanied by a genuine smile are." He took a step toward me and dipped his head to the side, his lips connecting with mine. I could feel his smile against my mouth. "Damn, you're beautiful."

"Cheesy." I placed my hand on his chest and pushed him back. "As much as I like kissing you, I want to play baseball even more."

"Fine. I'll grab some balls from the garage and meet you in the backyard."

"Okay!" With a skip in my step, I jogged from the kitchen toward Rafe's room, where I grabbed our gloves. Glancing at Rafe's closet, I made the quick decision to invade it, taking the first two hats at the top of a tall stack on the floor.

Rafe met me outside, an entire crate of white-and-red spheres laying next to his feet. The narrow yard provided just enough room for us to properly practice pitching. The rectangular area had a small strip of concrete next to the door, while the rest of the yard was covered in grass.

"Here." I handed him his glove while simultaneously placing a navy-blue cap on his head.

I shoved my hand into my glove, threw a black hat over my head, and stood in front of the green net next to the fence, a square taped to the lower middle of it to imitate the strike zone.

"We'll just start off light, yeah?" Rafe confirmed as he made his way to the opposite side, standing next to the makeshift mound his dad helped us make in middle school.

"Yeah, like usual."

We both stretched our arms a bit, Rafe more so. He grabbed a single ball out of the white box, tossing it in his hand for a moment, happy to finally be playing with me again. He cocked his arm back and leisurely threw it forward, the ball landing in the pocket of my glove with a soft noise on impact. I let out a breath, loving the feeling of the small object through the thick fabric over my fingers. I threw the ball back to Rafe with a loud smacking noise as he caught it in the webbing.

We played catch for a while, silently enjoying the slight tug in my shoulder and the bright sun blazing from above. Sweat trickled down my neck and into the collar of my shirt, but the slight breeze made it cool, like water was being poured down my back one teaspoon at a time.

"Want to pitch a bit?" I asked.

"Are you sure you'll be fine squatting? And holding your left arm up like that? It won't hurt?" The slew of questions flew from his mouth.

My pinched lips should've said enough, but even my words couldn't get through his tough head. "Yes, Rafe. My ribs don't hurt, and if anything, my shoulder feels better than it has in years. I'm good to go, seriously."

"Okay. If you say so," Rafe gave in, knowing I needed to practice one way or another.

I dropped into a squat, balancing on the balls of my feet. "Start with some fastballs," I instructed, placing my glove in the middle of what would be the strike zone of an average player.

Rafe nodded and strode onto the raised dirt. Changing his stance, he started with a slow wind-up, the ball releasing from his hand at nearly half his normal speed. I barely moved my hand to catch the ball. He threw a couple more slow ones before his arm was fully warmed-up. I moved my glove up and to the left, Rafe throwing at a faster velocity than before.

I sniggered when the ball made contact with my glove. "What happened? Your control is trash."

"Hey! I'm not wearing cleats right now!"

"You're one of the best pitchers in our age group in the entire country, literally known for your precision, and you're trying to blame it on a pair of shoes?" I joked, both of us well-aware that cleats played an important role in the matter.

Rafe glared at me.

"I'm kidding." I shook my head. "Don't worry about control right now, just throw it wherever you want. You know that I can catch anything you give me."

And that was the truth.

I'd been catching for Rafe since before either of us could read. I knew what every movement of his body meant—the way his shoulder launched behind his ear, the position of his wrist, his grip on the ball, where and how he released—I knew how all of it would play out in every scenario possible. No matter how perfect or how screwed-up a pitch, I knew exactly where my mitt needed to be. Nothing Rafe could do would surprise me, and I was prepared to catch whatever he threw in whatever way and form, regardless of the ball's trajectory or path. *Everything*. That was what happened when you played with someone for fourteen years. When you learned to play the game with and from them.

"Give me a curveball," I shouted from the other side of the yard.

Every ball I asked for, Rafe delivered, his pitches only slower and more out of control due to the awful grip of his sneakers.

"Lemme pitch a forkball." Rafe's nose dipped toward the ground, his toe kicking at the dirt.

"Your fork sucks ass."

"Yeah, and they'll continue to suck if I don't practice them."

"Come on, Rafe. Your fork is worse than your knuckleball, and that's saying something."

"Oh, fuck off. Knuckleballs are so much harder to throw than forkballs."

"Then explain to me why only your knuckleballs pass over the plate? I told you, your forkball drops too early. Give it another half of a second and it'll start its drop right before the plate and fall through the strike zone. If batters can see it coming, they won't bother swinging, and that gives them a free ball."

"I know that! I'm working on it, but Coach Gale refused to help me since I already have three main pitches."

"Maybe they'll help you out in college," I suggested.

"Well, it's not like I need another main pitch, but it'd still be nice to be able to use it when needed."

"Fine." I gave in. "Give me a fork, but make sure you don't slip; you can't mess up your elbow right before your season starts."

"Alright." Rafe flashed a bright smile. "Here ya go." He shifted his grip on the ball, placing it between his index and middle finger. In the pitch, he led more with his elbow than his other pitches, making me frown. The ball dropped too early and I had to catch it in front of where the plate would be.

"So?" Rafe called out.

"You saw the ball, so why're you asking me?" I grunted, throwing it back, still perched on my knees.

"That bad?"

"Worse than normal. Your biggest issue is that whenever you try throwing a forkball, your form changes. If you want it to be a useful pitch, the only thing that should be different is your grip. Anyone with eyes would be able to read what that pitch was going to be before the ball even left your hand. And if you keep trying to throw forks like that, you're gonna ruin your form," I lectured.

Rafe huffed, annoyed, yet also saw the truth in my words. We both liked to experiment with new pitches, but I always made him stop the second I thought what we were doing could jeopardize his already-solid pitching style.

"I'll give you three more pitches, but if you can't get your form under control, we'll move onto your slider."

"Yes, sir," Rafe snarked, adjusting the baseball inside of his glove. He glanced at me and then back at the ball a couple of times before getting off the mound and walking toward me. I hopped up and met Rafe halfway. "What do you think about my grip?" he mumbled, showing me exactly how he was holding the ball for his fork grip.

I hummed. "It looks okay? The issue might have to do with your grip strength? But that's not something you can fix right now, so maybe you should try focusing more on your release point. Or how soon you start to ease up on the strength of your grip."

"Yeah, I can try that."

"Okay," I nodded, turning my back to the mound.

I squatted again, raising my glove as Rafe dug his foot into the beige sand. "Focus on your form!" I shouted.

Rafe took a slow, deep breath, his eyes narrowing in on my glove. He raised his right leg into the air nearly up to his right elbow before his leg came slamming into the dirt, Rafe's left arm flying across his body.

My glove dropped and I caught the ball just before it hit the ground. "That was a hell of a lot better!"

"Let me get some more in while the feeling's still fresh."

Rafe threw twelve forkballs in total. Once I noticed his form starting to break, I decided we should move on.

"Do you want some water?" he asked.

"Sure."

I stood, my calves aching slightly from not having caught in weeks. My back was completely drenched in sweat, the summer heat getting to me. I moved toward the sliding door and sat in front of it, my legs sprawling out on the cool, shaded concrete.

Rafe left the door open while he went inside to fill up two plastic cups. Bringing them back out, he crouched down next to me with a grunt. "Here."

I took the cup from his hand and gulped down the contents. It was silent for a moment, both of us basking in the warm breeze. The beautiful flowers from his neighbor's tree peeked over the fence and into Rafe's yard, giving us the perfect view of the last bits of pink-and-orange petals that should've finished shedding at the end of spring.

"We should go on a date," I blurted. "Before we leave, we should go on a date," I said, quieter this time.

Rafe peered at me, pulling the water from his mouth and setting it on the ground. "We're leaving tonight."

"We have time."

Where I expected a reply, I was met with a blank stare instead.

I looked away, immediately regretting the question. It was stupid; if Rafe had wanted to go on a date, we already would have. Like always, I couldn't read between the lines. "We don't have to, of course. I'm fine staying in..."

"What? No, I was just surprised. I'd love to go on a date. Did you have anything in mind?"

"A trampoline park?"

"The one here or the one in Riverside?"

"Definitely Riverside. Theirs has the dodgeball court and foam pit."

Rafe's gaze shifted to the yard, a small smile playing on his lips as his eyes trailed the dents in the fence from when we were younger and tried free batting with no nets; we were lucky we didn't break any windows.

"So," I started, "when do you want to go? Do you want to pitch a bit more? Or take a shower first?"

"Nah, I think I threw enough today. And we'll just get sweaty again later. Do you want to head out now?"

"Sure."

Rafe stood first, leaning to each side and stretching a bit before reaching out a hand to help me up. I smiled, gripping his hand and yanking myself up. When I was finally standing, he didn't let go. Leaving our gloves near the door to his backyard, Rafe squeezed my hand and pulled me inside.

"You two look excited," Rafe's mom commented from the couch in the living room, *Narcos* playing in the background.

"We're going on a date," Rafe beamed.

"Oh? Alright, que la pasen bien." Even though I knew she was trying to hide it, I could see the corners of her mouth turning up and her eyes crinkling ever so slightly.

"We will." Rafe thanked her as he led me to the front door.

The second Rafe's hand wrapped around the handle, his mom shouted, "¡Y no vuelvas a casa demasiado tarde!"

"Okay, te veo esta noche."

Their words flew over my head, my two pitiful years of high school Spanish useless in practical situations. "Bye, Teresa." I managed to get a single word in before the door was closing behind me and Rafe was dragging me to his car.

"Someone's eager," I snickered as I pulled the seatbelt over my right shoulder.

"Of course I am, it's our first date. Plus, I want to get there while it's still relatively busy. We can't exactly play dodgeball by ourselves." Rafe put his car into drive and focused on the road in front of him, wordlessly allowing me to take over the aux.

"It might be a Sunday, but it's summer. I'm sure at least three birthday parties are going on right now."

"Okay, true. But it's also our first official date."

I rolled my eyes. "Yes, a trampoline park. How romantic."

"I'd rather go jump and throw foam blocks for three hours than sit down at some stuffy restaurant in the dark and pay for ridiculously overpriced food any day." Rafe briefly glanced at me, grinning.

I couldn't fight the smile forming on my mouth. "You already know I'm the same."

We were both extreme adrenaline junkies with a strong passion for competition. My definition of a romantic date was simply having fun and enjoying being with Rafe; I imagined his was similar.

"Have you finished packing?"

"Yeah, everything except my glove and some toiletries."

"Okay. We'll probably leave around five p.m. It'll take about an hour to get to the airport, and then the flight's a little less than two hours."

"That sounds good and all, but Rafe, how are we going to pay for everything? I know you said you'd take care of it for now, but still... car rental, gas, plane tickets, motel cost, and food—it's going to add up..."

Rafe let out a low hum. "I told you not to worry about it. Remember how I got a job last year because our landlord raised the rent and my parents were having a hard time covering the bills?"

"Yeah?"

"Well, they got pissed when they found out I was trying to help out, spouting some nonsense that I was just a kid and shouldn't be worried about that stuff; I don't understand how I couldn't be, it's not exactly fun watching them struggle financially. They managed to take care of it in the end and got everything under control without needing me to pitch in what I earned. So basically, now I have a couple grand in savings."

"And you're sure you're okay dipping into that for me?" I asked tentatively. It made me uncomfortable, siphoning money from Rafe and his family like a parasite, but as things were, it was my best option.

"Aspen, I'd spend it all on you if I needed to. Without hesitation."

Heat rose up my neck and toward my face. "Thank you."

Rafe turned his head to look at me, momentarily making eye contact. "Anything for you."

"You're really flirty, you know that? I don't remember you being like this before we started dating."

"In my defense, I didn't realize I liked you, and once I did, we started dating the following week."

"Fair enough."

"That, and I've never liked someone as much as I like you, and for some reason, I feel the need to express that all the time." Rafe always spoke so confidently, as if nothing that left his mouth could embarrass him.

"Ah, shit." I ran a hand down the back of my neck as I turned to look out the window. "Do you want me to look like a tomato?"

"I think it's cute how red you get when you blush."

"Fuck off."

"You're not necessarily pale, but you're white enough that you look sunburnt when you're embarrassed. It's cute."

I glared at Rafe, daring him to continue. "I'm not cute."

"You're right, Aspen—you're fucking adorable. Do you really need me to explain why?"

I recalled the way people treated me like their new puppy before I hit puberty, back when I was short and my facial features made me look an additional five years younger than I actually was. "No," I grumbled.

———

Rafe pulled into a narrow spot with two large SUVs on either side; both of the vehicles radiated Soccer Mom energy, probably carting boatloads of kids. He switched off the engine, and we both stepped out of the car, squinting at the harsh light shining down from behind the industrial building.

"Come on." Rafe smiled, heading toward my side of the car. As we moved closer to the entrance, I fell into line with him, his fingers playing against mine and subtly brushing against me with each step.

Once through the front door, we were bombarded with the incessant noise of high-pitched shrieks. We were greeted by the chipper receptionist, handing over a flat fee and signing waivers, not bothering to read what it said, already aware that it forfeited the park's liability if we were to get injured.

The lady working the front reached into a drawer and pulled out two sky-blue wristbands, asking each of us to hold out our right arms to place them around our wrists. "You're all set. When you get inside, there will be a locker where you can place any belongings you don't want to hold. I suggest keeping your shoes, phone, and wallet inside of it. And although shoes are not allowed on the trampolines, socks are required. Have fun."

We made our way inside, weaving through hordes of people surrounding tables with birthday cakes and balloons until we reached a wall with countless locker cubbies against it, right next to the bathrooms. We had to pick two in the bottom right corner, as there was a stretcher blocking the rest. On top of the yellow framework and white bed-pad was a teenager icing a broken and bloody nose, their ankle sitting in an unnatural position. We ignored the two EMTs standing by the kid, getting ready to wheel them out; I didn't think I'd ever been here when there wasn't someone being carted off to the hospital, nursing some sort of injury.

After pulling our shoes off and shoving our things inside, Rafe gave me a lopsided grin and grabbed my hand, dragging me farther into the large, open building. He was practically jogging as he pulled me toward the opposite end of the indoor park to the dodgeball court, placing us at the back of a long line. There was a group of three girls in front of us, all about middle school-aged, their hair pulled back into ponytails and braids. In front of them was a variety of other kids, both younger and older.

When we moved up in the line, we faced a worker wearing shorts similar to mine, along with a startlingly green T-shirt with the trampoline park's name splayed out along the chest. "How many? Two?" he asked, looking between me and Rafe.

"Yeah," I responded.

"Do you want to be on the same team or a different one?"

I glanced at Rafe and he smirked at me. "Different."

The man working at the line told me to go to the left side while Rafe went to the right. I walked onto the blue cushion lining the trampoline before stepping onto the bouncy black material, jumping up and down. Several platforms made up the court, each square separated by a foot of solid-yet-squishy foam platform material. The trampoline platforms became slanted when they bled into the wall, letting people bounce off the sides.

Kids continued to pour onto each half of the court until there were probably about twenty people on each team with numerous dodgeballs resting on the centerline.

Rafe and I stood toward the front, waiting for everyone to be ready.

"You're so screwed," Rafe laughed.

"Oh? What makes you think that?"

"I'm a pitcher, duh. You. Are. Fucked." Rafe's eyes twinkled.

If I wasn't so good at keeping my composure, I might've burst a blood vessel stifling my laugh. The fact that he thought he had an advantage over me was *cute.*

"You're a *big bad pitcher,* huh? Well, what does that make me? I've been catching everything you've thrown for years. If you think you've got anything over me, well, you are *terribly* mistaken." I leaned forward, whispering the last part.

Rafe cocked a confident brow. "I guess we're about to find out."

"Okay, everyone, stand behind the first square," the worker shouted from the side. Everyone collectively moved behind the first of the three trampoline sections. "I'll quickly go over the rules. Headshots don't count. Catching the ball means the person who threw it is out. If a ball hits your person anywhere below the neck, you're out. Do not cross the centerline, and you *are* allowed to block throws with another dodgeball."

And then his countdown started. Rafe and I both smiled like idiots, bouncing and ready to sprint for the middle.

"Three. Two. One," there was a slight pause when the man in the green shirt glanced around, trying to create some suspense, "go!"

I lunged forward, grabbing two balls and throwing a couple more backward for other kids to grab. Rafe also held a ball in each hand. He clenched the foam between his fingers, jumping gracefully around on a square with a little girl hiding behind him. He moved backward and almost tripped over her, gently placing an arm on her shoulder and chuckling an apology. While he was distracted, I took my first shot. I cocked my right arm back and sent the ball flying toward Rafe's side. Right when it was about to hit, he turned from the small girl, his left arms swinging back, my ball making contact with the one tightly gripped in his hand.

His head shot up with his mouth agape in surprise.

"You got lucky!" I yelled.

"Hey, now! Luck is also a skill!" Rafe's left arm came soaring from his side much faster than the ball I threw. I dropped my arms low and stopped his ball with the one in my hands before it could connect with my shins.

The number of people around us dwindled. A lot of the younger kids tried to take care of Rafe and me first as we were older, and thus the primary targets. I ran around from one side to the other, jumping against walls, trying to avoid the array of colors flying at me. All until it was just me with a younger guy and a girl against Rafe.

Then the worker stepped onto Rafe's side. "Just to even out the playing field a bit." He grinned. The guy was probably around my age, possibly a bit younger.

I hovered near the back and watched as Rafe and his new teammate pelted the two preteens on my side, quickly getting both of them out.

"I see how it is," I said, picking up two purple dodgeballs rolling around. "Still think this is even?" I taunted.

The two of them got closer together, each with a ball in hand. They whispered, not taking their eyes off me before nodding and going to opposite sides of the court.

There was a reason I called the shots on the field; Rafe's plans were see-through.

I dropped the dodgeballs I was holding. Rafe gave me a smirk, thinking he had me pinned.

"One!" the employee shouted. "Two! Three!" Both balls were launched at me.

And I caught them both. One in each hand.

Jaws dropped and I knew the smug smile on my face would make Rafe want to punch me.

Large hands, intense grip strength, and the instincts of a seasoned catcher. What could I say?

"I guess I won then."

"Shut up." Rafe shook his head as we started walking back toward the entrance where the front of the line waited for the next round. "What kinda live-action anime-type shit is this?" He grumbled, stepping off the trampoline.

"That was so damn cool," the worker commented, his eyes glistening, impressed.

"Eh, it's just 'cause I play baseball." I brushed it off, moving to the back of the line once again.

Rafe moved behind me until his chest was pressed into my back. His warm breath on my neck sent goosebumps down my arms, whispering in my ear, "That was really fucking hot."

I turned my head so that I could see his face out of the corner of my eye, winking as I spoke. "What can I say, I'm good with balls."

Chapter Twenty-Four

Aspen

I DOUBLE-CHECKED MY BAG, MAKING sure I had everything I needed. There was nothing left in the bathroom, everything already tucked away into a Dopp kit. I had one bag that specifically belonged to my baseball gear and an extra duffle for all of my clothes, which, at this point, were mostly just Rafe's.

"Aspen, come here for a sec!" Rafe shouted from the other room.

I stopped rummaging through my bags next to the shoe rack by the front door and jogged leisurely into Rafe's room. He stood near his desk with his hands occupied.

"Yeah?"

He turned to me and moved his hands toward my face, sliding a pair of sunglasses over my nose. "How do they fit?"

I grabbed the side with my finger and adjusted it slightly. "It's good. Thanks."

"Sure. I had an extra pair and thought you might need it." Rafe pulled his own pair onto his face. "They're both polarized too, that one's just a bit older." Neither had a colored lens, which I appreciated.

"Is there anything else you need to do? Have a change of clothes?"

"I'm set. All my stuff's already in the car," Rafe explained.

He wore a scandalously tight charcoal-colored T-shirt that outlined each and every one of his hidden muscles. That, along with one of the dozens of black athletic shorts he owned, endowed Rafe with the authentic style of a guy who did nothing but play baseball. Not that I could comment on it, as I was in the same shirt but white and with sleeves, and an identical pair of shorts; they were both Rafe's, after all.

"Let's say goodbye to my parents and then hit the road." Rafe stepped around me, walking out of the room. We made our way down the hall, where Rafe gently knocked on his parents' door. "Mamá, papá, ya nos vamos."

"¿Ya?" I heard feet shuffling toward the door from the other side.

"Sí. I booked a later flight so Aspen has an extra night before he has to play," Rafe replied as someone gripped the handle and opened it, revealing Rafe's mom with his dad right behind her. Rafe backed up, allowing the four of us to shuffle into the living room.

"Call me when you land," Teresa instructed as she grabbed Rafe's arm and pulled him into a hug. "You too, Aspen." She let go of Rafe and then wrapped her arms around my back. Keeping her hand on my shoulder, "Good luck, mijo. I know you'll do great!"

Her hand fell from my shoulder as Mateo gripped my other arm. "You're going to be amazing. Just give it your all and I'm sure things will work out one way or another."

"Thank you." I looked at both of Rafe's parents, momentarily wishing they were mine. Wishing that it was my parents giving me a pep talk before a big tryout like this. They used to do that, and if they hadn't found out I was gay, maybe they still would. I shook off the feeling, pushing it down even further than before. I didn't need distractions, and I was more than grateful to have Rafe's family here for me like this.

I picked up one bag while Rafe lifted his own, his mom asking a question as we slipped on our shoes: "¿Volverás este fin de semana?"

"I'm not sure. We'll probably head straight to Newhalm from the airport once we get back. We'll be home for a couple weeks after that before we head out for the Jackals' tryout."

"Okay, that's good. Remember, I want updates every day. I want to know how things are going."

"Of course, dad." Rafe began to slide outside, trying to end the conversation. "Love you."

"Drive safely!" Teresa shouted as we disappeared past the front door.

I squinted, the sun reflecting off the trunk of Rafe's car; he used his right hand to pop it open and throw in one of my bags. I followed closely behind him, stiffly lifting the bags when I paused, noticing an additional two bags.

"Why is your baseball gear in the trunk?" I asked with a scrutinizing gaze.

Rafe shyly scratched the back of his neck. "You caught me... I'm trying out with you."

I furrowed my brows, glaring. "What?"

"I'm going to try out with you," he said, slower this time.

"Why the hell would you do that?" I nearly shouted. "You have a DI school lined up for next year, why would you throw that away for a slim shot of playing fucking *Rookie ball?!*"

"Woah, okay, calm down. I'm not throwing anything away. I'm just taking a gap year. If things don't work out in the Minors, I'll start college next year with you. And if things do go well, then we'll still be on the same page."

"But why??" I asked, exasperated. "You could be setting yourself back an entire year or even more!"

"Why are you so upset about this?" Rafe asked calmly with knitted brows.

I ran a shaky hand through my hair. "I just... I feel like you're throwing away an opportunity."

"How is this," he gestured toward his bags in the trunk, "throwing things away? I'm not doing this for no reason—I'm doing this for you, Aspen."

His words somehow pissed me off even more. "*For me?* You could potentially be screwing up your career for *me??* I'm not okay with that, Rafe!"

I sighed and pinched the bridge of my nose, unable to explain my emotions. I was suddenly crushed by this feeling... like my presence in Rafe's life was becoming too overwhelming, like I was taking over and ruining things. Again. I always felt like I was ruining things. He had a solid game plan that would lead him straight to the Majors in just three to five years. But then I barged in with my fucked-up life and forced him into a position where he could no longer follow his plan—all because I couldn't follow mine.

It wasn't supposed to be like this.

Rafe took the bags from my hands and silently set them down inside the car, placing his hand on the hot metal of the trunk and slamming it closed, making sure it clicked. He turned and took a step forward, invading my personal bubble by sliding the sunglasses off my face and wrapping his arms around my neck. On instinct, I placed my hands on his waist, subconsciously taking a step closer to him.

Although I couldn't see his eyes, I knew he was trying to read mine. "Do you remember that promise we made—when we were sitting under that willow tree after playing catch, just the two of us?" He grinned at the memory. "We were getting ready for the summer season, our first year off of tee-ball. It was hot, but there was this breeze that kinda just made everything... peaceful. My back was pressed against the bark of the tree, my butt completely soaked from the grass, and your head was resting on my legs while you tossed a ball in the air, trying to see how much you could make it spin. And you asked me something. You asked how long we could play on the

same team—you asked if we could keep playing together, forever...
and I told you that we could, and we would."

With a small intake, I sucked all the air into my lungs I could and
held my breath.

"You told me we were best friends—that you would follow me
anywhere just so we could stay together, playing baseball. And now
I'm holding up my end of the promise; how could I let my best
friend move onto the next chapter of his life without me? So this
time... this time I'll follow you."

I chewed on my lower lip, my scab still visible but healed enough
that it wouldn't reopen so easily. "I didn't think you remembered
that conversation..."

"How could I forget it? Especially when you seriously did follow
me everywhere to play baseball together. Even when you made a
better team in ninth grade, you still decided to play on the one I
went with." Rafe let out a small laugh. "And then you proceeded to
take us all the way to Nationals, where we beat the team you were
originally going to join."

A smile played on my lips as I struggled to keep my face straight.

"And Aspen, you need to understand that there aren't going to be
any repercussions from us doing this, trying out for the Majors. If
things go south, we both have contingency plans. We can always
drop back down to play college ball next year. Things aren't so black
and white. There are several ways we can do this that will all lead to
the same place."

"Okay," I breathed out, giving in. "Okay."

"So, we're good? We're on the same wavelength now?"

"I'm sorry. Yeah." I shook my head, detaching myself from him.
"We should get going."

Rafe lifted his hand and settled it on the side of my face before
sweeping back and through the side of my hair. "Okay."

Damn—what did I do to deserve someone like Rafe?

The building in front of us was a big step up from the shitty motel I stayed at after getting kicked out, but it wasn't anything too fancy. Something along the lines of a Comfort Inn. It was a three-story building with light-grey accents here and there, the front entrance consisting of a stone arch, making it look much nicer than it actually was.

"Here," Rafe said, handing me my bag while grabbing his own, leaving all of our baseball gear in the rental car's trunk.

"Did you make a reservation?" I asked as we walked across the lot and through the glass doors.

"Yeah. I wasn't sure how booked they'd be 'cause of tryouts, so I made one just in case."

We approached a long wooden counter acting as the front desk. There were three workers spread out along the inside of the pen, each wearing cheap-looking black blazers with black slacks.

I followed behind Rafe as he stood in front of a red-haired woman in the middle, focused intently on a hidden computer.

"Hello?" Rafe spoke gently to get her attention.

"Hiya!" The woman beamed. "How can I help you today?"

"I have a reservation. For Rafe Alvarez." He placed his elbow on the granite top, leaning into it. I awkwardly shuffled my weight from one leg to the other while hovering behind him.

"Reservation for a single room with a king-sized bed, correct?" She glanced up and looked between me and Rafe. She gave us neither a knowing nor judgemental look.

"Yeah."

"And would you like one or two key cards?"

"Two, please."

"Alrighty. So, where are y'all coming from?" She made small talk, typing furiously.

"Cedar Heights, California. It's near Riverside." Rafe listed the closest big city; she'd be more likely to know where that was.

"What brings y'all all the way to Las Manos?" She spun around in her chair and placed two white cards into a small machine that made a noise similar to a car engine.

"The Knights tryout."

"Ah, yes. We have a couple of other guests here for the same thing. The Knights baseball team is the most interesting thing in this area, so a lot of the people are invested." She pulled both of the cards out after a low beeping noise erupted from the appliance. "Good luck to both of you." The cards were pushed toward the front of the counter in an envelope.

Rafe signed a couple of things and then we were off toward our room.

Stepping into the cool steel elevator, I tapped the button for the second floor. "What room again?"

"Uhh..." He flipped open the card stock holding the room keys. "Two-o-four."

A ding rang out from the speaker and the doors glided open. We stepped out and I glanced left and right, trying to figure out which direction we were supposed to go.

"This way." Rafe gestured toward the left after noticing two small silver placards with maps. The hallway had one long, continuous carpet that was somewhere between purple and brown, the walls completely grey, the door frames a stark white. He stuck the key card into the slot and twisted the gold handle once the light turned green. Rafe pushed his way into the room with his bag falling off his arm and dropping it right in the entryway with me following suit.

The first thing I could see was a small kitchen comprised of a cabinet, counter space the size of a school desk, a sink, microwave, and mini-fridge all stacked in a column. I walked down the narrow hallway squished between the bathroom door and square closet, leading from the entryway to the bedroom. A large king-sized bed took up the center of the room with nightstands on both sides. It was covered in several white sheets that matched the sheer curtains framing a window that gave us the stunning view of the hotel parking lot.

Naturally, the first thing I did was jump on the bed, flopping into the cushion face-first with my arms spread out like a bird, landing with a grunt. "I don't understand why sitting in a car is so tiring. I wasn't even the one driving."

Before Rafe replied, I was bouncing on the bed again, joined by his body beside mine. My face was shoved into one of the pillows while Rafe rested on my right side with his head laid on his hand and arm propped on his elbow. Rafe shivered with his back to the window, the night breeze blowing the curtains about.

"Because you're weak," he deadpanned.

"Shut up." I grabbed the pillow from under my head and shoved it into Rafe's face.

"Oh? So that's how you wanna play," he sneered before raising the pillow in the air and throwing it back at me, only this time, he didn't let go. Rafe mercilessly beat me with the pillow, repeatedly whacking my head as I struggled to suppress a laugh.

I lay flat on my stomach, eyes screwed shut, with my head facing Rafe, now on his knees. I jabbed my hand out, making direct contact with his stomach, forcing out a strong gasp. As the air was punched out of him, the pillow fight ceased. I took it as an opportunity to spring up and tackle Rafe to the bed, grabbing the pillow from his hands and smothering it into his face with one hand while tasing him with the other.

He breathlessly wheezed, trying to laugh but not finding the oxygen to do so. "O-okay! Enough," he stuttered through a smile.

I lifted the pillow, laughing along with him. "What? Can't take it?"

Rafe gave me a curious gaze, his eyes glistening as they trailed from my face... and down. I followed his eyes and realized I was straddling his stomach.

"I can *definitely* take it." He smirked at our current position, his hands reaching out and latching onto my hips. They moved down farther and farther until they gently rested on the outer parts of my ass.

"Are you sure about that?" I raised a brow. "You're already lookin' a little out of breath there."

Rafe let out a fake gasp. "You dare insult my stamina?" He squeezed the flesh between his fingers and I sucked in a breath. "Me? The person who consistently pitches full games?"

"Then prove it."

"Prove what?"

"That you've got good stamina. *Show me.*"

Rafe sucked his bottom lip into his mouth, softly taking it between his teeth. "You'd like that, wouldn't you?"

I leaned down so my face was hovering over his. "Maybe," it almost came out as a whisper.

"Hmm... I can certainly do that." Rafe craned his neck off the bed, his head lifting a couple of inches before his lips met mine in an open-mouthed kiss. Rafe pulled away, leaning back to look into my eyes with a seductive smirk on his face.

I licked my lips at the sight, placing my forearms on either side of his head and leaning down, not wasting any more time and reconnecting our mouths. Rafe hummed at the feeling.

I ran my fingers through his hair roughly, snagging his lip between my teeth and forcing my tongue into his mouth. Rafe ran his hands up and down my back under my shirt, setting my skin on fire. His fingers played on my flesh, right around the waistband of my shorts, before slipping under, forgoing my boxers. I let out a long moan into his mouth as he squeezed the bare skin of my ass.

"Off?" Rafe managed a single word as he detached his lips from mine.

"Yeah." My voice came out rougher than intended, a shot of nerves running up my spine. I wasn't sure if it was thrill or anxiety.

Rafe rose up, grabbing the hem of my shirt and tugging it over my head. The sleeves got caught and he pulled each off individually, the garment now completely inside out. Without skipping a beat, Rafe threw off his own shirt.

He stared at my chest, eyes lingering on my abs. "Fuck. You're so hot."

Somehow, the words did nothing to boost my confidence. I ignored the weird, unsettling feeling in the pit of my stomach. "I could say the same about you," I replied, my hands ghosting over the tight muscles littering Rafe's abdomen.

When Rafe's eyes raked over my upper body, my heart dropped in my chest and my face fell as his line of sight came to a halt on my lower stomach, unable to look away from the thin, white lines spread across the muscle, disappearing into the top of my shorts. "These..."

He hadn't seen me without a shirt on since I first got out of the hospital, and the insecurity immediately kicked my mind into fight or flight. I tried to press it down, playing it off like I always had. "It's fine," I tried to reassure him. "I haven't cut there in years. My belt would dig into it too much when I'd play, so..."

"Is that why you started doing it on your thighs?"

"Maybe," I shrugged, knowing my voice might crack if I tried to actually explain it.

Realizing I'd instantly stilted the heated mood, I lifted my leg with a huff, rolling over and falling in place next to Rafe, my arms covering my stomach protectively. Rafe turned on his side, his head propped up with his hand as he looked at me. Even with my gaze focused on the ceiling, I could tell Rafe was trying to get a read on me, searching for whatever it was he always seemed to find in my eyes. "Sorry," I murmured.

With a sigh, he said, "Aspen, we've been over this." He reached out and brushed his hand through my hair, my eyes fluttering shut at the feeling. "You have nothing to be sorry for, so stop apologizing."

"Still..."

Rafe grabbed my arm and brought it away from what it was hiding, my startled eyes snapping to his. He ignored it, kissing the corner of my eye as his fingers trailed down the underside of my arm, forcing my hair to stand on edge at the light, almost tickling touch. When his fingers got to my palm, they traced the lines and creases. The tip of his index nail teased, dragging across my skin before lacing his fingers with mine in a delicate-yet-firm grip. His other hand followed the top of my forearm that led to the appendage still trying to hide what it could, reaching my wrist and cupping the flesh, making no attempt to move or uncover what was below.

"I can see the scars, and I'll always be able to." My body stiffened, taking a rigid form at his words. "But they aren't the first thing I notice. Without your shirt, it's easier to see how you're thicker than me, in a buff sort of way. Your muscles are less defined than mine, but evidently larger. I've seen you in enough tight-fit shirts to know how broad your shoulders are and to understand how *dizzying* your body is. With and without your shirt. Because even though you have scars, they'll never be the first thing I notice, since there's so much else to see. So much beauty in the angles and curves that the scars may not add to, but they sure as hell don't take away from."

I chanced a glance at Rafe to test if I could see the lie in his face, *in his eyes,* but I couldn't, and a weird wave washed over me. Relief, perhaps? His words were genuine, spoken as a wholehearted truth from his mouth, but when the words echoed back in my head, this time with my own voice, they were lies. Lies because even if Rafe believed them, *I* didn't.

"I know what you're thinking." His words were nothing more than a whisper. "I've always been able to read you better than I can read any book. And even though my words will never be enough to convince you that your scars don't make you ugly, that they don't make you *less,* I'll believe it enough for the both of us."

Chapter Twenty-Five

Aspen

"I THOUGHT IT WAS GOING to be at the Knights Stadium." I glanced around at the enormous field in front of me.

Three baseball fields took up the corners of the park, each bleeding into the other, only separated by a short wire fence acting as an out-of-the-park home run and inside-the-park home run barrier. There was a single empty corner that housed a makeshift bullpen as well as countless batting nets. Bleachers surrounded the park, and endless rows of white outlined parking spots with "Danger: flying baseballs" signs littered all around.

"Their stadium isn't big enough for something like this," Rafe replied.

Toward the front, where the parking lot met the grass, were four large blue canopies, each with a short line heading out of the tent. Rafe and I waited patiently as we got closer to the front of the queue. It was eerily quiet around us, the players nervous and most likely trying to clear their heads.

We were in and out within minutes, only needing to check in our names since we'd already filled out all the paperwork for registration online.

Rafe and I exited from the back of the canopy and walked farther onto the grass field where other players gathered, jogging, stretching, and playing catch to warm up. Following suit, Rafc and I sct down our gear and pulled out our gloves, Rafe grabbing a ball from the bottom of his bag, and putting a suitable distance between us to leisurely play catch, occasionally taking a couple of steps back. It took another thirty minutes before one of the organizers, or coaches, or whoever was running this thing, came out onto the field, standing just in front of the tents with a white-and-red megaphone.

"Can everyone hear me?" the man shouted. He wore blue jeans stained with dirt, accompanied by a team zip-up jacket and sunglasses with red chrome lenses.

There was a chorus of "Yes, sir," echoing around the gathered players.

"I've been coaching baseball going on thirty-eight years—sixteen of them being with the Knights. This is my sixth year running open tryouts." He paused and sighed, pacing along the line of grass. "The number of players we'll be contracting to our Minor League affiliate teams depends on the level of talent we see here this week, meaning that there's no cap on the number of players we're willing to take. However, there is also no minimum number. I know zero sounds like a scary number, but at the end of the day, it doesn't change the fact that every single one of you may go home after this camp with nothing to show for your efforts.

"We selected around one hundred applicants based on experience and performance, placing importance on future potential. A number of people will be dismissed at the end of each day, and to start, we will assess basic skills. You'll be split up into three different groups that will rotate between fields where you'll be observed doing drills, each field focusing on different basic skills. Last names A–F to Field 1, G–O to Field 2, and P–Z to Field 3. Go!" he shouted angrily into the microphone, as if simply being in his presence was a major offense.

The eager testees quickly grabbed their bags and jogged to their respective stations.

"At least we're still together," Rafe mentioned as we ran in the center of the group headed toward the field in the left-most corner with a large green sign titled "Field 1" at the top of the chain link fence separating the catcher's box from the stands.

"Yeah, makes me feel a bit better."

Several official-looking men leaned against the dugouts, waiting for our group to arrive. Some held clipboards while others sported stoic expressions with their arms tightly crossed over their chests.

"Put your gear in the dugout," one emotionless voice commanded. "Leave everything in there and come back out."

Everyone hastily deposited their bags on and under the metal benches before rushing to stand in a huddle in front of the coaches.

The same man who'd spoken before—who looked like an army drill sergeant—shouted, "Start with a warm-up run. Two laps around the field!"

The thirty or so people immediately broke out into a run. The men at the front sprinted their asses off, trying to impress the coaches. Rafe and I stuck to the middle of the pack. Not too fast, and not too slow—just enough to get our hearts pumping without wasting energy.

I was focusing on my breathing when a guy slightly behind my right shoulder began to talk. "Did I tell you about what my friend Jason pulled off a couple years ago?" His tone was light and amused.

"No," another guy answered. "What'd he do?"

"Well, there was this chick he was into. She was fucking perfect, blonde, blue eyes, nice tits and ass, and he ran into one of her friends. And get this, he told her he was *gay!*"

"Okay, and?"

"And then he started getting invited to sleepovers and girls' nights because they didn't think he was into any of them! The girl he had the hots for changed in front of him and he secretly snapped some pics. Do you wanna see them later?"

"Hell yeah!"

Rafe's jaw tightened, his teeth grinding. I glanced down and his fists were tightly clenched, his nails digging into his palms. I tapped his shoulder to get his attention.

I shook my head. *It isn't worth it.* No matter how much I hoped they'd trip and break their noses, guys like them were far from rare, and Rafe and I both knew that. They were caught up in their egos and entitlement, and people like them—at the top of the totem pole and privilege scale—were nearly impossible to touch.

The rest of the two laps went fairly quickly, and within minutes, we were standing in front of the dugout once more.

"I want everyone to get into a line behind home plate!"

It was uncomfortably silent as the group shuffled into a long line going from home to third. I glanced at Rafe. Running through the line drills were a standard part of any tryout and I had no qualms about the procedure. The issue laid where none of the coaches had introduced themselves, now or earlier. I couldn't tell if it was because they were running late and rushing things, or expected so little of the players here that they didn't feel the need to bother. It was unorthodox and rubbed me the wrong way.

Two of the coaches stood at first base with stopwatches in hand while the rest stood back to observe.

"We'll be timing your speed. There will be four rounds, each round extending to the next base. Understood?" The lack of strain in his voice told me his words were far from his full capabilities, but the sheer volume had me tipping my head away, my ears searching for relief.

"Yes, sir," only a couple of the players replied.

"What was that?!"

"Yes, sir!" Now everyone responded.

"First up, what's your last name?"

"Johnson, sir."

"Johnson. Johnson. Johnson," he repeated as he flipped through papers, trying to find the last name. "Eric Johnson, Samuel Johnson, William Johnson, or John Johnson?"

"Will, sir."

"Okay, Johnson," the coach huffed. "Go when I say."

Will nodded in reply. With a short three-second countdown, Will took off from his position in the right-handed batter's box, sprinting as if his life depended on it. His long strides leapt through the ninety feet, only slowing down with a shuffle once he was well past the white rubber square. I faintly heard the beeping of the timers as the coaches pressed several buttons, resetting them and scribbling down his time.

The main coach who'd been speaking before huffed in disappointment and grumbled something to himself.

"Next," he shouted. "Three, two, one, go!" The duration of his countdown had dropped below three seconds.

The next runner took off, this time, from the lefty box. After the stopwatches beeped, the coach clenched his jaw.

One after the other, the coach was unsatisfied with the times and became increasingly angry. "Fucking hell!" he swore. "If I could, I'd fucking eliminate you right now, Hernandez!" Another and another. And then someone tripped over the base. "Fucking pussies! You'd think I was running a tryout for fucking women with the way y'all run!" He threw his clipboard to the ground. "What?! Want me to paint the base *pink,* so maybe you'll actually find it? If you can't run the distance of one *fucking* base, *go play softball with your little sisters!*"

Rafe glanced at me, giving me a *what the fuck* kind of look.

Uhm... That was concerning...

"Fucking next!"

And that would be Rafe... Meaning I was going to have to go soon. My biggest worry was that I hadn't gotten any actual practice in over a month, and unfortunately, that was enough time for me to get out of shape.

"Last name?"

"Alvarez."

He gave him no acknowledgment, "Go!" being spat from his lips.

Rafe gracefully spun from the left-handed batter's box to run toward first. He was visibly faster than the others, but then again, Rafe had been scouted by D1 schools and was probably already levels ahead of anyone trying out; our circumstances for being here were just a little special.

"Finally!" the coach boomed. "A real man has shown his face! The rest of you faggots run like women! Take Alvarez as an example; this is what a baseball player is supposed to sprint like."

The guys in line behind me grumbled at the insult, but I froze, staring wide-eyed at the man in disdain. Rafe fixated a harsh glare on him as he stalked back to the end of the line.

I then found myself in the middle of trying to calm an upcoming panic attack. *Damnit.* If this was going to be a repeat of what happened in high school, then I'd rather quit baseball altogether. But this was just one coach... and two players, but they technically weren't associated with the team. One person, and one individual alone, wasn't enough to dictate my opinion of an entire team, so I ignored it. I ignored it and ran. And ran again. And again. And one last time as my feet slid into home plate, my ears blocking out the incessant swearing from General Dipshit.

"Good work, everyone. You'll have an hour for lunch, after which, you'll go to Field 2."

The players quickly dispersed, some already groaning in soreness. I didn't even get a chance to talk to some of the other guys while I was in line; we were shouted at every time someone made noise. It was a little excessive.

"Did you bring any food?" I asked Rafe. "I didn't think I'd be running so much first thing in the morning."

Rafe rolled his eyes. "We barely ran more than two laps around the infield."

"I mean, yeah, we've run like twenty times that in some shitty practices, but that doesn't change the fact that we had to run before the sun came out," I huffed as we grabbed our bags, the gear feeling like dead weight since we hadn't needed any of it yet.

Rafe rolled his eyes. "It's past noon. The sun's been out for hours."

"Well, hearing Sergeant Asshat use slurs made the weather seem a bit cloudier."

He averted his gaze, unable to comment on that.

"I have a couple bars in my bag." Rafe shifted his bag so it was over his shoulder, now resting on his stomach instead of his side and back. He unzipped a pocket and pulled out two protein bars, handing me one and then repositioning his bag to its original spot.

I ripped the top of the plastic, peeling the edge away and sliding the bar up so I could take a bite, my fingers firmly gripping the surrounding wrapper.

"Want to stop by the bathroom?" I asked with a full mouth before vulgarly stating, "I don't want to feel like I'm going to piss myself when I bend over to pick up a grounder."

"Sure. I think I heard someone say that the only open bathrooms are the ones inside the public locker room."

"A bathroom's a bathroom. Better than peeing in a bush." I quirked a smile.

Rafe groaned. "I thought we weren't going to talk about that anymore."

"Hey," I raised my hands in defense as I bit off another chunk of my lunch, "it's not my fault you didn't go far enough off the trail."

"You could've warned me that there was an entire family right behind us! Do you know how many people saw my dick that day?!"

I snickered, "Too many. The look on that old lady's face was priceless."

"Fuck you," Rafe spat.

"Later," I teased.

"You're impossible."

"You love it."

"Of course I do."

There were several other players in the locker room, most I assumed were also here to use the bathroom. Once I finished my business, I met Rafe at the sink to wash my hands, my ears honing in on one of the several conversations happening in front of a set of lockers.

"Nah. Nah, man! He said he was bi!"

"He's just in denial," another guy snorted.

I furrowed my brows, glancing to my right and noticing Rafe scrubbing his hands just a little too hard.

"My cousin's gay."

"Oh shit, you have one in the family?"

"If he's gay, he probably has AIDS! Fucking nasty."

"Does it work like that?"

"I dunno, probably. I heard all gay guys have AIDS."

"Serves 'em right."

Rafe stared himself down in the mirror, his hands clutching the edges of the white sink. His jaw ticked to the side, fingers tapping the inside of the square bowl, faster and faster, like he was about to explode.

Once was a chance. Twice was a coincidence. But three times was a pattern.

Yeah… this wasn't going to work out.

I grabbed Rafe's arm and tugged him harshly toward our gear. I threw his bag at him, picked mine up, and pulled him to the exit. I dragged Rafe past the field and canopies, my grip strong on his forearm, leading him to the parking lot.

"What are you doing?" he asked, glancing back at diamonds in the background.

"We're leaving. This team isn't for us."

"But—"

I cut him off, "If we stay here, one of two things is going to happen." I stared him dead in the eyes as I opened the trunk of the rental car, tossing my gear inside. "Either you're going to get into a fight, or we're going to get *hate crimed*." Been there, done that. And I wasn't interested in a repeat.

Rafe opened his mouth to argue, but he knew what I said was true.

So I repeated myself once more. "*This team isn't for us.*"

Rafe sighed, taking off his hat and running a hand through his coarse hair. "Yeah, you're right. We'll try again with a different team, and if it's like this, we'll just have to try again."

"That's the spirit."

I was so used to hearing these kinds of things—at school, at home, from friends and family—that it didn't affect me like it should. Not like Rafe, who was probably hearing homophobic things like this for the first time since he realized he wasn't straight.

It might not have affected him as much before, but sometimes things changed when they were directed at you. Because that was how the world worked—people didn't care until it was about them.

Chapter Twenty-Six

Aspen

"Hey, Rafe?" I started as Rafe tapped his finger mindlessly along the stitching of the steering wheel.

"Hmm?" He nodded lightly to the rhythm of whatever song was playing quietly in the background.

I hesitated before speaking. "Can I ask you something?" Rafe's eyes snapped toward mine at my hushed, somber tone.

He quickly turned off the music, looking back at me and then the road, doing so several times. "What's wrong?"

My words came out slowly, my voice sounding deep and tired. "Nothing's wrong, I just... keep thinking about when we were still in school. All our friends would constantly say awful things about gay people. And I know you never started those kinds of conversations and you didn't really join in on it—but I have to ask, why didn't you say anything?"

Rafe opened his mouth, but no words came out.

"I thought you were homophobic," my voice was nearly a whisper. "I thought you were going to hate me when you found out... and now—now you get mad when you hear anything bad about people like me, but you never did before. I know, I *know* it's not personal. It just feels like maybe you didn't care until it was about you, too..."

Rafe pulled his lips into his mouth "Honestly, I'm not sure."

That wasn't what I wanted to hear. I didn't know *what* I wanted to hear.

"I was so confused when you kissed my forehead in the hospital," I confessed. "Besides the disorientation from just waking up and the fact that *you* were kissing *me,* I didn't understand why you were so okay doing that to another guy all of a sudden." I let out a humorless laugh. "I thought it was a joke."

Rafe's brows set into a heavy crease, his mouth in a deep frown. "You thought I was *joking?*" he repeated.

"I didn't know what to think. So yeah, I thought you might've been mocking me, maybe trying to get back at me for pretending to be straight, playing me because you were disgusted that I kissed you —*that your best friend kissed you.*" I shook my head. "But then you came out to me, said you felt the same. And I found out that you'd accepted your newfound sexuality"—I snapped my fingers—"like that. It got me thinking: If you were so okay with being attracted to guys, why were you so okay with listening to our friends saying gay people should *go kill themselves?*"

He let out a solemn whisper, "I'm sorry."

I sighed, running a hand through my hair. "I'm not mad, Rafe. Our relationship just happened so fast and it's hard for me to understand how or why."

Why was he okay with me liking men? Why was he okay dating a man? And why was he so okay with dating *me?*

"Maybe it was because I grew up with everyone around me saying that stuff, so I was used to it, that it was such a normal thing to hear at that point that those words didn't have that much weight—that much meaning—and didn't seem as bad as they actually were." Rafe wrinkled his nose in thought; it reminded me of something I did when I'd get that strange feeling at the base of my nose, the one that made me feel like I was about to cry. "Or maybe it was the

Internalized homophobia and I was subconsciously trying to make myself fit in. I'm not really sure.

"And when I think back on it now, I wish I didn't just go along with whatever they said. I didn't think it mattered, that what they were saying would really affect anyone. But now I know—" his voice cracked and he sucked in a shuddering breath, "I know how much it affected you... how hard it made things for you... and I wish —*fuck. I wish I could go back and stand up for you.* I wish it didn't take a *sexuality crisis of my own* to see how fucked everything was. Maybe if my head wasn't stuck so far up my own ass, I could've helped you, could've been there for you more than I was..."

I didn't know what to say, truly. I had no response. There was nothing for me to respond to. I wasn't mad about his explanation, I wasn't angry, and I wasn't looking for an apology. I wasn't happy with his answer either, but it was in the past, and there wasn't anything he could have done to change that. So I simply nodded, a heavy mood settling between us.

"I'm sorry... I ruined the mood, didn't I?" My face fell even further, thinking about how it was a little unfair to ambush Rafe like that; he'd been nothing but supportive and accepting.

"Why would you be sorry?" Rafe sighed, seemingly sensing the things going through my head. "You're right. I was ignorant and I wish I'd done things differently. But I didn't. All I can do is be better now."

"You weren't bad... just confusing..." I mumbled.

"I didn't think about how that kind of stuff affected people, but now that I get it, now that I know how much it hurts people, I can't just stand by and listen to it anymore. I've already done enough of that."

"How do you expect to do that while closeted? The whole reason I always keep my mouth shut is that sticking up for gay people makes people think you're gay, even if you aren't."

"My sexuality isn't anyone's business. I don't care what people say."

"Does that mean you want to come out?"

"I'm not against it. There are pros and cons..."

And yet, that somehow made me feel like I was holding him back. Being out would remove this heavy weight constantly pulling me down. I wouldn't be so stressed about how others saw me. I could be myself without feeling suffocated by secrets and webs of white lies. But even then, I couldn't. Because for all the good things that would happen, there'd be ten times more bad things. What price would I need to pay to be myself? At what cost?

I could answer half of that. I did pay—I had to trade my family, friends, and livelihood for my sexual orientation. But that was how life was. You had to pay for everything. Pay for food or starve to death. Buy clothes and shelter or suffer from the elements. All things necessary for survival, and all things every human needed. And nothing could change that. Just like how nothing could change the fact that I was gay, yet for some reason, I still had to pay. I had to pay and sacrifice and pick my battles, all just to be who I was.

If I were to come out, I could lose the few things I had left, like baseball. I knew Rafe understood that; he knew just as well as I did what it meant to be a gay professional athlete. We both knew how bad homophobia was in sports, particularly male sports. It could mean more than just being ostracized or physically harmed by teammates—I could be dropped from the team completely. They'd say they had protections against LGBT discrimination and that a queer person couldn't be fired for just that, but there were so many ways around it. They could slap on a label, say I wasn't performing like I was expected to. They could lie and say I quit because of an injury. Or they could say I did something inappropriate and unacceptable, creating a scandal out of nothing.

And what could I do about it? *Nothing*. Absolutely nothing.

What, should I take them to court? Try to fight for my rights? I was me, and the head of whatever team or league had the kind of money and power I couldn't begin to fathom.

Okay, sure. Say I did have enough money for a lawyer. What then? I won and went back to a team that didn't want me in the first place? Spend my days warming the bench, since they wouldn't be obligated to play me as long as I got paid? Watch from the sidelines until my contract was over, only to never touch a live ball?

Yeah, my thoughts were a little extreme. But then again, when weren't they? Thinking of the worst-case scenario helped me prepare. If things went south, I wouldn't be surprised, and thus, I wouldn't be as hurt. And if things went well, then I'd get to enjoy that moment. Setting my expectations low was—yes, self-destructive—a means to protect myself from the shitty reality I'd already become acquainted with.

"You need to stop thinking so hard. With the way you're pushing your eyebrows together, you'll have wrinkles before you're twenty." Rafe drew his eyes away from the road for a second. "Look, Aspen, I'm not saying I want to come out to everyone. All I'm saying is that I don't want to just sit and watch people walk all over you; I don't want to see it eating at you. If I can do something to keep you from getting hurt, I will. No matter what it is. You deserve to have someone that will stick up for you."

Except I didn't want anyone to stand up for me, especially not if it was going to put Rafe in a difficult situation.

"I like who I am. I like being with you, as your best friend, as your boyfriend. All I've ever wanted is for you—us—to be happy."

"But my happiness isn't your responsibility." God, I was so tired of feeling like I was dragging Rafe down, holding him back.

"This relationship isn't an obligation, Aspen. I want to be here. With you. Even if you broke up with me for whatever reason, I'd still want you to be happy. I'd still try to make that happen however

I could. And I would still protect you from anything and everything."

I fought the smile climbing onto my lips, the corners of my mouth twitching upward. "You're such a sap. You need to stop reading literary fiction. People aren't that blunt in real life."

"I'm just trying to be the main character," Rafe quipped. "I think I'm rather poetic," he smirked. "Plus, I like seeing you blush."

"You are something else. Only you, Rafe. Only you."

"Don't lie, you love it."

I cleared my throat. "No, I don't... okay, maybe."

Rafe snickered at my affirmation. "It always starts with denial."

"Hey! I got over my gay denial phase ridiculously quick for a kid with religious parents!"

"I did, too! Okay, how about this? As a reward for having parents that told us we were going to burn in hell for being queer, we should go on a date."

"You don't need an excuse to take me on a date."

"We've been best friends for fourteen years. Practically everything we've done together is a date."

"Well, geez, sorry for not having other friends and forcing you to hang out with me," I joked.

"Do I seem upset to you? I loved it, felt like I got to monopolize you, keep all your attention for myself." Rafe paused for a second, thinking about what he just said. "How the hell did I only just realize I like you?"

"That's what I want to ask," I laughed. "Damn, I wonder how long we could've been dating by now."

"It would've been before my first girlfriend, so probably middle school."

"You're totally right," I hummed.

"Oh!" Rafe startled. "I know what we should do! Laser tag!"

The game with fake guns and light beams was a regular stop for our baseball team when we were fourteen; all the guys constantly talked about wanting to date a girl that would get into the competitive spirit with them. Little did Rafe know, all he'd had to do was look to his left, and he'd have found exactly what he was looking for.

"Las Manos is a pretty small town. Would they even have a laser tag place here?" I asked.

"Try looking it up. I'll take us back to the hotel so we can change into some actual clothes."

I took Rafe's phone from the console and tapped in his six-digit password. A simple two-keyword search was quick to reveal that basically nothing intriguing existed in the barren Arizona town, but a twenty-minute drive to the next city over would lead us to a chain site that had a location we'd played at back in Riverside.

Chapter Twenty-Seven

Rafe

THE WALLS OF THE LOBBY were adorned with neon drawings and patterns that glowed under the black light. Various arcade games were shoved into the corner, a set of street racing machines so popular a small crowd had formed to watch. Parents huddled around the doors to various party rooms, nearly as loud as the children running around with cake on their faces, fueled by sugar rushes.

"We're going to be the oldest people here," Aspen whined, but the glint in his eyes betrayed him. The bright green lit up his entire face, making his dark circles nearly nonexistent and projecting his excitement.

"That didn't seem to be an issue while you thoroughly enjoyed pummeling a bunch of six-year-olds in a game of dodgeball at the trampoline park."

A burst of chatter caught our attention, a group of guys popping out of a door to look at a scoreboard being broadcast on a large television hanging above a claw machine, a stacker game, and a series of gashapons. If their beards were anything to go by, I'd say they were probably at least a couple of years older than us.

"Those weren't kids. They were devils, Rafe. Goddamn devils. They had it out for me from the beginning."

"You gave one of them a bloody nose!"

Aspen shrugged. "I regret nothing."

I shook my head in disbelief, placing my hands on his shoulders and steering him toward the line in front of the attendant. "I'm so glad you were too busy playing baseball to get the summer camp counselor job you were thinking about."

Once at the front, the worker spoke first, launching into a speech about the different game packages they offered, and knowing Aspen, a single game wouldn't be enough—I ended up paying for three back-to-back rounds for both of us, reassuring my boyfriend that we could always buy more after if he still wanted to play. I had a feeling he'd teeter toward the game room without complaint, although I wasn't exactly sure that'd be the cheaper option.

"What would you like your codenames to be?"

Aspen turned to me. "Are we trying to be cool, or going middle school-style and making up for what we missed?"

I snorted, "Trying to pick a 'cool' codename is why everyone on our team teased you, Lord DragonFire."

The brunette rolled his eyes. "Don't act like you were any better, Sir PuppyEyes"

"You're the one who picked that for me!"

"And it still suits you and your puppy dog eyes," he cooed, speaking in a baby voice and pinching the side of my cheek.

"Alright, alright!" I swatted his hand away. A swell of bliss bloomed around my heart, my eyes crinkling in adoration. Aspen was never like this in public, keeping our relationship confined inside the walls of my house. The fact that we knew no one here and wouldn't be staying created a sense of relief and freedom he wasn't familiar with. It was an opportunity, and I'd try to absorb every last ounce of affection I could get.

"We're totally using our shitty middle school codenames. I'm not taking no for an answer." Aspen then rambled off the embarrassing names we'd picked years ago, ignoring my protests.

A monotone voice blared through the speakers, "Attention all players. All those participating in the next game, please proceed to the briefing room. Attention all players, please proceed to the briefing room."

Aspen gave me a smug smirk when he was handed two bright yellow plastic sticks, tapping my nose with the cool, silver button on the end.

I snatched it from his fingers before he had the chance to pull back. "Okay, Lord DF, the first game is 'every man for himself,' so how are we doing this? Enemies or allies?"

"Hmm, that's a tough one." Aspen looked up, pretending to be deep in thought as he pondered his options. "Truce. Just because I know you suck and would come in last place without me."

"You always did take laser tag ridiculously serious."

"Of course I did. I was trying to impress you." Aspen winked as he slipped past an eight-foot-tall door.

Wow... that's a shot right through the heart. I trailed after him with a skip in my step and a smile that wouldn't falter even if someone were to punch me.

We entered the large square room along with everyone else playing this round. The floor was obscured by clouds of smoke from what I'd guess were at least four fog machines. Once everyone had flooded inside and the massive door closed, Aspen took one look at me and blanched. "You gotta be shitting me."

My chin dropped to my chest and I took in the bright purple glow of my white shirt, my eyes instantly glaring at the purple fluorescent lights above.

With a tsk, Aspen said, "I take it back. Enemies, we're enemies. I can't be in a truce with an idiot."

"No take-backs! You already knighted me with your glow stick! Our alliance is official. Going back would be the ultimate betrayal. I never took you for a traitor, Aspen. Are you turning into a traitor? Because that's a major red flag right there. I don't think I could date a backstabber."

"Being with you is like waving a white flag. You're literally a walking sign saying, 'here! I'm right here! Shoot me, please!'"

"So be a good boyfriend and protect me!" I cheered. "Prove your undying love for this defenseless damsel in distress and maybe, just maybe, you'll win his heart."

Aspen grumbled, crossing his arms over his chest.

I gave him a victorious, toothy grin and wrapped my arm around his neck, resting it on his shoulder as an employee made their way onto a raised platform. They read the rules of play and made everyone chant a pledge to get adrenaline pumping and competitive spirits up.

A large door allowing the width of five people shoulder-to-shoulder to funnel through receded into a wall. We rushed down a mirrored hallway until we reached another room where twenty or so packs were perched on hooks as the sound of a bomb siren wailed, throwing my heartbeat into a false state of emergency. I glanced down at the stick in my hand, a faded twenty-eight written in Sharpie at the bottom. My eyes poured over the numerous barely visible numbers on placards until my eyes landed on Aspen, who'd already found his: number twenty-nine.

He already had the thick vest strapped on, the laser gun dangling at his side. "Come on, Rafe! Get your ass moving or we won't be able to snag a good sniping spot!"

My fingers fumbled, pulling the heavy set off the rack, the dim lighting making it nearly impossible to see where it was clipped in.

I barely managed to connect the pack to my codename using the metal end of the plastic stick before Aspen stopped me with a sigh. "Come here."

I turned to him with a questioning glance, but before I could speak, he was taking the clunky gear from my hands, lifting it over my head, and adjusting the straps.

With the gear covering the graphic design of Aspen's shirt, he was completely shrouded in darkness, the black light picking up nothing on his person. He nodded in approval at the pack covering a fair portion of my glowing clothes before making his way toward the red numbers counting down until the game started and the lasers went live.

Aspen extended his arm, and I gave him a quizzical look as his hand reached up and cupped the side of my face. With the most earnest expression he could muster, Aspen told me, "If you trip, I won't hesitate to leave you behind." And with that, he turned on his heel toward the arena, expecting me to follow.

My jaw dropped. "Love you, too," I muttered under my breath.

Just steps behind Aspen, we entered what looked like an enormous maze. Black buildings and ramps to second floors blocked my view of the ground paths. The only lighting was the black lights illuminating the special paint marking corners and the edges of walls. Players scrambled to find the best starting places, and with how much we used to do this when we were younger, Aspen and I didn't even need to agree on a spot, immediately searching for an empty second floor we could use as a base. We rushed up and down steep ramps, cutting through occupied spots until we found a building near the center of the arena with an open cutout where the windows would be, giving us prime sniping visibility.

"You'll cover me?" Aspen asked as he crouched next to the window, peeking his head out to keep the sensors on his chest gear covered as the clock hit zero and automatically switched to twenty minutes. We always did it this way when we played team games; half of the guys would snipe and the other half would hold down the fort and take out any intruders.

"I got you."

Aspen handled his gun carefully, never letting it out in the open long enough for someone to get a hit on it. Since we were placed in the middle of the zone, more people tried to take over our spot than I'd anticipated, and with only two of us to defend it, other groups that had formed alliances overwhelmed us.

"God, you'd think with how good your pitching control is, you'd have at least decent aim with a gun!"

"The two skills have absolutely nothing in common!" I quipped back, the LED lights on my pack flashing bright red with yet another life lost.

Aspen cursed and left his post at the window, dashing to a wall next to the entrance and peering around the corner at where another group was hiding, biding their time for an opening to rush in. With a loud beep, the lights on my chest and gun lit up once more, only this time, they didn't turn off. I was out. With a twisted smirk, a girl no taller than four and a half feet slipped past me, lowering her gun to Aspen's head like she was about to execute him, before shooting his shoulder pad.

"Rafe! What the hell, man?"

"She got me out too!"

The girl claimed the spot next to the window, scouring for her next victim. "Don't be such a whiny bitch. Suck it up and accept defeat." The high-pitched voice had me biting back a snicker while Aspen glared daggers.

"Next time we play 'every man for himself,' I'm using you as a human shield." Aspen walked off, no lie in his words.

"Good to know I'm still of some use," I scoffed. "And they score based on how many other people you hit, not how early you get out."

Strutting out of the area, placing our gear back on the hooks, and exiting the room, Aspen took one look at the live scoreboard and said, "If I accidentally kick you off of the bed tonight, just know that it was on purpose."

"Try me. I'm in the mood for snuggling, and you know better than anyone that I have a hell of a grip. If you try to push me off, you're coming right with me."

Next to second place in bold, white letters was "DragonFire," just below a codename that undoubtedly belonged to a certain foul-mouthed child, with "PuppyEyes" ranking somewhere in the middle.

"Clearly, you're too unmotivated. Maybe an incentive will help." Aspen uncrossed his arms from over his chest and unclenched his teeth. "How about this? If we come in first during the team round, I'll give you a prize."

"Oh?" I raised a brow. "I'm listening."

He took a step toward me, and then another and another, not even checking to see if others were looking. He leaned in, his mouth ghosting my nape, and teeth just barely grazing the skin.

I gulped, eyes wide.

Aspen pulled away from my pulse point. "Only if we win. And you have to rank above *her*."

"I swear, you're more childish than any of the actual kids here."

Chapter Twenty-Eight

Aspen

"Okay, so this should be a much, *much* more pleasant experience." Rafe stood tall, both of us stiffly holding our bags.

"Are you sure? Can you guarantee we won't hear slurs in the first twenty minutes like last time?" I gave him a sarcastic, questioning glance.

"I'm sure it'll take at least an hour."

"You're joking, right?"

"Of course I am. Armada is supposed to be one of the most open and accepting teams in the league," Rafe stated.

"Sure, sure. Do tell me, how many gay players do they currently have employed?"

"Come on, Aspen. That's not a fair question. We both know there aren't any uncloseted MLB players right now. But Armada donates to charities and does fundraisers and campaigns and stuff—and not just during pride month."

"Okay... if you say so."

"If there's any team we're to get hate crimed on, it *probably* won't be Armada."

I snorted. "How reassuring."

"I'm sure things will go better here. Let's go in with a good attitude; maybe we'll be able to manifest it."

"Well, it can't get any worse than it was in high school, and I don't plan on telling anyone here, so it should be smooth sailing. But seriously, if I hear anything related to a slur or STDs, I'm out."

"If that does happen, make sure to drag me out before I get into a fight and get myself blacklisted," Rafe pleaded.

I agreed with a huff, "There's a reason I stayed in the closet."

"Guess it's time for me to join you. Narnia, here I come."

"Is this a community center?" I asked, taking in the deep mud-brown of the building in front of me.

"Yep, Newhalm Community Center. There's supposed to be a decent field here."

The parking lot led directly to the front of the main building, which was surrounded by five others.

While walking to the Recreation building, I caught a glimpse of an enormous pond surrounded by a large, vibrant grass field. Closer to the cluster of buildings were murals and random pieces of artwork as well as a giant fountain spouting artificially blue water.

A sign next to the door with a large arrow pointing inside was labeled "Newhalm Armada Tryouts." We followed several more signs, trailed by other players, that led us down a maze of hallways until we were in a large room with wood floors and a stage at the front. A couple hundred chairs were spread out, a good portion of them already taken by guys in full uniform with their bags sitting on the floor by their feet.

Next to the door was a table of two people sitting in foldable chairs with boxes of blank paper and safety pins, instructing, "Please write the initial of your first name and your full last name as large as you can. When you're done, take some safety pins and secure the nametag in the center of your jersey. Please keep this on until the tryout is over."

Rafe and I took Sharpies out of a plastic cup acting as a container as they marked us present on the roster.

After a few quick glances around the room, we took our seats. It looked like Rafe and I were among the youngest here. Legally, guys as young as sixteen could try out, but realistically, most people that came to these things had hit dead-ends in their careers or were having trouble getting noticed in their leagues. Usually a combination of both. There may have been a couple of other people like us here, but it was hard to tell.

Soon enough, a woman wearing black slacks and a pale-pink blazer came onto the stage with a microphone in hand. "Hello everyone," she chirped.

The men went silent, abruptly ending their conversations. Some replied to her, but most stayed quiet.

"My name is Lucy Kay and I'm one of the many coordinators for the Newhalm Armada's Recruiting Department."

There was a short applause after her introduction.

"I'm very excited to have all of you here with us today—albeit not as excited as our coaches—to see what new talent may pop out." With a wide smile, she gestured toward a line of older-looking men standing off to the side of the stage, eyeing the players in front of them. "This morning, I'm here to give you all an overview of what to expect from these tryouts that will take place over the next couple of days. Then, the coaches will introduce themselves and explain what they are looking for.

"This tryout will take place anywhere from two to five days, depending on how much of you our beloved coaches would like to see, which all rests on you, the players, and what you show us. And I'm sure you've all been to your fair share of tryouts throughout your careers, but here, we look for specialty skills over basics. We don't need players that can simply meet the standard requirement; we need players that excel in certain places in ways others cannot. I wish you all the best of luck out there!" Lucy tilted her head in a bow and walked off the stage, handing the microphone over to one of the three men standing to her left.

The new holder of the mic cleared his throat as he moved to the center of the platform. "Hello, my name is Morgan Richter, or Coach Rick. I'm the head coach of Armada's Single-A team, the Finches. To my side is Coach Bashir of our High-A team, the Pizzly Bears, and Coach Brooks of our Rookies, the Glacial Giraffes." The men waved when their respective names were mentioned.

He continued, "We also have Triple-A, Double-A, and Low-A teams, but the head coaches are unable to make it today. They may stop by later in the tryouts. However, it's unlikely our Triple-A and Double-A coaches will show as their teams are both away for games."

I deflated a bit at his words, but in the grand scheme of things, this didn't change my plans. I need to start somewhere, and if that was at the Rookie level, I'd take it.

"Our assistant coaches and various Armada scouts will help with this tryout," Coach Rick went on. "We'll be splitting into two groups for today. Pitchers and catchers will stay at the Community Center and the fielders will head to the high school down the street. As for cuts, there is no set number; if there's a substantial lack of talent, we'd be willing to end this tryout tomorrow and not take on any new players. But we could also take several of you depending on what's needed on our rosters. All we want from you is to give us your best. Show us what you're made of and what you can add to Newhalm. Thank you." He exited the stage, handing Lucy the mic once again.

"Okay, everyone! Please head to your assigned fields. I recommend jogging there to warm up." She smiled, dismissing us.

Slowly filing out of the double doors, we made our way into the scorching summer sun. The bright uv rays pelted my skin, raising alarms in my head of how I didn't put on any sunscreen. With a hushed curse, I grumbled to Rafe about how I'd look like the uncooked side of a steak within a couple of hours.

We stopped our jog at the dugout, putting our bags down on the metal bench.

Snickering, Rafe pulled something out of his bag and held it up toward me. "Close your eyes."

Seeing the sunscreen in his hand, I squeezed my eyes shut, struggling to close my mouth over my smile. The cool spray hit my face and neck before Rafe asked me to turn around.

"What am I, a rotisserie chicken?"

"You will be if your little white ass doesn't let me do a three-sixty degree spray."

I rolled my eyes, rotating around in a circle with minuscule steps. "Okay, *mom.*"

"You're the one who was complaining about looking like raw meat. Now, rub it in."

I gave him a fake scowl, reaching my hands behind my neck and making sure it properly covered the small amount of skin not covered by clothes in slimy grease. I aggressively rubbed my hands on my pants, hating the feel of the sunscreen.

After a couple more minutes, Coach Bashir found his way onto the dirt with a binder and clipboard in hand. "Can I have everyone grab their gloves and join me behind home plate?" he instructed, stomping over to the backstop.

I glanced around and everyone seemed to be grabbing their position-specific gloves. Rafe had his pitching glove clutched in his right hand, so I grabbed my catcher's mitt and followed the rest out onto the field.

"Hello," the coach started as he counted the number of people herded together, glancing back at a piece of paper and nodding in approval. "I will go a bit further into what this tryout will look like. First, I'm going to have you all pair up and toss the ball around a bit to warm up. We'll begin this with a focus on the pitchers, having each of you give a quick summary and show of the pitches in your arsenals.

"After we get a feel for what the pitchers have to offer, we'll join back with the fielders and test you in a scrimmage against our very own Finches. Find a partner you'd like to play with—you'll be sticking together all day." The men hectically glanced around, frantically trying to pick someone while hoping that they were at least decent at the game. Unsurprisingly, no one approached Rafe or me, probably put off by our age and thus lack of experience. That was fine with me; I didn't need to awkwardly refuse anyone. "If you don't have a partner, come to me and I'll have someone from the Finches assist you today."

Out of all the pairs, only one pitcher stepped forward, the odd man out. In some ways, his position was rather favorable. He got to team up with a catcher who had real experience in a professional league.

"Okay, now that everyone has a partner, catchers, go put on your gear. Once you're ready, go out onto the field. After about fifteen to thirty minutes, we'll have each of you try the mound."

It took less than a minute for me to get all my equipment on, everything perfectly adjusted to my fit. Grabbing my mask, I jogged out of the dugout and met Rafe on the grass, my back to the fence just past the first base line. Some other players soon joined us, the group splitting between sides, all purposefully placing the catchers to the fence to block wild pitches.

We started with light catch, making sure our shoulders were warmed-up. A lot of the coaches paced back and forth between the groups. I speculated that they were writing our names and descriptions of what we were wearing so they could pick us out of a crowd if they couldn't see the name tags on our fronts.

I liked this. Slightly differing from a standard tryout, the procedure was refreshing and new, but still professional, the coaches hard and realistic, yet also present. They were putting effort into trying to find talent.

"Ready for me to sit?" I shouted to Rafe.

He gave me a nod. "Yeah."

I backed up farther, now standing on the dirt. Rafe also moved a bit, eyeballing the correct distance as if he was on a pitcher's mound and I was behind the plate—about sixty feet.

"Don't go all out yet!" I yelled to ensure he heard me. "Make sure your shoulder's fully warmed-up."

He gave me a thumbs-up as he kicked the grass a bit. This wasn't the best place to pitch, since he had no elevation and a bad cleat grip from the textured greenery underfoot.

Some of the assistant coaches drifted behind Rafe, watching as I dropped fingers between my thighs in various combinations before one of them began to stalk toward me. "Did you two agree on signs beforehand?" he asked.

"We played together before this," I explained.

"I see. Could you tell me the signs? I'd like to know what he's trying to throw."

I agreed, rambling off a list of every possible ball Rafe could throw, which included several more that I'd theoretically have him throw in a game, even if they weren't his best.

"Thank you." Just like that, he moved back to the other coaches.

They did a similar thing to the rest of the pairs, making quick conversation and returning to their posts.

"Okay, everyone, huddle up," Coach Bashir shouted from beside home plate. The players jogged over in a stressed silence. "What we're going to do now is have each battery go through the pitcher's best pitches. For now, only pick your top three, and if you don't have three, then just show what you *do* have. You'll only get twelve pitches, since we need to get through all the players here before lunch. Remember, everyone! This is your chance to show technique! We'll have someone stand in as a batter so we can clearly see the strike zone. Now, who wants to go first?"

Several hands shot up, but I grabbed Rafe's sleeve and shook my head. It was better to observe first and gauge the coaches' reactions. I wanted to see if I could tell what would impress; I'd rather not go in blind.

Most of the people who went before us made their pitches known, shouting out the type of pitch and the zone it was supposed to be in. No one stood out. Most of the players had shaky control at best, and those who had good control lacked speed. There weren't as many wild pitches as I'd expected for batteries that had never played together before—that was what stood out the most. The catchers all went one step further, desperate to show something of themselves amid a pitcher-centric evaluation.

"Okay, next group." I raised my arm in the air with no hesitation. I'd seen all I needed to.

"Uhh," the Coach drew out, craning his neck to see our name tags. "Ace, Alvarez."

I slapped Rafe on the shoulder as a means for reassurance, quietly whispering, "You got this. You're better than everyone that's gone so far," before we parted.

The catcher that went before me said a quick, "Good luck," while passing.

I took my place behind the plate, adjusting my legs until I was used to the ground. Rafe did something similar, making himself comfortable on the unfamiliar mound.

"You have signs, correct?" Coach Bashir asked.

"Yes, sir," Rafe replied.

As the stand-in batter made his way into the righty box, Coach Bashir adjusted his position from behind the pitcher's mound so he could better see what I was calling for. He took out a different piece of paper, the one the assistant coach who'd talked to me earlier had written all of our signs on. That was good; it meant I could call for strategic balls and still show Rafe's control.

The man in the box raised his bat, giving us an intense stance. He genuinely looked ready to hit the ball, which was great since it gave us a more realistic simulation.

I wanted to start off with a strike. Something that would make a statement. A fastball, high and inside, close enough to the batter's face it'd push him back. It was ballsy, but it'd leave an impression.

And Rafe gave it to me, exactly where and how I wanted it. The Finches' batter threw me a stern glower with a clenched jaw and pinched lips, knowing I was responsible for the call.

This was where I was going to be different from the others that went before. I wanted to switch up what Rafe gave me, pretend this was a proper game, as if we were practicing a winning combination of pitches.

I threw the ball back, giving the signal for a breaking ball. A slider.

His speed dropped its normal amount when pitching this specific ball. It was routine for him, practiced and perfected. We went through the motions. Rafe was familiar with how I liked to do things and was prepared to pitch whatever I wanted. And for the final pitch, I wanted to give them a show. I signed for a fastball in a location that would, worst-case scenario, jam him. Right at his knees, low and inside, barely in the zone. I gave Rafe that look, making eye contact until he got it. *Give me everything you've got,* it meant. The fastest ball he could pitch, right here, right now.

And boy, did he deliver. The sound the ball made as it smacked into my glove felt like heaven on Earth. Ecstasy in the form of a white ball stitched in red.

I tried to hide my smirk as Coach Bashir left his place and jogged toward the assistant coach on the side. The head coach leaned over his shoulder to look at the speed sensor. He took off his cap and rubbed a hand through his hair, looking at the miles per hour on the screen and then glancing back at Rafe.

"What's your average fastball?" he shouted.

"Around ninety-eight, but I can hit a hundred."

"Yes. I can see that... your control's not bad either."

"Thank you."

Coach Bashir nodded at Rafe, the two of us leaving to join the rest of the group.

"You did great," I praised.

"You think?"

"*You think?*" I mocked. "You're the only guy the coach even mildly reacted to. That's a good sign if I've ever seen one."

"I was kind of nervous," Rafe admitted shyly, rubbing the back of his neck.

"Really? It didn't show at all."

"It helped that you were there."

I glared at him for flirting with me in public, desperately trying, and failing, to hide the small smile gracing my lips.

As the rest of the pairs went, Rafe and I commented quietly, making critiques and evaluations of our own.

"Alright, that's a wrap, everyone! Great job. We saw some good stuff out there today. What we're going to do now is split the group. The names I'm about to call will go to the other field for their scrimmage." He went on to read about twenty names. "You have forty-five minutes for lunch. Good luck to those of you I won't be overseeing for the rest of the day. Hopefully, I'll get the chance to talk to some of you again tomorrow."

The players parted ways, most people going back to their cars to either get food or move fields. Rafe and I stayed in the home dugout along with a couple of others. I pulled a leftover sandwich from yesterday out of my bag and dug in, making some small, pleasant conversation with the other guys trying out. Before I knew it, our lunch break was over and the fielders were wandering their way onto the dirt.

After throwing my trash away, I joined Rafe in the crowd of people. There were probably around seventy additional players here on top of the twenty pitchers and catchers. Recalling the number of people in the room we gathered in before tryouts, I wondered how many people were told to stay at the other field. It had to be near a hundred. I had no clue how they'd manage that.

From the corner of my eye, I saw a small swarm of light-blue-and-white uniforms walking into the away dugout. Their uniforms had "Finches" printed on the front. It looked as if the entire team had come.

"Can everyone hear me?" the man who'd been running this side of tryouts shouted. Before he could get a response, he continued, "We'll now be starting a friendly scrimmage against Armada's affiliate Single-A team. We expect everyone to play clean. And, although this is a tryout and we want to see everyone's best, do not do anything to risk injury. Trust me, it isn't worth it.

"This won't be like a normal game, so here's how we're gonna do this. You'll stay on the defensive, only fielding, while the Finches will only be batting. We'll play in rotations, those on the field playing in rounds, three innings at a time before switching with the next group. They'll all be back-to-back so you'll need nine outs total, but the people that may or may not be on base will reset every three outs, just like a normal inning change," the Pizzly Bears' head coach rambled on. "Any questions?"

A hand shot up from the back of the group. "Will there be any opportunities to play more than the three half-innings? Like if you don't get a chance to touch the ball?"

"That's a great question, and for today, no. But there will be more chances tomorrow, so don't worry. Just do what you can. Be attentive and ready for anything.

"I'll read off the first group of players," he said, and proceeded to call both my and Rafe's names. "I'll be acting as the coach for those trying out. For those of you who just got here, if you're not playing, you can wait in the stands."

A storm of dust was kicked up as most of the fielders made their way to the bleachers.

"Do you think they're any good?" Rafe asked, gesturing toward the Single-A team.

"I'm not sure," I replied honestly. "I can't imagine they're anything ridiculously special. I'd normally say we should start off more cautious, but you're throwing well today. First impressions are important, so let's start off with a bang."

Rafe hummed in agreement. "On your call."

"As always." I looked up from Rafe and noticed that the others had already taken their positions. I'd wanted to have a group huddle and get some camaraderie going, but it was too late and I'd have felt awkward calling them to the pitcher's mound now.

I clumped leisurely to home plate, one of the assistant coaches finishing putting on the umpire's protective gear while others made their way onto the field to act as the base umps.

"Ace!" Coach Bashir called to get my attention. "You're calling the pitches here!"

"I was planning on it, Coach!" I said, slipping into a crouch.

Things progressed quickly from there. The Single-A team was at a level far below my expectations and Rafe was getting strikeout after strikeout. I knew the coaches were surprised, staring at the two of us intently as Rafe got his seventh out in a row. So far, this was a no-hit, no-run game and we'd already gotten through the core of their batting lineup.

I was caught off guard when Coach Bashir rushed out of the dugout, pausing the game. "I'm subbing the pitcher and catcher! Rimon, take the mound. Cortez, get behind the plate." He frantically scribbled things down on his clipboard.

My brows furrowed as I glared at the coach. Rafe was more confused than anything, glancing at me while we jogged back to the dugout.

"Why'd he sub us? There are still two more batters and we haven't gotten hit off of yet." Rafe's voice was filled with concern that I wished I could soothe.

All I could do was shrug.

After he finished writing something down, the coach motioned for the ump to resume the game, heading back into the dugout and sitting on the bench next to Rafe and me.

"How old are you, son?" he asked, looking directly into my eyes, which were partially hidden behind my mask.

"Eighteen..." I trailed off.

He turned to Rafe, "And you?"

"Also eighteen."

He nodded, chewing on his pen as he stood. "Don't take your gear off." He pulled his phone out of his pocket and stepped out of the dugout, his back to the game.

"Why do you think he pulled us out?" Rafe leaned over to me, whispering.

"I'm not sure. It's not like we were doing badly. Maybe they didn't think the rest of the inning would go any differently and wanted to see someone else? I don't know, but it seems like he's planning on putting us back in."

"We *were* having a good game..."

"Well, this isn't exactly tough competition. I'm a little underwhelmed," I admitted. Rafe and I had both played at higher levels with more intense competition.

There could also be other factors contributing, like how they may not have been putting in a real effort since they had nothing to lose. The Finches had no reason to perform to the best of their abilities; a lot of the players seemed bored, their overall team dynamic looking calm and tired. While the players trying out were shouting and cheering our side on, the Finches were near-silent. They didn't want to be here, and that was evident in their playing, although that wasn't to say the outcome of Rafe's pitching would've differed even if they were putting in the work.

There were two players on base now, and the fielders were finally seeing some action. Things were much more exciting to watch when it wasn't such a one-sided game.

Several more innings passed, and the groups rotated at least three times. It started to get darker out, the sky dimming until the field was veiled in a dusk light that messed with depth perception. Once the field lights turned on, the bright LEDs illuminated the diamond in a blinding manner, resembling several suns sitting stagnant in every direction.

Just as the catcher on the field stood, shouting the number of outs to the fielders, I noticed a large, dark-skinned man wearing a purple hat and neon-yellow shirt with purple lettering. I recognized him from some games I'd watched on TV; he was the Rumbling Hornets' head coach, Jackson Zambler.

He strutted silently into the dugout, avoiding the gazes of the players in the stands whose focus was solely on their competition, the people they were fighting against for a recruitment spot.

Jackson Zambler went straight to Coach Bashir, tapping lightly on his shoulder to get his attention. "What was so important that I needed to rush over here before the Hornets' game was over?" He spoke in a hushed tone, a deep, resonating whisper that did nothing to stifle the clarity of his voice. I sat right behind them, so it was easy enough to understand.

I slapped Rafe's leg to get his attention, jerking my head toward the coaches.

Coach Bashir cleared his throat, glancing in my direction before standing to be at eye level with the Triple-A coach. He leaned in so his lips were next to the new coach's ear. I couldn't tell what they were talking about.

"Ace, Alvarez," Coach Bashir started, "get back out there."

We jumped off the bench and jogged back onto the dirt. "He called the Triple-A coach over?" Rafe asked, confused.

"Looks like it."

"Maybe they wanted an extra pair of eyes?"

"Maybe," I echoed.

I held my glove up in the air, Rafe hitting it with his own before heading to the mound, taking the ball from the previous pitcher.

I turned to the umpire, asking, "What's the count?"

"Three-one, no outs."

"Thank you." I shouted the count to the rest of the fielders, making sure Rafe knew where we stood in the inning.

Things went just as smoothly as before. The batters were up and down, one after the other. I worked them, having Rafe pitch a variety of balls and strikes, using different pitches to confuse and bait the batters. We were five consecutive strikeouts in before the Triple-A coach left the dugout, his voice resonating across the field. "Pitcher change!"

I jogged up to meet Rafe as he headed back to the dugout. "You killed it. Seriously."

"All thanks to your calls," Rafe smirked.

I went all the way back to the dugout with Rafe, meeting the coach right in front of the fence with a new pitcher in tow.

"Ace, right?" Jackson Zambler asked.

"Yes, sir." I took off my mask to see him more clearly, running a hand through my hair to push the sweaty strands out of my eyes.

"You and that pitcher... Alvarez?" He questioned the name. He glanced behind him to look at Rafe. "Yes, Alvarez. You two have played together before?"

"Yeah," I kept my response short and simple.

"Okay, okay," he hummed, moving to pat my shoulder. My head ticked to the side ever so slightly—my lame attempt at covering a flinch. "I'd like to see how you perform with a pitcher you're not as used to. See more than just how you call."

"Hi, I'm Aspen," I introduced myself to the new pitcher, glancing into the dugout to see Rafe giving me an encouraging nod, and the Triple-A coach opening a little book, pen in hand.

"Sammy." He stuck his hand out for me to shake it, his grip strong.

"What kind of pitches do you throw?"

"A fastball, changeup, and a cutter."

"Okay, nice." It gave me room to work. "And how are you at hitting the zones?"

"My control is decent," he said confidently.

"So I can call for corners?"

"Yeah. Should be good."

"Okay." I slapped his shoulder with my glove. "Good luck, man."

"You, too."

He returned to the mound, throwing a couple of practice pitches as the next Finches' batter took some swings off to the side.

Sammy raised his thumb into the air, signaling that he was good to go.

I had to disagree. His pitches were all off—he hadn't found his rhythm yet and was practically begging to get smacked by their batting lineup. The balls were wild and inaccurate. His cutters were just a shittier version of his mediocre fastball. Every time I gave him the signal for a zone I knew the batter would have trouble hitting, he'd shake his head and throw whatever the hell he wanted.

I dropped my fingers below my thighs and gave the simple sign we'd come up with for a fastball. He shook his head. I then tried for a cutter, but he shook his head again. It was stupid—he was stupid, and it was beginning to piss me off. Their batters had cycled through several times now and I'd seen how they fared against different types of pitchers; the guy in the box hadn't missed a changeup yet.

But with no other options left, I called for a changeup—he pitched a slow fastball through the middle of the strike zone.

The batter dropped his elbows, keeping them tight near his hips. The bat cut through the air, and with his legs fully pivoted, the ball went flying. Farther and farther until I thought it was going to go over the fence in left-center field.

I stood up, watching as the center fielder sprinted with all he had. His body crashed into the short wire fence, sending him toppling over to the other side. He recovered quickly, jumping in the air with the baseball in his glove. Cheers and shouts followed the play.

A wide grin spread across my face. *Nice save.*

I pumped my fist into the air with one finger up. "One out!" I shouted.

The players on the field all parroted what I said, shouting their own words back and slapping their gloves, high off the exciting catch.

I settled back into my position, eyeing the next batter. He wasn't good with inside pitches; he'd gotten jammed on them every time Rafe pitched it. Sammy nodded, finally agreeing with my call on the first try.

I shifted slightly to my left, placing my glove just below his knees. *And the pitch went outside...*

The ball cleared the third baseman; the left fielder who was playing too far back had to run in order to scoop the ball up. By then, the batter had already rounded first and was sliding into second.

A double. One out and a runner on second.

Sammy's control was practically nonexistent. It could've been due to nerves or something else affecting him, but either way, he wasn't pitching well.

I called for a time-out, running up to the mound and placing my glove around my mouth. "What's going on?"

"I dunno," he muttered, kicking the dirt with his cleat. "My control just isn't on today."

"Is that why you're rejecting all my calls? Because you don't trust your control?" My tone was sharp.

It was tough love. He needed to perform well so I could also showcase how I played. This was a two-way street, and without Sammy on his game, I would look like half the player I actually was.

"No, no. I just thought that a different ball would be better—"

I cut him off. "And is that working out for you?"

He was silent.

"Just trust me on this, okay? I want to see you play well just as much as *I* want to play well. This is a team sport and we need to work together. Pitching and catching is a duo game; it'd be near-impossible for one to get noticed and not the other in a drill like this."

"Yeah, yeah. You're right. Sorry. I just wasn't sure because you seem like you're pretty young…"

"I am. But you have to understand that they'll know if you're getting hit off because of my calls or because you're ignoring my calls. This is only going to hurt you. If you get hit off of when I'm calling, then you can put all the blame on me. Sound good?"

"Okay…"

"Okay."

We moved on to the next batter in a decent position. We weren't cornered until he threw three wild pitches in a row, almost all of which I had to block with my body or stand to reach.

And damnit, Sammy was not ready to play in the Minors, let alone Majors.

The batter popped the ball into the air; it would've gone foul, but I knew I could catch it. I threw my mask off with vigor to get better visibility on the ball, leaping from my squat and diving to my right, four feet behind the Umpire. I caught the ball in midair, landing roughly on my stomach.

The second I touched the ground, I jumped to my feet and threw a bullet to second base. My speed was similar to that of a pitcher's, allowing the second baseman to catch the ball as the runner frantically scrambled to get back to the base. But he was too late. The baseman tagged the base with the ball in his glove before the runner could get his fingers on the white rubber square.

That play would've been impossible if it weren't for the runner's error. It was a rookie mistake that shouldn't have happened at this level. Tagging up was a basic. But I'd take the out any day; what that runner did made me look good, and that was the whole point of this tryout.

Those in the stands whistled and cheered at my double out. The Triple-A coach had a smug expression as he marked something in his book. Very few catchers could throw like I threw, and they knew it.

My eyes searched for Rafe, finding him with the proudest look on his face. I felt tingles spread through my body, an electric buzz lighting me up with adrenaline. A smile tugged at my lips—nothing got me more excited than impressing Rafe.

Chapter Twenty-Nine

Aspen

THERE WERE NOTICEABLY FEWER PLAYERS gathered in the same room we'd met in yesterday morning; a fair number of people had been cut.

Lucy Kay stayed on the sidelines as the Triple-A coach walked to the front. "Hello," his low voice boomed, echoing through the room. "My name is Jackson Zambler. You can refer to me as Coach, Coach Jack, or Coach Zambler. My boys all call me Zam, but that name is reserved for the men that play under me.

"Some of you may have seen me stop by toward the end of tryouts last night, which may have been a bit of a surprise since I originally wasn't goin' to come, but I thought it'd be fun to see you all for myself. That being said, I'm goin' to explain what today will look like. It'll be similar to yesterday where you warmed-up and then went into a scrimmage, except today, the focus will be on battin'." The room suddenly became loud with chatter and groans.

"Now, I'm aware that some of you may not have gotten a chance to show your fieldin' capabilities yesterday, so today, we'll be splittin' the fields. Those of you who want to continue fieldin' will head over to the high school field, and those who are confident in what they've shown thus far and are ready to move onto battin' will stay at the Community Center's field. Coach Richter will continue with the high school group, and Coach Bashir will remain here with me."

At Coach Zambler's mark, the players dissolved, a majority leaving immediately, already knowing which field they wanted to go on.

I stood slowly, turning to Rafe and speaking in a hushed voice. "We should bat now, right?"

"Yeah."

"I think so too. But there's one small problem."

Rafe furrowed his brows. "What?"

"Wood bats?"

"Oh, shit..."

"Yeah, *oh, shit.*" I rolled my eyes.

The weird thing about baseball was that players used aluminum bats from little league through college. There was an abrupt switch to wood in the MLB since grown men playing pro ball tended to have better hand-eye coordination and bat speed when hitting. Because of that, Rafe and I only dabbled in the usage of wood bats when we were messing around in batting cages. Neither of us even owned one.

"Welp... we're quick learners." Rafe didn't even need to feign confidence, his nonchalant grin genuine and fearless.

I laughed. "Okay, then. We'll have to wing it."

"Worse comes to worst, they'll cut us because we don't know how to swing a wood bat. If we field today, we'll still have to bat tomorrow and we'd be cut then, anyway. Let's just get it out of the way and try our best."

"Wow," I raised a brow with a slight smirk, "nice pep talk there, big guy."

"What can I say," he shrugged, "I almost became captain one time."

I snorted. "Shut up. We were five and you somehow still managed to lose to the kid that broke his leg during the first game of the season."

"Hey!" Rafe mocked hurt. "That's not fair! It was rigged from the beginning! He was the coach's son!"

I placed my hand on his shoulder and looked away, giving him a slight push to get him moving toward the door. "Come on, Mr. Almost Captain."

We trailed behind a stream of thirty or so guys going to the same field as us; the number was substantially lower than yesterday. Now, we neared the normal size of a team, giving us more than enough space for everyone to squish into the dugout. There were several coaches already there—a couple were the assistants from yesterday, plus an additional five others. If I were to guess, I'd say they were batting coaches.

Once on the field, the Triple-A and High-A coaches hovered outside of the dugout fence.

"Good morning," Coach Bashir greeted.

He was followed by a chorus of "hellos" and such from the players.

"I see some familiar faces from yesterday... as well as some unfamiliar ones." His eyes narrowed in on a guy sitting in the very center of the bench. "How old are you, son?"

Other players blocked my view so I couldn't see him when he spoke. "Sixteen, sir."

"Sixteen," Coach Zambler whistled.

"You're a sophomore, then? Junior?" Coach Bashir asked.

"I'll be a junior, yeah. I play on my school's team."

"You're pretty young, huh? Is there a specific reason you wanted to try out for the Majors?"

"Do you want an honest answer?"

"Of course."

"I was curious. I wanted to see how you'd run a tryout and how good the players here would be. That and... I had the week off from my part-time job and needed something to do..."

Some people laughed at the last part.

Coach Bashir was thoroughly entertained. "Son, have you ever even used a wood bat?"

"... no," his timid voice replied.

The rest of the players had a field day with that, bursting out into laughter, all in good fun.

"Alright." The High-A coach clasped his hands together and studied the faces of the players lined up on the bench. "Is there anyone else here who's never used a wood bat?" he asked sarcastically.

He wasn't serious, but I glanced at Rafe and he let out a puff of air. I bit my lip and raised my hand, soon followed by Rafe doing the same.

"Oh? Looks like we have two more," Coach Bashir mumbled.

We got strange glances from the guys next to us. We didn't exactly play like guys fresh out of high school.

"Right, uhm..." He turned to the other coach. "How should we go about this?"

Coach Zambler surveyed us with a skeptical look and then spoke in a hushed voice, not nearly as quiet as he thought he was. "You called me down here to see some young guys destroyin' the Finches' battin' lineup." He scratched his beard. "So how 'bout we put 'em in a corner with the other kid and they can toss balls for each other while they hit into the net. Get 'em familiar with the bat and then have 'em join the rest of the players."

"Yeah, let's do that." Coach Bashir turned back to us. "Do any of you need a bat?"

I smiled sheepishly and rubbed the back of my neck. "That'd be great. Thank you."

"Alright. I'll explain how we're going to do this and then I'll send you boys off to the bullpen. There's a net in there that you can use.

"Okay, everyone. Listen up! Things will be somewhat similar to yesterday's setup. You'll be batting and the Finches will be fielding. There are still going to be innings, and after every three outs, we'll reset. All runners still on base will go back to the dugout and we'll simply continue where we left off in the lineup. Everyone should be able to bat several times today. And remember, your goal is still to score. That's how you win a baseball game, after all." Coach Bashir talked a little more before sending Rafe, me, and the sixteen-year-old off to the bullpen, each with a borrowed wooden bat.

We rotated who tossed and who batted until each of us were making solid contact. It took longer than I'd planned to get used to the weight and feel of the bat, and I couldn't predict how well I'd do against actual pitching, but this would have to do.

"Boys, you good to go?" Coach Zambler shouted as we walked back into the dugout.

"Yes, sir," Rafe responded.

"Okay, Alvarez. You're next, get on deck."

Rafe nodded in acknowledgment.

I gripped his shoulder and whispered in his ear, "Don't stress out. Stay relaxed. You got this." I wanted to give him more advice, but even I wasn't feeling super confident with the bat change.

I watched intently as Rafe took a couple of practice swings before stepping into the left-handed batter's box. He exhaled slowly, steadying his nerves. He watched the first strike go by, trying to get a feel for the pitcher since we weren't able to watch him before.

A couple of balls were thrown before Rafe made up his mind. If the next pitch was good, he'd go for it. And he did. He hit it slightly more inside than he would've liked, but his form was nice and he drove the ball into shallow right field, the ball stopping where the dirt shifted to grass. It was a solid single; he was safe with seconds to spare.

"Ace, you're up." Hearing my name had me snapping my head up to meet the gaze of the Coach Zambler.

"Alright." I threw my helmet over my head and adjusted my batting gloves; the white-and-grey nylon fabric slipped over my fingers with ease.

I stepped out of the dugout and repeated the same actions as Rafe, swinging my bat a couple of times, still trying to familiarize myself with it.

I took a deep breath and entered the box, shuffling my feet as I stared at the pitcher. My bat loosely wobbled behind my head while I found the perfect grip. I stood in position, waiting for the ball to release from the pitcher's hand.

My eyes followed the first ball—and I went in hard. I swung, clenching my teeth as I sent the ball into the outfield... into foul territory.

I shook it off, getting ready for the next pitch. This time, I hit the breaking ball into the opposite side of the outfield, foul once again.

The count was zero-two. I couldn't get any more strikes; I really wanted to join Rafe on those bases.

My eyes narrowed in on the ball and everything else went fuzzy, fading into the background. I led with the knob of my bat, following through and making contact with the ball with the center of the barrel.

I dropped the bat and started sprinting to first, watching the ball to see where it went. And I kept watching it—and watching and watching and watching—until it was gone, straight over the fence at the back of center field.

A blinding smile overtook my face as I slowed into a leisure jog around the remainder of the bases, ignoring the dull sound of clapping from the other players in the dugout. Rafe waited for me at home plate, my hit having brought him in. The second my foot touched the white pentagon, Rafe placed his hand onto my back and pulled me into a tight hug. I chuckled and lightly slapped his ass before he let go.

One of the great things about baseball was that players were often really close and it was normal to celebrate things with touch. It was all fun and games, mostly just teasing, so no one would bat an eye at the PDA. With our shoulders constantly bumping, Rafe and I walked back to the dugout.

Coach Jackson had his phone in hand, his contact app open. "Ace!" he called me over.

I left Rafe, breaking into a trot. "Yes, Coach?"

"I want you to be honest with me. No bullcrap."

I squinted in confusion, waiting for him to go on.

"You've never used a wood bat before? Is that completely true?"

I pulled my helmet off and rubbed the back of my neck, wiping away sweat. "I've used wood at the batting cages a couple times. But never during an actual practice or game."

"Okay," he said. "Thank you." Without a second glance, he stepped out of the dugout and lifted his phone to his ear.

I sat back down next to Rafe while we waited for another at-bat to come around. I couldn't say this was the most efficient way to do things, only looking at one player batting at a time, but there were also some perks. Like being able to see how the player runs the bases and how they handle the pressure of outs and strikes versus balls. Adding a bit of realism to the drill also allowed all the coaches to focus and see the same things, making it easier for them to come to the same conclusions about a player's skills.

"Pitcher change!" Coach Zambler stomped back through the dugout and onto the field, followed by a grumbling man wearing a Rumbling Hornets uniform.

"I don't understand why you called me here! It's my only day off this week and this"—he pointed toward the guys on the bench without so much as sparing us a glance—"is a *Rookie* tryout."

"If you don't quit complainin', I'll bench you tomorrow. Give you that extra day off you seem to be covetin'," the coach grumbled.

"Zam!" The player gave him an exasperated look.

"One innin'. Pitch one innin', that's all I'm askin'."

"But why?" He protested some more as Coach Zambler walked him to the mound where he replaced the Finches' pitcher.

"It's obvious, isn't it? This is a tryout, and I need to test some players."

"Micheal is a damn good pitcher—"

"Micheal is a damn good *Single-A* pitcher. You, son," Coach Zambler grabbed the player's glove and shoved the ball inside, "are a *damn good pitcher.*"

The guy on the mound sucked in a breath, looking like his head was about to explode. "One inning?"

"One innin'," the Triple-A coach confirmed.

"Fine," he sighed. "But you're buying me dinner. And I expect steak, the expensive kind. And get me some fine wine as well."

"What, you invitin' me to a candlelit dinner or somethin'?"

"No, you're sponsoring a candlelit dinner for me and my wife. Keep in mind, she has a sensitive palate." Coach Zambler rolled his eyes at the man's words. "One inning."

"If I'm payin' for a fancy meal, you better make it two. Don't go easy on 'em," he warned. "I'm not kiddin'. I need to see how some of 'em will do against a pitcher with one foot in the Majors."

"Alright, Zam. Now get off my mound, I need to warm up."

"Take this seriously. You'll get embarrassed if you don't," he cautioned, resigning himself to his prior seat.

I turned to Rafe and whispered in his ear, "You put this team on the list because you knew there'd be an opening for a pitcher on their Triple-A team, didn't you?"

"Well," he shrugged. "It's certainly had an appeal. A hole in the Triple-A roster means that someone's getting moved up from somewhere, meaning there's an opening for me."

I chuckled. "Now I know what you were doing instead of studying for finals last semester."

Rafe smirked. "What can I say? I've got my priorities sorted."

"Your mom would throw a shoe at you if she heard that."

He snorted, "She already did."

The sound of the ball slamming into the catcher's mitt distracted me. I focused on his pitching. "What do you think he's throwing? Ninety-five?"

"Looks about right."

We sat in silence for a minute, watching the Rumbling Hornets' pitcher warm up his arm and get used to the field. Once he was ready to go, he went through the lineup like it was a stale pack of gum. One up, one down. He didn't seem as focused on strikeouts as he was on getting outs in general. He utilized the fielders as best he could, controlling his pitches and forcing batters to hit easy pop-flies and grounders.

Rafe was the first batter he allowed on base—only a single. He didn't get out and that was the important thing. Being on base meant he could still score, which was a plus mark on whatever score sheet they were using to grade us.

I stepped up to the plate, taking a sharp inhale. This guy's demeanor was completely different from the previous pitcher. He oozed confidence, and that was reflected in the pitches he threw over the plate.

I planned on watching a couple of pitches before I committed to a swing, but they had no stats on me and I saw a ball low and outside with my name practically scrawled into the red webbing. Instead of keeping my elbow tight to my side, I reached for it, allowing my grip on the bat to loosen as my body twisted.

With a satisfying smack, the ball sailed into right field. I watched as the pitcher's head turned, following the ball. I rounded first before the ball hit the top of the fence, bouncing past the right fielder in the opposite direction he was running. I was past second by the time he caught up to the fast-rolling ball, and when he finally threw it to the second baseman positioned right behind his base, I was halfway past third. They tried a quick relay, throwing it as hard as he could to the catcher, but I was diving headfirst, stretching my arm out as I slid past the catcher and reached back to tag the plate.

Safe.

I jumped up with the widest smile on my face. I bounced on my feet, Rafe wrapping me in a tight hug—*and I just found a new incentive to hit home runs.*

I glanced at the pitcher; he looked pissed, about ready to throw his glove on the ground. His jaw was tightly clenched, holding in a humorless laugh.

I wanted to flip him off. It was his own fault for underestimating people he'd never seen play before. He called us rookies, but *that* was a rookie mistake. Confidence was necessary, but he was too full of himself to the point it became a flaw. But then again, it was a good pitch. So it may not have been his error, but rather my skill. But hey, two two-run home runs in a row was pretty great.

I unfastened the velcro strap of my batting gloves, flopping onto the bench next to Rafe. We grinned like idiots, high off adrenaline. I shoved my helmet onto the space next to me, chatting with Rafe as I continued to watch the pitcher, curious as to how the other guys would fare against him: a lot of outs and not a lot of running. There was a pause once the pitcher's second inning was over, only allowing one more base hit before he was able to get the last out.

He strutted off the field, unsatisfied with the outcome. "Thank you for this. I appreciate it," Coach Zambler said as the Hornets' pitcher exited through the dugout.

The moment he was out of sight, the coach turned on his heel and looked directly at me. We held awkward eye contact as he closed the distance between us with just a couple of steps. "Ace, grab your gear. I'd like to have a word."

I froze, my mind and body both on pause. Rafe shoved my shoulder and eyed me, snapping me out of it. I quickly pushed all of my stuff back into my bag, leaving the bat. I fumbled getting up as I struggled to grip all my gear, my head spinning as I followed Coach Zambler from the dugout and toward the Community Center.

After going through a set of automatic doors, he led me down several halls. We passed the large gym-like room we'd gathered in before, heading into a smaller room with a circular desk in the center surrounded by several file cabinets.

"Have a seat here. I'll be right back." He gave me a curt smile before closing the door, leaving me by myself.

I set my gear on the ground and awkwardly lowered myself onto a stained, grey-cushioned chair. I tapped my fingers on the wood of the table, making a rhythm to soothe my mind. I would've checked my phone if I had a working one, but even if I did, it wouldn't have been able to distract me from this.

He pulled me away from the group in the middle of the second day of tryouts. That was either really good or extremely bad. Except, I knew I played well—better than most of the others I'd observed— and if they were going to cut me, it'd be at the end of the day when they cut everyone else. They wouldn't pull someone aside just to tell them not to come back the next day. They wouldn't, right?

I chewed on my thumbnail as the fingers from my other hand strummed on the hard surface beneath it.

This has to be a good thing.

There's no way it isn't.

I jumped when a series of knocks erupted on the door.

"Hello?" Lucy Kay peaked her head inside.

"Hello..."

She took a seat across from me, Coach Zambler following behind her and pulling a chair out for himself.

"It's so nice to meet you, Aspen." She held her hand out for me to shake. "I introduced myself earlier, but my name is Lucy Kay and I'm in charge of recruitment for Armada and their affiliate teams."

"Right. Recruitment..." I spoke slowly, the words still processing in my head.

"Let me get straight to the point." The coach's deep voice distracted me from my confusion. "I want you to play on the Rumblin' Hornets for me."

I gulped, my voice coming out uncharacteristically high. "Okay."

"If you were to accept our offer, you'd join others for our Minor League season. Durin' this time, you, as well as all players not already signed to a Major League contract, will play under Armada's Minor League associations. You'll get moved around to different affiliate teams depending on performance."

I nodded along, trying to keep up. Although I already knew most of this, it was a formality in the offer process. When there was a natural pause in his words, I spit out the most important thing in my head. "The pay..." The question came out half-baked.

"The salary changes depending on the level, but on the Rumbling Hornets, you'll be paid about fifteen thousand a year, plus discounted housing accommodations," Lucy chimed in.

"What about medical insurance?"

"We provide both health and life insurance for all our players. If you have any dependents, we'd have to discuss things further with —"

"I don't have any," I interrupted, not needing to hear more. A strange sense of relief pooled in my stomach, knowing I wouldn't have to go into extreme medical debt if... *something* were to happen to me and I *didn't* die. If she'd told me the best option was to stay on my parents' medical insurance until I was twenty-six, I might've been needing that medical insurance sooner than they'd think...

"Alright," Coach Zambler huffed. "It'll be rough. It'll be hard and you might get moved down a level, moved back up, moved back down another two, or dropped. But if you're willin' to put in the effort, work hard, and give it your best, then I think we can expect some great things from you."

"That would be amazing, thank you." I was always awkward when I tried to be formal, not sure how much to smile or how much enthusiasm to pour into my words.

Lucy beamed. "I will get in contact with HR who will then send you everything they will need from you, including a final offer form." She grabbed a blank piece of paper and a pen, handing them to me. "What is the best way to contact you?"

"I'll write down my email. And thank you so much. I really appreciate the opportunity."

"Of course! It was great meeting you, Aspen. I hope to see more of you in the future." Lucy stood and we shook hands once more.

I repeated the motion with Coach Zambler after wiping my hands on my pants to get rid of the sweat, then leaving the room a clammy and jumbled mess.

Once in the hallway, I glanced to my right and noticed Rafe waiting in one of the chairs lining the wall, his leg bouncing up and down.

The reason for his presence dawning on me, I grinned from ear to ear. Hearing the door open, Rafe looked at me with wide eyes. I winked and gave him a thumbs up. His eyes sparkled at the gesture, making him look like a puppy that just got its first bone.

We somehow managed to get on the same Minor League team; I wasn't sure if it was because of talent or sheer luck, but either way, the fact that I'd get to keep playing with Rafe had me buzzing with euphoria.

Chapter Thirty

Aspen

I PACED BACK AND FORTH, waiting for Rafe to exit the room, not knowing what to do with myself.

Was this really happening?

The door creaked and Rafe popped out with the brightest smile on his face.

It was happening.

"Yeah?" I whispered, trying to confirm what I already knew.

He nodded aggressively. "Yeah. Yeah."

I wanted to kiss him right there and then, but I'd managed to hold myself back all these years, so another thirty minutes wouldn't kill me.

I barely lasted the half-hour. The second the door of our motel room closed, my mouth was on his and clothes were being tossed to the side without a care in the world. A foreign sense of confidence from the adrenaline and sheer astonishment of it all tackled my insecurities and pinned them to the ground. But not hard enough— they wormed their way through the tiniest of openings, but that was okay. Rafe made sure I knew it was okay. And that resulted in the best celebratory sex I'd ever had. Well, it was the only celebratory sex I'd had. I kept my shirt on, knowing I didn't have to take that step yet and there'd be plenty of time for me to get there in the future.

We drove back to Rafe's house the next morning, spending the following week filling out paperwork and packing. Everything went smoothly. We moved into the Rumbling Hornets' dorm and spent the summer playing in official games, the season having started in April while we were still in school. Falling into the routine was easy, a necessity for my mind. It kept me grounded, in a way, busy. I worked my ass off to keep myself occupied, to make sure I had something to do at all times. Practice, play, eat, sleep, and repeat. Rafe, being the loving boyfriend he was, joined me on our few days off to keep practicing, because I wouldn't stop. I spent all of July and August like that; baseball, baseball, baseball.

When September first rolled around, we were back in Newhalm and warming up for a game. Home games were my absolute favorite, allowing me to sport a purple jersey with a neon-yellow long-sleeve underneath instead of the inverse, which made us look like a bunch of off-brand highlighters.

The autumn sun beat down on the small field named after one of the team's sponsors, the onlookers flocking to the corners of the stands with slivers of shade. The number of fans reminded me of high school games just after playoffs began; a constantly increasing number of people, but never quite enough to fill the stadium.

Rafe and I were in the bullpen; I was set to start and Rafe would most likely take the mound at the end of the game as a closer if our other pitcher needed relief. Rafe had been pitching a lot lately, so the plan was to give his shoulder a rest. The pitcher I was catching for was someone who'd been moved up from Double-A just three days prior, and we were still a little awkward, just beginning to set the right pace for our play style.

"Ace, come 'ere for a minute." Zam didn't look up from his cell as he called me over.

I tossed the ball back to the pitcher and walked around the bullpen, following the coach through the dugout and into a barren hallway in the stadium.

My cleats clicked on the ground with each step, my leg guards rustling against the white pants underneath. I held my mitt in my right hand and had my mask clutched between my elbow and side.

Zam finally looked up when I asked, "What's up?"

"We have a problem," he huffed, rubbing along his jaw, and going back to his phone, studying a string of text messages.

I straightened my back, his tenseness seeping into me. "What is it?"

"Look, kid. I know you were supposed to play here today—helpin' assimilate the new pitcher and everythin'—but I'm gonna have to send you off."

My mouth parted slightly as I tried to form words, but nothing came out. "You're sending me down?" I struggled to swallow the forming lump in my throat.

"It's an emergency situation," Zam explained. "I know it will be a little stressful but—"

"Where am I going? The Finches?"

He ignored me and kept going. "Your contract was purchased," *Oh, shit! Did I just get fucking traded?* "... and Dan won't leave my phone alone." *Dan? As in Dan Bernstein? Armada's head coach?* "Sheb and Jones are both stuck at an airport because of delays, and Kim, who was on an outright waiver, just got picked up by another club. You and Elias are the only catchers on the forty-man roster, but Elias has food poisonin'. Looks like this is your big break."

I pointed my finger at my chest. "Me?" My voice cracked and rose five octaves. "You're sending me *up?*"

"Yes. You're goin' up. Straight to the main roster."

"Okay... should I leave now or..."

"Yes. If you leave now, you might still have time to warm up there." He told me to grab my gear and then meet our assistant coach in the parking lot.

With a single glance back at Zam, I jogged to the dugout. I took my gear off and shoved it inside my bag, throwing them over my shoulders.

"What did Zam want?" Rafe stood on the dirt, leaning into the dugout. He noticed I'd taken my guards off. "Are you going somewhere?" He furrowed his brows.

"They called me up," my voice rose at the end, making it seem like a question.

The forty-man roster was a confusing mess that even the most dedicated fans didn't understand. Major League teams carried twenty-five players, but in August, they expanded their rosters to forty, keeping up to an additional fifteen players as a type of reserve. The second the month changed to September, the roster became finalized and players from the forty-man roster could be brought up to the main team if someone was injured, demoted, or traded. I had no idea why I hadn't been informed of my contract change, but I could only assume it was a last-minute decision made within the past few days.

"And holy fucking shit, I'm about to play in the Majors and I don't even know who they're playing or what Armada's pitchers throw or how the team works together and I'm going to fuck everything up and ruin this chance. I'm going to bomb this and get sent back down on optional assignment—"

Rafe wrapped his arms around me and squeezed me in a tight hug. I buried my face in his shoulder, taking a deep breath.

"You're too good at baseball to mess anything up," Rafe chuckled, sending a pleasant vibration down my spine. "Just approach it as you would any other game. Don't overthink it. You'll get in there, surprise the shit out of everyone, show them that age isn't everything, and give the other team hell. Right?"

"Right," my voice was muffled.

Rafe pulled away from me. "Aspen, look at me." He placed his hands gently on either side of my face, forcing me to stare into his eyes. "You can do this. I know you can. And *you* know you can."

"I've never played at this high of a level before..."

"So? Aspen, when you play, you either *set the bar* or go above and beyond it to join the others on your team."

I let out a shaky breath, taking a step back. "You're right. Okay. I've got this," I tried to give myself a mini pep talk. "I should probably go."

"Good luck."

"You, too."

I scratched the back of my hand aggressively while walking to the parking lot, and I didn't stop even when I sat in the back of the car. I could only hope that I didn't draw any blood without noticing.

My nerves killed any conversation and congratulatory talk from the assistant coach, my silence converting the mood and sweeping us into a stiff ride.

We pulled into the underground staff-and-players-only garage at Newhalm Park. Rushing out of the car and into the building, I followed him across the charcoal-colored carpet and through cream-colored walls. My ears were filled with the echo of fans filtering into the stadium, the smell of stale office and blasting AC burned my senses, forcing the hair on my arms to stand on edge. His pace increased, and after a couple of minutes, we were practically jogging. He stopped abruptly in the middle of one of the halls in front of a large navy-blue door, grabbed the handle and opened it, sunlight momentarily blinding me.

In front of me was a small set of stairs with only a couple of steps, leading right into the home dugout, which was filled with players and coaches. All heads turned to me and I stood in place, frozen and wide-eyed at the attention.

Someone came rushing toward me, grabbing my hand and shaking it. His eyes darted around and he spoke frantically, in a rush. "Aspen?"

"Yeah," I replied, taking in the packed seating on the opposite side of the field.

"Great, the game is starting in five minutes. Take this," he shoved a jersey into my hands, "change and then get out on the field." He left with no further instruction.

I unfolded the shirt; it was Armada's signature home-game jersey, a solid maroon color with "Armada" written in bold black letters across the chest. The lettering was slightly slanted, the end of the word higher than the beginning with a thick line underneath. It had my name on the back with the number forty-four written below in black with a white outline. I'd requested the same number for every team I'd ever been on; 44 looked like my initials, A.A. When I gave the Rumbling Hornets' manager my preferred jersey number, I'd been told it was already taken. It seemed like that wasn't the case for Armada. I threw off my shirt, ignoring how the purple socks and neon-yellow long-sleeve didn't match. I pulled the jersey over my head, not wasting my time trying to undo the invisible buttons that blended into the reddish purple. I tucked the jersey into my pants haphazardly, practically throwing myself on the bench to put on my catcher's gear.

Someone who looked like a coach walked past me and I rushed a set of words out of my mouth. "Excuse me! Do you have a card with Armada's plays on it? And something I can look at for the other team's batting stats?" *Other team? Damn, who were we even playing?*

All of Armada's starting players had already taken their places on the field, the other team getting ready with their bats in hand. I squinted at their green-and-gold jerseys—the Fort Canton Leopards.

The man seemed surprised at my request, but he nodded and quickly pulled up a player profile list on a tablet. I looked at the numbers and tried my best to memorize them and what balls they did and didn't hit well. I only got to look at it for a minute before I had to put it down. I'd be winging this for the most part. Again.

Just as I finished putting on my Rumbling Hornets chest protector, black with purple lining, a man I recognized as Dan Bernstein approached me. "Aspen Ace?"

"Uhm, yes, sir."

"Okay, good. I know this is last-minute, but thanks for coming."

"The pleasure's mine," I gave him an awkward smile, attempting to talk formally once again.

It was pure luck that Armada and my Triple-A team were both in Newhalm today, because if not, this promotion may never have happened.

"Grab your mitt." He gestured for me to follow him.

I stumbled out of the dugout and followed the coach onto the dirt and up to the pitcher's mound.

"Aspen, this is one of Armada's pitchers, Wendell Rowe." The man was maybe an inch or two shorter than me, but visibly older with a dad bod-esque physique that was still athletic and fit.

"What the hell is this?" Wendell's eyes narrowed in on me.

"It's nice to meet you," I greeted, trying to break the ice.

He ignored my extended hand and glared at Dan Bernstein. "I know you said you were going to bring someone up, but I thought you were going to call Elias! At least most of the guys here have played with him before! What are you thinking, bringing up some random *kid?*"

I bit my tongue, willing myself not to say something that could land me in hot water with the team.

"Oh, stop your whining. Elias is sick. He can't play even if we wanted him to. And Zam personally recommended Aspen for the extended lineup. He was the only choice. So, get over it, suck it up, and play nice. Give him a rundown of your signs." Coach Bernstein ended the conversation and walked off the mound, loudly smacking some gum.

Wendell cleared his throat, composing himself. "Hi, welcome to the Majors, kid."

I suppressed my grumbles at the discreet disrespect, deciding to pick my battles. It'd be of no help to get off on the wrong foot with a pitcher I'd have to continue working with in the future.

The older man simplified the combinations as best as he could and I ran them through my mind, trying to memorize the details to match them with the small card I'd slipped into a band over my wrist.

"Got it?" he asked.

"Yeah, got it."

I couldn't remember a math formula to save my life, but baseball always seemed to stick.

They placed me at the bottom of the batting lineup. I went up three times throughout the game and managed to get two doubles and one single.

We won.

And I helped them do so.

I'd already taken off all my gear, sitting in a daze on the padded bench with my mismatched jersey colors. Most of the guys had already funneled out of the stadium and back to their cars or the bus to take them to the dorm. Although, at their pay level, most of them didn't need to take the dorming option and just rented apartments.

"Ace, you're still here?" Coach Bernstein noticed me sitting by myself at the back of the dugout and took a seat next to me.

"I'm waiting to see if the guy that drove me here was going to come back and give me a ride to my dorm."

"You don't have his number? Wasn't he your coach?"

"I would call, but I don't have a phone..." More like my number was momentarily out of commission.

"You don't? That's kind of an essential here. You'll need it for communication."

I fidgeted in place. "Right, but money's a little tight at the moment..." I had the option of picking three meals a day or a phone plan. I had no hesitation in choosing food.

"Alright." He gripped my shoulder and gave me an understanding smile. "If I have someone bring a van to the Hornets' dorm, do you think you could fit all your stuff in the back?"

"Excuse me?" I sputtered.

"Well, since you're not on the Hornets anymore, you'll probably have to move. They only give discounted housing to players on their current roster, and if you're tight on money, staying there wouldn't be ideal."

My mouth hung open and an uncomfortable feeling settled into my stomach. My current monthly salary barely covered a third of a month's average rent in Newhalm; I wouldn't have enough to stay anywhere until October. Some guys on the Hornets who had families needed to pick up part-time and sometimes even full-time gigs on top of baseball to pay for everything. I wouldn't be able to do that; I'd crash and burn within the first week.

"Armada also has some cheaper living options, so don't stress so much," he laughed at my scrunched-up face. "How about this: I'll get you in contact with someone from management that can help you sort this out. She'll be able to get you the best deal possible."

I dipped my head. "Thank you, Coach Bernstein."

"Call me Dan."

"Right, Dan. Thank you."

"Sure thing, kid. And while you're here, don't let anyone give you shit for being young. They should be impressed you got here at this age, and don't let them forget it." I ignored the hypocrisy of him referring to me as a kid. "I'll make sure to send you the schedule tonight. I'll see you tomorrow." He pulled his phone up to his ear, disappearing into the stadium and leaving me by myself with only the fleeting noise of fans remaining.

I rubbed my face in shock before leaning forward and placing my elbow on my knee and resting my chin on my hand. I looked out into the field, water peeking out from over the top of right-center field. Newhalm Park was right next to the bay. I couldn't hear it, but I could feel the cool air and damp wind despite it being a sunny, cloud-free day.

The door creaked and a young woman walked out; she looked to be in her mid-twenties. Her straight black hair was tied into a slick ponytail that fell just above her waist, a single mole under her left eye. She wore loose jeans with a tucked-in Armada T-shirt. She almost tripped walking up the five steps leading to the dugout, the tips of her high top Converse catching the edge of the step.

"Are you okay?" I asked as I stood to help her.

She brushed a cluster of baby hairs out of her eyes. "Mhmm, yep. I wasn't looking where I was going. Nice to meet you. I'm Piper Zhang, the team manager," she paused and looked up, "not—not the field manager. That's someone else. Dan. Dan's the field manager. I'm more on the PR side. I act as a kind of buffer between the players and things they may need."

I nodded along as she continued.

"Like, for example, I'm the person you would call if you needed to get in contact with someone to deal with social issues. Something like media and damage control for scandals or if you cheated on your wife. I'm like a contact app; I get players connected to the right people."

"Cool..."

"And right now, I'm here to help you move." She began to walk out and I followed her with my bags in hand.

"Right... apparently, I'm being evicted? With no notice?" *Is that legal?*

"There are several options, the most common being renting an apartment. But I understand that rent in this area is kind of absurd and a little unrealistic for most people. Dan mentioned that you were a little tight on cash."

That's putting it lightly.

"You won't need to worry about money so much for now. I was told that you only just got put on the forty-man roster, so you might not know about the salary raise. However, that raise is next to nothing compared to the split pay you'll be getting now on the twenty-five-man roster.

"Armada also has its own dorm building that a lot of the players stay in. It's kind of like college; there are different levels of housing depending on what you choose and pay for."

"I've never been to college."

She hummed, "You can have your own suite, but single rooms are pricey, or you can room with someone else. I personally recommend rooming if you're on a budget, or at least until your contract is settled and you've been on the team long enough to go for something else."

Money talk had me cringing, thinking about my barren wallet with nothing in it but my ID, my debit card linked to an empty pool, and the credit card I was too scared to use.

"The only issue here is the *moving* part of it. I brought a car but..."

I snickered. "Don't sound too upset. All I need is a ride—I can carry all of my stuff in one trip. It won't take long."

"Oh, thank god," she sighed in relief. "Last month, I had to help someone switch from the Single-A to Double-A dorm, which are literally three hours apart, and by the amount of stuff that man had, you'd think he'd been living there his entire life. It was like a new episode of *Hoarding: Buried Alive.*"

"Damn. That sounds awful," I grimaced at the thought. "I don't have much with me. I can fit it all in three bags, and I'm already carrying two of them."

"Right. I heard that you just signed on."

"Yep."

"Must be exciting! You don't see people rising to the Majors so quickly. Two months? Even the best scouted and drafted players usually spend a couple of years in the Minors."

"There are always exceptions."

"True."

"If I'd played for a college, I'd probably be drafted in a couple of years, anyway. Although I don't know which team it'd be for."

"This is me." She unlocked her car, the double flashing light illuminating the concrete wall in front of the small, silver SUV. She opened the trunk and I tossed my bags inside.

Once seated and buckled, she pulled out of the garage and began our drive to the Rumbling Hornets' dorm. It was on the opposite side of Newhalm and I hadn't really gauged how much of the hour-long travel time could be attributed to atrocious traffic.

"Sometime within the next few days, you'll receive the rest of your Armada gear. There'll be three jerseys. The maroon one you're already wearing, a black one, and a grey as well. You'll receive an email with an attached PDF of all the things Armada players are allowed to wear so you can pick undershirts, gear, and other apparel you'd like for games and practices."

"Good to know. I felt ridiculous wearing neon-yellow—I stuck out like a sore thumb."

"Really? Besides the color difference, I thought you blended in pretty well with the team."

I felt a blush crawling up my neck at her words. I didn't fit in with the Cedar Heights team, and I wasn't close with the club I played for, but god, I wanted to feel a sense of belonging here.

Piper waited in the car while I went to go pack, getting my new housing situation set up.

Once inside, I went straight to Rafe's room and knocked on the door, hoping he was already back from his game. He opened up with nothing but a towel wrapped around his waist, his hair dripping wet.

"How'd your game go?" I asked as he let me inside, closing the door behind me.

"We won. The new guy did good. I didn't need to go in." He moved to grab a change of clothes. My eyes raked down his body as he dropped his towel. "But enough about me, I want to hear about your game." Rafe slipped on a pair of boxers and looked me in the eyes. "So?"

I tried to fight the smile on my face, but Rafe caught on, and soon enough, he was hugging me, wrapping his arms just below my butt and lifting me into the air.

I giggled and brushed my fingers through his black locks.

"Holy shit!" He set me down.

"I know!"

"You actually did it!"

"I know!!"

"Oh my god, Aspen! You're a Major Leaguer!"

"I know, I know," I laughed. "They're having me move today. Literally no warning. I actually came here to grab my stuff, I'm supposed to move into Armada's dorm."

"When do you need to leave? If you have time, we could—"

"Now. I'm supposed to be leaving now. Someone's in the parking lot waiting, so I need to get a move on. So hurry up and put some clothes on." I pecked him on the lips and swiftly left the room.

I went through all the drawers in my small closet-sized room, grabbing my clothes and toiletries and shoving them into my duffle bag. It took less than ten minutes to compile everything I owned—I didn't know if that was efficient or kind of sad.

Rafe entered through my opened door and watched as I zipped everything up. "I got some news after the game. Me and a couple other guys are on the forty-man roster, too. If something happens, I might get moved up."

"You better." I glanced at the clock and sighed, "I should go." I shoved my catcher's bag into Rafe's arms. "Help me carry it to the car."

We met Piper out front and she popped the trunk, Rafe and I not-so-gently placing my stuff inside.

I want to hug him so badly. I didn't know when we'd both have a day off, and I didn't know when I'd see him next. Would it be next weekend? Next month? Would he drive to come to see me? Would we crash at each other's dorms?

I gave him a look that told him all I wanted was a smothering bear hug, but here, in public, all he could do was give me a reassuring nod, his eyes telling me he wanted to do the same.

I slid into the passenger seat and watched Rafe through the side mirror; he gave me a small wave before the car turned the corner. Traffic was heavier now since it was getting closer to rush hour, but once we pulled in front of the tall building, dread began to seep in. A roommate meant that I'd have to change in the bathroom, even in my own room. And if he found out I was gay and tried to hurt me while I was asleep... there were a lot of ways this could go south.

She made a beeline to the front desk in the middle of the lobby. It wasn't as fancy as I'd imagined; it felt like a normal apartment complex, just five times larger. Her shoes squeaked against the chevron tiles, drawing the attention of the person manning the front counter. Once Piper checked me in, I was handed a thick packet: my lease agreement.

"Do I need to put down a deposit," I leaned toward Piper, whispering not-so-quietly, "because it will take some time before I can get my deposit back from the Hornets' dorm, and I don't have enough to pay for another until then."

"You can hold off on the deposit for a bit, although you might get spammed with emails asking for payment."

"Is that supposed to be reassuring? And aren't I supposed to make a deposit *before* I move in?"

She waved me off. "Semantics."

If my salary was going to see the major increase I was thinking it would, I could stop rationing my money for food and sign up for a phone plan. Maybe the wants no longer had to be optional in order to afford the needs.

Afterward, I was handed a slip of paper with a series of codes on it. Room number and passcode, wifi, and building map. Giving all residents access to a gym, pool, and dining hall, the dorm was a noticeable step up from the Rumbling Hornets' dorm.

"Let's knock so we don't scare the shit out of your roommate for just barging in. I really don't want to walk in on another buck-ass naked married man."

I laughed, "Sounds like you've got a story there."

"Ugh, don't even get me started. I'd rather burn my eyes out than think of that hairy motherfu—" she cleared her throat. "Let's just say there's an image seared into my brain that I could've gone a lifetime without."

"I could also go a lifetime without seeing my new teammate naked." I knocked on the door.

The handle clicked and slowly turned, the head of a young man peeking out. "Hello?"

"Cameron, hi! It's nice to see you again," she beamed.

"Hey, Piper," he gave her a heart-eyed smile. "How's it going?"

"You just got a new roomie! Congratulations! Now you'll both get to make up for the college dorm experience you oh-so sadly missed out on!"

"You're being sarcastic, right?" He furrowed his brows, his tone light and playful.

"Nope!" She turned to me, taking a card out of her pocket and placing it on top of the duffle stacked in my arms. "Take that, it has my number if you need anything. I'll see you boys at the next team picnic!" Piper left me awkwardly standing in front of the ajar door.

"Uhm, hi," I greeted.

"Right... hi." Cameron opened the door to let me inside. "You can take the bed next to the window."

"Thanks." I threw my duffle on the bed and placed my baseball bag, covered in dirt and dust, on the carpet.

I turned around to see the brown-haired male looking at me with a scrutinizing gaze. Something finally clicked, "Oh! You're the catcher from today!"

I looked down, realizing I was still in uniform. "Yeah, that was me. I didn't get a chance to introduce myself earlier. I'm Aspen."

He reached out to shake my hand. "Cameron Cuff."

"Piper mentioned something about college..." I attempted to make conversation.

"Yeah. I lived at home while I played in college, and then I got drafted after my second year. I'm twenty-one now, so I've been playing in the Majors for about two years. I was just traded to Armada in the spring. What about you?"

"I just graduated high school. I got in through tryouts a couple months ago."

Cameron let out a long whistle. "Damn. And I thought I started young."

Chapter Thirty-One

Aspen

"So this is the newborn baby catcher Dan decided to adopt?" Zander Sheb pulled away from the line of guys as we shook hands with the other team.

"He's eighteen," Cameron defended.

"Yes. A baby. That's what I said, Cam."

"Zander's right. Eighteen's as fresh as it gets 'round here." I recognized the voice as Daunte Walker; he'd been Armada's primary left fielder for over half a decade.

"I'm eighteen, but I still managed to get here, didn't I? And Cam started when he was what? Nineteen?"

"Maybe, but you're the youngest here, making you the baby," Zander teased.

"Then should I be calling you grandpa?" I fired back.

He chuckled, "I'm not *that* old."

"But in *my newborn eyes...*" I got several laughs from surrounding players.

"So, fresh outta hell, huh?" Daunte asked as we grabbed our bags from the dugout and started walking toward the locker room.

"What?"

"Hell. High school. My lil' bro uses the words interchangeably."

I grumbled at that. "I do, too."

"Aw, shit, Daunte, don't start with your little brother rants again." Cam turned to me. "He's obsessed with high school baseball because his kid brother plays. Daunte probably knows more about high school leagues than the one he's been playing in for the last fifteen years."

"Shut the hell up, Cam! My brother's a champion! A goddamn champion!"

"Yes, yes. His school won Nationals this year. We know," Wendell huffed like he'd heard the story a million times.

"Aye, you just graduated, right? Maybe you've played them. He goes to Springfield."

"Oh, yeah. I think I've played them. I'm not really sure, there are a lot of Springfields, so..."

"He was so surprised when they won States. Called me crying like a baby. Kept talking about how his team was supposed to lose to the top-seeded team, but that school ended up losing in the second round because their pitcher and catcher weren't there."

His words had me turning my head. "That sounds awfully familiar."

"Oh? You heard about it too? Well, my bro kept saying it was a really big deal and if you played, you'd probably have heard it, huh? Apparently, the guys that dropped out played on that 18U club team that's won Nationals three years in a row," Daunte whistled.

I held back a snicker. "Wow, that catcher must be amazing."

"I've seen a couple of his highlight reels, and I gotta say, he's real fun to watch play."

"Thanks! I appreciate it, man." I slapped him on the shoulder with a dopey smile, enjoying the confused expression on his face.

"What?"

"That school your brother was talking about, Cedar Heights, right?"

"Yeah, how'd you know?"

I raised a brow, smirking. "I played for Cedar Heights."

"Seriously?! My brother would be so excited to hear we're playing on the same team. The kid was short-circuiting trying to figure out what happened to the wonder kid catcher. Probably never would've guessed you were here instead."

"I actually had some issues with some players on the team and quit before States started." I was using the term "quit," loosely. "And our pitcher is here, too."

"Seems like y'all didn't need that national title since you both ended up in the Majors right outta high school, anyway."

Our conversation slowed as I followed behind the team while they funneled into the locker room, right on Daunte's tail. It was my first time in Armada's locker room, although I'd been in other Major League and college stadiums for some big tournaments in the past.

The lockers were similar to cubbies, lining the left and adjacent wall. I glanced around, noticing all the players going to a rectangular locker with their last name on a black-and-white placard at the top. It wasn't hard to find mine, the first one on the left; they were in alphabetical order. The far right of the room contained the showers, a line of individual white boxes that were several steps up from my school's showers, but were clearly meant for nothing more than a quick rinse to rid oneself of the stench of sweat.

Although I didn't catch today since Zander was back, Dan had me pinch-running for Wendell. I enjoyed myself, diving and getting dirty. I even had some sand in my hair from when my helmet flew off as I jumped headfirst into third base, trying to beat the baseman to the bag. I was safe... mostly because I rushed into him so hard it was practically a tackle, but I got him to drop the ball from his glove, so...

The guys around me all undressed, heading to the showers half-naked, I'd work around that, I always did. I grabbed a fresh towel from a pile, taking the clean set of clothes I'd brought and walking to a stall in the middle. The only thing separating me from them was a flimsy curtain, but I'd make do. I hung my towel and clothes, clean and dirty, over the bar holding up the drape. I hastily made use of the large containers of soap stored on a metal tray screwed into the wall, scrubbing my body while burning water trailed down my back. The steam was palpable and made it difficult to breathe—just how I liked it.

I washed my face, eyes still squeezed shut when my hand flailed around, looking for the handle to turn off the stream of water. I shook my head back and forth, rubbing at my sensitive eyes, the feeling of foreign liquid making them itch. Because of that, when I first turned around to grab my towel, I thought it may have blended in with the walls due to my blurry vision, but as my pupils returned to normal, none of my stuff was on the bar.

I peeked my head out of the side of the curtain to see if it'd fallen on the ground; it hadn't.

I looked from side to side. I could still hear water running, but no one was walking back toward the main room, so I shouted, "Did someone take my towel?"

There were snickers in the background but no response. *How juvenile.*

"Seriously, guys. Can I have my stuff back?" I tried to sound nonchalant, but there was a slight ringing in my ears. I knew exactly what it was, but I tried to ignore it, push it down deep below the surface.

My fingers subconsciously picked at their ridges and the pace of my blinking awkwardly increased. I stood in silence, my arms beginning to tremble. *Now was not the time for this, Aspen.*

"Hey, Ace! What's taking you so long in there?" Wendell implied something dirty and I winced. That line of thought was exactly what had Devin swinging a bat at my skull.

I opted out of picking at my nails and instead began to harshly rub at the skin of my forearms, pacing the small distance of the ever-shrinking cube. I felt trapped; they didn't actually expect me to go out there naked, did they? They'd see everything, not just my—

I couldn't *breathe*.

I tried to suck air into my lungs, but it got caught at the top of my throat. My right hand fell to the tiled wall next to me in an attempt to hold myself up, but it just slipped down.

"Don't be a wuss!" someone yelled, their voice echoing through the locker room.

"He must have a small dick."

Stopstopstop.

"Gonna call mommy and daddy to come save their little kid?"

Too much laughing.

Too much noise.

They were joking. *It was just a joke.*

It wasn't funny.

"Come on, guys, cut him some slack." There was a string of people calling Cam a "buzzkill" telling him he was "ruining their fun."

Footsteps approached, soon followed by a towel flying over the top of my stall. I wanted to thank Cam, but my voice wasn't working.

And it was only a towel, just big enough to cover what my underwear hid.

Only one thing pumped through my mind, one single thought: *scars.*

Scars.

Scars.

Scars.

Everywhere. *All over.*

There was no way to hide it.

Why couldn't they just give me back my fucking clothes??

I snatched the towel before someone else could take it, tightly wrapping it around my waist and securing it so it wouldn't fall.

I couldn't go out there. *Everyone would see.*

My fingers clawed at my throat. *Why is it so hard to breathe?*

Why was it *always* so hard to *breathe?*

Why did this keep happening to me? Why was it always me?

Why couldn't I move on? Why does everything Alex did keep coming back? Why wouldn't it all just leave me alone??

Whywhywhy?

"Aspen, what are you doing? If you don't hurry up, you'll miss the shuttle," Cam spoke.

The bus to the dorms... fuck! All I wanted to do was curl up in my bed—*my bed.*

Where was my bed? The mattress I'd slept in for a total of one night couldn't count, especially not when I was sharing the room with a stranger. No, not sharing, I was a guest. He was there first and I was the one on a short-term contract. I'd be the one leaving if they cut me from the team.

Rafe's bed? It was practically mine, *except it wasn't.*

Home. I wanted my bed at home. I wanted to pull *my* blankets over my head. I wanted to soak in the warmth of *my* heavy comforter. I wanted to return to the only place that had offered me any semblance of comfort for years. But it wasn't *my* bed anymore. Maybe before, but not now.

Where did that leave me?

Where was I supposed to go if I didn't *even have a bed?*

I looked down and wrapped my arms around my waist. I wanted to hide it. I'd always hid it.

I covered the scars on my abdomen with my forearms as best I could, pressing the entire length of my arms into my skin in an attempt to hide the marks. *They'd still see.*

With a shaky hand, I pulled the curtain open. My hair dripped into my eyes as I kept my head down, walking right past the eyes I knew were glued to me. Maybe curious as to why I was so quiet at first, but now most certainly drawn to the scars on my back.

I clenched my teeth as I approached my locker. None of my clothes were there.

"Where's my stuff?" My voice cracked, showing so much more vulnerability than I wished.

A finger pointed toward an abandoned bench. I bundled the clothes in my arms, trying to get them all into my locker so I could sort my uniform from my change of clothes. I couldn't hide the insides of my arms and move everything all at once, resulting in all my clothes dropping to the floor at the foot of my locker.

Fuck! I hit the side of the cubby with my hand, leaving it resting above while I tried to suck in air.

For the first time, I looked up. Half of the team was gone, but the other half stared at me like I was a zoo animal on display.

"What are you all looking at?" I seethed at their silent response. "Uncomfortable? Well, it's your own damn fault." *I tried to change in private...*

I bent down to grab my clothes, throwing them into my locker. I shrugged on my boxers before dropping my towel—they could probably see the thick, angry lines on my thighs and stomach too...

I slipped into a loose, long-sleeved shirt and pulled up a pair of Rafe's shorts. I looked at no one as I left. I couldn't tell if I was going to cry, but a panic attack was bubbling inside of me.

Why can't I catch a break?

I sat on my bed. No, not my bed. A bed. I sat on the edge of a bed and stared at the wall, the plain beige helping to dull the thoughts in my mind.

Things were better now. Things were *different.* So *why?* Why was I still like this? Why was I still so ashamed? Still so scared of everyone and everything?

Why did I have to live like this?

The door squeaked, Cam shuffling in with his backpack; we had practice tomorrow, so we all left our baseball gear in the locker room. Our next game would be the following day at a different stadium, hours away.

"Hey."

I didn't respond

"Earlier..." he spoke hesitantly. "The guys were just trying to play a harmless joke. It wasn't to single you out. They haze everyone when they first come on, happened to me a couple months ago. I got locked in a supply closet and missed my surgery to get my wisdom teeth removed; I'm still trying to reschedule it. They, uhm, they wouldn't have done it if they knew—"

I stopped him there. "Can I borrow your phone?" My voice was raspy, still fighting against an ever-so-present lump threatening to spill tears from my eyes any second.

"Yeah. Yeah, sure. Here." He handed me the device. "What do you need it for?"

"Just calling a friend real quick." I kept my sentence short, not in the mood to talk. Or be here. Or be awake... or alive...

My foot shamelessly tapped against the carpet, my knee bouncing up and down as my fingers pinched the bridge of my nose.

"Hello?" came Rafe's voice.

"Hey..."

"Aspen? Did you get a new number—"

"Can you please pick me up?" My voice broke, my panic getting closer and closer to the surface. Soon, it'd break free. And then it'd break the skin on my wrists.

"Yeah, of course." I could hear him grabbing his keys in the background, his door slamming shut. "Where are you?"

"My dorm."

"Aspen, what's wrong? You're scaring me."

"I just... can I stay at yours tonight?"

"You can stay whenever you want." He didn't press his previous question.

I glanced back at Cam, knowing he was watching me, listening. I tried to pretend he wasn't there, my voice coming out in a hoarse whisper. "*I just—I feel like I might do something I'll regret...*"

Chapter Thirty-Two

Aspen

NOTHING, AND I MEAN *NOTHING,* was more awkward than being surrounded by a bunch of grown men too prideful to apologize, but visibly guilty. They didn't want to be here, and neither did I. It felt like I'd ostracized myself from yet another team. Yay me.

Wonderful, absolutely fucking wonderful. Scars exposed. Mental breakdown witnessed. And admitted danger of relapse. Between all the players on Armada, every individual had seen one to three of those things. Lovely.

Some of them avoided me at all costs, like they were worried I wanted to get back at them for pulling a shitty prank. Others, like Daunter and Zander, moved on like nothing had happened, making me thankful that at least some of them were mature enough to know when certain things should be left alone.

What caught me off guard was the end of the high-tension practice when Wendell took me to the side before I left, shyly apologizing for being a dick. My nonconfrontational self accepted his words, of course. Because even if it still wasn't okay—if *I* wasn't okay—I could certainly pretend like it was. For the team's sake, and to protect myself from more issues, I could act like it was water under the bridge. No harm, no foul. Except there was harm and what they did was most certainly a foul, but I'd just leave it as having a bad ref that favored one side over the other. I could be okay with that; it wasn't my fault, and it wasn't anyone else's either. I was simply unlucky with the cards I'd been dealt. I'd coped with it in the past, with things not going my way and keeping my mouth shut, and I could continue to do so for however long and for whatever reasons I pleased.

And at the end of the day, the general consensus was that yesterday didn't happen. No one made any mistakes, and no one saw anything they shouldn't have. I wasn't sure if I liked that or not, but it was fine. It was always fine.

"You think he's done for the season?" Zander perched his foot on the bench, untying the laces of his cleats.

"Probably more than just this season. You don't recover from something like that in just a year. The physical therapy will definitely take up next season too." Cam frowned.

"What happened?" I asked, appearing out of the bathroom stall in a fresh set of clothes with only a couple of eavesdropped sentences for context.

"Owen got put on the sixty-day injured list," Zander supplied.

"He was a sidearm pitcher, so I can't say I'm surprised, but I thought he had another few years before he'd need another elbow surgery," Daunte said.

"I didn't see him yesterday..." I trailed off, confused.

Daunte explained, "Happened last week."

"Does that mean there's an open spot for a pitcher?" I probably shouldn't have sounded so enthusiastic at the mention of another player's serious injury, but my mind went straight to one potential outcome in particular and it sent a spike of excitement through my gut, bypassing my filter.

Zander raised an eyebrow and looked away. "Probably."

That sounded an awful lot like a "yes" to me. I'd take it.

I had Rafe on the phone, hunched over the tall counter attached to the side of our kitchen, getting an ample view into the room that smelled like Cam's awful attempt at making brownies.

Rafe had gotten moved up last week with a full sit-down promotional talk with coaches, HR, and lawyers present after hitting a grand slam into the water behind the park... and on account of Owen's injury opening up a slot. Rafe saw the opportunity and capitalized on it. He took the same housing deal as me, on a budget nearly as tight as mine, and moved in with a roommate. He considered sharing an apartment with me, but thinking about spending all that money—that we didn't even have yet—to live in a city we'd barely be present in, was more than off-putting. Only half of our games would be played in Newhalm, the other half spent in different cities around the country for away games.

Cameron called my name from his bed across the room.

"Hold on a sec, Rafe." I pulled my phone from my ear as I craned my neck to see Cam lacing up his shoes.

"I'm going to get some drinks with the guys, have a little fun before we hit the road."

They'd done this a few times, even inviting me in the beginning, saying they'd buy something for me since I was only eighteen. But I'd refused the second I heard "alcohol."

"What time do you think you'll be back?" If he was coming early enough, I could wait to go to bed so he wouldn't wake me up trying to sneak in.

"I probably won't be, if you catch my drift." He winked.

And that was how I knew where they were going: a nightclub.

"Alright, see you tomorrow, then." I gave him a small wave as he grabbed his things and slipped out the door.

I turned back to my phone, putting it on speaker. "Hear that?"

"Your roommate's going to be gone all night?" There was a mischievous tint to his voice.

"Come over?"

A string of laughter erupted from the other end of the line, footsteps already thumping down the hall and stopping right in front of my door.

I grabbed the handle, allowing Rafe just enough room to step inside before I pushed him against the door, closing it in the process. His phone fell from his hand and landed on the ground, forgotten.

My mouth was on his within seconds, a slow, satisfied hum making its way up Rafe's throat. I moved to his jaw, nipping at the skin with my teeth. Rafe's fingers swept through my hair, holding me still as he forcefully removed my mouth and pressed a harsh kiss to my lips. We stumbled backward until the side of my leg hit the bed. The moment my head fell onto the middle of the mattress, Rafe was clambering over me.

"God, you look so beautiful like this," Rafe whispered as his hands wandered south.

"Like what? On my back?"

"Hmm. That, too." He pressed a light kiss against my jaw. "But I'm talking about your face..." Another kiss on my dimple. "How you get all flushed." A soft press of his lips against my eye. "The way your skin heats up at my touch." He lifted his face mere inches from mine, an adoring smile overtaking his features before he tenderly pressed his mouth against my forehead. "But most of all, the way your eyes light up like they have everything they've ever wanted in life. Like they're *truly happy.*"

I dreamed of stupefying things that night. A world where I wasn't—legally speaking—homeless. Where I had unlimited food and the clothes on my back were my own, not stolen from Rafe's closet. Where no one laid a finger on me with the intent to harm, and talk of gay and queer people ranged nearly nonexistant to quiet support in passing conversations. Where my best friend stayed by my side, offering limitless love and support. Where I wasn't surrounded by constant hate and fear, and had the genuine opportunity to enjoy what life had to offer. A world where everything was falling into place.

———

I woke up to the sound of *Angry Birds* and hushed cursing. Even though I hadn't opened my eyes, I knew it was bright out. Instead of the black solace my eyelids were supposed to offer, the insides were painted a blinding orange, the early morning sun assaulting my face. I groaned and turned my head the other direction, burying my nose in the crook of Rafe's neck.

I listened to his heartbeat, hoping the calm, sleeping beat would lull me back into unconsciousness.

But then my mind registered that Rafe was still asleep.

Yet the sounds of video games and frustration filled the room.

My heart leapt in my chest and I reluctantly peeled my eyes open. My head shot up and looked directly at the source of the noise. "Cam?"

Oh, shit.

"Mornin', Aspen. Have a fun night? I know I did, but I'm starting to think it wasn't nearly as great as yours," he chuckled, comfortably tucked into his bed.

"What?" My voice cracked.

"I'm not the cleanest guy myself, but can I at least ask you to try and get your condoms in the trash? I almost stepped on one at like four a.m."

Rafe stirred at the talking, his morning voice hoarse and rough. "What's wrong?"

"Mornin', Rafe." Cam waved as Rafe craned his neck to see who was in the bed behind him.

Rafe muttered a quiet, "Fuck," before rubbing his eyes and sitting up. The cover fell past his torso and revealed the excessive number of hickeys he'd gotten last night.

"So you two…" Cam crossed his two fingers and then proceeded to use his index finger and thumb to make a circle while a finger from his other hand entered and exited. "You two fuck buddies?"

I blinked rapidly, unable to process his calm. "No, uhm—we started dating in high school…"

"Oh, right! I remember you saying you two were best friends or something." Cam glanced back at his phone. "I hate this game. Can't get past this damn level." He shook his head in disapproval.

"You—you don't care that we're…" I trailed off, my words implying all they needed to.

"Dating? Why would that matter?" Cam didn't look up, but he did look about ready to throw his phone at the wall.

"Because, we're both guys… uhm, I don't know. Forget it." If he had no qualms, I had no reason to dig deeper.

My roommate swore, flipping his phone onto the bottom of his bed. "This is what I get for re-downloading all the games I used to play. I should just go back to *Cut The Rope* and *Doodle Jump*. Oh, right!" Cam looked at us. "I do have a couple of rules for… *this*." He gestured to Rafe and me.

I frowned, my heart rate picking up.

"Number one. Do not, under any circumstances, ever, have sex on my bed." Cam shuddered. "Ever. And number two. If you want some space to do whatever, give me a heads-up so I don't walk in on anyone with their dick out."

"That's it?" Rafe asked.

"Sure. Unless something else comes up."

"You won't—you won't tell anyone about this, right?" I hesitated to ask.

"Fear not, my closeted companions, your secret's safe with me."

Chapter Thirty-Three

Aspen

My face set into a deep frown as Rafe continued to explain things to me. I knew he was right, but leaving was harder than it should've been. I was doing better, but sometimes that wasn't enough.

"I know, Aspen, I know, but my roommate's coming back tonight. You *know* why you can't stay."

"The prick should've stayed with his family for another week," I mumbled. "Who travels to a different country and only stays two days??"

"It's been a couple days now. Cam probably won't be taking that medicine anymore. I didn't even need any after I got my wisdom teeth out."

Yeah? Well, I finished the whole damn bottle...

"You can stay here as long as you want, hell, you can keep sleeping here, but one of us would need to sleep on the floor. I can get some pillows and blankets from your room and put together a little makeshift cot." Rafe rubbed the back of his neck. He was trying to find a solution, but I didn't like any of his answers. "I think you should go back." I opened my mouth to protest, but Rafe continued. "If it's too hard, just call me. Come back here. I'm not going anywhere."

"Okay... I'm sure it'll be fine, I'm just overreacting."

"You're not overreacting. But avoiding Cam like this isn't going to help."

I sighed. "I should probably go before your roommate gets here. I'll see you tomorrow."

"I love you, and text me how it goes."

"I will, and love you, too." I stepped into the hallway. The carpet quickly began to stretch, a couple of doors turning into dozens and then hundreds. My head spun and I placed a hand over my eyes.

My finger hovered against the keypad. I clenched my teeth; *what I wouldn't give for a little liquid courage right about now.*

I typed in the code, giving way to a quiet beep as the door unlocked.

"Aspen?" Cam seemed surprised to see me.

I stepped past his bed, barely sparing him a glance. "Hey."

"Where've you been? Haven't seen you since before I had surgery." His words were slurred, cluing me in that he still had gauze shoved into the back of his mouth and most likely looked like a chipmunk.

"I was with Rafe."

A look of understanding dawned on him. "Ah. Gotcha." He tried to wink, but his face was still too numb and I was rewarded with an aggressive blink.

I headed to the bathroom, noticing the orange-and-white bottle displayed for all to see on the counter. I sucked in a breath, tightly closing my eyes. I took care of my business in the dark; not seeing it made things easier, but simply knowing it was there was enough to remind me of things I'd rather not think about.

The last time I took something like that, I almost died in a motel, loathing everyone and everything. *Including myself.*

I couldn't do this.

THE SMILE HAS LEFT YOUR EYES   333

I burst out of the bathroom and rushed the length of the room, getting ready to fly through the door.

"Where're you going? Something wrong?" Cam was alarmed by my panicked attempt at escape.

"I-I'm going back to Rafe's room. I'm going to spend a few more days there."

Worry etched itself into Cam's eyes as he got out of bed and moved toward me. I froze with my hand holding the door handle and eyes locked on my unmoving limb. *Why can't I turn it?* My heart picked up in my chest.

"Aspen, are you okay?" He pulled the gauze out of his mouth to make sure I could understand him, his cheeks considerably slimmer.

"Y-yeah. I'm fine-fine."

"Dude, what's wrong? You're getting really pale." He grabbed my shoulders. "Here, sit down for a sec." Cam guided me to the chair at one of the desks in the room. "Do you want me to get you some water or crackers? I think we have some orange juice in the fridge, too—"

"No. I-I'm al-r-right." My hand rested on my thigh and the tips of my fingers itched. My nails subconsciously worked at the skin just above my knees, picking and scratching.

"You're clearly not." He whipped his head around to look at his bed. "I'm calling Rafe." He rustled through his sheets, looking for his phone.

My voice cracked. "I'm okay. You d-don't need to call him."

He peered at me with a skeptical look, hesitating before he straightened himself out. "You were jittery when you walked in, but now you're stuttering and you look like you're about to pass out. If you don't want me to get Rafe, I don't know what to do."

"You don't need to do anything," I sighed, rubbing my hands over my face roughly. "I just... could you do me a favor?"

"Yeah, of course."

"The prescription meds you got from your dentist—hydrocodone or Vicodin or whatever—could you, uhm..." I gulped, choking on the words. "C-could you keep them somewhere else? A-and I know it's inconvenient, but if you kept them in some-someone else's room or y-your lock-locker, I'd really appreciate it..." I fidgeted with my hands, unable to look up to meet Cam's eyes.

"You're like this because of... *opioids?*" I couldn't tell if his tone held severe judgment or something else.

I glanced up at Cam, meeting his eyes before quickly dropping mine again. "Look, I've been clean for a few months now. A-and I'm not saying I'm going to steal them or take any, okay? It's just hard being around it. Brings up some not-so-fun memories."

"I'll toss them, it's not a problem. I don't need them anyway, ibuprofen has been doing the trick." My hands shook and I tried to keep my breathing even as Cam pulled up a chair next to mine. We sat in silence for a minute before he spoke. "Does this have to do with the scars? I didn't mean to see them, but then the locker room thing happened... you don't need to answer if it makes you uncomfortable. I'm not trying to pry."

"No, I uhm, yeah. It's related, I guess. My life was kind of a shitshow. Things have only been kind of okay for about four months now. I'm still... *working* on some things."

"This is why you reacted so badly when I offered to buy you drinks... sorry..."

"It's fine. It's not like I go around advertising that I'm a recovering addict."

"What happened?"

Just like the night I was drunk and high, confessing my darkest secrets to Isa, I felt a cloudy buzz giving me the courage to let the words fall from my mouth. Only this time, I knew Cam wasn't going to turn on me. "Oh, you know, just the standard homophobia, blackmail, and attempted murder."

The room stilled and Cam stared at me, mouth agape with a look of horror. "Excuse me?"

I gave him a brief description of the shit my old teammates pulled, being vague and avoiding descriptive details. After, Cam threw the bottle away, either in someone else's room or a public trash can. He shoved gauze back into his mouth and crawled into bed. He fell asleep before I could even thank him.

I was about to join Cam, thinking he had the right idea in taking a nap, but my phone vibrated. It was Daunte in Armada's group chat, his text directed at me. "Yo, Aspen! Get your ass down to the common room. Got your first batch of fan mail."

Some of the other guys chimed in as well, Zander making another jab at my age. "Aww, baby's all grown up!"

I rolled my eyes, my thumbs quickly tapping the screen of my phone as I made my way toward the first floor. "I'm not even the youngest anymore. Rafe is."

This time, it was my boyfriend who replied. "Not my fault you never lost the baby fat on your cheeks."

"Fuck you," I shot out.

I got a separate message from Rafe, not on the group chat. "If you insist," with a winking emoji at the end.

I laughed, shaking my head as I walked into the common room directly connected to the front lobby. In the center was a large, circular table where a couple of guys were gathered, sifting through lumps of envelopes.

"Look who finally showed his face. Here ya go, Mr. Popular." Daunte handed me a large stack of what I'd guess was at least twenty letters. "You'll be getting more and more every day, and honestly, we don't look at most of them. But the first time's always fun."

I gratefully accepted the colorful array of papers, dumping them next to Rafe where he'd already started opening and reading some of his. "Anything interesting?" I asked.

"Mostly just appreciation notes and tips from baseball dads on how I can 'improve.' Oh, but get this!" Rafe picked up an opened envelope from inside a large box he'd set apart from the rest, pulling a full canvas out and showing me a painting of the two of us. It was from the perspective of a fan sitting right behind the backstop. It was probably based on a picture; the ball had just released from Rafe's hand, my glove steady and waiting for its arrival.

"It looks like professional work. Something people would commission an artist for."

"The letter that said she's a painter and loves creating things related to baseball in her free time. I can't believe she sent this. I'm going to hang it up."

"You should send a picture of it to your parents, they'd love it." After going through a couple of letters of my own, I snorted, "You get a whole damn masterpiece meanwhile I get poorly drawn stick figures." It was from a young boy, so I wasn't expecting much. The legs were drawn too far up the line for the back, giving the figures mini-dicks. The action itself was nice, but I was a little jealous of Rafe.

"No love letters yet?" Daunte cackled from a lounge chair in the corner, a thick book in hand.

"Ha ha, very funny." I rolled my eyes, flipping through the envelopes to figure out which to open next, hoping one would catch my eye.

"Just wait until you get yourself a stalker... sending packages with dead animals and bloody tampons," Wendell whispered the last part, a haunted look consuming his face.

I turned to Rafe, mouthing *what the fuck.* He shrugged, a little disturbed.

A lavender envelope turned my thoughts. It was familiar, eerily so. I bit my lip, hoping it wasn't what I thought it was.

I didn't know why I bothered with thoughts like that. I'd always known things like hope were fucking useless. My hand clamped onto the stiff paper, crumpling it. My lungs felt constricted in my chest, a tightness wrapping its way around my heart.

"What's wrong?" Rafe's gentle hand on my arm did little to comfort me.

"Nothing," I muttered, stomping out of the room and shoving the letter into the trash can.

Today has been a complete shitshow.

I tried to ignore the rustling of the trash bag followed by an "Oh, shit" from Rafe.

"Who's it from?" someone asked.

"Just, uh, someone Aspen cut ties with a while ago."

A while? Try four months. And *she* cut ties with *me*. My life was spiraling and she let that bastard kick me out. And right when I was starting to get better, just learning to function like a normal person, she sent me a letter, trying to drag me back in.

I didn't need to hear more of their conversation, so I left. Anything my mom had to say to me was surely full of shit, therefore it belonged in the trash.

Rafe caught up to me right as the elevator doors were about to close. He shoved his hand over the drifting metal door, causing it to recede into the wall. He calmly entered the small box, standing next to me.

I didn't start talking until the doors shut. "Does it make me a bad person?"

"You don't owe your mom anything, not after what she did. She made her choice back then, and I doubt a letter would change anything."

"Was throwing it out the right thing to do?"

"You're not obligated to read what she sends just 'cause she's your mom." Rafe sided with me, but I knew he hadn't thrown the unopened envelope away. He'd shoved it into his pocket, keeping it for who-knows-what.

Chapter Thirty-Four

Aspen

THERE WAS A REASON I was never interested in social media, and now, looking at my phone, I was given a cruel reminder. I should've known people from my hometown wouldn't have stayed quiet, especially now that I was on TV where they could see me and be reminded of my existence.

I couldn't be sure if my old friends did things out of jealousy or hate. Maybe it was both. They confused me; what was with their obsession with my sexuality? It seemed to be so important to them that everyone knew about it, going as far as to out me online.

I woke up to numerous posts, mostly anonymous, from guys I went to high school and played baseball with. A lot of the posts were things along the lines of "I can't believe they let a fag play in the Majors." Or things like, "I bet his teammates don't know he's gay." Those were some of the *less* vulgar ones. Some even tried to make claims about things I did, but those posts got a lot less attention, thankfully. But once it started getting traction, news outlets started to pick up on the rumor. There weren't an overwhelming number of articles, but there were enough that I wanted to crawl into a hole and die. Literally. *I'd have no complaints being six feet under right about now.*

Some guys on the team saw the articles, and some hadn't. I was snappy and scared, not talking to anyone unless it directly related to the game we were in the midst of. They all got the point and didn't approach me with anything that wasn't relevant to baseball.

Rafe hesitated, too, worried more than anything else, but the articles were just rumors. Some he said, she said.

I played more aggressively than I should've, and that threw off the balance our team had found. The rhythm we'd settled into while playing was disrupted, the tension palpable. I wanted to be unaffected; I tried to not let it get to me, but I was terrified. I was absolutely terrified of a repeat. What if someone assaulted me again? What if the homophobia directed toward me became widespread rather than just from a couple of people? What if, what if, what if?

Did people believe the rumor? Did they even care? Or was it just fear taking my mind too far? But then again, if that were the case, my sexuality wouldn't be in the discussion section of tabloids.

My mind was elsewhere the entire time I played, and if I was being honest, I was probably responsible for our loss. I felt even worse after the game. Before, I used to pride myself on my ability to compartmentalize my issues when I played. But I couldn't do that today. I was distracted, making mistakes left and right, accidentally ignoring Coach's batting signals, and not going along with his plays. A record number of pitches got past me, resulting in more runs than I'd have liked to admit. Wendell looked like he was about to blow a fuse, maybe even punch me. But I'd asked Dan to switch me out after a number of innings and he'd refused, telling me I needed to get past my mental blocks before any important games came up. When Rafe was in, he tried to reassure me that everything was fine, but it wasn't.

Nothing was fine.

I wasn't fine.

I'd been dealing with my issues, facing and handling them, but because of that, I was having trouble focusing on anything except for those damn articles all teetering toward the negative.

After shaking hands with the enthusiastic group of Manatees, I brushed past my teammates, slamming my glove on the bench, kicking the sturdy seat with clenched teeth.

"It's fine, Ace. Everyone's got their off days. They won't be smiling tomorrow when we whoop their asses," Daunte tried to cheer me up with a firm hand clasped on my shoulder.

The most I could manage as a reply was a firm-yet-reluctant nod.

The guest locker room was dead-quiet. Armada hadn't lost a game this badly all season. And it was against fucking Tampa of all teams. If anything, we should've won in a shut-out, but no, I had to go and mess things up. *As always.*

The entire team funneled out of the stadium to board our bus to go back to the hotel. I lingered at the back, wishing I could disappear. It was unprofessional, letting my personal life affect me like this. They were paying me a shit-ton of money and I was giving an awful performance in return. I wanted to go back to how I did things before, pushing back my emotions, holding them by the throat, and keeping them in place while I was around others, suffocating them until I was in my own privacy where they could suffocate me back. But I worried about doing that. I worried about doing anything like I used to for fear of falling back into old habits. I wanted to let go of the past. I wanted to move on, to enjoy life. I wanted things to be better, but everything kept coming back to bite me in the ass. It felt like I was cursed to be miserable. Like I was climbing a ladder, each step up leading me closer and closer toward being okay. But then I'd miss a step and fall, ending up bruised and scared to try again.

My hands shook and my fingers went lax.

I don't want to do this again.

I won't be able to handle all of this a second time.

My bag fell to the floor, the noise startling me. I realized I hadn't been moving with the rest of the guys, almost everyone loitering in front of the doors of the bus or already inside while I still stood at a distance. Even Rafe had moved forward with the group, awkwardly standing in the middle of them and me, eyes locked on my figure and waiting for me to catch up.

I opened my mouth to speak, but the tension in my chest kept the words inside. I bit my lip, chewing the tissue raw. I bent down to pick up my bag, but for some reason, I couldn't lift it. My arms felt numb. And then my legs did, too. I fell the short distance to the ground from my squatting position, my legs tingly and trembling.

"Aspen," Rafe called as he jogged over, grabbing the attention of a couple of players that hadn't yet boarded the bus.

Rafe gripped my elbows, hauling me off the ground. Tightly grasping my shoulder, Rafe struggled to hold me up as he checked all over my face, looking for a sign of something, but I didn't know what.

"What happened?" His forehead creased in worry, his frown lines deep and unflattering. This. *This* was what I hated—seeing Rafe upset and sad because of me. I should've done a better job at hiding it, but what was the point? Rafe saw through me like I was a clear sheet of glass.

"My legs're jus' a little..." I slurred my words together, speaking in a hushed murmur.

A voice sounded in my head, an echo—a remnant—of noise that stained my mind like wine on a carpet. An unsettling sensation swept through me, completely taking over. It felt as if my heart had dropped into my stomach, the beat thumping in a place it shouldn't. I shook, and not just a little; my whole body was nearly vibrating. I didn't notice when breathing became impossible, my normal flow of oxygen obstructed by short, labored breaths. The voice called my name again, louder, closer. *It wasn't in my head.* My lungs shot into a state of hyperventilation. *Something was wrong.* I *knew* something was wrong. I whipped my head around the near-empty parking garage in a panic. My grip on Rafe's shirt tightened when I saw the reason for my anxiety.

What the fuck? What the fuck?? Oh my god, no no no—

"Alex, w-what're you doing here??" No one was supposed to have access to this area; security was blocking the doors and exists to make sure the players didn't get ambushed by fans.

Hearing my brother's name had Rafe snapping his head up. He shoved me behind him roughly, reaching his arm back and holding onto my elbow. It was a constant, steadying touch.

"Vacation," Alex replied.

I glanced back and noticed some guys from my team were watching us now.

"Get the hell out of here!" Rafe spat.

"Shut the fuck up. I'm here to talk to Aspen. Get out of my way, Rafe." I listened to Alex's tone, but I couldn't look him in the eyes. I stared into the back of Rafe's shirt, focused on where the collar met his neck.

"Leave before I call security," my boyfriend seethed, looking like he was getting ready to fight.

I heard footsteps shuffling behind me.

"He's a fucking faggot and doesn't deserve any of this, why the hell are you protecting him?" Alex paused for a second before he began to snicker. "No way! Are you a fag, too—" there was a crack followed by lots of shouting.

I moved away from Rafe and saw Alex on the ground, Zander gripping his shirt with his left hand while his right drilled into his face.

Alex was bleeding.

There was blood.

Blood blood blood.

I fell to the group on my hands and knees. I couldn't control the bile working its way up my throat, my retches followed by sobs.

It was like I blinked once, and then Zander was off Alex, who was being dragged away by buff men decorated in light blue and walkie-talkies.

A hot hand rubbed against my back as the last of the vomit spilled from my mouth, finally allowing me to breathe. I heaved, the picture of crimson coating my mind. It wasn't me under someone's fist, but Alex instead. Yet somehow, it threw me back to how things used to be. To what Alex used to do to me.

I shivered even though it was hot, Rafe's gentle hands helping me off the ground. He grabbed my hands, wrapping my fingers around a bottle of water.

"Drink," he instructed calmly.

I swished the water around in my mouth, spitting it on the black-painted concrete before allowing some to spill down my throat.

"Are you okay?" Rafe asked in a hushed voice.

I looked at Zander; he shook out his blood-covered hand, his knuckles already bruising. Cam, Daunte, and Wendell surrounded the older catcher, quietly talking amongst each other, and glaring at the direction my brother left in.

"I just—" my voice cracked. "I just don't understand why he came here. What more does he want from me?" I rubbed my palm against my eye and let out an unsteady sigh. "I'm so sick of this shit."

It felt like my family was trying to worm their way back into my life. Like I was the long-lost family runaway they'd been searching for. Well, they were the ones that pushed me away. They had no right to see me now to... to... to what? To force me into the church? Make me their perfect little straight Christian boy? To beat me up when I couldn't be what they wanted?

Oh, wait. Check, check, and check. Been there, done that.

"Come on." Rafe grabbed my gear, layering it on top of his as he pulled me toward the bus.

We went straight to the back, sitting on the left side in a row of two. Rafe let me take the window seat to help if I got dizzy or needed to barf again. The seats were made of fake leather, but the material was comfortable enough that I was able to drift off with my head leaning against Rafe's shoulder. He threaded his fingers through my hair, and with the team quiet and doing their own things and the subtle hum of the engine, I was gifted a nightmareless sleep. For all of what seemed to be thirty seconds.

Rafe tapped lightly on the right side of my face as I drooled onto his shirt. I grunted and made no attempt to move.

"Aspen, wake up."

I lifted my head and glared at Rafe with half-closed eyes.

He chucked and rustled my hair. "God, you're adorable."

I swatted his hand away and rubbed my sleeve against the side of my mouth, sighing as I moved to follow Rafe and the trail of players off the bus. I was the last one out, leaving me to stand behind the small crowd waiting for the bus to be unloaded. I placed myself at the back, already uncomfortable being around everyone with all that happened today. I'd made a big scene; rumors consuming the news, practically throwing the game, my brother showing up... it kept piling on and on.

"Hey, man." Daunte spotted me and shoved his way toward me, wrapping an arm around my shoulder. Several other guys, like Wendell, Cam, and Akio Sato, our first baseman, joined him, forming a somewhat-circle.

"Hey..."

"So," Wendell started. "If what the articles said is true and you are gay, we just want you to know that we don't care. If it's real or not, you don't need to say anything, just that it doesn't matter." The way he said it lacked any awkwardness and held genuine undertones. He gave me a curt smile, as did the other guys, as they stepped away with their gear in tow.

I bit my lip, nerves bubbling in my gut. But it didn't feel like the normal nerves, it felt... different. Less unpleasant.

Grabbing my gear from the bottom compartment of the fancy bus, I slung the bags over my shoulders, finding Rafe waiting for me. "Go shower and change, and if you want, you can come to my room. Or I can come to yours," he suggested.

"Can you come to mine?" I mumbled.

"Sure, just text me when you're ready." Rafe ruffled my hair again, this time gentler and more soothing. It was the most affection we were comfortable showing in public. For now, it was enough. I wanted to push my head into his touch, to bask in the warm comfort he always offered. But instead, I moved from him and we went to our separate hotel rooms.

My shower was quick, yet by the time I was out, my arms had been rubbed raw, deep scratches parallel and perpendicular to the scars. It felt like I needed to endlessly scrub my body. Like there was this dirt—*filth*—that I couldn't get rid of. Like something was stuck on me—under my skin. Like there was something wrong and the only way it could be right was to get it out. But it was in my head: the image of fists slamming into jaws and bone, and blood... so much blood. And that—*that* was something I *couldn't get out.*

Alex always made me bleed. And then he'd make me want to bleed.

I stood in front of the steamed mirror, tapping my fingers on the counter. I thought about wiping the condensation away, but I didn't really want to look at myself. I didn't want to see what kind of expression my face had taken. I didn't want to see the reflection of the scars Alex left on me, or the ones I left on myself because of him. I wished I could erase that part of my life. I wished it didn't happen, or that I could at least pretend it didn't. But I couldn't do that—I couldn't erase all the damage they did to me, so instead, I wished I could erase myself.

I wished things would stop following me wherever I went. I wished I could escape... and I already knew the best way to do that, to escape. It wasn't an easy way out, it was in no way *easy*. But it called to me. It called and it called and it called. Over and over again, relentlessly. Relentlessly for *years*. And whenever I answered the call, it seemed to hang up from the other end before I could finish the conversation, before I could finish trying to... now it was calling again, and I wanted to answer it. I wanted to escape, to erase myself from *all of this*.

"Aspen?" A voice and loud sequence of knocks startled me, my arm flying into the wall as I turned.

"Fuck!" I shouted, holding onto my throbbing hand.

There was more knocking and I cursed again, running out of the bathroom and throwing on some clothes, the ends of my dripping hair tickling the bottom of my neck.

I peered through the peephole and I was more than confused to see Zander. I quickly unlocked the door, my brows furrowed. "Hey..."

I was met with silence, the corners of his mouth downturned.

"Uhm... do you need something?"

"Can I come in?"

"Sure?" I opened the door wider, allowing the man to come in before closing it behind him.

Zander sat at the desk chair across from where I placed myself on the edge of the bed. "About earlier... the guy I punched, he was your brother, right?" Zander tried to look me in the eyes, but at the mention of Alex, the only thing my eyes found interesting was the floor.

Alex's words rang in my head. *"Always look down when I'm talking to you."*

"Y-yeah... how'd you know?"

"You have some similarities in your faces."

I didn't reply, simply nodded.

Zander sighed, "I came because I wanted to make sure I didn't punch him for nothing. I was watching from afar at first, and I couldn't help but notice your body language, and then I heard him call you... that. I guess what I'm trying to say is that I put some of the pieces together, and I thought it'd be better if you're aware that I know."

"Know what?" I croaked. I knew where this was going, but I didn't know what exactly that meant.

"I only started playing baseball because of my dad. He loved the sport, but he blew out his knee in college and had to quit. He wanted nothing more than for me to do what he couldn't, and he did whatever he could to make that happen. My old man was obsessed, a complete control freak. He'd beat the living daylights out of me whenever I made an error—it made me hate baseball just as much as I hated him. I tried to quit too, but he never let me. And things kept going like that, through high school, college, even when I made it to the Minors.

"When I got traded from the team in my hometown, I got to experience what life was like without him threatening me for everything I did. I got to try baseball without my dad whispering over my shoulder. Without him there, I learned that I actually loved baseball, so I stuck with it and cut all ties with him." I looked up for the first time, and Zander was there waiting, his eyes immediately making contact with mine. "He tried to find me, too. And he did, and it nearly tore down everything I'd done to rebuild myself."

I opened my mouth to speak, but it was so hard and I couldn't understand why. My throat hurt, but it shouldn't have. "How—how'd you do it? Get over it, I mean."

"Hmm... I don't think it's something I'll ever truly get over." My shoulders sagged at the confession. Of course. *Of course,* it wouldn't get better. I knew that—I'd *known* that. It wasn't news to me, so it shouldn't have hurt this much. "But that doesn't mean things don't get better. Because they do. It gets better, in time. You'll feel a little lost at first. Confused, maybe even guilty. But then you'll start to get comfortable. You'll fall into a routine, you'll make friends, discover yourself and who you want to be without the fear of others... you'll heal, in time."

"And if I can't? My life right now is better than it's ever been. I mean, before I was here, I got kicked off my team and suspended from school. I was fucking homeless, sleeping in motels or at Rafe's. I didn't have a single dollar in my pocket. And now... now I'm working my dream job, making almost half a million. I live somewhere that looks like it's right out of a movie. And I have food and *no bloody clothes.* I have everything I've ever wanted, but things are still... hell, I even have Rafe—" The sentence got caught off in my throat, my brain freezing. *Ah, shit.*

"It doesn't matter that you have everything now, because the damage's already been done."

I gulped, "I..."

He offered me a warm smile. "Calm down, kid. I already know you and Rafe are dating."

"Huh?"

"Not all of us are oblivious." A small smile quirked onto his lips. "I've seen the way you two are glued at the hip. The hushed laughs and prolonged touches. It's not obvious to most people, but it wasn't too difficult to figure out."

"Does anyone else..." I left the question unfinished. "Was it that easy to..."

Zander shook his head, snickering. "I'm just yanking your chain. I was heading to Akio's room the other day to play some poker with him, Wendell, and Daunte, and we saw you dragging Rafe into your room. It was kind of cute, I'll admit, seeing you two holding hands like a couple of lovestruck puppies."

Chapter Thirty-Five

Aspen

"CAN I HAVE THE LETTER from my mom?"

Rafe's brows knit together tightly.

"I know you kept it. I just," I took a breath, "I need to see what she wrote."

"If you're sure... I don't want you to get hurt."

I bit my lip and nodded, completely understanding where he was coming from. In fact, I agreed with him so much to the point where, if he insisted, I wouldn't even touch the damn thing.

Rafe stood from his bed and opened the drawer of his bedside table, unveiling the purple envelope. He reluctantly handed me the slip, watching intently as I opened it and pulled out a folded piece of paper with a handwritten message.

Hello, Aspen.

I know it has been a while since we've been in contact. I've tried to reach you on your phone, but I know your father disconnected the line. I was happy to see you playing on TV, and I want you to know that I am so proud of you for making it this far. The second I saw you, I immediately began to write.

I miss you and I'd love to see you again. I spend every Wednesday morning at The Swiftly Café in Arkaley, it's about an hour from

Newhalm. If you'd ever like to talk, I'll be there from ten a.m. to two
p.m.

I hope you're doing well.

Love, Mom.

"She's probably still there." I glanced at the time as Rafe read over my shoulder.

"Do you want to see her?"

"I mean, I miss her, yeah."

"Even if what she says will only hurt you?"

"But what if we can fix things?"

"If you think you can mend your relationship with her, you should go. And if it can't be fixed, I think you could use the closure."

"Our game's at six o'clock, right?"

"Yeah, there's more than enough time for you to go and come back before warm-ups. Do you want to borrow my car?"

"That'd be great, thanks."

Rafe fished his keys out of his pocket, handing me the lanyard they were attached to. "Text me if you need anything?"

"Of course." I gave him a chaste kiss before I left his room, heading toward the parking garage.

I took a deep breath as I opened the door, trying to calm my nerves. So much could go wrong, but I had to know if this was salvageable. My mom was amazing and did everything she could for me growing up. Until she found out I was gay, that was. If she could somehow get over her bigotry and try to understand and accept me for who I was, I'd want her back in my life in a heartbeat.

———

Arkaley was a mid-sized, somewhat-small town sitting somewhere between city and suburbia. The cafe my mom mentioned was on the outskirts of the downtown strip, placing it in a peaceful area that still had decent foot traffic. The Swiftly Cafe reminded me a lot of where Amelia took me to get ice cream, the sign made of soft pastels and the windows covered in beautiful chalk art. I stepped into the rectangular shop, a white divider directly in front of me, separating the small space to my right that would guide the line to the register, and the seating on the left that took up a majority of the cafe.

I was confused when I glanced around the barren interior, with few customers sitting at the tables and booths. I couldn't find my mom's blonde, bobbed curls, nor the vintage-style clothing she always wore. I hovered by the front, beginning to think she'd already left despite it still being before noon. And then I spotted it, a wavy head of ash-brown hair tucked behind a woman's ear, the ends resting below her shoulders. Gone was the person imitating the image of a 1950s housewife, no pearls in sight. Now, I took in the long, flowing navy-blue skirt with a comforting flower print mixed with a white blouse. A relaxed smile rested on her face, a cup of coffee, and a small paperback book in hand. This wasn't the Madeline Ace I'd always known.

I hesitantly stepped toward her two-person table next to the window. "Mom?"

Her head shot up in my direction, wide, startled brown eyes boring into mine. She gasped, dropping her book and losing the page. She jumped from her seat and encased me in a bone-crushing hug. On her tiptoes with her arms wrapped around my neck, my mom sharply inhaled. "Oh my goodness, you—you came! Oh, sweetie, I missed you so much."

I didn't hug her back. *I couldn't.*

"You dyed your hair back..." I'd never seen her without the dry blonde curls, powdered face, and red-painted lips. She had makeup on now, but her abundance of freckles shone through and her lipstick matched the soft rose color of her eyeshadow.

She pulled away from me and checked my face, her fingers gently gripping my cheeks. "Aspen, I can't even begin to tell you how much I missed you."

I didn't say it back. *I couldn't.*

"We should sit down." I tried to make my voice sound hard and stern, but the shock of seeing her like this had me faltering.

"Yes, yes. Of course. Would you like some coffee? Or a hot chocolate?" Her voice was warm and sent a shock of comfort down my spine. I was tempted to accept, wishing more than anything that I could sit down and have a conversation with my mom like we did before I was outed. Back when her only feelings toward me were love and adoration.

"No, I'm okay." I took the seat across from her. I wanted her to speak first, to explain herself.

"Alright." Her eyes sparkled with something—happiness, maybe?

"Why did you want to meet?"

"I wanted to see you... and to talk with you."

"Talk about what?" I scoffed, biting my tongue and struggling to keep things in.

But then I realized that I needed to do this. I needed to get things off my chest, and there'd never be a better time than now.

"Do you know how hard I tried to be straight? I tried so, so hard to love women and only women, and I hated myself more than anything because I couldn't. I was convinced that I was sinning and damned to an eternity in hell. Do you know how damaging that is to a person? A child? Believing that when they died they'd rot in pits of fire only to be tortured in reprise?

"But then I had another thought. I started questioning things. If being gay was a sin, then why was I born like this? Why would God make me gay if it was a sin?" My mom kept her eyes steady on me, her expression unchanging. I let out a humorless laugh. "I came to two conclusions back then, and even now, I still think they're both right. For starters, *being gay is not a sin.* And second, there is no fucking God. Because if there was, he wouldn't have let all this happen to me. He wouldn't have punished me for being myself."

She placed a hand over her mouth, and I took it as a sign to continue talking. Once I started, I knew I couldn't stop. Everything had to come out, and it was going to whether or not I liked it and whether or not she wanted to hear it.

"You have no idea what Alex did to me, do you? You have no idea how every single time you rushed me to the hospital for breaks, fractures, sprains, and gashes that wouldn't stop bleeding, was all because of Alex." I tried to keep my voice even, to not let the painful lump in my throat win. "You know I was invited to play on the Olympic team as a bullpen catcher last summer, right? But I had to withdraw because I broke my arm. Don't you get it? *I didn't break my arm,* Alex did! He took so much from me and you had no fucking clue.

"So let me ask you this: why did you come here? Is it because you saw the rumors in the news about me being gay? Are you here to tell me that I should deny it—to save your reputation, or spare you the shame of having a gay son? Well, it's already dying down. No one gives a shit. And it isn't a rumor, because no matter how much you wish it was, *I'm still gay.* So why are you trying to mess things up? I'm the happiest I've ever been in my entire life! No one is forcing religion down my throat. I'm making a career for myself... I have a boyfriend too. And most of all, Alex can't *hurt me* anymore. So why are you doing this? I'm so tired of people in my family ruining me! What did I do that was so wrong? What did I do to deserve all of this?!" Tears welled in my eyes and I tried to force them back down as my fingers scratched at the backs of my hands under the table.

My mom nodded, pulling her lips between her teeth while her eyebrows dipped inward. "I filed for a divorce."

"What?"

"I quit working at the company and moved out two months ago."
My mouth hung open. "I-I don't understand."

She took a deep breath, her shoulders tense below her ears. "After you left, I sought out Father McCarthy for guidance... and I hated everything he had to say. Hearing people insult you, saying the same things I had said, put things into perspective for me. When I approached your father with this, it didn't go well. We fought quite a bit, and I started to realize that something was wrong with our lifestyle, not yours. I began doing some research about sexuality and I reached out to parents with gay children and even joined some groups to help me better understand it.

"And then—" she choked back a sob, her voice quivering alongside her mouth, "and then I found out Alex had been hurting you. And he was *proud*. He was *so proud* of what he'd done for our family and the church. I was horrified. The man Alex has become is a stranger to me. And Garret *approved*. That was the last straw. By then, I knew what had happened was wrong and I no longer wanted to associate with people holding such beliefs. True believers of God spread love, not hate. So, even if you'd never see me again, I still picked you, because what they—we—did was wrong, and I want to fix it. I want to be in your life. I want to support you and love you regardless of anything. I want to find myself and discover what I truly want to do with my life without the influence of strict Christianity pushing these ideals of what and who I should be as a woman and mother. I know what religion means to me, and now I'm figuring out how it fits into my life, because the type of Christian I want to be, is not the one that I was."

The information was overwhelming. *What was I supposed to do with it?* My mom no longer had the blonde hair that so many men seemed to desire and she looked to be dressing for herself. The expressions on her face were the most relaxed and at peace I'd ever seen. She radiated a calm energy that drew me in. I came in thinking

I'd get everything out in the open, say a final goodbye while she'd rot with guilt... but now...

My mouth parted and my leg bounced relentlessly, my knee tapping the bottom of the table. "So you're leaving dad?"

"I've already left him."

Chapter Thirty-Six

Aspen

"SHE'S SPAMMING ME!" I GROANED to Rafe.

He laughed, "What the hell is she sending?"

"Like a bajillion videos of my best plays from each game, links to articles about me, and even baby photos of us playing together when we were four."

"Aw, but that's cute."

"Yeah, but all I asked was what she was doing for dinner."

"Cut her some slack, she's recently single and you're the only family she's still talking to. You're basically your mom's best friend."

"I mean, it's nice of her, yeah. But I had to put my phone on 'do not disturb' because of all the notifications."

"She's putting in an effort." Rafe gave me an incredulous look.

I sighed, "I know, I know. It's just hard to get used to. She went from zero to a hundred real fast."

"How is she, though?"

"She seems happier. Happier than I've ever seen her. Freer, too. She's traveling for fun for the first time in her life. Just sent a picture of herself in Times Square. She also started going to a new church and keeps sending me pamphlets, trying to get me to go with her," I mumbled the last bit.

"She's still on that? I thought you made things pretty clear."

"I did, but she's all excited because this church is accepting and what not. She's doing better, but some things'll never change, I guess." I cleared my throat. "Anyway, what are you bringing to the barbeque?"

"I told Wendell I'd bring soda, and that asshole gave me a list of specific brands I could and couldn't get, the number of bottles that should be in each pack, and the exact number of ounces the bottles need to have down to the decimal place. I swear, that guy is anal-retentive about everything."

"You're lucky it's just Wendell getting on your back. I have five different guys blowing up my phone with different steaks and burger types they want me to get. They're worse than my mom."

"At least you're not like Akio. The poor guy is in charge of the sauces—he's got a list of over fifty different bottles he needs to get. I tried to help him out, but he's too much of a pushover and already said yes to everyone's requests, saying he couldn't go back on his word."

"He's too shy for his own good."

"What time do you want to head over?"

"I told Cam I would get there early to help set up."

"Cam's going early?" Rafe raised a questioning brow. "Cam? Getting out of bed before ten a.m. of his own volition?"

"Piper's going to be there."

"Ah." A look of understanding dawned on him. "Of course. Does this mean we get to watch her reject him again?"

"Probably."

Rafe checked his clock. "Do you need an extra pair of hands?"

"No. But I'd like it if you came."

"Alright." Rafe gave a soft smile, pecking me on the cheek before slipping his shoes on.

Once I was facing the door, there was a puff of air and then a light weight on top of my head. I turned around to Rafe with a jaw-dropping smile on his face and a hat sitting backward on my head. "Gotta protect those pretty eyes of yours."

"By putting it on backward? Sure, let's go with that," I snickered.

Ever since I'd departed from my baseball hat collection in my closet at my dad's house, Rafe had been like this. He tried to make up for what I lost by replacing my things with the familiar. That mainly came in the form of caps, Rafe randomly placing his on my head whenever he got the chance. I'd gone from wearing baseball hats nearly everywhere I went to not owning a single one, and before I even knew what I was missing, Rafe had taken care of it. The habit stuck.

I could buy my own hats now, but that didn't stop Rafe. After a while, I realized he did it because he liked to match in some way or another. The black hat on my head with a dark-green bill coordinated with Rafe's grey baseball hat by whatever terms the color schemes in his head followed. It was his discreet way of showing affection and it always made me feel warm inside. Like the cold could never get to me as long as I had Rafe by my side.

The drive was quick, the park only a couple of blocks from the dorm. The several fields were full of vivid, luscious grass, and while the drought and complete lack of rain should've been the death sentence expected for a field like this, the park overlooked the bay which provided a misty, salty wind that kept the greenery alive and well. Lining the several fields were footpaths of gravel and dirt, and if you followed them all the way down, certain ones would lead you to a set of concrete steps that took you to a small beach.

The park itself was a viewing spot for people to picnic, relax, and look at an array of breathtaking flowers and trees, offering an overload of colors and smells that either resulted in enlightenment or a severe allergic reaction.

We headed toward the field in the middle, sections of it blocked off between flower beds and picnic tables made of rubble and stone pieced together. Zander was already at the grill, working alongside Daunte in setting them up.

Daunte whistled when he saw me, two coolers of meat stacked in my arms, completely obscuring my face. "Think that's enough?" he quipped.

"I'm taking utensils next time," I grunted as I dropped the heavy weight onto the table next to Zander. "I'm not doing this or paying for all your fat asses again."

The second Rafe got the drinks on the table, Wendell was at his side, inspecting the soda. "What the hell is this, Rafe? I *specifically* told you that it *has* to be ten ounces!"

"They don't make soda in ten-ounce bottles!! What did you want me to do, manufacture the fucking things myself?!"

"Yes! Spend your money on something useful instead of a goddamn five-pack of lube."

"Hey! You promised you'd let that go!"

"It's not my fault they sent it to the wrong room."

"It had my name on it! And my sex life has nothing to do with your OCD."

Zander cackled at the two as they continued to argue.

Soon enough, Cam came over with the expression of a kicked puppy. I quirked a brow in question and he shook his head.

"You need to give up, man. It's not going to happen." I patted his shoulder.

"You don't know that..."

"Yes, he does." A cheery Piper threw two canopy tents shoved into bags on the ground. "I have a boyfriend."

Cam's jaw dropped. "What?"

"Yep. Met him last month at a meeting when he spilled his drink on me. We got dinner the next day and now we're going steady." She smiled, a light blush coating her cheeks.

"Congrats," I spoke with amusement in my tone.

"Yeah..." Cam said weakly. "Congratulations."

"Aw, cheer up. There's plenty of fish in the sea." I tried to comfort him, but my gaze shifted to the ocean and Cam caught on. The shortstop couldn't swim, meaning there'd be no catching fish on his part.

"Aspen!" he gasped, clutching a hand over his chest and mocking hurt. "Just because I don't know how to swim doesn't mean you need to rub it in my face."

"You live next to the ocean! Who lives next to a bay and doesn't know how to swim? If there's a tsunami," I dragged my hand across my neck, making a clicking noise with my tongue, "you're dead."

"Not all of us grew up in California. Some of us are from states where the largest body of water is the pool at the closest high school!"

"Hey, guys!" I cupped my hands around my mouth and turned to the several players that had begun to show up, lighting up the park with noise and laughter. "Next time, let's go to the pool! We'll get to see Cam with floaties!"

"I'll lend you my daughter's!" Akio sniggered with a beer in hand. "She's got these princess ones she outgrew last year. I'm sure you'll love them!"

"Screw you, I'd look fucking hot in princess floaties!" Cam paused and looked at Piper. "Right?"

She scoffed and rolled her eyes. "Whatever makes you feel pretty."

The sun beat down on us, the sky a blinding blue with nearly no clouds in sight. Despite the sunshine, the breeze from the ocean sent shivers over my arms and legs, making my hair stand on edge. The atmosphere was playful and energetic, people doubled over in laughter left and right, burgers being handed around, and burly men stuffed to the brim with red meat and whatever sides had shown up throughout the afternoon.

Everyone bubbled in the jovial environment with bright grins on display, myself included.

My eyes were sunken into my cheekbones, hidden from the wide smile showcasing my dimples. The corners of my mouth were upturned as hearty laughs escaped my mouth.

I was laughing.

I was happy.

And I was damn good at faking it.

Chapter Thirty-Seven

Rafe

I BOUNDED DOWN THE HALLWAY, giddy with excitement as I made my way to Aspen's room. His mom had sent me a picture of the most beautiful fan art I'd ever seen. It captured everything I loved about Aspen: bright, gleaming eyes, a genuine smile, and positive, open body language. He'd just hit a grand slam, his first home run of the season, straight into the sandy water outside the park. Teammates surrounded him, thankful to have him on the team, and accepting of everything that made Aspen who he was.

He was finally finding his place, finding peace within himself and the people around him, and the piece of art nearly captured it better than my own memories.

I walked past the last couple of doors before I found myself in front of Aspen's room. My eyes were focused on my phone as I raised my hand to knock when I realized the door was open.

"Aspen?" I called, gently pulling the door open to let myself in. He'd never leave it open, and Cam usually didn't, either. "Aspen, your door's open..."

There was no one in the main room, both beds messy and unmade. The desks looked like they always did, full and stacked with random appliances. I checked the small kitchen next, thinking maybe Aspen was listening to music while making lunch, but no one was in there, either. I questioned if a fan had gotten into the apartment building and broken in, but then I got to the closed door of the bathroom. I knocked once again. "Aspen, are you in there?"

There was no reply. I was met with silence; the only noise was the ventilation from the other side of the door. I clamped my hand around the handle, the metal creaking under my turning grip. Yellow lights shone down from above the mirror, lighting the bathroom in a warm hue that altered the natural color of the room.

All the cabinet drawers had been pulled out, the shelves on the wall void of their normal products. Things were sprawled over the floor, some even floating in the toilet. The bathtub was filled to the brim with clean, soapless water, and towels lay crumpled next to the sink. Alongside the white pieces of cloth discarded on the tiled floor was a trash can. My eyes would've simply scanned over the metal bin... but I saw something familiar. Something I hadn't seen in a long time, but the memory of it clung to my mind, flooding my head and kicking my heart into an irregular rhythm. Balls of toilet paper were tucked into the trash, squished between wrappers and other wads of the thin paper.

With an unsteady hand, I reached for one of the balls floating atop an empty carton of something. I found the edge of the roll and slowly began to unwind it, layer after layer. And what I found in the center had my heartbeat stuttering, a nauseating sensation winding itself around my gut. A pounding noise filled my head, unhelped by a stream of static noise blurring my hearing.

A retractable utility knife, the blade safely held within the black plastic handle. Except, I couldn't see the silver of steel... All I saw was red.

Red, red, red.

A deep, ugly hue.

A liquid seeping from the pores of the blade.

Blood painted the toilet paper red. It coated the razor as if it was its natural color. Like it was *meant* to be red.

The knife clattered into the sink, my fingers unable to keep their clutch on the blade. Unable to keep holding onto something coated in blood. *Aspen's blood.*

I fumbled with my phone, clicking on Aspen's number. I paced the length of the small room, my phone pressed to my ear as the incessant ringing became unbearable. "Come on, Aspen, pick up." It went to voicemail. Again and again, there was no answer. "Pick up, damn it!"

I stumbled out of the bathroom, nearly falling to the ground as I pushed my way out the door. My legs trembled as I rushed from Aspen's room to the elevator. I pressed the button frantically, waiting for the doors to open, but it was taking too long. I glanced left and right.

Fuck! What am I supposed to do?? The thought sprinted through my mind on repeat. *Shit! Shit! Shit!* I couldn't think, nothing was coming.

It was taking too long...

Stairs. I'd take the stairs.

My footsteps echoed in the cool stairwell; the only noise beside the sound of my shoes slapping against the ground was my uneven breath. I burst into the lobby, running into the common room where I knew several players would be.

"Has anyone seen Aspen?!" I bit the words out. My voice sounded angry, but I knew my face held nothing but panic and fear.

"I saw him in passing like an hour ago. Tried to say hi, but he didn't say anything back, so I think he was listening to music or something. He was kinda in a rush, had a weird expression, too," Daunte supplied.

"Do you know where he was going?"

"Looked like he was heading downtown."

Downtown? "Downtown... like he was going to cross the bridge?"

"Uh-huh. Looked like that."

"Rafe, what's wrong?" Cam had turned the volume of the TV down as low as he could, a full room of people suddenly looking at me.

"Cam, I... I need you to call 911. Have them send an ambulance to Newhalm Bay Bridge, okay?" I'd already begun to move from the room and toward the exit doors. "Alright? I-I need you to do that *right now.*"

I turned my head, ignoring the scraping of chairs against the floor as people stood in confusion. I ignored them, taking off in a full sprint.

It wasn't too late, not yet.

I could still make it.

I had to...

But what if I couldn't? What if I was too late? He almost died last time... and who was to say this time would be different?

Because he'd tried before, and even though he'd never succeeded... well, Aspen always liked to say there was a first time for everything. All I could do was hope that this wasn't the first time. Because he could only die once, and no matter how hard I tried, it seemed like there was nothing I could do.

Like it was fate.

Aspen was destined to die by his own hands, and I was destined to watch, helpless no matter the effort I put in to change things.

Was there really nothing left I could do? Was there anything I *hadn't* done? Was there anything left *to* do?

Run. I could run. If I got there in time... maybe—maybe I could save him again. Maybe this time he wouldn't leave me.

My feet ached in my shoes as my arms pumped by my sides. I passed bikers and joggers alike. Tears streamed down my face, the harsh ocean breeze adding an unpleasant sting.

The sun was out, but dark, grey clouds blocked it as if fate knew what was going to happen today. As if it was setting the mood, like a cruel, cruel joke. Fog swept the bay, cascading the bridge in an opaque mist. I couldn't see more than five feet in front of me, forcing my eyes to focus on the lines carved into the sidewalk of the metal bridge.

I kept my eyes wide, hoping I'd see a shadow near the edge before it was too late. And I did—a shadow caught my eye. It was on the opposite side, not more than two and a half feet tall. It could've been a dog or a small child, but something was pulling me toward it. Dragging me toward the shadow and forcing me through the oncoming traffic. I weaved through cars, ignoring the fact that they wouldn't be able to see me in the low light of the day. But I didn't care. I didn't matter. Not here, not now.

It didn't matter when a Camaro honked at me. Or when a Prius swerved out of the way. I didn't care when the Lexus slammed on its brakes, the car behind it nearly crashing. Or when the fog didn't allow a Camry to see me before it could stop, ramming into my side and knocking me to the ground. It didn't matter because my pain was nothing compared to Aspen's. It didn't matter because the adrenaline could get me through it. Because I didn't care what happened to me as long as Aspen was okay.

But he wasn't okay. Which was why I had to be.

I clenched my teeth, grunting as I made it to the other side of the wide bridge with next to no visibility. The shadow hadn't moved, its form becoming more and more clear. It was on the outside of the rails, sitting on the ledge with its legs dangling over the water.

The white T-shirt had me doubting the shadow's identity, but the locks of ash-brown hair had my heart sinking in my chest.

"Aspen," I croaked.

All I got was the slow turn of a head and a quick glance before his eyes fixated once more on the incoming cargo ships and the paddle boarders crossing underneath.

As I got closer, I realized the white shirt wasn't white. It should've been, but it wasn't. The shirt acted as a blank canvas, and Aspen's blood the paint. His hands were cradled near his stomach, the front of his tee a wet, deep crimson, his fingers unmoving, so still it looked like they *couldn't.*

I approached the bars separating us, not daring to place so much as a hand on his shoulder. I was scared—*terrified*—of what would happen if he felt cornered.

"I'm sorry." I barely heard the whisper over the rumbling of waves and engines of cars.

"Why would you be sorry?" I chuckled, not a hint of humor in my voice. "You have nothing to be sorry for."

"I tried."

"We can keep trying!" I attempted to reason, my breath hitching in my throat.

"For how much longer?"

"Aspen... *don't,*" my voice broke.

"*I have to.* It's the only way." His voice was strained. It lacked no emotion, holding everything I could think of: pain, hurt, exhaustion, and so, so much more.

"It's not."

"You don't get it. It's the only way to make it stop! I can't—I can't get the damn voice out of my head," he said through clenched teeth. "No matter where I am, what I'm doing, or how I'm feeling, it's like this voice follows me around. Like it's whispering in my ear, coaxing me to *just do it. What does it matter? Just do it. You should just die. End it here. You're exhausted, so just stop already. Kill yourself.*"

"Please..." I gasped weakly.

"I thought I was getting better. I really did. I truly thought I was happy. Everything is better now, so why doesn't it feel that way?

Why is life just as suffocating now as it was before? No, it somehow feels *worse* than before, and I don't understand *why.* I want to go back to how things were. When things didn't hurt. When everything was numb and it felt like I was floating. Because at least then it didn't hurt. But now... now I don't know what to do. I don't know how to get rid of this... *this feeling* that the world is crumbling around me.

"I used to think that getting out would be enough. I used to think that a handsome prince with tan skin shielded in impenetrable armor would come rushing in, save me like a damsel in distress. I thought that he'd make all my problems go away, like being loved would be a cure-all. But even when the prince came—" Aspen's throat sounded as if it had been through a shredder, the words escaping came out rougher than they ever had. "Even when the prince came... and *saved me,* and took me away from hell, and showed me how *beautiful* life could be in a castle full of love, the voice wouldn't leave me alone. That feeling in my chest wouldn't *leave me alone.*

"I'd look at everyone around me, happy and living their lives, and I'd wish I could have that, too. But then I realized—*I did.* I had it all, but I still wasn't happy. My prince had saved me from the things tearing me apart, bit by bit. But I figured out that he couldn't save me from this thing destroying me from the inside out. You can try to help me, Rafe, but you can't save me from myself. You can't take me away from the voice in my head, because it's my *own voice.* My *own* thoughts."

Aspen sucked in a breath, his chest rising uncomfortably. His voice was raw, broken, and chopped up like the words were killing him. "So, Rafe, you have to promise me something. You have to *promise me* you won't blame yourself. Because *this...* this isn't something you can save me from."

He slipped off the edge.

Chapter Thirty-Eight

Rafe

A BLOOD-CURDLING SCREAM LEFT MY throat as I rushed toward the bars, getting ready to follow into the icy water.

Strong arms wrapped themselves around my waist, hauling me a couple of inches into the air as I kicked and flailed until my feet landed on the ground.

"Rafe! Come on, man!" The arms wouldn't let go. They held me still, dragging me to the ground where I dissolved into a useless puddle of sobs and tears, wails wracking my body.

"No. No. No. No! I-I can't! I can't! Let me—let me go! Let me go! Let me fucking go! Let go, let go!" I couldn't stop shouting, trying to tear my way out of Zander's grip. "Stop, please... just let me go after him. Please, let me go..." My voice lost its strength, as did my body. Flashing lights of red blinded my vision, my words lost in the sound of sirens.

"Rafe, listen to me. The Coast Guard is already here. They'll find him."

They'll find him? Find him after he's already dead? After either the impact killed him or hypothermia stopped his heart?

A weird wave of calm washed over me. No, calm was the wrong word. *Defeat.* There was nothing I could do... there was nothing I'd ever be able to do. I wanted to be enough for him. I wanted to be enough for Aspen to stay. But I wasn't, and I'd never be.

The tight grip around my torso loosened and Zander removed himself from under me, standing to join a couple of other guys that had followed me out. I stared out at the bay, a stillness in my body that made me feel more lifeless than a living being should. The only thing reminding me that *I* was here and Aspen *wasn't*, was the pounding of my heart, sending shock waves of burning fire through my body and sweat down my temples. It seemed like even the frigid air wasn't enough to quench the heat in my body.

This wasn't supposed to happen. Things were supposed to be better. I thought they were better... I thought I knew Aspen enough to see through his charade... but he'd fooled me. I believed things were okay, and if I'd just noticed that they weren't, I could've done something. *Could I, though?* Time and time again, I had proved to be useless. Last time, I'd known something was wrong, yet did nothing to stop it. And this time, I was left in the dark. I didn't notice, leaving me unable to prevent it from happening. Again.

Again and again. He would keep doing this, wouldn't he? Aspen would figure out his tells and learn to hide them. He'd choose to suffer in silence over confiding in me. Because there was something about me that Aspen didn't trust. Maybe something in the way I handled things that felt too suffocating. Maybe I was too overbearing... or maybe too loose and distant. Maybe I was part of the problem, one of the things forcing him into this corner where he felt like there was no other option.

Should I have been more positive with him? Or more realistic? Maybe I should've forced him to deal with this sooner, in a safe place. Had him go to a therapist, or talked to my dad more about how I could help.

There were so many places I could've gone wrong, I just didn't know where it was. I didn't know what else I was supposed to do. I didn't know how to handle this, and I didn't want to. I didn't want Aspen to be so sad. I didn't want him to cut. I didn't want him to fake his smiles. I didn't want to see the dull look in his eyes that seemed to spill his deepest secrets... the light in his eyes that I'd somehow failed to realize was going out.

There was a buzzing noise in my head, drowning out the surrounding chatter. I could see the police cars sectioning off this portion of the bridge. I could see my friends and teammates with worried expressions, talking to cops and EMTs. I could see them, but I didn't really *see* them. They were there, but it felt like they weren't. It felt like I was stuck in a bubble where the only thing in my eyes was Aspen jumping with no hesitation. Like there was nothing for him to stay for.

"Rafe! I've been calling your name for the past two minutes! Come on, they got him. We need to go!" Cam gripped my arm and yanked me off the ground.

"He-he's..."

"They already have him in an ambulance going to Newhalm Central." I was dragged away from the scene, taken to a car, and pushed into the backseat. I was squished between people, the driver running red lights like he could afford a million tickets.

I tapped my fingers against each other relentlessly, trying to find comfort in the rhythmic pattern as the pad of my thumb lightly touched each individual finger on my hands. It reminded me of some of Aspen's habits...

"I called Piper, she's going to connect you with Armada's public relations department. It'd probably be best for Aspen if none of this leaked to the press." Wendell held his phone out for me to take.

I stood from the cushioned chair in the waiting room, Zander, Daunte, and Cam seated around me with their legs bouncing and tense expressions on their faces.

I didn't thank Wendell as I grabbed the black device, leaving the room wordlessly to find a more secluded area of the hospital.

I pressed call on the number Wendell had pulled up in his contacts, a man from the other end answering with a confused, "Hello?"

I cleared my throat, trying to find my voice. "This is Rafe Alvarez. I got your number from Piper and was told I should call…"

"Just a second, please." Mumbled voices filled the background before he returned to speaking. "Could I call you back in an hour? I'm in the middle of a meeting with—"

"Not really." I interrupted with a strained voice. "If we wait another hour, this will be all over the news."

"If it's urgent, we can speak now."

"Uhm…" *God, how should I even start this?* It wasn't my business to share, but I could already see cameras pointed at the players in the waiting room, unsuspecting people having recognized us and more than curious about the grim expressions on our faces.

I knew Aspen would understand. He'd much prefer a few strangers within Armada to know about this than an entire world full of scrutinizing sports fans. I kept things brief, only mentioning things that held importance—things Aspen might've found important in keeping to himself. I skimmed over his history with self-harm and suicide, informing the man of Aspen's latest attempt.

In a grave tone, he told me that he'd get started on this immediately and ensure that none of this would get out; they'd cover it with an official-yet-vague statement to the public that Aspen was taking some time off for personal reasons.

I headed back to the waiting room and slumped down in the chair. My hands raked over my face; we hadn't received any news in hours. Fucking *hours*.

It paralyzed me. Made my lungs stutter and gut twist in an unseemly way. Forced all thoughts in my head to cease.

Last time—*fucking hell! Last time, last time, last time!* Why did there even have to be a last time?!

Last time... he was only in surgery for two hours. This time, it'd already been five.

Five hours of nothing. Radio silence. Vague updates from nurses saying "He's still in surgery." How bad was it? How much damage did he do? Was it from the cuts? Broken ribs from landing in the water? A punctured lung? I just wanted to know what was wrong. I wanted to know if he was going to be okay. Or if—or if this time would turn into the last time.

I didn't know what I'd do if this was—*if this was truly the end.*

I don't want to do this without Aspen.

Without him, what was the point?

He was my everything and always had been. Without him, it'd feel like I had nothing at all. With every touch, Aspen had gushed about how *warm* I was. Like I'd been thawing the wall of ice he'd built to protect himself. I knew going in that there was a chance his cold would overpower my heat. That the warmth I tried to spread wouldn't be enough... and I was okay with that. I was okay freezing. But it wasn't supposed to be like this. If the cold won, we were supposed to freeze together.

I was supposed to freeze with him...

Chapter Thirty-Nine

Rafe

WAITING ROOMS. I FUCKING *LOATHED* waiting rooms.

The blindingly white walls directly contributed to my splitting headache. A flickering light above had me squeezing my eyes shut. The anxiety wafting over from my teammates experiencing this for the first time sent my nerves into overdrive, and the distinct-yet-familiar smell of antiseptic had bile rising in my throat.

It was dark out now, ominously quiet, the only sounds were the squeak of sneakers as nurses and doctors walked across the freshly waxed floors.

I'd called Madeline crying, not sure how to confess that Aspen had tried to kill himself. *Again.* I didn't know how to break it to her that her son had been suicidal for years. That he'd tried to kill himself countless times under her roof, some probably while she was there.

Her voice trembled like the world was crashing around her. A small confession that she was still in New York for an art exhibit ended abruptly when she'd hung up, already getting in a cab and heading to the airport.

Then I'd talked to my own parents, resulting in a much, much worse breakdown, drawing unwanted gazes from startled people around me. Despite being outside and finding an abandoned corner to pour my feelings and fears out, people still found me. People still passed and whispered and secretly took pictures on their phones. It had me questioning what was wrong with humans. What made them think taking a picture of a crying man standing outside the emergency room of a big city surgical center was an okay thing to do? No matter who I was, I still found the gestures inappropriate and indecent. It felt like Aspen's hatred and overall distrust toward people was rubbing off on me. My normal indifference was gone, and instead, I found myself wound up, agitated and on edge being around others.

I spoke longer to my dad than my mom, wondering if there was something wrong with me—If all these things in my head were foreboding. A sixth sense foreshadowing my loss of the only person I'd ever loved.

He told me it was guilt... I was feeling guilty.

But I'd already known that. I already knew that I was going to blame myself. How could I not? Especially when I was the one closest to him. When I was the person who was supposed to be watching over Aspen, making sure he was okay, happy, and healthy. And I'd failed on all fronts.

I'd failed. It was my fault. I blamed myself. And I was riddled with guilt.

Although I didn't know what, I knew there was something more I could've done. I wasn't good enough, and I didn't catch myself lacking. I didn't pick up my slack to make sure Aspen was in the right headspace to be here, doing this. Doing anything. I didn't pay enough attention, too focused on my own life and my career furtherance.

I was selfish, and now, Aspen would be the one to pay for my mistakes.

The door to the private room they'd given us creaked open, a woman with a soft expression poking her head in. "For Aspen Ace?"

"Yeah!" Cam immediately straightened his back from the uncomfortable slump he'd been in before.

"Alright." There was a small smile ghosting her face. *That's good.* That had to mean good news, right? "Is there any immediate family here? This information is private so—"

I raised my hand like a schoolchild. "I am. I'm family."

She gave me a questioning glance. It was clear we weren't related, so I wasn't surprised by the confusion on her face. But Aspen was my family, and I was his. Once Armada had set up his insurance, Aspen had put me down as his only emergency contact, as well as his medical proxy, if needed. I didn't know he'd done that until we'd gotten to the hospital. In fact, I hated that he did that. Like Aspen knew this would happen again. That he'd be incapacitated, unable to make decisions for himself, and knew he'd need someone to do it for him.

I stood from my seat and followed her outside the room, so we stood just in front of the wooden door. "The surgery went well."

I let out the biggest exhale of my life. All the tension fell from my shoulders and my mind clouded over, finally allowing some ounce of exhaustion to seep in.

"He inhaled quite a bit of water, and his lungs are struggling to work on their own. Thankfully, the doctors aren't worried about secondary drowning, so you shouldn't either. He's lucky he picked the Newhalm Bay Bridge, and I really hate to say this, but if he'd jumped from Newhalm Narrows Bridge, he probably wouldn't be here right now. All Aspen has is a broken clavicle. None of his organs were punctured.

"The bigger issue is his wrists." She paused for a second, thinking of how to word the next thing she was going to say. She began to speak in a much quieter, softer tone. "When Aspen cut himself, he severed several tendons in his left wrist. The doctors did their best to repair them, but even with physical therapy, there's a chance he may never have full function of his fingers and hand again. Now, this isn't to say he won't make a full recovery, because that is also possible. It depends on how his body heals and the steps he takes to get better physically.

"He hasn't been out of surgery long, and we're not completely sure when he'll wake up. But once he does, he'll be held on a seventy-two-hour suicide watch. If there's reason to believe Aspen may hurt himself again when he gets home, a doctor may decide to have him committed as an inpatient to receive psychological help."

"Is he allowed visitors yet?" I rushed out.

I needed to see him. I *had* to. With my own eyes. I had to see for myself how he was doing; the words of doctors and nurses weren't enough to calm me down.

"For now, yes. Two people can go in at a time, but you'll need to be quiet. And when he wakes up, we'll talk to Aspen and then see how he's doing."

"Alright." I rubbed my fingers against each other. "Can I see him now?"

"Sure." She motioned for me to follow her. "Before you go in, please understand that he is currently intubated, and it might be difficult to see him like this."

I muttered in response. "It's not the first time."

The nurse gave me a pitiful glance, leading me to a private recovery room in a dead-silent ward. She gripped the handle and slowly opened it for me, gesturing for me to go in first.

The room was freezing, so cold I could almost smell it. It was a stale stench that burned my nose and eyes. The lights had been dimmed as low as they could be, giving just enough brightness to maneuver in the room while allowing Aspen to rest comfortably.

His head was tilted back against the pillow, a clear tube shoved down his throat. I could've sworn a tear dripped down the side of his face, but that could've been due to a factor of things: the cold air, or simply the fact that he was lying down.

The black strap of a sling poked out from the top of the white blanket draped over his body that rested just below his neck. His left arm was trapped in the brace, making a small outline in the cover just over his stomach while his right arm laid limp by his side.

I sucked in a sharp breath of air, pulling my lips between my teeth. The tension in my forehead told me my brows were deeply furrowed, and there was this weight building in my chest. My eyes burned ten times more than when I'd walked into the room, salty water dripping down my face and lighting up stripes of my skin with an icy sensation.

A small hand found its way onto my upper back, rubbing soothing circles over the fabric.

"When'll he wake up?" My words slurred together, talking expending much more energy than it should've.

"It's hard to tell. It could be in an hour or a day. He's not in a coma, just sleeping, so he's catching up on some much-needed rest. His body is physically and mentally exhausted."

"Right..."

"There's a nice chair over there," she pointed toward a cushioned, recliner-looking chair in the corner. "There are also normal chairs along the wall, and if you'd like, you can move one closer to him."

"I, uhm... I can't hold his hand, can I? 'Cause of the bandages and cuts..."

She peered up, a look of realization and understanding dawning over her before she quickly masked it. "I'm sorry, but no. It could cause additional pain. However, it should be alright for you to rest a hand on his leg or offer him light touches. In fact, it's encouraged. Sometimes a familiar touch can be comforting to patients."

I nodded, not bothering to blink back the tears as they fell freely down my cheeks.

"Okay," she whispered. "I'll leave you to it."

"Thank you," I somehow managed to croak out.

The second the door closed behind her, my hearing focused on the rhythmic beeping of the heart monitor. It was what told me he was alive and breathing, a lifeline that allowed my heart to beat along with it.

I placed a chair by his torso, trying to keep my voice straight, strong. "God, Aspen... what did you do." It wasn't a question.

Watching his motionless body made me realize how badly I wanted to talk. Made me aware of the urge to fill the silent void that felt like it was killing me. But when I focused on the fact that he wasn't breathing on his own, that his wrist had been sliced so deep he may never be able to use it quite right, and that having a better life didn't really mean *Aspen* was better, I was unable to utter a single word.

The room was peaceful and the beat of Aspen's heart was lulling me to sleep, forcing my eyelids to flutter shut involuntarily. Despite the calm supplied by the safety of the hospital, there was this sense of unease settling in my stomach, something that didn't seem as if it'd be going away any time soon.

I laid my head on the outer shell of the mattress, the top of my hair flush against Aspen's thigh, the right side of my face squished into my arm as I peered at the boy from an angle that only awarded me the haunting image of the bottom of his chin and an enlarged throat because of that damn tube. I let my right hand cradle Aspen's leg just under his knee, and at this point, it was more to comfort myself rather than Aspen.

When my eyes finally closed, I opened them a second later. Or so I thought—the hallway lights seeping through the cracks of the door starkly overshadowed the dark, daunting night light hidden by an outlet. Not to mention the fact that the lights of Aspen's room were also on, creating a rough shadow on his face. But then again, that shadow could just as likely have been from the dark circles clouding the bottom of his eyes.

His opened eyes.

I jolted up in my seat. Aspen was elevated, sitting up as a doctor on the other side of his bed checked the wounds on his right arm.

"We tried to wake you, but you didn't budge, so we let you be," the doctor remarked.

The man in the white coat wasn't the only person in the room. In the chair next to the space I'd dragged mine from sat an older gentleman with a white beard and an aged beige cap. He had a flannel under a black, soft-looking vest. It was an odd combination, but he exuded a gentle aura. I gave the stranger a scrutinizing glare, confused as to why he was in the room.

The doctor spoke before I had a chance to ask. "Everything's looking alright for now. A nurse will bring you food and snacks throughout the day, and there's a button right here," he pointed to a panel on the adjustable bed, "that will call a nurse in. This is for emergencies only. If you're in an excess amount of pain, we can give you a stronger type of pain medicine—"

"I don't want any pain meds," Aspen spoke with a firm-yet-gruff voice, his throat hoarse and probably in pain from being intubated.

"Yes, but with your injuries—"

Aspen cut him off once more. "Look at your damn chart, it'll have certain medications I can't take."

"Of course. I noticed that it's not allergy-related, so there could be exceptions if you're unable to handle the—"

He was not having this doctor's ignorance. "I just fucking relapsed with self-harm and tried to kill myself. Would you like me to relapse into my drug addiction as well?" Aspen spat.

"I understand." The doctor lowered his head. He looked young, probably a resident just starting out. "My apologies." Suddenly looking uncomfortable and probably realizing his mistake, the doctor scurried out of the room, leaving the chart at the foot of Aspen's bed.

"Well," Aspen paused, his voice full of dry humor, "this is a new low. Even for me. Looks like my baseball career is going to be over before it even starts. Wonderful. Absolutely fucking wonderful."

"The nurse said that—"

"I know what the fucking nurse said, alright?!" I flinched at his outburst. "Fuck the nurses and fuck the doctors! Don't you get it, Rafe? I can't feel my fucking fingers! You know what that means: nerve damage, possible paralysis, decreased motor function, and absolutely zero chances of being able to play!"

"With time—"

"Time?" Aspen scoffed. "How much time? You think Armada would keep a rookie with permanent damage to his hands and signed to a one-year contract on the roster?? I was trying to die, not make things worse while living!"

I wanted to tell him to "stay positive" or "be optimistic" and that "everything will be okay," but I couldn't. Not to Aspen. Even I wasn't sure he could play again, not because I didn't think the physical therapy wouldn't help, but because I knew Aspen. And I knew he wouldn't let himself heal. If anything, he'd relish the oncoming struggle. He'd take the pain like it was the only emotion he had access to, which could very well have been true. He'd sabotage himself, either by giving up or trying again. And when I said trying, I didn't mean trying to get better. I meant trying to make things better in his own way, which translated to putting *everything* to a stop.

He could do it. I knew he could recover. But I didn't think he'd even *want* to, and that was what hurt the most.

Aspen tried to put on a front, but I could see him blinking back tears. "I'm so tired, Rafe. I don't... I don't understand why I keep doing this shit to myself. And I can't seem to stop, no matter how hard I try or how much I want to, I just *can't*. We need to break up."

My eyes widened in horror. "W-wait! Why would—that doesn't —why?"

He sucked in a slow, hard breath through his nose. "I heard that you got hit by a car... and you tried to jump in after me..."

"Aspen—"

"No, Rafe. I knew this would happen. I just knew that my fucked-up mind was going to rub off on you. You were perfectly fine before I dragged you into this... and now you're being reckless without a care for your own life. This is my fault, Rafe. Don't you see it? Can't you see how being around me is affecting you? You were willing to *die* for me. That's not healthy, Rafe! And I know I'm not the poster boy for healthy mindsets, but you were! You *should be*. But you're not, and that's my fault."

"And you think breaking up with me, distancing yourself, would help that?! You think I'd be okay if you just left me? That I wouldn't worry myself to death not being right next to you?! I know I'm not doing great! I know, okay, I *know*. I know I'm fucked-up now, but it was going to happen, anyway. It was bound to happen eventually—"

"Because you're around me!"

"Because you're my best friend and I'm in love with you! I've always been like *this* because of you! Even when we were little, you were the only thing on my mind. This isn't anything new, Aspen! I've always cared more about you than myself, and sure, maybe it's getting worse, maybe I'm obsessed, maybe I'm completely fucked-up too, but that's been an issue for fucking years. Nothing's going to change by breaking up with me because I was like this before we started dating.

"If we break up, I sure as hell won't get better, and neither will you. It's been fourteen fucking years, Aspen. You can't leave me here, not now. My shit is on me, so just... just get better. I'll be okay, I'll figure things out on my part and I'll be okay. But I *need* you to be okay, too."

"I can't let you become like me..." His eyes were downcast, his voice nothing more than a whisper. "This thing, it's like a contagious disease. And Rafe, you caught it. I can't let it kill you too..."

"I'm here because I won't let you die. Sure, maybe I was reckless, but I don't regret it."

"I'm not going to get better, Rafe. *I'm not going to get better.* You're going to try and save me when you *can't,* and you're going to get worse. You're going to depend on me, and when I'm not there anymore, *you're going to get worse.* I can't let you become like me."

"I won't. *I'm fine,*" I emphasized.

"You're *not.* And you know how I know that? Because I *know* the signs. I've been *through* the signs. And I can see the warning lights flashing whenever I look at you."

A gruff voice interrupted before I could get another word out. "I feel like now would be a good time for me to step in."

Aspen and I both snapped our eyes to the man sitting in the back of the room with a pained look on his face. I'd forgotten he was there.

"I didn't mean to sit in on that conversation, so I apologize. I was in a meeting with our coordinators when you reached out to our PR manager." He looked at me.

"I'm sorry, but who are you?" Aspen narrowed his eyes in annoyance.

"Sean Murphy." *The fucking owner...*

Aspen visibly bit his tongue, holding in whatever string of curses he wanted to let out.

"Once I heard what happened, I couldn't sit still and wanted to see how you were doing with my own two eyes. Intruding was not my intention. But since I heard some rather... *personal* things, I think I should make a couple of things clear before you two keep arguing." Sean frowned, disturbed by the reason for his presence. "Aspen, I can assure you, you won't be dropped. You'll be moved to an injured list where you'll remain indefinitely until you're healed. We have a lot of options for physical therapy, and once you're good as new, you'll pick up right where you left off. You've got potential, and it won't be wasted while you're with Armada.

"But before you can play again, you'll need more than just physical clearance. We have a lot of mental health resources available for players. There's a wonderful therapist with our team, and I think you'll find her helpful. You'll play again, I believe that with every bone in my body. But before then, you're going to get the help you need, because we won't let you play like this. The mental state of our players is our number one priority, and I think it should be yours as well. Even if you don't want it, which seems to be the case. But as long as you're on our team, I think you'll be required to get it.

"And Rafe, I think you should talk to our therapist as well. You're taking on a responsibility that isn't yours to bear, and that guilt you've got fogging up your brain, it can be dangerous."

Epilogue – Aspen

Two Years Later

"Now, Adam, normally these two teams have a very visible and aggressive rivalry, but that is clearly not the case tonight." The announcer spoke into his microphone, his commentary broadcast on both the radio and over the footage of the game.

"Yes, that's right. The Vale Beach Mavericks and Newhalm Armada are neighboring teams, creating fierce competition along the bay. This time last year, we'd normally be seeing nothing but scowls and possibly even another fight!" Adam responded.

"The biggest difference this season is that the Mavericks scooped up a couple of Armada's players. Most notably, Rafe Alvarez and Cameron Cuff. After Armada won the World Series last year, the Mavericks offered trade contracts that neither player could pass up. In fact, I've heard that Rafe Alvarez still lives in Newhalm, and since the cities are so close, getting to Vale Beach is no trouble."

"Yeah, Matthew. His decision to stay in Newhalm is very unique. But either way, Rafe Alvarez, as a player on both Armada and the Mavericks, has given us quite the show. He made up half of the youngest, and one of the strongest, batteries the MLB has ever seen alongside Aspen Ace. But what I find even more entertaining is watching the two play against each other. This is their third year in the Majors and first year on different teams. We're only halfway *through the season, and neither player has hit anything less than a home run when facing the other. It's quite remarkable!" Adam's deep voice held a layer of excitement that had a special way of enticing viewers and listeners.*

Matthew spoke, "I was looking at an interview the two did together a couple of weeks ago, and this may be old news to some, but I found out that the two had been playing together since Pewees! Now, I'm quoting Rafe Alvarez, 'We've played on the same team since we were four years old. There's no call Aspen could make that I wouldn't anticipate, and there's no pitch I could throw that he wouldn't see coming.'"

"They're one of the most experienced batteries in the league. Fifteen, nearly sixteen, years made them unstoppable in the World Series last year and is now making them the most entertaining opponents. Not just for the gameplay, but because of the player interactions—"

Matthew interrupted Adam, "Oh! Look at them now! The Armada bench is challenging the Mavericks' shortstop, Cameron Cuff, to a dance-off!"

"I remember a time last year when the entire Armada team bedazzled their helmets in Disney princess stickers, courtesy of Akio Sato. I heard they got into a bit of trouble with their higher-ups for that one. And there was also that instance when they got the entire stadium to do the Macarena with them after winning the World Series! Cameron Cuff was also part of that group!" Adam let out a full-hearted laugh at the memory.

"If you'll look down at the field, it looks like Rafe Alvarez is teasing Aspen Ace. He stole his glove... and is running around along the third-base line!" the announcer cackled. "And now Aspen Ace is sitting on the dirt with his arms crossed over his chest."

"Is that what I think it is? Is he... is he pouting?"

"I think you're right, Matt. And now Rafe Alvarez is walking back over. It looks like he's going to give him back his glove and—

nope! He faked him out and is now running away again. Aspen Ace has grabbed his leg and is clinging to it like a koala!"

"Oh! It looks like the umpire is coming over to break things up to get the inning started. He's trying to be serious, but we can see him laughing from here!"

"I can't believe that out of everything we've done on the field, *that* is what they decided to air on TV. I look like a little kid," I huffed, shoving my hand into a large bowl of M&Ms.

"Well, I think it's adorable," Rafe mumbled, burying his head into the back of my neck and tightening his grip around my waist.

I was nestled in his lap on our couch, my back pressed against his chest, sitting between his legs. It was one of the most expensive pieces of furniture we owned, able to move and adjust the different pieces to change the shape of the sofa. The white-and-grey piece was currently set up like a rectangle, minus the fourth strip closing it in.

"Hot, Rafe. I'm hot. Not adorable, *hot.*"

He chuckled, the vibrations resonating down my spine. "You'll always be hot. But don't kid yourself, even those tattoo sleeves don't make you less cute."

"The love letters would have to disagree."

Rafe rolled his eyes. "Jesus fucking Christ, the amount of fan mail you got the first time you didn't wear a long-sleeve under your jersey haunts me."

I sighed in agreement. "Yeah... that poor mailman."

I glanced down at my bare arms. I still hadn't gotten used to wearing T-shirts in public, but now that I'd covered up my scars, I felt confident enough to go outside without the fear of curious eyes and blunt questions.

I wanted to get the sleeves done sooner, but I was only able to finish the last session several months after this season began. Even after I started therapy, it wasn't easy and I relapsed a couple of times with cutting and alcohol, but after I'd gone a certain amount of time and my wrists were thoroughly healed, I was able to start the process of getting sleeves.

I wasn't exactly "okay," but I was a lot better. Some days, it didn't feel that way, but when I looked at the bigger picture, I knew that things were. I could feel it in the way I carried myself, the way I talked to people, and the way I flinched less and less around others. With me getting better and seeking help of his own, Rafe was also doing well; he got his head on straight and started caring for himself like he should have.

"When you said you wanted to take me on a date, I didn't expect it to just be us sitting on the couch and watching reruns of our games." Rafe was unimpressed.

"What else were you expecting? A picnic by the ocean? In this weather?"

"Well, we could..." he trailed off, walking his fingers up the side of my arm.

I chuckled, "Sorry, love. Not tonight. You can email your complaints to my therapist." The antidepressants fucked with my libido, but hey, you gotta pick your battles.

It took a long time for me to come to terms with the side effects of the meds, and even longer to find the right ones. Some would leave me a carcass, no energy to do anything, and no will to play baseball. Others had no effect, and some felt like they made me worse. There were times when I'd stop taking them, just because I wanted to feel something other than nothing, or because I was struggling so much with the fact that I could rarely get it up, and most of the time, didn't want to. I'd questioned if Rafe would get sick of a relationship where he couldn't have sex very often, then I'd stop taking the anti-depressants, and I'd spiral. Well, a lot of things made me spiral, and sometimes that "thing" was nothing at all.

"That's alright." He kissed the top of my head. "I'm happy just holding you like this."

"Who's the koala now?"

"That's Zander Sheb giving signs from the dugout," Adam noted. "He announced that he'll be retiring within the next couple of years in an interview at the beginning of last season."

"Right. That was directly after Aspen Ace returned to Armada after taking some time off. Just before Aspen's second year in the MLB *started, Zander Sheb said, now that Aspen is back and better than ever, he feels comfortable leaving Armada's future in his hands. It seems like Zander Sheb may look into coaching as the next step in his career, but he still hasn't officially retired yet so we may get to see another season or two of play from the star catcher."*

"That was a great game," I hummed, thinking about the thrill of winning the World Series. The intensity was like nothing I'd ever experienced, and I itched to go again.

"I can't believe we pulled it off, too. Neither of us played too much the year before that, especially while you were in PT. And then, bam, we were both regular starters the next season."

"Yeah. And then you left me," I spat, my voice lacking venom as I teased him, "for the fucking Mavericks!"

"I wasn't the only one! Cam left too! And you totally would've gone if they'd offered you as much as I'd gotten. Since Vale Beach is less than an hour from Newhalm and I could still live here with you, there was no reason to turn them down."

"Except for the fact that we only ever see each other when we're on the field playing each other, or by some miracle, both have home games!"

"Aww," Rafe cooed. "You could've just told me you missed me."

"Fuck off."

"Do you really want me to stop hugging you?" he asked with a smug look.

"No," I grumped back, burying myself farther into his hold.

"Matt, get a load of this! Daunte Walker is having a staring contest with the camera!" The dark man stared wide-eyed, unblinking with his arms over his chest. His eyes followed the camera even as it moved and tried to pan to another player in the dugout.

"And Akio Sato appears to be trying to stack cups on top of Wendell Rowe's head," Matthew added.

"This is a pretty normal day for Armada. They always have lots of fun in the dugout."

"Ugh," Rafe groaned, rubbing his eyes. "I miss them."

"What? Regret switching teams?"

Rafe eyed me and grinned. "Never."

"Oh my god, that's not what I meant. And you didn't even switch teams! You started playing for both."

"I don't regret going to the Mavericks. I like it there. But that doesn't mean I can't miss the guys here."

"You should come hang out with us tomorrow night. The guys are throwing Zander a birthday party. Daunte ordered a cake with the message 'Congratulations! You're one year closer to death!' instead of 'happy birthday.'"

Rafe snorted. "Sounds like Daunte, alright."

"Bring Cam with you, too."

"Don't you talk to him enough? I swear, you FaceTime him more than you talk to your own boyfriend."

"Rafe," I gasped, "are you jealous of a straight boy?"

"I'm jealous that he's taking up all your time."

"Well, if you want more of my time, come back to Armada!"

The room got quiet for a minute, forcing me to move slightly away from Rafe to look at him. He was contemplating something.

"When my contract with the Mavericks is over..."

"You'll come back?!" I jumped in my seat.

"Yeah. If Armada offers me a contract, I'll take it. Even if it isn't as good as another team's offer. Playing on the Mavericks is a good experience for me and I'm happy I'm doing it. The coach was the best pitcher in the league when he played and I feel like I'm learning a lot. But at the end of the day... I want to be with you and I want to play with you."

"If I ask Sean, he'd probably do it. Even if we don't need another pitcher, he'd make you an offer if I asked him to."

"Slow down there, sparky. No need to pull your connections just yet. I still have a couple of years on my contract. I'm not a free agent yet, so don't get ahead of yourself."

"But you'll come back, right? You'll stay with me this time?"

"Of course, Aspen. At the end of the day, I'll always pick you."

THE END.

.

Acknowledgments

Thank you to my amazing early readers! To those of you who read the first draft while I was still in the process of writing it and encouraged me to keep going, this story wouldn't be here without your wonderful comments. Thank you to my outstanding beta team who not only caught grammar, spelling, and plot errors, but pitched ideas to make my story the best version of itself. Another huge thank you to my lovely ARC team for their support and honest reviews. Thank you, mom, for being there for me throughout this whole process. Ryan Boyd, thank you for editing my work and making me a better writer. And thank you so much Myriam Strasbourg for the absolutely stunning cover!

About The Author

Danielle N. Dawsen was born and raised in Northern California and now lives in San Luis Obispo, where they attend California Polytechnic State University. As a complete and utter homebody, their favorite pastimes include cuddling with their mini bernedoodle, Koda, consuming all kinds of fiction (television, manga/manhwa, books, etc.), and writing emotional stories with the goal of making their readers ugly cry.

CONNECT WITH DANIELLE:
daniellendawsen.com
TikTok, Instagram, Twitter: @daniellendawsen
Goodreads, BookBub: @daniellendawsen

Lightning Source UK Ltd.
Milton Keynes UK
UKHW012026120122
397037UK00004B/1159